Plays
Well with
Others

Plays Well with Others

A NOVEL

Sophie Brickman

WILLIAM MORROW
An Imprint of HarperCollins*Publishers*

PLAYS WELL WITH OTHERS. Copyright © 2024 by Sophie Brickman. All rights reserved. Printed in the United States of America. No part of this book may be used or reproduced in any manner whatsoever without written permission except in the case of brief quotations embodied in critical articles and reviews. For information, address HarperCollins Publishers, 195 Broadway, New York, NY 10007.

HarperCollins books may be purchased for educational, business, or sales promotional use. For information, please email the Special Markets Department at SPsales@harpercollins.com.

FIRST EDITION

Illustrations by Alex Testere

Library of Congress Cataloging-in-Publication Data

Names: Brickman, Sophie, author.
Title: Plays well with others : a novel / Sophie Brickman.
Description: First edition. | New York : William Morrow 2023. |
Identifiers: LCCN 2023046403 | ISBN 9780063371200 (hardcover) | ISBN 9780063371231 (ebook)
Subjects: LCGFT: Novels. | Epistolary fiction.
Classification: LCC PS3602.R531256 P53 2023 | DDC 813/.6— dc23/eng/20231211
LC record available at https://lccn.loc.gov/2023046403

ISBN 978-0-06-337120-0

24 25 26 27 28 LBC 5 4 3 2 1

For Ella, Charlotte, and Jules

To know your enemy, you must become your enemy.

—Sun Tzu, *The Art of War*

PROLOGUE

In the dream, she's at the playground with her children, happy shrieks merging with the jingle of the ice cream truck, the newly installed rubber ground squishy to the touch as kids tumble down and then, in slow motion, seem to bounce right back up again. But then it registers, as she swims through the woozy state of dreamland, that she is feeling the cold, knobby rubber flush to her left cheek, pressed hard and flat against it. Deep from the city's core, a rumbling vibrates straight through her throbbing eardrum. *The subway?* she thinks, still unafraid.

But she's also aware of another sound, far off, high and ethereal, like the baby singing through the monitor on her bedside table back home, even though that makes no sense, because she's here in the playground, she can see her own body now, the vantage point having suddenly swooped to reveal her limbs way down below, spread like a chalk outline at a crime scene. It seems curious, but more in an intriguing way than an alarming one, to be watching herself from above—if that noise from the monitor, or from wherever, would just stop already. But no, it's persistent, getting louder and louder.

And so, with great effort, she forces herself into a seated position, and as her distorted perspective rights itself and the blood roils in rolling rhythm in her ears, she realizes that she has not been dreaming at all, that the noise is coming from a siren, that an ambulance has arrived, that people are running toward her, and that something is terribly, terribly wrong.

First Semester

SEPTEMBER

Dear Mother Inferior,

We've tried everything! Sitting outside her door, sticker charts, pacifiers, no pacifiers . . . and somehow, my toddler just won't go to sleep on her own. Bedtime starts at 6:30 p.m. and ends at midnight, with one of us sleeping on the floor. I know that I'm supposed to set limits, but I feel so broken, I don't know where to start. SOS!

Love,

Conked in Ronkonkoma

P.S. Not to point out the obvious, but it's exceedingly difficult to have sex with my husband when we are in different rooms.

Dearest Conked,

Not to point out the obvious right back atcha, but you made a sort of joke in your sign-off, and I think that places you squarely outside of SOS territory! I'll cheers my Chardonnay to that, Momma! *laughing so hard you cry emoji*

So first things first, there is no wrong way to parent. If it's working for you, who cares what all the other mom-shamers out there think? But you're clearly feeling that it's time for a new era to dawn in the nursery, and for that, another cheers to you. The first step toward making a change is admitting that you want one. And four years ago, when my Sam was about a year old, before we'd added not one but two(!) other little ones into the mix, I was done. Exhausted. Spent. Subsisting on a few two-hour chunks of sleep each night. A friend of mine told me that in France, mothers leave their hubbies alone to sleep train the kids and take a "spa vacances" by themselves, a little payback for nine months of gestating their child. And we had to try something. So off I went for a long weekend with my girlfriend and my pump, my bosom inflating and deflating every few hours like a mini, two-balloon-only Thanksgiving Day Parade. When I returned, boom, Sam was sleeping through the night, and you'd best believe nothing is sexier than a father who's just sleep trained your child, even if he looks like a raccoon.

There are a handful of tried-and-true sleep training methods—I could list them but I know you've already googled them all, *Conked*. Maybe you're a cry-it-outer. Maybe you're a gradual extinction-er. Maybe you're a co-sleeper, and about to click buy on that California King, just willing your husband's penis not to shrivel into a raisin. But I can tell you one thing I knew for certain, the minute I read your letter: a change is gonna come (sing it, Sam Cooke! *microphone emoji*). You just want the courage to make that change happen. And can you hear that? It's our community of mothers, cheering you on.

As I say time and time again: you got this. *small explosion emoji*

Love,

Mother Inferior

• • •

From: Ash Wempole

To: Annie Lewin

Subject: Your column!

Annie!

Your adoring editress here, back and fully restored after spending Labor Day weekend at a mud spa in the Catskills—I spent HOURS caked in mud and could literally feel my toxins being leached out of my kidneys and bloodstream and through my pores. HIGHLY RECOMMEND.

But down to biznass: loved, loved, loved this column! So full of upbeat positive energy, just what every mother needs as we hurtle into the school year. And SO. RELATABLE. I know, I know, I don't have kids of my own but literally moments after reading your words (literally) I told my boyfriend I needed him to support me more on social, the way Dan supported you when sleep training Sam. I really think it resonated, because he even posted a pic of the urn I just sculpted and put up on my Etsy store! (No pressure but if you're in the market for an urn—they are so not just for funerary purposes anymore, you can use them for all kinds of things—I got you, girl! Use the discount code ashsplash for 10% off, only for my fav writers!)

Will get this bad boy posted up on Rawr.com's homepage tomorrow a.m., can't wait for it to set the world on fiyah with its speak-truth-to-power rawness!

P.S. You are literally the only one of my writers who refuses to join Slack. I write emails for you, and you alone. *pulsing heart emoji*

Ash

She/They

Editress. Wordsmith. Potter.

@RiseFromTheAshes

Etsy store: TerraCottaAndAsh

• • •

The morning the private school kindergarten applications went live—nine a.m. sharp the Tuesday after Labor Day—Annie Lewin found herself in a preschool classroom that smelled of glue and Cray-Pas, a tiny chair digging into the small of her back. Throngs of overeager parents, she knew, had just been unleashed to start filling out essays espousing the uniqueness of their progeny, but this was the only slot when she'd been able to schedule her son's classroom meet 'n' greet, which was necessary "to acclimatize children to their new surroundings before the first day of classes," or so said preschool literature. So here they were in the fours homeroom, Sam playing on the rug nearby, Annie tamping down the distorted feeling she always associated with this munchkin land, as Miss Porter pushed a packet of papers across the table.

"Of course, this year is slightly different because there's the exmissions process," she was saying—*like something that afflicted the marshlands after Deepwater Horizon*, Annie thought, willing herself to pay attention. "You'll have a more formal conversation with Headmistress Halpert in a few weeks about applying out, but we've compiled some information about it here, for you to review before."

Annie had spent the summer listening to a podcast about a wildly wealthy banking family that had lost its riches after investigators discovered that the patriarch had been Ponzi-scheming it all along. The main character, his daughter, had used an Italian word over and over again to describe their upbringing: "abbondanza." Abundance. Lavish richness. Access. To Annie's unseasoned eye, all the independent schools seemed to be variations on a theme, the theme being "abbondanza." The only thing that appeared reliably different were the uniforms: this one's made the boys look like corporate raiders, that one's hewed closer to a monastic vibe, that other one was more yacht-chic, all madras all the time.

It wasn't just that the New York City kindergarten application process seemed, to Annie, like something lifted from an *Onion* headline—"Four-Year-Old Receives Admission to Premier School Based on His Playing of the Moonlight Sonata on Kazoo"—

or that it forced her to confront her ambivalence about weaving her child into a particular swatch of the fabric of a city where she still felt the outsider, despite nearly a decade spent calling it home. It wasn't just that she couldn't quite believe her baby boy was almost ready for kindergarten. It was also that her bandwidth for wrestling with big questions was basically nonexistent. There was the stress of getting settled in the new apartment—something she'd allotted two months to do, but somehow, five months later, she was still unpacking—combined with the general state of the world and a phone full of depressing news, but also specific things, like the weekly column she had to file, and that no matter how hard she tried, she couldn't get more than two hours of uninterrupted sleep. Just the night before, seemingly moments after calming her mind enough to rest, she'd swum up out of a dream to a presence standing by the bed.

"Mama, I fell out," her middle child, Claire, had whispered hotly onto her cheek. So Annie had reluctantly swung her legs out from under the warmth of the covers for the seventh—*eighth? ninth?*—straight night in a row and padded her daughter back to her room, tucking her in and wondering, blearily, how on earth to keep a mobile individual within the confines of a room until the sun rose.

"Mama, you sit in da chair, with BOTH feet on da ground," Claire had dictated, as she did every night. "And don't close ya eyes. And head up. And den you stay a *long* five minutes." Whatever that was, some nonsense measurement her child had concocted to make sense of a nebulous world she could not yet understand: a short time that you could somehow extend into a long one, an Escher painting where days and mornings and afternoons and evenings looped around, contracting and expanding at random. Had this bedtime begun a short or long two hours ago, with the fifth last book and third absolutely-no-more-songs-after-this-one rendition of "A Bushel and a Peck"? Had she been a mother for a short five years or a long five years?

When Claire's breathing slowed, Annie had tiptoed back to bed, willing herself to drift easily to sleep, but of course her uncooperative brain whirred away, amped up on scattered to-dos and disconnected thoughts, crushing the prospect of sleep as if it were a juice box in a compactor: she needed to get Claire clothes that fit her properly, that didn't cut deeply into her wrists at the cuffs; the sticky thing that went on the bottom of the tub to prevent slips was getting moldy—How much mold was okay? Or was that mildew? What was mildew, exactly? What were the downstream health consequences of packing the kids salami sandwiches for lunch again? Would their preservative intake eventually allow them to be embalmed, like Lenin, but sans any added chemicals? It was all Annie could do to stop herself from sling-shotting out of bed to start preparing breakfast and troubleshooting by moonlight.

And on her husband, Dan, blissfully snored, cocooned in his clearheadedness, as her cloudy head spun circles.

"I imagine you'll be taking advantage of Sawyer's early application option for Sam, since Mr. Lewin graduated from there, right?" Miss Porter continued, dragging Annie back into the classroom.

Sawyer. Right.

Because Dan was an alum, Sam had access to a special preapplication pool at the city's most coveted school—everyone just knew, of course, but there was also the *U.S. News & World Report* rankings—which was open to all alumni, siblings, and staff members, with admissions decisions relayed a full four months before general applicants. Annie had first learned about it when Sam entered the twos class at the Bartleby Neighborhood School and she'd been invited to the mom-only, school-specific WhatsApp chain. Though she'd quickly muted the "Bartleby Babes," that frenetic, disembodied Greek chorus that lived in her phone, when she had the bandwidth to dive in, it had proven endlessly fascinating to watch the queen bees buzz about. Clicking open the chain was akin to unleashing the Furies—best done purposefully, and with full awareness of the emotional consequences. Conservatively, half the things written there could be lifted and leaked to the *Post* for a tidy sum, and Annie often found herself taking screenshots and texting them to her college friend, Camila, so they could have a laugh together about the insanity of her new reality. Camila's son would go to the local, bilingual public school in Berkeley. No connected families, no unconnected families, no interviews or letters of recommendation, no admissions or exmissions. Just: school.

The so-called double-or-nothing incident had dominated the admissions chatter that first year.

MAYA: Babes, do I have some news for you. Strap in those seat belts, or clip into that Peloton.

CHRISTINE: *ear emoji*

LEONORA: *ear emoji*

BELINDA: *ear emoji*

YAEL: OMG lol am actually on a Peloton now, I see you, Samira *high five emoji* #rideordie

SAMIRA: *high five emoji* *flexed bicep emoji* #yesoryes

MAYA: Mmmk, so ladeez, remember how Peter Park had that clause in his nanny's contract that if Leo got into Sawyer, they'd give her a $15k bonus? And how the nanny spent that whole admissions year doing STEAM enrichment with him in the park?

(Flurry of thumbs-ups)

YAEL: Ahem, he referred to her as a "governess," she did have that PhD *omg emoji*

(Smattering of ha-ha's)

MAYA: So the day they got the acceptance letter, the Parks offered her double or nothing if she could get Leo's cousin in this year! She just told my nanny at the playground!

(Explosion of exclamation points)

MAYA: She took the bet!

CHRISTINE: [GIF of a googly-eyed Aziz Ansari making it rain dollar bills]

Back then, the entire premise had seemed utterly preposterous—*Prepping a child for a kindergarten interview? Paying your nanny to do it for you?*—but as Sam graduated to the threes classroom, and then onto the fours, as Claire joined the school, as baby Max was born, all but ensuring a full five years as a Bartleby family, Annie came to realize a singular truth about how its community viewed kindergarten admissions in the most cutthroat city in the world: that every part of the process was an opportunity to massively bungle something that would then set one's child on the wrong path to the wrong life. Slip on one banana peel, and bam, it was ta-ta, Ivies, and hello, Bucknell, which might as well have been hello, ditch digging. Letter of recommendation from someone too famous, but not intellectual enough? Ding. Someone intellectual, but too obscure? Ding. Ninety-second video too blurry? Too professionally produced? Ding, ding. Parents' job too middle manager-y? Ding. College alma mater too midwestern? Ding, ding, ding. And why not just sidestep the private school rat race and send your child to public school, where Annie, herself, had received a perfectly adequate education just forty miles outside the city? Bartleby parents often claimed they had "mixed feelings" about not honestly considering that route, but then conversations—after the obligatory guilty-with-an-explanation throat clearing about the system being broken—tended to boil down to, *Are you really going to deny him the chance to take a class in high-end sneaker development?*

Yes. Shoe designing.

A click through Sawyer's website revealed that since Dan's time there three decades before, the school had completed four capital campaigns. The new and improved campus now boasted two separate rooftop turfs, a state-of-the-art music wing where the sixth-grade choir recorded its annual multifaith holiday album, and a five-thousand-square-foot "maker's studio" where students could learn how to make 3D-printed custom Nike sneakers from an actual ex-Nike designer.

"Why on earth does he need to learn how to make shoes?" Annie had asked Dan that August, just weeks before the application portal opened up. Her great-grandparents had been shoemakers in Poland. *Wasn't the idea to be upwardly mobile?* "Is he going to be a cobbler?"

"It's not about the shoemaking, it's about the exposure," Dan had said, furiously pecking out a message on Slack. "You want him exposed to all sorts of things, to figure out what strikes the passion, the fire. I loved my time there, and honestly, Annie, most mothers would kill to have an in at Sawyer."

"I'd literally—*literally*—kill for Greg to have gone to one of these schools," Belinda Brenner had just about echoed at last year's preschool benefit (theme: Burning Man on Park Avenue), with a little knowing wink, as if Annie had married expressly with this moment in mind, like a Victorian heroine securing her fate with the right dance partner. "Us unconnected families who have to apply with the masses, we're like ships out at sea, just looking for a port in the storm. We're not even gonna *try* at Sawyer. I've run the numbers, and with all the connected families this year, there's just no way." She then turned on an Oliver-Twist-cum-Eliza-Doolittle accent, hands clasped in supplication. "Please, sir, educate my baby! Please teach him his letters and numbers!"

Crazy. These people were all crazy.

Yet Annie had been led to understand that an acceptance at Sawyer would be the golden ticket. And a rejection, particularly given Dan's connection, the ultimate mark of failure. Statistically, various reporters crowed, it was harder to get into Sawyer than it was to get into Harvard, but a spot at Sawyer almost guaranteed a spot at Harvard, so it was like taking out two particularly rare birds with one stone.

Even the non-crazies seemed to be in agreement. Laura, the only other mother at Bartleby Annie had ever actually liked, had grown up in the city and attended the premier all-girls' school.

"Look," she'd told Annie one day at the swings, "if Jack weren't 'exceptional,' which is what we're calling him now, I guess, and going the specialized school route, I'd absolutely be considering Sawyer. It's a great school, it really is—the facilities, the faculty, the best of the best."

Annie had always assumed that, like her, her children would go to the local public school. But falling in love with Dan and moving to New York City had, like a choose-your-own-adventure fork in a book, hurtled her down a different storyline, and then— with the sudden windfall he'd made a few months before application season, and the purchase of the apartment just outside the school district with the wonderful public school, and into one with middling scores—onto a different bookshelf.

"But what do you even mean when you say 'best'?" Annie had countered, snatching Claire up just before she got clocked in the head by Max's rapidly descending feet. "Aren't there many things that make the 'best' environment for a kid? And don't all those studies show that when you control for income and if the parents went to college and stuff, it basically wipes out any tangible differences between private, public, homeschooling, whatever?"

"Oh, c'mon, Annie, let's be real," Laura had replied, giving Jack a shove. "Everyone knows that school choice is where values and principles go to die. You don't sacrifice your own child at the altar of ideals, particularly if that child is Sam and is basically already reading. The worst sin would be putting him into an environment where he'd be bored out of his mind. You really want him to be the smartest kid in the room, like you were?"

Annie thought the system had worked for her until she arrived, Bambi-like, on Harvard's campus, the first graduate of her suburban New Jersey public high school to get into an Ivy in years. Her own mother still worked as the librarian there, shelving books and making recommendations in the comforting room where Annie had sat after school studying each day, a social outcast just waiting to find her people. It didn't happen immediately, the loss of innocence. Almost instantly, she fell in with a group of friends at the *Crimson*, so couldn't have cared less about the fancy social clubs that lined Mount Auburn Street, where various heirs and roman-numeral-affixed classmates held court; or about the ritzy prep school kids, like her freshmen-year roommate, a well-meaning but wildly dysregulated girl who was unsuccessfully trying to hide an eating disorder, which led naive little Annie to scatter peanut butter sandwich squares in the common room in the hopes that she'd be moved to ingest a nibble of something, anything, more caloric than straight vodka and the occasional handful of raw almonds. Take your black-tie parties; Annie was fine in the stacks or the dorms, drinking cheap wine and having pseudo-deep conversations with similarly nerdy friends.

But eventually, she started to internalize that while there were doors that were obviously shut to her due to factors way beyond her control, there were, too, doors that she didn't even know existed. Doors that people were opening, in houses that had been built in different solar systems.

"It's like the secret menu at the fast-food place," Dan would say, whenever she expressed ambivalence about sending Sam into the belly of the beast. "You want him to know it's there. What he does with it is up to him."

Annie forced her focus back to Bartleby, pulling two pages at random from Miss Porter's folder. One was titled "Kindergarten Independent School Application Essay Pointers," another "How to Dress for Success: Your Kindergarten Interview."

"So whichever route you choose, you're going to need to write a personal statement expressing why it is your top choice," Miss Porter continued, as Annie's eyes scanned the words "Peter Pan collar" and "culottes." "And you're going to need to include Sam's favorite extracurriculars, his strengths and weaknesses, that kind of thing."

His extracurriculars? Didn't you need curriculars to have extracurriculars?

"And I always tell parents at this point in the process," Miss Porter continued, "before it's really started up in earnest, that it has gotten more vicious than it's ever been. More and more people are having two, three, sometimes four children, and so all the siblings suck up spots at the schools because of preferential treatment, plus there are the last-minute donations from heavy hitters." She smiled conspiratorially. "You and your husband, as double Harvards, would ten years ago have been put in a special bucket but now, crazy as it may seem, there are so many of you!"

The horror.

The two women turned their focus to Sam, who was happily constructing a tower out of unit blocks. Sometimes his beauty, his perfection, temporarily blinded Annie, made it so that when she looked away again, every time she blinked, she'd see different perfect parts of his body projected on her eyelids. The gentle taper of his eyebrows. The arrowhead-shaped birthmark on his left shoulder blade. His tiny earlobe, begging to be nibbled. At just four years out of the womb, he was still close enough to the other-world to be pristine and unmarred by all this bullshit.

She was just a suburban public school kid, swimming upstream in a world Dan understood intimately. *What did she know? Maybe Sam would be the next Manolo.*

"We're gonna have a fun year together, aren't we, Sam?" Miss Porter called over to him.

"Can't wait!" her charmer chirped, flashing a big smile.

• • •

BARTLEBY NEIGHBORHOOD SCHOOL

14a East 77th Street

New York, NY 10075

"Where Play Is Work"

KINDERGARTEN INDEPENDENT SCHOOL APPLICATION ESSAY POINTERS

Dearest Fours Parents,

We are excitedly readying the classrooms for the first day of school and eagerly await your smiling faces in the halls. One order of business before we get to the meat of this note: We are—can you believe it?—already starting to plan for our annual gala, which will be themed "Gatsby (the Baz Luhrmann Version)"* and held at the Cosmopolitan Club before Christmas break. A quick reminder to check the Google spreadsheet with designated tasks on it, and email the planning committee at GatsByBaz@BartlebyNeighbSchool.edu with any queries.

Now, to the matter at hand: In addition to your in-person interview, your family's personal statement is one of the most important parts of your kindergarten application. It allows you to tell the school, *in 500 words or fewer*, what makes your child unique and wonderful. We are proud of our exmissions record, which remains one of the most successful in the city, and are excited to help you and your family find the perfect match. While there is no one right way to write an essay—we even had one family secure a spot at their top school with a submission that was written entirely in iambic pentameter—we urge you to consider the following guidelines when crafting your statement:

• Make sure you answer why your child is an ideal fit for this school of all schools, and *please remember to change this section of the essay for each school.* Look up the school's motto. Is your child scholarly? Kind? Independent? Traditional? Faithful? Include anecdotes of your child that connect specifically back to the values of that school.

• If you are applying to a coeducational school, please make sure you mention why exposure to the opposite sex is important to your family. If you are applying to a single-sex school, talk up the virtues of your child's sex while incorporating acknowledgment of gender fluidity, and the evolving definition of gender.

• Is diversity important to you? Please think about how to address this in your essay, particularly if you identify as a nonminority. Note: for a concise and simplistic refresher on anti-racist literature, feel free to browse the two anti-racist shelves in the children's library.

• Show, don't tell. If your child plays music, which piece is her favorite? If your child likes to build, what monuments is he working toward with his MagnaTiles? If your child is learning chess, which opening sequence is their favorite and why? If your child is doing none of these things, find a way to introduce a similarly enriching activity into their lives, in an organic way. While Bartleby is founded on the understanding that play is a child's work, you want to signal that your child is ready to actually work in kindergarten.

• And most of all, have fun!

We will read up to four drafts of your essay and offer detailed feedback on two of them. All four will be read by your assigned Kindergarten Admissions Delegate (KAD), and your first and last draft will be collaboratively edited by a committee formed of two former heads of admissions, three teachers, and four former or current parents (fours parents are not allowed to edit, for obvious conflict of interest reasons) who are professional writers, or tangentially related to the publishing industry.**

Good luck, and we look forward to this school year!

Sincerely,
The Exmissions Team
Bartleby Neighborhood School

---

* Not to be confused with an earlier Bartleby gala, "Gatsby (the Robert Redford Version)."

**This year, two have been published in *The New Yorker*, and two are on the boards of international media conglomerates!

• • •

From: Ash Wempole
To: Annie Lewin
Subject: Click click womp

Dearest Annie,

Starting with a truth bomb: I was so excited to see how the sleep-through-the-night piece would perform, but it sort of just . . . lay there, like me in my mud bath (cue time travel music, fade to me back in the Catskills, LOL). Despite your absolutely sky-high levels of awesomeness, and how even non-parents can find takeaways from your thoughts (hello, right here, waving), your numbers have stayed pretty steady! They've even declined a little bit from this time last month. (Womp.)

I'm wondering if we might find a way to jazz it up, so we can compete with the other mompreneurs out there, who are kicking ass and taking names, or at least *making* names, if they're not taking them (you know, via branding). The reason we wanted you on our site was because your *Times* piece was so raw, so real, it had no choice but to go viral! We gotta tap back into that rawness! And with four months under our belt, let's get into raw egg territory, so raw you might get salmonella, nameen?

So I'm thinking we do something totally wild, like bare (bear? I always mess that up!) with me here, turn each of your advice columns into thirty-second TikToks? Let that marinate for a bit. Could really foster an amazing sense of community if people can mime their problems at you, and you can mime/rap them back? Not exactly sure what that means, but I'm just the big ideas person.

For inspo, linking to a video that went viral of Korean moms doing a dance battle to a remix of Coolio's "Gangsta's Paradise," played by their children on pan flutes. A-DORBS. (37 million views in 24 hours, just sayin'.)

Back at you soonest, and still awaiting any urn queries you might have! Just got one out of the kiln.

Ash
She/They
Editress. Wordsmith. Potter.

@RiseFromTheAshes
Etsy store: TerraCottaAndAsh

From: Annie Lewin
To: Ash Wempole
Subject: re: Click click womp

Ash!

Thanks for the kind words re: this week's column, I appreciate it. Honestly, I am not exactly sure what my voice is supposed to be in these pieces—upbeat and chipper and full of "mommas!" and "you got this!"? Because I sure as hell don't feel upbeat and chipper. (I don't even drink Chardonnay. I drink bourbon, but that somehow feels off brand.) All-knowing and wise? See: above. Are you still sure I'm the right person to be giving advice to mothers? It's not the blind leading the blind here; it's worse, like Stevie Wonder trying to juggle flaming batons on a unicycle—maybe just not the right fit?

I don't know the first thing about TikTok. Do you imagine I'd write my column and then rap it to the camera or something? I'm such a Luddite when it comes to social media, and honestly it scares me! But I will think. And try to figure out a way to get those pesky numbers up, sigh. Even if it involves learning how to play the pan flute.

Apologies for not responding to your earlier urn comment. What kind of non-funerary purposes do you recommend?

Best

A.

From: Ash Wempole
To: Annie Lewin
Subject: re: re: Click click womp

LMFAO, you're a riot! And of course we still think you should be our parenting advice columnist. You're a mother! You have opinions. Just write what is in your heart. If you can't write it, maybe you can TikTok it. :)

dancing red dress emoji *small explosion emoji* [GIF of Taylor Swift throwing a grenade behind her and the landscape exploding into flames]

And thanks for being urn-curious! So while indeed most urns are either used to hold actual ashes of a deceased loved one, or mementos of that dead person, there's been a new wave of filling them up with potting soil and planting flowers right out of the top, kind of this gorgeous way to say, we're flipping this object associated with death on its head and making it all about life and rebirth. I have a few avocado trees growing out of urns right now, and they look beautiful. You could fill them up with Christmas ornaments, or hook decorative gourds on the top ('tis the season, motherfuckers!—sorry, if you didn't get that, it's a reference to an article from McSweeney's *hyperlink* that everyone I know finds absolutely hilarious, I'm even drinking coffee right now out of a mug that says "it's decorative gourd season, motherfuckers" on it). But really, the urn is your oyster. Find its pearl!

And I read somewhere that the stress of moving is NO. JOKE. Like, actually, hold up.

(Pause for googling)

Yeah, so these researchers quantified stressful events on a scale of 1 to 100, with 100 being the death of a spouse, and 10 being "going on vacation" (um, more like a negative ten in my book, amirite? Def at least negative 15 if we're talking a Catskills mud spa) and if you add up a handful of things I know you're going through at this very moment—moving, having not just a new baby but another two kids under five, plus lack of sleep—it's like Dan has died . . . (pause for calculation) . . . three times. OOF.

Gurl.

Self-care. That's the name of the game.

Gtg, this is the longest continuous set of sentences I've written since college. lol *laughing so hard you cry emoji*

Ash

She/They

Editress. Wordsmith. Potter.
@RiseFromTheAshes
Etsy store: TerraCottaAndAsh

• • •

Annie didn't realize how much she'd missed her morning commute with Sam until they were out on Madison Avenue that first day of school, him scooting just a smidge ahead, the late summer light projecting their shadows out long in front. His presence made the walk turn their neighborhood into *Mister Rogers*, with doormen waving kindly as they passed, and passersby picking up shreds of the songs he'd sing, full-throated—mostly age-inappropriate musical numbers they listened to in the car, like "I'm just a girl who cain't say no" and *Guys and Dolls*'s "The Fugue for Tinhorns," since Annie couldn't bring herself to play "Baby Shark."

"'This guy says the horse can do,'" Sam belted out, as they crossed Seventy-Sixth Street and turned down the side street toward Bartleby's friendly flag waving out front, a mass of strollers and scooters crowding the sidewalk.

Everything was very gentle at Bartleby, part of the reason she loved the preschool so much. For the youngest kids, this would be the first day of a three-week separation period, each morning in the classroom increasing by fifteen minutes, to ensure both that the most anxious two-year-old would feel supported as she began that year's classroom journey, and that the working parents all lost their minds. Sam's first day in the twos had lasted just twenty minutes.

"Twenty minutes?!" a besuited fellow parent had scoffed, as the classroom teachers began to lead the children in the goodbye song, just moments after singing the welcome song. "This school's hourly rate is higher than my lawyer's!"

When they arrived, Sam ran to greet his friends, and Annie looped his cow-print helmet over the scooter handles, consciously trying to blend in with the crowd of buzzing parents, unleashed after a summer apart with the rabidness of dogs at a racetrack.

"Annie Lewin, well, aren't you a sight for sore eyes!"

Welp, that was a fail.

"Loved your latest column! Absolutely adored it." A sharp barking compliment that always sounded, somehow, like a judgment.

Belinda Brenner.

Texas Tuxedo was what they called a jean jacket over jeans. *Was there a name for a leather jacket over tight leather pants?* Annie wondered as she shoved Sam's scooter in with the rest, burying a flash of shame that she still dressed like a seventh grader: mousy brown hair shoved into a messy bun, oversize button-down paired with leggings draped on her slight frame, diminishing boobs supported by what was definitely more sling than bra. Even so, was a double-leather getup appropriate attire for Belinda's job as the premier celebrity divorce attorney in the city? Where she spent her days cracking a whip in the air and screeching into the ether (or so Annie imagined), "Take him, take him for all he's worth!" as underlings cowered beneath her, supplicating senators to her unhinged Caligula?

"Belinda!" she replied, plastering on a smile and reluctantly turning up toward the entrance, where Caligula was standing, lips bloodred, not a hair out of place.

"You know, we still haven't figured out the sleep training thing," Belinda chattered on. "Brando still wakes up three times a night because we just can't seem to institute limits! But my hours have been so nuts that if my baby crawls into bed with me at midnight, I'm just happy to be able to hold him, you know? Like, with my case, I literally can't remember the last time I made it back for bedtime—it truly blows."

A four-sentence master class in how to assert status. *Sun Tzu could learn from her*, Annie thought, snorting internally at Belinda's use of "my case." As if anyone didn't know that referred to her representing the wife of the former tennis world champion in an extremely public divorce. It was plastered all over every news outlet, Belinda's perky ponytail bobbing and swaying as she deflected nosy questions from scrums of reporters.

Unspoken after those four sentences was the comment that Belinda had drunkenly lobbed out the previous year during a Mom's Brunch Out, after one too many Bartleby Bellinis: "Wouldn't it be nice to have a flexible career like Annie's, one where you never had to be crunching through documents late at night, then back in court the next morning?" And no, Annie had never forgotten it, not just because she sensed Belinda had brought it up as a slight dig to assert her own professional status, but also because it felt—particularly now—so true. Belinda hadn't actually called her career "cute," but she may as well have.

Brando stood next to his mother, hair spiked slightly with what any sane person would assume was jam or slime, but Annie suspected was actual hair gel, because of course Belinda would appropriately coif her child.

"Hey, kiddo—excited to be in Miss Porter's class this year?" she asked him. Brando shrugged back, grimly.

As far as Annie knew, Belinda thought they'd first crossed paths when the boys had just started in the toddlers, and they'd both volunteered in the library, checking out books and reshelving others in the meticulous system that, instead of adhering to Dewey, was organized based on subjects pertinent to the four-foot-and-under crowd (Bunnies, Trains, Dinos). But Annie remembered her from the spring before, during that first info session on the roof terrace, Astroturf crunching underfoot as prospective parents listened to Headmistress Halpert and her sidekicks wax poetic about the Bartleby philosophy. She'd had no idea how pedigreed the institution was when she signed up for a spot at an open house—during which she fell for it hook, line, and sinker, most impressed with the serious, smart, yet playful demeanor of the veteran faculty—just liked that the school appeared, in online photos, to be bright and airy, and was only a few blocks' walk away from their previous apartment. The parents in attendance seemed a bit more put together than she'd expected, but that had been her experience in nearly all New York City interactions—heels at lunches, lipstick at the gym, accessories at the playground. *Was this any different?*

It was when they reached the question-and-answer portion of the evening that she started to understand that the nervous laughter accompanying every question was a thinly veiled attempt to disguise frayed nerves. Sipping from her plastic glass of tepid white wine, she suddenly became aware that nearly every woman in the room was vibrating like a tuning fork. From one, dressed in a professionally distressed thick white work shirt, white oversize cropped jeans, and black combat boots, which made her vaguely resemble a designer plumber: "May I ask, is there a wait list, and if so, how long is it, and how aggressively does it move?" From a British-accented waif in a caftan: "Say you have an applicant who is born on September first, right at your birthday cutoff, but he's proven to be particularly gifted and advanced—like say he is already reading to himself, and not just *Pat the Bunny*, but *Olivia* the pig books—would you still insist on redshirting?"

Redshirting, Annie later learned, was a term borrowed from the sports world, a practice in which certain college coaches pulled scrawny or underdeveloped athletes out of competition for a year so that they could get bigger and stronger, then be unleashed on the field the following year like raging bulls. In the academic world, redshirting applied mostly to boys, considered to be slower to develop than girls, less verbal, more emotionally erratic. Though technically private school kindergarten classes would accept students that had turned five by September 1 of a given year, often "summer boys," those born in June, July, and August—like Sam—were recommended by preschools and kindergartners alike to spend one extra year in preschool before taking their official education by storm. Annie couldn't help but wonder how this practice manifested itself in the later years, when tiny, prepubescent winter boys had to get changed in the locker room next to manly, redshirted summer boys.

But it was the comment from the woman with the perky ponytail—Belinda Brenner, Annie now knew—that stuck with her the most, after a father raised his hand and asked a question about the afternoon versus the morning toddlers' program. As far as Annie could gather, you could apply to either, but it was markedly more difficult to get into the morning, since many children were still napping during the afternoons. "If he gets in, we'll just force him to drop his nap, I mean it's fucking Bartleby," she overheard Belinda whisper-hiss to her husband, a short, reedy man who looked vaguely stoned, eyes perpetually at half-mast. "One brutal year of overtired tantrums at night? Totally worth it."

Sam, at that point, was not yet two years old. One of the happiest parts of Annie's day was going to get him from his afternoon nap, his cheek warm against hers, his curls stuck to the side of his face, his breath mild and sweet, like he'd been eating bowls of strawberries in his dreams, the humidifier pumping a comforting stream of mist into his junglelike bedroom, the outside world and any other obligations all but excised from their little cocoon of softness. Wrenching him away from the nap that he so desperately needed, that she so fully enjoyed, simply so he could build blocks for a measly two half days per week under the supervision of professionals that might—she was gathering was the general understanding in this particular, deranged, room—dictate the course of the rest of his life? *Screw that.* The school seemed charming and gentle, the teachers wonderful, and even if the prospective parents were nuts, Sam wouldn't have to deal with them. But if he didn't get into the morning class, she'd just see what other options were in the neighborhood.

Of course, then Sam got into the mornings, Brando got into (and took) the afternoons, and Annie found herself in the same community as Belinda. She'd managed to mostly avoid her in the intervening two years, the administration perhaps aware that they'd be like oil and water. ("We love normal parents like you," the head of the PTA gushed to Annie at the accepted parents' spring cocktail reception, which Annie decided to wear as a badge of pride, and not some nebulous denigration marking her a normal blob in a sea of extraordinariness.) There was the library day, during which Belinda kept stepping outside the room and whisper-yelling into her phone about some client, while Annie read *The Tiger Who Came to Tea* alone to Sam's class, entertaining that the tiger might, in fact—as the Babes had suggested during one hilarious thread—represent depression and alcoholism. There was the travel mug of piping hot liquid Belinda carried with her everywhere, which Annie and Camila liked to joke contained not coffee but Red Bull—something that could caffeinate, but also burn nose hairs off and strip paint in a pinch. There was the yearly gala, which Belinda always took way too seriously. (See: her hideous yellow checkered skirt suit most recognizable on Alicia Silverstone in *Clueless*, which she wore at the "Gettin' Jiggy at the 90s" benefit. Her husband arrived in his normal jeans, sneakers, and T-shirt, a Clinton inauguration sweatshirt tied like an unappealing and clown-size cravat around his neck.) There was the *flexed bicep emoji* plus *fist pound emoji* plus *small explosion emoji* trifecta that Belinda liked to deploy on the chat, a little sprinkle of participation that kept her in the mix but with a distance that assured her status as too important to actually put thought into the words she was deigning to write. The other Babes, though sometimes irritating, seemed innocuous. Belinda, Annie could sense, was tactical about everything— every comment, every outfit, every interaction. Now, in Sam's final year at the school, it appeared Annie's Belinda-free luck had finally run out.

"Did you sign Sam up for group music classes at Harmon-Strauss this year?" Belinda continued at 1.5x speed, taking a sip from her travel mug and wrenching Annie back into the conversation. "Brando will be doing violin, like I did, and you know, we opted out of solo private lessons at home because Harmon-Strauss has the concerts at the end of each term and I just think the important thing is that they perform, it's good for them to have that experience, don't you agree? Plus, it'll only help our applications, I figure. But what do I know, I'm just a country bumpkin from Connecticut!"

She made it sound like she was born in a pasture and raised without running water.

Greenwich. Greenwich, Connecticut.

Annie felt her brain start to rev into gear, searching for the right response to this land mine of a comment. Brando had been, all the mothers knew, studying Suzuki violin since he was two. It was rumored he practiced an hour a day, and since the method required the parent to learn along with the child, or at least be engaging with the instrument as the child did, Belinda's husband dutifully took on the task. Annie hadn't signed Sam up for music classes because she was so overwhelmed, she had not yet found the time to unpack her underwear, which was floating around in a box somewhere covered in dust—an apt metaphor— let alone figure out after-school activities for her children. She'd been so drawn to the arts that she'd devoted most of her career to them, moving from the culture beat at the *Crimson* to a job as a cub reporter for the *New York Times* arts section and working her way up, often finding herself gobsmacked, as she interviewed a director or sat in a darkening theater with her notebook, that this actually constituted work—particularly since her practical- to-a-fault father, as in-house counsel to a national office supply company, had, to her knowledge, enjoyed not a single day of his professional life. But now, she couldn't figure out a way to artic- ulate why the idea of forcing young children to perform for an audience was so godawfully repellent to her, why she hoped that simply exposing Sam to Rodgers and Hammerstein would, via osmosis, be enough.

Her brain whirred and whirred, almost short-circuiting, as Belinda stood there waiting for a response, and as she waited, Annie suddenly became aware that something was off, but she couldn't quite put her finger on it. The ambient noise from Mad- ison Avenue had suddenly vanished, replaced by a sort of dull roar, and she got the surreal feeling that she was floating, as if in a swimming pool, that perhaps her heels had started to lift, just a bit, from the insoles of her worn Chucks—but before she had a chance to truly panic, the comforting pressure of a hand came to rest on her shoulder, and she dropped back down again.

Laura. Always there at the exact right moment.

"Hi, Belinda," Laura said, squeezing Annie, "looking amazing as ever in that leather getup, and cool as a cucumber, even in this heat! I accessorized with a little maple brown sugar oatmeal in my hair, as you can see."

Annie caught a whiff of eau-de-Quaker-Oats-fake-maple flavoring as a thin film of sweat bloomed on her skin, her heart pounding. *What in the hell had that just been?* The opening bell rang, and Laura, effortlessly gorgeous, and partial to expandable pants and roomy sweatshirts from the various colleges where she'd studied or served on the English faculty, navigated the two of them up into the main hall. There, they encountered a riot of children and caregivers—that clinical word that took the caring right out of it—that had already divided, to the knowing eye, into different cliques: the working mothers, the gently employed mothers, the stay-at-home mothers, the fathers who participated, the nannies, and the hot au pairs.

"I totally blocked out *that* bullshit," Laura whispered to her, head jerking toward Belinda, who was now holding court on the stair landing. "But thank god we're in the same class. We can handle her together, don't worry."

"That was the craziest thing," Annie replied softly, the floating sensation lingering in her lower extremities. "Just now before you came over I had this sort of . . . hallucination. Like, I was actually spinning out into the ether as Belinda was yapping at me. You don't ever have them, do you?"

"This morning, I hallucinated I was dressed but in fact was halfway to the elevator before I realized I had no pants on," Laura said. "Does that count? C'mon, sweetie."

Annie hadn't even seen Jack, Laura's little genius, pressed up against her leg—a small, earthbound koala. She leaned down.

"Don't worry, buddy, I'm overwhelmed, too." He flashed her a weak smile.

"Jack!! C'mon, let's build a castle!" Sam came barreling in, took the koala by the hand, and yanked him up the stairs to their classroom. Clearly a better tactic. Her good-hearted little angel, who did the right thing in the right way without even knowing it was the right thing or the right way.

"Thank god for him," Laura said as they trudged up the stairs behind the boys. "Seriously. Without the promise of Sam at his side I don't think I'd have been able to get Jack out the door this morning."

• • •

Back at home, Maria—their once-a-week cleaning lady back before they were married, who'd seamlessly transitioned to taking care of the babies as they were born, and served as Annie's co-parent more than she'd like to admit, even sleeping over some nights when Dan was away for work—had drafted three-year-old Claire into helping shell some peas, while baby Max took his morning nap. It was in this short window when Annie carved out time to write, a sacred three-hour slot before Sam's pickup and the chaos of an afternoon with three children descended.

As she headed up the stairs to her office, Annie still couldn't bring herself to call it home—a disconnect that surely contributed to her inability to unpack fully and "nest," or whatever the interior design blogs were calling it these days. The penthouse had been owned for three decades by a banking heir and his Botox-loving wife, who'd raised four children in the cavernous rooms, then the minute the youngest was in college put the house on the market and got a divorce. Annie viewed it as a sort of parable about the perniciousness of money.

Then, the fateful one-two punch, which shoved her directly into the parable:

1. A tanking real estate market.

2. An apartment-size windfall, made by her husband, after he invested in cryptocurrency through his fund, catapulting them into the highest echelons of the social pyramid literally overnight.

Dan. A Manhattan kid, born in the white-hot center, and perpetually striving to get closer and closer to its burning core. He just couldn't help himself, after what had happened to his family, the tragedy of it all. Plus, he couched the need for the apartment in some argument that it was the financially responsible decision. She'd been pregnant with Max, Claire was sleeping in a Pack 'n Play in their bathroom, and they did, honestly, need more space. Just not so much. As they passed through the mudroom during the tour with the real estate agent, she'd wondered aloud if this was a Manhattan apartment or an Irish hunting lodge. But Dan rightly pointed out that their hall closet was overflowing with tiny shoes, and no one in their right mind would pass up extra square footage in a city where it was a rarer commodity than kryptonite. And so, four months after Max's birth, they headed a few blocks north and a few blocks closer to the park, that one Pac-Man move on the city grid taking them a single, impossibly final, step away from her squarely middle-class suburban childhood.

"We can, you know, throw money at the problem now and just hire more help," Dan had told her the night before they moved, while she was thinking aloud through drop-off logistics now that they'd be farther away from Bartleby. "Maria is mostly tied to the baby, anyway—you don't have to be so granularly involved."

But even the idea of Maria, lovely, charming Maria, folding her socks and underwear into perfect little parcels made Annie feel uneasy. *Two people to help with the children that no one had forced them to have? And wasn't granular involvement part of the gig?* So she'd organized her life to be able to work (kinda) and parent (kinda), off-loading tasks to a cadre of helpers as inconceivable to her as never writing another word in her life.

Squirreled away in what the previous owners had used as a storage closet for luggage, Annie had set up her workstation. Dan's office desk was a jumble of paper piles, files and folders strewn everywhere, crumpled-up receipts sprinkled around as garnish. He was comforted by the detritus of his life. Annie, on the other end of the spectrum, worked best in ascetic environments—she'd even abandoned the noisy newsroom of the *Crimson* for the Widener stacks when she was on deadline. All she had in her closet-office was a wooden chair with a thin cushion on top, an IKEA computer desk just slightly wider than her computer, and a phone charger plugged into an outlet on the far baseboard, to keep distractions out of reach.

She was working on a piece about how to get children to eat a wide variety of foods, not all beige-colored or sweet, after skimming the Mother Inferior slush pile for the right email to serve as a jumping-off point for this week's column, which came from someone who signed off as Engaged to Beige. Even though the only way Annie ever got her children to eat non-beige foods was to bribe them with the promise of beige foods, something she'd read was horrible parenting—the quid pro quo tactic.

"Dessert should be offered, family style, at the same time as vegetables and main courses," one parenting guru had opined in a widely circulated *Wall Street Journal* piece that had been making the rounds recently. "Studies show that restricting food intake, and only allowing sweets after other more quote-unquote healthy food has been consumed, leads to disordered eating and a preoccupation with treats. Don't make sweets a big deal. Trust your children's bodies to tell them what they need."

She'd tried this tactic the day before, in the spirit of research, and Claire's and Sam's bodies had both told them to consume a dinner of rainbow sprinkles served in bowls, eaten plain, and guzzled like a frat boy with a forty, hold the salmon and peas thanks. As for not making sweets a big deal, their eyes bulged out of their sockets like Roger Rabbit looking at Jessica's gazongas whenever a gummy bear was within spitting distance, something that appeared to be innately wired and immutable.

Engaged to Beige, she began,

Jessica Seinfeld wrote a whole book about blending vegetables into foods and making them disappear. And trust me, I'd do that, too, if I had the time to blend.

She paused. The tone was all off. Too angry. What people wanted was positivity, with a dash of commiseration. She was writing for clicks, but clicks came when the community felt seen and heard, Ash had said as much. She deleted and began again.

I hear ya, Momma, she tried. *And can we all raise a glass of Chardonnay to Jessica Seinfeld who, bless her heart, wrote a whole cookbook on how to hide blended vegetables into foods so that Jerry could get his daily beta-carotene intake through spinach- and carrot-puree-filled brownies?*

She highlighted "Chardonnay," deleted it, tried "Chard." Cocked her head. *Did that make it sing?*

Long sigh.

The upside of this job was that she could do it in her daily three-hour slot, with a few editing hours late at night, after the kids had gone to bed. The downside was, well, so many things. Just a few years ago, she'd been sitting at the *New York Times*, energized at edit meetings, pitching profiles on obscure talents she adored, who, after profiles with her, became no longer obscure. She helped put actors, directors, playwrights on the map. She'd worked with an editor in her seventies who'd been at the *Times* for longer than Annie had been alive, who referred to her as "kid," and pushed her to make her prose sharper and leaner. It was a match made in editorial heaven. Then came the op-ed she wrote two months after Max's birth, and everything had changed.

"Mother Nature's Myth" had been one of the most read of the year, eliciting more than three thousand comments from parents around the world. The time peg of the piece had been the recent resurrection of a term coined decades earlier by a medical anthropologist: "matrescence," or the life stage of becoming a mother, which, in many ways, paralleled adolescence, or so were arguing a cutting-edge group of academics at Oxford. Within hours of publishing, the article had whipped up the waves of social media and gone viral, and then an email from Ash popped up in Annie's inbox, full of emojis and exclamation points, asking her to join a new media startup.

In certain ways, the timing could not have been more fortuitous. Her *Times* editor had just taken the first of what promised to be many buyouts, and the Arts staff was shrinking by the week, reporters scattering to web-based enterprises that promised more nimbleness in a bleak media landscape. Add to that an infant who was not yet sleeping through the night, two other children under four years old, and a husband who kept telling her to see the writing on the wall re: legacy publications.

"You think next-gen AI programs won't completely obliterate the newsroom?" Dan had asked rhetorically one morning, scrolling through the myriad tech newsletters that flooded his inbox, the logo of one emblazoned on the fleece vest he wore over a polo, fitted jeans, and designer sneakers, completing the classic VC uniform. "Fat chance."

And so, after Ash agreed to match her *Times* salary plus give her equity, the startup bankrolled by the wife of a Brazilian banker who viewed it her calling to preserve the type of American magazine content she'd grown up on—*YM* and *Sassy* magazine being her touchstones—Annie took what she assumed was a life raft and created a millennial-friendly persona she named Mother Inferior. The every mother. The mother who'd give you advice with a healthy dollop of reality mixed in. The mother who would never encourage you to put chocolate cake next to broccoli and hope that your child would just willingly choose the crucifer, because that tactic was sanctimonious horseshit. And yet, three months in, she still couldn't figure out just how to fulfill her own mandate and also give Ash the clicks she needed, all the while ignoring blaring headlines that, due to various next-generation AI chatbots, she was walking around with a target on her back.

Had she made a terrible mistake? she wondered as she settled on "Chardonnay." *Should she have remained a holdout at the* Times, *fighting against the dying of the light, battening down the hatches as AI bots swarmed the elevator banks?*

• • •

From: Annie Lewin
To: Camila Garcia Williams
Subject: OMG Belinda

I know how you've missed our installments of "Annie tries to fit in at pre-school" the past couple months, so, picking up from June: the Divorce Doyenne was the first person I saw at drop-off today and she asked me if I wanted Sam to enroll in some fancy music school not just because it would help his kindergarten application, but because, and I quote, "the important thing is that they perform."

THEY. ARE. FOUR.

Isn't the important thing for them to, I don't know, love music? Or am I getting it all wrong? Should I start taping a violin bow to one of Max's hands in the crib, like Andre Agassi's dad did with the Ping-Pong paddles??

Belinda. ARGH. Fitting that her name literally means serpent. *Hisssssss.* The Brenners, apparently, just returned from the French Riviera where they spent two weeks at "family tennis camp," whatever the f that is. To think my child-hood summer trips involved taking a sleeping bag out into my backyard. Gasp.

Anywho, part of me looks at her and just wants to CRUSH HER. Please keep an eye on me. I'm literally spewing advice that I don't even follow myself to a bunch of mothers on the internet, while someone else takes care of my children half the time! Should I have stuck with pre-med and been a doctor? At least then I'd rest easy, knowing I contributed real value to the world. The last meaningful piece I wrote was the *Times* op-ed, nearly six months ago now! When I stop to think about it too long, I want to crawl into a hole.

Speaking of hole crawling: Did I tell you about the sneaker-making class at Sawyer? They can . . . make sneakers. Starting in third grade. It all seems ridic-ulous, but I watched Sam, for a long while yesterday, construct a pretty wild contraption using this new STEAM toy he got that has pulleys in it, so that he could catapult his stuffed animals from the floor to the top of his bunk bed with-out climbing the ladder. And I thought, I don't know, if he's in an environment where they nurture that innate creativity, will he become the next Einstein? And if he's in the wrong one, will he be fated to live life as a patent clerk? Laura told me the other day that you don't "sacrifice your child at the altar of ideals," but what about sacrificing him at the altar of the privileged, where he grows up surrounded by children who were born assuming sneaker making is their God-given right? Will no doubt have to come to terms with that in time for our "connected family Zoom" presentation with the administration, sigh.

Paging Dr. Freud: My nails are a physical manifestation of my psyche. I gnaw them down to the quick and have now started to bite the skin on the sides. *puke emoji* And I'm def taking this anxiety out on my Gen Z editor. Poor girl.

Dying to hear all about your very civilized life in Berkeley.

Xoxo

A.

P.S. Have you ever hallucinated during broad daylight? Asking for a friend.

P.P.S. Looked up the causes and the most likely, according to the NHS, are schizophrenia, Alzheimer's, or anxiety/extreme stress. No need to point out that I haven't slept more than a few hours at a stretch in, oh, four and a half years and feel so stressed I might spark. Or that my great-aunt Esther actually was schizophrenic, and maybe hallucinating runs in the family?! (Am I just a few years away from being wheeled out at the sanatorium for some fresh air during your monthly visit? You will visit, won't you?)

P.P.P.S. re: losing one's mind, did you see the article in this week's *New Yorker* about T. S. Eliot's *The Waste Land*? Apparently Eliot was on the brink of mental collapse for two full years (!), until he finished the poem. But check this out: it's Ezra Pound's response to Eliot after reading the first draft. "*Complimenti*, you bitch. I am wracked by the seven jealousies." Isn't that just . . . amazing? I'm gonna try "*Complimenti*, bitch" out as my sign-off for the column. Feels better than the rah-rah "you got this" that Ash suggested. Ezra Pound: the original bad biatch.

P.P.P.P.S. But honestly, name one mother who doesn't have anxiety.

P.P.P.P.P.S. You don't count.

P.P.P.P.P.P.S. *Complimenti*, bitch.

...

Mother Nature's Myth

by Annie Lewin

New York Times *Opinion Section Archives*

I caught a fleeting glimpse of my maternal instinct in the first few moments of my son's life, that primal, atavistic sense I'd assumed would color the rest of my interactions with this new human. The doctor whisked him away for what I later realized was an Apgar test, and though it couldn't have lasted more than a minute, as I watched him on the scale with a warming lamp above him, his little body writhing, his mouth opened in furious protest, I found myself suddenly irate along with him—but in a foggy, disassociated way that was no doubt colored by the hormones flooding my body. He needed my touch, and they were separating us, which was cosmically unjust. Of that I was certain.

Thanks to the epidural, I was hooked up to a catheter and didn't have feeling back in my legs, yet I was prepared, like a mother who summons the strength to lift the rolling car off her child, to push myself up, to fight the drugs, to make my way to him against the odds—but as I was about to yank the catheter out (yes, really), his comforting weight was returned to my chest, and the world heaved back onto its proper axis, my heart rate slowing as I marveled at his minuscule tricep, covered in a soft down.

In the coming days, though, that utter certainty of what he needed and how to give it to him all but dissipated. Wasn't I supposed to know, innately, how to nurse? Wasn't I supposed to understand, reflexively, what his cries meant? Wasn't I supposed to be able to snap to in my new, most important role, with a clarity and purpose reserved for the most profound things in life?

Thankfully, the answer—as a consortium of psychiatrists, neurologists, and anthropologists at Oxford has argued in a new paper—is a resounding no.

"No, maternal instinct isn't innate, and no, you new mothers are not going crazy, and yes, this entire life stage has been wildly misunderstood for centuries," the lead researcher, Dr. Rebecca Calandra, told me. "This is why we hope our findings will help incorporate the term 'matrescence' into the mainstream."

The idea is simple and—for this mother, now of three, who is still figuring out just how to be a parent—wholly comforting. As the researchers write in their paper, "The Parent Trap: A Recasting of Matrescence from a Neurological, Psychological, and Anthropological Perspective," when someone becomes a mother, they "experience seismic changes in their biological, psychological, social, and spiritual makeup," all of which takes quite a bit of time and experience to settle into a new normal. In many ways, this parallels adolescence, which we only designated as separate from childhood and adulthood starting in the early 1900s. Over a century later, we're coming to understand that the years spent as a new parent need their own designation as well, something the researchers are hoping might reframe how we view everything from childbirth, to childcare, to postpartum depression. And while these early years affect all parents, they're particularly charged for the primary caregiver, who by and large is the mother.

Like with a Magic Eye puzzle, once you've seen the similarities, they're impossible to unsee. As in adolescence, a mother tests out different personas—is she going to be the emotionally tuned-in nurturer who'll ask her toddler what he's feeling after he's smashed the other kid over the head with the toy bulldozer in the sandbox? Or the tough love momma who'll yank him into a time-out because engaging with a toddler's feelings is tantamount to negotiating with a terrorist? (I toggle between both, often depending on how caffeinated I am.) As in adolescence, mothers find themselves wholly ambivalent about their new place in society, embracing responsibility while also willing it away. But unlike in adolescence, the accompanying volatile temperaments—while neurologically and psychologically sound—are often misunderstood. If a teenager dyes his hair blue and goes goth for a semester, it can be chalked up to "testing boundaries." If a mother wildly changes her appearance and demeanor, she's one step away from a call from social services.

"Years ago, before we truly understood what was happening in those formative adolescent years, we thought teenagers were exhibiting signs of going crazy on their way to adulthood," Calandra told me. "It's natural to draw parallels to modern motherhood. For sure mothers who experience postpartum depression will identify, but I think you'd be hard-pressed to find *any* mother who doesn't feel the very real stressors brought upon by the birth of a child, which, of course, is when the mother is born, too—something we tend to lose sight of. The baby must grow up, but so, too, must the mother, and that growth takes time."

I love each of my children with a fierceness that, I hope, would allow me to lift a car off them, but sometimes (perhaps most of the time) I have no idea how to handle the day-to-day stuff—how to navigate bedtime antics, how to shut down negotiations at mealtimes, how to relax into my new job enough to enjoy it, and not miss the forest (earth-shattering love) for the trees (how many broccoli spears constitutes "enough"). Now that a cadre of Oxford academics across disciplines has confirmed that I'm not lacking something I'm supposed to have, that my maternal sense will form with time, the hope is that I will be both more patient and kinder to myself.

And yet: I can sense, even through the internet, a collective sigh and rolling of eyeballs. What good does being patient, and kind, do? Don't we need to recenter the conversation about motherhood, take a wrecking ball to the old society and build a new one that values child-rearing, that supports mothers and gives them the time to make this transition, that doesn't do away with abortion rights, that doesn't pay an average of a measly $500 per year for each American toddler's care, compared to other rich countries' $14,000? And why must the burden of blaring the alarm about this fall to those of us who are most tired, vulnerable, and covered in spit-up? It feels like righting the course of an oil tanker with a canoe paddle—on two hours of sleep.

So, I suggest starting small. Perhaps you write down a calendar reminder to cut yourself some slack, every day around 4 p.m. Perhaps you volunteer, to the mom in the elevator, that you, too, are overwhelmed, and open up an avenue for conversation and commiseration. Perhaps you start to view social media posts of mothers in diaphanous caftans nursing their children on lily pads not just as false advertising, but as a form of mother-on-mother crime. Perhaps we can use that canoe paddle to start a small wave, that will, like a butterfly flapping its wings on the other side of the world, lead to cosmically powerful effects—because what are we mothers, we car lifters and life creators, if not cosmically powerful?

Here's to hoping.

OCTOBER

Dear Mother Inferior,

School started up a few weeks ago, and while I love my daughter's teachers, I just can't seem to find my parent crew. More to the point, I can barely make time for anything that falls outside the three realms of work, childcare, and sleeping. Which means, no, I barely even see the friends I already know and love. Should I invest the time in this community, or forget it?

Signed,

Asocial in Atherton

Dearest Asocial,

When my eldest entered preschool, I was super gung-ho about making new parent friends. I didn't necessarily think that just because we'd all had unprotected sex in the same few months, we should stand in a circle, swaying back and forth singing kumbaya. But I craved the support of other mothers who were going through the same things I was—the sleepless nights, the refusing-to-eat-anything-but-Goldfish sagas, the isolation.

So off I went to Sam's first day, and within two minutes, I realized that I would never, like *ever*, gel with any of the other parents. One had enrolled her child in "Russian Math," whatever that was, and the kid introduced himself by reciting his times tables (note: he was two years old). One father was videoing the entire first meet 'n' greet on his phone, as part of a project in which he was planning to record the pivotal moments in his son's life and then splice them all together in time-lapse before he went to college, starting with his son's head emerging from the birth canal. Suffice it to say, I decided to completely distance myself from the parent community there and focus on the friendships that I knew would sustain me—particularly my far-flung college friend, who wrote me emails every week. I found convenient excuses to miss various moms' nights out and parent potlucks and felt pretty smug about it all. Sartre famously said that hell is other people. Well, for me, hell was other parents.

And then the next year my second child, Claire, started going to preschool, and, would you believe it, crazy Russian Math mother had a younger child who was in our class, too (apparently we both boned, unprotected, at the same ten-month interval). Sweet. And our daughters became friends. At that point, three years into motherhood, I'd whittled down the people I interacted with on a daily basis to my children, my husband, and Abdul, the coffee guy at the corner bodega who caffeinated me twice daily. Did I have friends? Yes, I kept insisting to myself. But if I took a hard look at it, they existed exclusively on my phone.

Cut to the first of many playdates Claire has with this new friend, and in walks Russian Math mother. She's carrying a bottle of wine in her purse. It is four p.m. on a Tuesday. She asks me if it would be wildly inappropriate if the two of us crack it open, right then and there, and fishes out some cheddar bunnies and Fruit Roll-Ups deep from her purse and offers them up for our impromptu aperitivo hour, because she's forgotten to eat lunch. We kill the bottle of wine, then order pizza and continue to talk. I bring up Russian Math. She laughs. She says that introduction mortified her for months, and that her son is actually kind of brilliant and has this freakish obsession with numbers, so freakish he scares her sometimes, particularly since she's not math-y at all. But she's realized doing math puzzles is one way to keep him calm and focused, so he attends this math school that is for kids way older than he is, and she stays up at night fretting about his ability to fit in with other children.

Anyway, this woman has since become one of my closest friends and dearest allies. And that she is part of my child's school community is a critical part of our friendship.

"Antisocial behavior is a trait of intelligence in a world full of conformists," Nikola Tesla once said. All you need is to find your fellow nonconformists.

With love, antisocial internet hugs, and a rousing *complimenti*, bitches—
Mother Inferior

• • •

Annie had taken up running in the year after Sam's birth, her long, languid stroller walks morphing—as she weaned him off various midday nursing sessions and started to carve out more time for herself—into short jogs, then longer ones, then actual forty-minute loops around the park. She couldn't motivate herself to go to a gym class—the transportation to and fro, the changing in the locker rooms—and could never find the appeal in the myriad app-based workouts that had taken the world by storm, tiny coaches yelling into your earbuds that you were crushing life, when in fact all you were doing was holding a plank in your bedroom. Running she could do. Fresh air. A cognitive break. A chance to listen to truly terrible pump-you-up music when she was on her own or, now that she'd befriended Laura, to socialize with an actual real live person who was her own age and could commiserate about the challenges of having two kids so close in age and, well, everything else, too.

On days when the stars aligned and schedules synced up, they'd meet at the Met steps, dodge tourists and ice cream carts, and shuffle-jog their way up toward the reservoir, which they'd loop, then head down to Seventy-Second Street or, when they were feeling particularly ambitious, all the way down to Fifty-Ninth. Then, an iced coffee reward before returning, sweaty and wrung out, to their respective computers.

This Saturday morning, Dan had taken the kids to his new favorite activity—rock-climbing at a nearby gym—which Annie feared was his go-to because he could put Sam and Claire into harnesses and literally tether them to a wall while he sat tethered to his phone nearby, Max asleep in the stroller. *But who was she to quibble with a free weekend hour?*

"My department head put me with this *very* uppity, *very* woke Gen Z teaching assistant who makes me feel like I'm an actual crone, writing with quills by candlelight," Laura told her, through stuttering breaths, as they passed the hulking black mass of Mount Sinai Hospital, where, collectively, they'd birthed five children.

"I'm sorry, at least you're not supposed to be TikToking your lectures," Annie wheezed in response, causing both of them to snort. "And on the home front, your angelic children actually listen to you when you tell them to stop doing something." She told Laura about the previous night, when Claire had been coloring the living room walls—again—which Annie had missed because Sam had covered Max head to toe in Desitin, the reasoning being that, "If it's good for his butt, isn't it good for the rest of him?" The stuff was like cement, and by the time she'd scraped the baby off, Claire had made some serious progress. "When I asked her to step away from the crayons, swear to God," Annie said, as they passed the reservoir gatehouse, "she looks me dead in the eyes and says, 'I'm not coloring, Mama,' while continuing to color."

"Little psychopaths," Laura puffed out. "Why don't they ever warn you that living with a toddler is like sharing a house with Norman Bates?"

The pride Annie felt for her friend ran deep and curdled, when she was being honest with herself, with a significant dash of envy. It wasn't just that Laura was clearly firing on all cylinders professionally—her first academic book was set to come out in the next year, and she consistently got rave reviews from students who rightly thought she was one of the coolest, most motivating teachers they'd ever had. It wasn't just that being affiliated with a university gave her a clear status stamp, a place to hang her hat, smart colleagues to banter with, schedules that were imposed from on high and gave order to her day. It wasn't just that "upper echelon academic" appeared more immune to the influx of AI than "internet mommy blogger." ("Okay, ChatGPT, write me a 100,000 word book about Carto-Geographic Consciousness and the Dawn of Early Modern English Literature.") Most enviable to Annie was the clear trajectory of to-dos, marching orders that would, so long as Laura did what was expected of her, spit her out in however many years a wizened professor with soft, wrinkled hands, surrounded by books, many of which she'd written, and various speaking engagements that she could use as anchors for family trips around the globe. Or so it seemed to Annie, who looked at her own career and could only see a black morass ahead. Female writers in her circle, by and large, wanted to channel Nora Ephron. Would Ephron have found herself helming an internet advice column and avoiding social media at all costs? Highly doubtful. She'd have figured out a way to harness the medium to her advantage, she'd have embraced using her own life as copy, she'd have created multiple hashtags and maybe even made a cute Memoji of her pixie cut peeking out from atop a black turtleneck that would, inevitably, find its way onto tote bags sold at the Strand.

"Seventy-Second or the whole shebang?" Laura asked as they got off the reservoir by the big tree and started their way south on the bridal path, dodging horse poop as they passed the swings, a few babysitters absentmindedly pushing their charges while they stared at their phones or talked animatedly into thin air to far-flung friends or family. Annie was, technically, on deadline and really should be home continuing to grind through a piece about how to keep postpartum sex alive, something she felt uniquely unqualified to answer.

"Seventy-Second," she said, then, "How often do you guys do it?"

An article had been making the rounds that fall, written by a woman with three school-aged children whose husband had asked for a threesome for his fortieth birthday present. She'd interviewed various candidates, found someone she felt comfortable with, and then the three of them had met at a pied-à-terre and spent an afternoon together.

The responses split mostly into two camps, with *How brave!* on one side and *What a jerk* on the other. Annie sat right in the middle. She'd be horribly offended if Dan asked for a threesome—you want an experience for your birthday, go to a baseball game—but she'd also understand his desire to spice it up. The last time they'd had sex in earnest was to conceive Max, a grueling, military-grade affair fueled by a fear that she was nearly forty and her own mother's recent admission that they'd wanted more children but had waited too long. Annie had always liked the idea of three. It was impossible for a three-legged table to wobble. And so with a prayer to the fertility gods, and perhaps a little earlier than she'd have liked, they started to try again. She remembered those few weeks of sustained sex as a to-do at the end of a long list of to-dos—dinner, bath time, bedtime, eat cold leftover Spinach Littles over the sink, strip down, pretend to be really into it for the first five minutes, then will your husband to perform. *Mechanical* was the word that came to mind. Now, toggling between nursing and sex seemed as natural a progression as Max skipping crawling and cruising and going straight from tummy time to driving stick shift.

"Whales sleep with half their brain, so they can keep moving forward!" Sam had once announced to her, amazed, after a trip to the Natural History Museum. *If only she were a whale.*

Exhaustion was but one hurdle. Dan had FaceTimed early the other week from the Virgin Atlantic lounge at Heathrow, en route to Berlin and sporting an excellent new haircut. "One of the perks of this lounge is there's a barber!" he'd said, grinning, as he took a sip from what appeared to be a Pimm's Cup, a round of cucumber perched on the rim. It was like a Zen koan: If a new haircut turned you on, but you were five time zones apart, was your libido actually still kicking?

Sometimes, she'd get herself in the mood by thinking of Dan having sex with someone else. She imagined that orgy scene from *Eyes Wide Shut*, with her walking around in a mask and coming upon him in ecstasy with a leggy woman wearing a bird's beak, after which she'd slink upstairs and relax into a plush chaise lounge. When she finally got her act together to go to therapy, she'd try to remember to bring it up, plumb the depths of her soul to figure out why dozing off with no one touching her was her sexual ideal.

Laura scoffed, jerking her back into their run.

"I mean, unless we set an alarm to do it in the morning before the kids wake up, which is about the least sexy thing I can imagine, we have at most three slots per week: Monday after class,

Friday night, and Sunday night." Her husband, a doctor, was in a particularly brutal period of overnights, and combined with Laura's teaching schedule, they were often like ships in the night, blindly passing children back and forth between them like batons. "I figure one out of three is commendable, right? So, I don't know, we try for that. I tell myself this is just a, um, fallow life period, sexually."

What woman in her orbit actually had a screaming hot sex life? Annie wondered, as they passed the swans in the pond, happily paddling languid circles next to their life mate. Even Belinda, the mother who had it all, the mother whom she'd witnessed lasciviously and theatrically squeezing her husband's butt at a school function while emphasizing some point, to the delighted shrieks of a doting crowd, had told her directly that she was only home for five hours a night, to refuel between ball-crushing in court—in what scenario were she and her lizardlike husband getting it on?

Annie vaguely remembered reading somewhere that Balzac had abstained from sex during particularly creative periods, masturbated just to the point of orgasm and then lunged for his quill, shot up on adrenaline. Maybe, unconsciously, her own relatively dead sex life was inching her closer to Balzac? But out of breath, instead of saying any of this aloud, she only grunted to Laura in agreement.

• • •

Financial Times Saturday Profile

SPOTLIGHT ON: BELINDA BRENNER

Age: 42

Occupation: Divorce Lawyer

Alma Mater: Princeton B.S., Yale J.D.

Hometown: Greenwich, Connecticut

Currently based in: New York City

Lives with: her husband, Greg, and son, Brando, 4 years old

Favorite Quote: "You don't know a woman till you've met her in court."
—*Norman Mailer*

Sitting on Belinda Brenner's desk in her fortieth-story Midtown Manhattan office is a small picture frame displaying a torn, splattered piece of lined paper, ripped out of a notebook. On it is a grid labeled "Prisoner's Dilemma," a staple of game theory that addresses cooperation, punishment, and self-interest.

"I grabbed it from a sticky, beer-soaked table at Mory's after my mentor drew it out for me, however many years ago," Brenner explained, referencing the historic New Haven watering hole while sipping a piping hot beverage from the travel mug that is never more than an arm's length away. "I refer to it every single day. Clients come to me feeling like they are in prison, and I point to this and I say, *Don't worry. Either we'll find a way to make your spouse cooperate, or we'll drop-kick them off the Verrazzano Bridge!*"

The Prisoner's Dilemma has long been a tool used to better understand decision-making in politics and economics. It was Brenner, in a move that exemplifies the outside-the-box thinking that has earned her clients some of the highest alimony settlements in the field's history, who brought it into divorce court.

The premise: A bank has been robbed and the cops have arrested two people, who are in separate interrogation rooms. If they remain silent and refuse to confess, the cops will give them each three years in prison on a lesser charge (the exact times vary, depending on the version). If they both confess, they'll get five years in prison. But the cops then also offer each a Faustian bargain: if one confesses and the other remains silent, the confessor will be released as a reward for cooperating, and their accomplice will serve ten years. The findings of playing out the dilemma show that, even though actors should go for the mutually beneficial outcome, and stay silent, they won't; they'll both confess, because people act in self-interest.

	SILENT	CONFESSES
SILENT	Both get 3 years	Confessor: 0 years Silent: 10 years
CONFESSES	Silent: 10 years Confessor: 0 years	Both get 5 years

Caption: Brenner's framed desk art

How does this relate, precisely, to divorce?

"When you get married, you enter into one long prisoner's dilemma," Brenner explained.

Marriages start with each party trying to keep the other happy, cooperating, working together. This often boils down to making a sacrifice here or there. You don't want a situation in which one person is bleeding the other dry any more than you want one in which neither is contributing to the greater good.

"The dilemma is a framework for understanding how rational actors behave, but by the time clients end up in that chair across from me, they are no longer acting rationally," Brenner continued. "They want their spouse to, effectively, get ten years while they get off scot-free." Her job, as she sees it, is to work with the other party's lawyer to pull her client back off that ledge, since the most lucrative settlements happen when people stay out of court and cooperate with each other—particularly when children are involved.

"But if we can't do that," Brenner said, "well, then I'll do everything in my power to, metaphorically speaking, send their spouse to prison not for ten years, but for life!" Then she let loose the high-pitched laugh known to any of the reporters who prowl the halls of the downtown courts, looking for stories.

"She'll never break the law, but, man, does she know how to bend it," said Michael Feranti, who wrote *Happily Never After*, a *New York Times* bestseller about divorce court. "She bends it beautifully. For top attorneys, sitting on the other side of the desk from Belinda is like playing chess against a Grandmaster—terrifying and thrilling. She has an uncanny ability to see into the soul of her opponent, and then use their weaknesses to crush them."

Brenner now helms her own firm, Brenner and Associates, built on an eat-what-you-kill model. A summer internship with the firm is one of the most coveted for top female law students who eschew the masculine white-shoe culture typical of most New York City firms for a chance to cut their teeth at a place where they'll get exposure—and potentially a piece of the winnings—right out of the gate. Multiple sources took pains to point out, however, that Brenner retains a vise grip on the most granular functions of her firm, interviewing summer associates herself and even cite-checking briefs, a task typically delegated to junior employees.

Since giving birth to her son four years ago, it's impossible not to note a through line across many of her victories: she's taken to using children in her negotiations, which is why various lawyers are speculating they may play a role in her upcoming case, in which she will be representing Manon Moureau against her longtime husband, tennis champion Gui, a fashionista who, rumor has it, staffs his houses exclusively with young, attractive men. The Moureaus have two sets of twins, one identical, one not.

"The statistical chances of a double twin natural birth are one in seven hundred thousand, give or take," said another high-profile divorce lawyer out of Hollywood. "How likely is it that their children were conceived naturally? I bet IVF plays a role here. Maybe they're not even his kids! Has anyone seen them hit a backhand?"

"I can't disclose any details here," Brenner demurred when asked about the case directly, "other than I will do everything in my power to make sure Manon, who's played second fiddle long enough, gets her due."

In many ways, that framed little scrap of paper is a nice metaphor for Brenner's philosophy: anything—however cheap, dirty, crumpled up, and forgotten—can become a touchstone if you put a wide matte around it and dress it up nice. And, similarly, anything bright and shiny—even a former No. 1 world champion—can become fraudulent and dull, so long as you spin the right narrative.

You'd think, with her complete and utter devotion to the field, she might have some personal tie to divorce, but her parents are still happily married, and she says she couldn't function without her husband, Greg.

"When I met my husband, it was like finding the other half of my soul in another person's body," she said, paraphrasing Aristotle. "But Joan Didion famously said that 'marriage is the classic betrayal,' and as long as that's the case for my clients, I'll keep springing out of bed in the morning, ready to help."

• • •

From: Ash Wempole
To: Annie Lewin
Subject: A breakthrough idea!!!!

Star momma! Loved how raw you were in this week's column. But honestly, we need to get down to brass tacks, as they (who? I've literally never heard anyone say that! And what even are brass tacks? LOL) say: Your talent is just. Not. Translating. Into. Clicks! What a bummer. I've been trying to come up with ways to target those younger mommas, and I had an idea that did not involve TikTok or putting your kids online, a way to make you sound a little more "with it." And I realize this might be a legit big ask because proper grammar is, like, your *thing* *dancing woman in a red dress emoji* but a lot of younger millennials are putting j' in front of verbs, like sort of making it French. So sophisticated and cute! It's easier to just do it than explain. So it's like:

Did anyone see the Super Bowl commercial with the grandpa? J'cried!!!

Or, *I know some of you go for Eggs Benedict for brunch, but j'bageled.* (I saw j'bageled and just thought it was so brilliant and hilarious, both with the sophistication of the j' but also the cleverness of turning eating a bagel into a verb. LOVE!)

Do you think you'd be open to doing something kind of funky like that in some of your posts?

J'hope so!

What we're seeking here is some sort of retweet that will make you go viral and draw readers to you. Influencers like @TequilaMom are a great first tier of people to try to get into your orbit. Then, the dream: @ChrissyTeigen.

Also, any urn thoughts? You could pop an avocado seed in there and then watch it grow with the kiddos . . . make those 'cado memories . . . Just sayin' . . .

Ash

She/They

Editress. Wordsmith. Potter.

@RiseFromTheAshes

Etsy store: TerraCottaAndAsh

From: Annie Lewin

To: Ash Wempole

Subject: re: A breakthrough idea!!!!

Forgive me for inching into territory you might term "too real," but the kids were up throughout the night so I may have lost my filter. Just pulling a few things from your email:

(1) You're mistaking garden urns for funerary urns that have been repurposed. They've been a fixture in gardens for centuries, even dating back to early Greek and Roman gardens. These have very little to do with funerary urns and are in fact simply used because they are aesthetically pleasing. Originally, ancient urns also held wine. Could I buy a few of your urns to drink wine out of? LOL.

(2) Brass tacks: Here *hyperlink* is a picture of a brass tack. The consensus from various historians seems to be that it has to do with the brass tacks historically used to affix upholstery to furniture. However, the explanation I prefer has to do with coffins. When you pass away, the last thing that will happen to your coffin—unless, of course, you're planning to use one of your own urns to do the deed!—is that brass tacks, or nails, will be driven into the top to secure it. In this instance, the meaning references a man faced with his death, and thus approaching the world as it is, with no bullshit.

(3) Grammar! So pesky, that little thing. Well, *je refuse*. (That is actually French.) I tried signing off with j'cheers but most of my readers will likely assume I've had a seizure while typing. I mean, I look at the word *j'bageled* and think . . . Just, no. Maybe there's some other thing we can try? I know you keep asking me to be more raw, but honestly, I feel as raw as a chicken

drumstick in a deep freezer. I'm just not the kind of person to lay that rawness out there for everyone to see. I'm doing my best!

Thanks for your patience and guidance in this brave, new, click-driven world,

Annie

• • •

Annie recognized his voice before she could place it, a gravelly huskiness she reflexively associated with high school bad boys and teen angst—and then she saw him, tugging a little girl's coat off and pulling her sleeves up for a hand wash in the tiny bathroom with the tiny toilet, baseball cap pulled over hair now graying and wild. When it came to Claire's turn, just as Annie was getting the paper towel ready for her, the name poofed into her brain. *Shawn Axel.* Two prolific Bartleby Babes, Yael Fogelman and Christine Hodges, waiting down the line, raised eyebrows at her when she passed, both jerking their heads toward Shawn, like twin meerkats. Annie knew it was just a matter of time before the WhatsApp chain had a collective orgasm.

She'd had movie posters of Axel pinned up all over her room in middle school—the one where he broadcast an illegal TV show from his parents' basement, the one where he moved in from out of town and incited the popular girls to throw their queen bee under the bus, the one where he spent most of the time sneering his lip and tossing his thick hair behind him, hands shoved into ripped cargo jeans, as he played an unlikely child prodigy. How many nights had she gone to bed dreaming of him, writing diary entries in her locked journal about how life would be different when they could finally run away together? He'd grown up in a town a few over from hers—it could happen. To signify just how angsty and nonconformist she was, she'd even had her father tack up the double-sided posters backside front, so the image and writing was flipped, the effect being that her bedroom always felt slightly off-kilter.

After drop-off, she clicked through to the Bartleby Babes, and sure enough, there was a flurry of activity.

CHRISTINE: Um, shame on you, Leonora, for being PTA president and not telling us that SHAWN AXEL is a new parent! I must have missed that on the class list because Chance is in his kid's class!!!!!

(Shower of exclamation points)

SAMIRA: Shut. Up. Are you kidding me?

YAEL: I masturbated to him so many times.

LEONORA: *stop sign emoji* *puking emoji*

LEONORA: Sorry for the delay, but you know Bartleby values discretion above all else, I figured I'd wait until he made an appearance. *dancing woman in a red dress emoji*

CHRISTINE: OK just checked the class list and his name and email isn't listed. Just hers. I figured that kid had a single mom. *crying laughing emoji*

YAEL: Possible for me to ask for Levi to be held back a year and repeat the 3s?? He def doesn't know all his colors yet. God, I'd kill to sit through curriculum night with Shawn at my side. Swoon.

LEONORA: *warlock emoji*

(Five question marks)

LEONORA: Whoops, sorry, gals, was searching for *tongue out emoji* *fire emoji*

YAEL: PREACH. *eggplant emoji*

SAMIRA: To think I was jealous that Bartleby didn't get Alec and Hilaria's seventh child!

CHRISTINE: [GIF of young Baldwin in *Glengarry Glen Ross*, in the "Always Be Closing" scene]

YAEL: LMFAO. Why isn't he living in Brooklyn and sending his kids to school with the Sarsgaard and Damon girls?

MAYA: His wife apparently has had a soft spot for the UES since she rented a studio here as a teenager and got signed by Wilhelmina (thanks, Google *wink emoji*). They moved in Sept.

YAEL: The wife. I'm listening . . . *ear emoji*

CHRISTINE: Recently started some kind of kids' toy company, according to her Insta. I'm already plotting how to make sure she's part of this year's benefit.

SAMIRA: How much would something signed by Shawn Axel rake in?! Gotta get Bartleby that rooftop garden, biatches!

CHRISTINE: Maybe they could donate a night with him.

LEONORA: Sign my bosom, Shawn!

CHRISTINE: Always be closing.

BELINDA: *flexed bicep emoji* *fist pound emoji* *small explosion emoji*

(Heart overload)

Outside, at pickup for Claire, he was there again—sitting on the front steps and sucking on some sort of vaping cartridge that looked like a jump drive, still bad to the bone, but now with a tasseled little girl's scooter in one hand. The doors opened and the threes poured out, Claire decorated with a light dusting of glitter, carrying a thick roll of paintings in one hand and dragging a boy with the other.

"Mama!" she crowed. "This my new friend, Oliver!"

As Claire and Oliver started to run tight circles around her, Annie watched Shawn push himself up from the steps and jam the cartridge he'd been sucking into his pocket, just in time to scoop up a little girl who'd barreled down the stairs. He had a gut, and was wearing a lumberjack shirt, but was still the guy from her posters. Her heart fluttered a bit, and she hated herself for that flutter.

"And who's that?" she prompted Claire, as Shawn and his daughter made their way down the block, out of earshot.

"That's . . ." Claire thought. "That's Amoeba."

"Amoeba," Oliver echoed, nodding.

Hmmm. Hollywood. There'd been a Moon Unit, there could be an Amoeba.

Before they'd reached the end of the block, Annie had googled her way through the intervening thirty years, during which Shawn had been admitted to rehab, took on a few supporting roles in universally panned films, met an ex-model—at one point famous enough that she went by a mononym—on the beach in Ibiza, then gotten a divorce and moved across the country to pursue true love. "Shawn Axel and Clementina welcomed their first daughter, Amelia Luce Axel, in August," read the *Post* headline. Just two weeks after Claire.

Well, he already left one woman, Laura texted back, after the Axel update. *You never know.*

Yeah, right. The issue wasn't him leaving his wife—it was Annie cheating. She was the kind of person who never drank or ate after a visit to the dentist until the allotted three hours had passed, who'd always done her homework first thing on Friday afternoons, who would be too petrified of getting caught doing the wrong thing that even the thought of misbehaving made her feel guilty.

Which didn't mean she didn't contemplate it.

That night, with Dan off at another work event—*At what point did those become, professionally and financially, optional?* she wondered—Annie had a dinner of leftover kids' food, a dessert of Cheetos fistfuls, washed it all back with two generous glasses of cheap pinot noir, then opened up Netflix and typed in his name.

Oh god. She'd forgotten all about *Kiss from a Rose*. It was one of his last films, when he'd transitioned out of teenage hunk status but before he'd fully become a no-longer-employable druggie. In it, he played a gardener who tends the estate of an aging heiress. The first half of the film, which Annie rewatched at 2x speed, was mostly shots of him striding up and down hills in dirty jeans, a shovel slung over his shoulder, or wiping his brow with a muddy hand, observing his rich employers from a distance. Then the heiress's daughter comes to visit, allegedly because the heiress is getting older and can no longer take care of herself. But after making love on a pile of freshly lain sod, the daughter admits to him, weeping—and in keeping with the dramas of the day—that the reason she came home was not to take care of her mother, but because she herself has cancer, that rare kind that afflicts only willowy, early-twenties movie heroines. The last shot of the film is Shawn meticulously planting tulip bulbs around a gravestone, squinting into the sunlight as Seal's "Kiss from a Rose" swells in the background.

That song—like Proust's madeleine, zipping her back to the air-conditioned summer theater, watching the movie with a middle-school crush—made about as much sense as the movie it scored.

"But did you know," the cool voice crooned over the credits, "my eyes become large and the light that you shine can't be seen."

Huh? she thought sleepily as she drifted off.

• • •

Annie identified Max's cries immediately as she came up out of a deep sleep a few hours later. Dan, who'd snuck under the covers god knows when, was breathing deeply, and she tamped down her urge to kick him, hard, and force him into a moment she seemed biologically programmed never to sleep through. But seconds later she found herself down the hall, fully consumed by the intoxicating scent of her baby's eight-month-old body, a baguette fresh out of the oven, and forgot all about score keeping.

As she cradled Max and hummed "Rockabye, Baby," he gazed up at her, his eyes big and round in the dark, then started to coo along like a little dove, his body vibrating against hers. For the first few months out in the world, he'd done nothing but stare up at her as she sang, unblinking, as stone-faced as an Olympic judge, still so close to the pre-world, the state of infinite knowledge, as to appear wise in his silence. But lately, he'd begun to sing back, tapping into a primal mother-child bond that had sustained centuries of sleepless nights and kept people procreating. Tonight, it only took a few minutes for exhaustion to overpower him. He stuck his chubby index finger into his mouth, turned his head in toward her like a little panda bear preparing to somersault, and drifted off. As sometimes happened, she was overcome with an almost pre-nostalgic feeling, that her son would soon reach an age when he'd no longer fit so perfectly in her arms, when his limbs would spill out like an octopus's tentacles and he wouldn't be caught dead singing a duet with his mother, when he'd morph into a lanky, smelly teenager who sported sweaty, hairy extremities and had no comfort objects save for some sleek tech gadget. And so, long after his breathing had steadied and she was certain he was fast asleep, Annie stayed in the dark quiet of the nursery, swaying back and forth like a languid pendulum in a grandfather clock.

Which is when it happened a second time.

She turned to check the time on the glow-in-the-dark clock, but instead of finding its neon face, she saw pinpricks of stars shining through a deep black that now engulfed her, the soft whoosh from the noise machine having crescendoed into a dull roar. With dawning dread, she sensed that she was back in that in-between place she'd dipped into at first-day drop-off, when Belinda had been chattering on about music school. *Not again*, she thought, suddenly realizing, with a sickening stomach drop, that Laura wasn't there to bring her back to reality, that Dan was fast asleep, that she'd have to navigate this bizarre moment alone. But as she looked down to see her nightgown swaying in a breeze beneath her, in her peripheral vision she sensed she wasn't, actually, alone. There were other nightgowned figures treading air next to her, all of them straining futilely to escape the pull of being sucked into the super-massive black hole just over yonder, like water down a drain, which would drop them straight through to . . . what? Something scary and cosmically overwhelming, the antithesis of the sun, so dark you couldn't look directly at it.

She wasn't sure how long she hung there in the balance—could have been a few seconds, or an hour—but when Max shifted in her arms, her bare feet dropped down softly onto the carpet, and she found herself once again in the nursery, sound machine humming, glow-in-the-dark hands showing it was three a.m. *Maybe this was just exhaustion speaking?* Heart pounding in her ears,

Annie quickly placed her sleeping baby back safely into the crib, then tiptoed her way to bed, where, like a trembling deer, she lay awake until dawn, every shadow, every creak jolting her into tightly wound awareness.

• • •

From: Maya Goodson
To: Class 204 Mommas
Subject: Class spa eve (+ dranks!!)

Dearest Mommas of Class 204,

I'd like to introduce myself as your new class rep (woot!) and invite you all to a get-to-know-each-other spa night. Figure we all could use a little pampering, so I've hired a few girls from a new service, SpaTinis™, to come and do an at-home session for all of us lucky gals. (And yes, 'tinis will be had!)*

A little about me: my eldest, Byron, just started at St. Edward's after three wonderful years at Bartleby, and my baby, Darwin, is in class with your lovely children. I've served as a class rep for two years and have volunteered for a third year because little brings me more joy than getting to hang with you lovelies and then pester you for holiday gifts. (Lol—but seriously, we should chat about what we want to give our teachers this year. Was thinking perhaps Hermès totes with the faces of our children embroidered on them—I know an amazing embroideress, just left Madame Paulette's and is now a free agent, squeeee! If so, will need a high-res digital file of your child's headshot, shot straight on, smiling, and with hair brushed and neat. The embroideress is *very* literal, so will actually embroider stray hairs onto the bag!)

Anywho, the deets:

Who: 204 Mommas
What: SpaTini™ home visit
Where: Maya's event space (address provided upon RSVP)

When: Next Thursday at 6 p.m.

Why: Spa! 'Tinis! SpaTinis!

To do: RSVP with your preferred service. Menu attached. Please note: the "fish pedicure," in which so-called doctor fish eat the dead skin off your feet, will *not* be an option, because Byron is allergic to freshwater fish and I can't risk contamination. (I won't get into details, but we learned this the hard way on an off-season trip to Telluride last summer!)

Can't wait to bond!

Xo

Maya

*We have totally lucked out by having Christine Hutton Hodges as a fellow class mom. Christine's longtime housekeeper, Ayu, periodically has her family overnight fresh fruit from their farm outside of Bandung in Indonesia, which I swear tastes better even than those $20-on-FreshDirect Oishii berries. Meaning: get ready for lycheetinis.

• • •

"Don't do da Scottish accent!" Annie heard Claire protest through the monitor at bedtime as she unpacked upstairs. But Dan started up his guttural Loch Lomond anyway, heavy on the brogue, and by the time he got to the chorus and those bonnie bonnie banks, Claire had quieted down, well on her way toward drifting off to dreams about dead Jacobites taking that low road of death back to Scotland—or so Annie assumed. Though Dan had made noises about joining a local choir in the city after graduation, work had descended, his star had ascended, then Sam had arrived, and where was the time? Annie couldn't help but think, as she placed sweatshirts in vaguely color-coded piles, that their lives were like some sort of depressing graphic that accompanied an *Atlantic* piece about middle age—the older you got, the more circumscribed your interests, friend circle, world. At least she could still reap the benefits of his a cappella training at lullaby time.

When writing a column about the power of singing to your children, she'd come upon a study that said it might be an adaptive trait: the better of a singer you are—whether bird, whale, or human—the more attractive of a mate you become. She wondered, occasionally, how it would have gone that first night they'd met if his voice had been horrific. But at the concert she'd been sent to cover for the *Crimson*'s Arts section, he'd seduced not just the entirety of Sanders Theater with his rendition of "Down by the Salley Gardens," but—she realized, as she followed him to the after-party, baffled and against her better judgment, and then his room, where his concert-mandated tuxedo quickly came off— her, too.

In her mind's eye montage of that first semester together, they barely left his bed, the sheets a constant tangle on the floor, the dust motes swirling in the long shadows of the sun the only indication that another day had begun. She must have gone to class, continued to file articles for the *Crimson*, attended Dan's last few concerts. His roommates must have been in and out, but mostly, she remembered lying there, discovering each other's bodies and eating takeout from the Thai place across the street in their underwear, accompanied by a soundtrack of Dan singing Mose Allison songs to make her laugh.

Annie had studied piano, dutifully but unremarkably, as a child, and could sum up her own musical talents with a single anecdote: to fulfill an arts requirement in high school, she'd signed up for jazz band, figuring she'd read sheet music for one semester and check that box. But when she realized she was also expected to solo, tinkling the ivories with melodies she'd create on the spot, she spent nights painstakingly transcribing the piano solos of great musicians, then playing them note-for-note in class. During the sophomore Christmas concert, the teacher was so impressed with phrasing that she'd cribbed, but exactly, from Al Haig—one of Charlie Parker's bandmates—he assumed she'd reached some sort of jazz nirvana, and, grooving to the music, signaled with a spinning index finger that she should take a second solo. Having no other option, she awkwardly played the same exact lines again, actively ignoring her teacher's flummoxed expression.

Dan, unlike her, was naturally gifted, equally able to follow along or riff. He'd found his passion back in elementary school, when the music teacher recognized that he had a particularly good ear and could parrot back any number of musical phrases she threw at him. As a high schooler, he was given the coveted "O Holy Night" solo at St. John the Divine and would take the bus across town each week to practice, Jesus gazing down from his cross at this Reform Jewish kid belting out in full-throated, eyes-closed commitment about falling down on his knees in rapture to Jesus.

"It was never about the girls," he'd told her. "It was always about the music. It was not considered a cool thing to do. Ever."

This became ragingly apparent at the group's after-parties, all held at a grimy karaoke bar in Harvard Square. Instead of following sake bombs with off-key renditions of Queen and Miley Cyrus in the hopes of getting laid, to date the only way Annie had ever seen karaoke approached, that first one she attended, she'd walked into the packed room to find a quartet singing "Midnight Train to Georgia." They'd somehow procured four microphones, instead of the standard two that came with the room, and as the soloist sang the top line with all the swagger of the Empress of Soul herself, three backup singers swayed back and forth, doing bland but highly specific locomotive moves, and singing call-and-response in tight, practiced four-part harmony, no part overshadowing the others. She later learned this was called "blending," a coveted musical combination that a cappella singers speak about with a reverence usually reserved for scripture. It was then, as her future husband flashed her a sheepish grin and shrugged, surrounded by other highly trained singers eagerly awaiting their turn at the mic—not one of whom cared even slightly how others might judge him for his love of Scottish ballads and old standards—that it dawned on her just whom she'd begun to fall for.

Her friends joked that it was like *Pretty in Pink*, her from the wrong side of the tracks and wearing sweats, him an adorable, wealthy Andrew McCarthy, perpetually striding around campus in a tuxedo—though he only told her the truth later on. *Wouldn't the story end with her alone at the prom?* But there was something so refreshing about proximity to someone who wasn't pretending, who enjoyed the finer things in life and was both unabashed about—and clearheaded in—his desire for them. For while he was a naturally gifted singer, she grew to understand that for Dan, even the a cappella wasn't just about the music.

"Oh, yeah, it's dorky even if you're not from suburban New Jersey," he confirmed one night after coming back from performing "I Wan'na Be Like You" from the *Jungle Book* at Alan Dershowitz's birthday party at the Faculty Club. Though Harvard was perhaps the only place in the world where a cappella trumped football on the prestige ladder, there was still a whiff of nerdiness about it. "But I now have Dershowitz's personal email, should that ever come in handy. Honestly, what other college hobby has an endowment and an alumni network full of titans of industry?"

Annie had never considered college to be anything other than a place to double down on academics, and, if you were lucky, find other birds of a feather doubling down next to you in the stacks— but, of course, as the *Boston Globe* incident went on to teach her, even if you had the chops once you walked through the door, you still needed to find a way to pry the door open first.

In many ways, it had formed the foundation for their relationship. Junior spring, a few months after she and Dan had started dating, she'd flopped down on the bed in his dorm room, dejected that some middling student in her journalism seminar had secured a summer internship at the *Times*, simply because his uncle's name was on the masthead.

"The *Globe* didn't even respond to my application letter!" she'd humphed, ripping the aluminum foil off a burrito and taking a furious bite. "It's infuriating. His stories are so overwritten, and he always gives the best lines to himself, never lets his sources have them. That's, like, the cardinal sin of reporting."

After a minute of silent googling, Dan looked up. "I found the managing editor's direct email online. It's right there on the staff page," he said. "Just send her a cover letter and include your story that just ran in the *Crimson*, the one about the decline in humanities enrollment. It's all anyone's talking about. You're obviously more talented than anyone in your seminar. Just see if they can make room."

Make room?

"But the applications were due two months ago, the decisions have already been made," she'd protested. "There are no more spots. Plus, I'm sure the managing editor isn't involved in granular stuff like summer internships. Isn't it a bit . . . presumptuous to just go over the top like that?"

"What do you have to lose?" he'd countered.

That night, he helped her craft a letter, the electronic whoosh as it hurtled into the cloud filling her with a mixture of hope and nerves and dread. The next day she had a phone interview, and the week after that, an internship. Et voilà, a new storyline, created by sheer force of will.

After graduation, Dan spent a chunk of his signing bonus on a trip for them to Europe, during which he mostly stared at her in charmed awe as she stared at various masterpieces in air-conditioned museums, and on the plane ride home, he told her she should quit screwing around and just move in with him. He'd rented a studio apartment in a modern high-rise with a washer-dryer down the hall (swoon!) near his office at the bank, and she could bike to work, and, honestly, were they really going to be spending enough nights apart to justify it financially? And she'd thought, *Well, that does sound practical. Not to mention better than splitting a one-bedroom with three girls in Bushwick.* When her mom had trained into the city to visit one Saturday and taken in the sweeping views, her eyes doing the awooga thing that cartoon characters do, Annie found herself saying, defensively, before she'd even uttered a word, "Mom, I realize it's really nice, but it makes financial sense, I can explain."

"It's just amazing to me, that's all, to be able to wake up to this view every morning," her mother had replied, recovering quickly. "It's fine to like nice things, sweetie. All humans have a little hedonism in their DNA." Then, gesturing to the expanse of the city, Annie's childhood split-level home lying somewhere beyond the glittering Hudson, "What luck!"

Luck for her, yes, but in Dan's case, strategy, too. When he left the bank to start his own fund, knocking on yet another door she hadn't known existed—*People their age could be their own bosses? Who would trust a kid like him with their hard-earned cash?*—he started wearing a wedding ring to investor meetings, long before he proposed and simply, he explained, to help his baby face command a bit more respect at the negotiating table. She'd balked—*wasn't that an easily verifiable lie?* But no one so much as batted an eye, prospective investors were drawn in, and a few years later, they were married anyway. She found it astonishing, and also comforting, to see someone will a life into existence.

"Man, she was a lot tonight," Dan said, as he walked into the room after three "Loch Lomonds" and two "Danny Boys," gaze shifting from his phone to his Apple Watch as he collapsed into bed, where he clapped his hand over a message as if killing an errant mosquito.

She was about to bring up Sam's application essay, due at the end of the month, when the sound of something crashing emanated from Dan's phone, then another, and then he let forth a cackle.

"Holy shit. Annie, you gotta see this," he said, eyes glued to his phone. "It's the former Flexport CEO with his Porsche. He's going to go Ferris Bueller on it, I swear. Ohmygodohmygod."

She didn't even have to ask.

The TechCrunched channel was a subgenre of YouTube destruction videos in which tech entrepreneurs and employees who'd made windfalls of money publicly destroyed expensive items they'd purchased in the glow of an IPO—Patek Philippe watches were popular, as were Waterford vases. The first post, which kicked it all off, famously featured a college dropout CEO of a Fintech company who—after his company went public and he, personally, made a fortune that rivaled the GDP of Vanuatu—destroyed his hydrofoil using a homemade slingshot and rocks smoothed by the tides of Lake Tahoe. The channel had risen in popularity in concert with inflation, now boasting millions of views per post, soaring ever upward like a unicorn valuation.

As with any trend, the media would not tire of writing think pieces on what it meant about the world, writ large: that it was a comment on the emptiness of capitalism; on the destructive power of wealth and the havoc wrought of massive income inequality; on the angst felt by the alienated masses who, no matter where they sat on the socioeconomic spectrum, believed they'd been sold a bill of goods when it came to the promised fulfillment of work; on the universal lack of meaning felt by a generation that was approaching forty but still identified with being in its twenties. *Perhaps.* But judging from how many dads in her cohort watched the videos, Annie suspected it had more to do with a primal need for catharsis craved by all these digitally castrated men, stuck in their Slack channels and Gmail portals and Twitter threads all day and unable to let loose in real life.

Huge crash.

"In. Sane." Pause. "I gotta go let off some steam. I'm gonna do a Peloton."

Bye, she was about to say, but he was already gone.

• • •

From: Camila Garcia Williams
To: Annie Lewin
Subject: re: OMG Belinda

AHHHH, how I've missed my crazed NYC dispatches! Is Belinda still drinking scalding Red Bull every morning? LOL.

So sorry for the massive response delay, I can barely get out the door in one piece with just Elio. And you have three. Blergh. But I remain ever so glad to get these long missives in my inbox! (Are we the last two people on earth to write longer than a tweet? Thankful the time difference forced us into this antiquated mode of communication after graduation, fellow crone.)

Some thoughts, in no particular order:

(1) That guy Scott who was the head of the Harvard Republicans when we were sophomores: I saw him at Dolores Park the other day when we were picnicking—he'd come from brunch at the hot new restaurant with $30 entrees and I was like um, no, I'm cool with this homemade sandwich not only because it tastes good but because I am actually proud to work at a nonprofit (unspoken: you jerk)—and he asked me what Elio's extracurriculars were and I actually said, throwing rocks in puddles and chewing on crayons. He did not laugh. Apparently *his* two-year-old, Hudson, has been taking chess classes since he could grip a rook. Gag. So, the crazy is bicoastal. Take comfort in that. We may be the only two weirdos left who want our kids to just be kids.

(2) You going off the reservation: You've been writing your column for just about four months now. Remember how excited you were when you started? Excuse me while I cut and paste from an email in July: "There's something so freeing about writing for a non-legacy publication, where I can just try stuff out and get immediate feedback, and be humorous, and really let my voice shine." Is that still possible? Also: I know we're not supposed to bring this up, but what about the agent who reached out to you about turning your op-ed into a book? Could you maybe noodle on that for a little bit every day and see where it leads you? Could give you something bigger to sink your teeth into.

(3) Hallucinating in broad daylight: Dying to hear more, but before we head straight to the sanitorium, when was the last time you got a full night's sleep? Ate a proper meal, not over the sink after the kids were tucked in? Had date night? Just take care of yourself a little!

(4) Remember that insane lecture in the Science Center when the professor made us watch videos of frogs jumping out of pots of water to demonstrate that the "frog in boiling water phenomenon" is not thermodynamically sound? Just, um, remember that frog, as you navigate these moneyed waters, okay? Maybe, like an actual frog, you'll jump out when the water gets too hot, but maybe, like the metaphoric frog, it will creep up on you . . .

(4a) Speaking of, re: sacrificing your child: Sacrificing?! What a word.

Wouldn't exposure to an environment where there isn't, gasp, a shoemaking class or a pool help shape a far more resilient, interesting child who will eventually become the kind of adult you want them to be? I started wrestling with this stuff before I was even pregnant with Elio—we could have gotten a much bigger plot in Oakland or El Cerrito but only looked at Berkeley because of the public schools. So yeah, our mortgage is higher, but so be it. As for this fear you have that Sam might be bored in a non-rigorous school, I mean sure, I was wildly bored in public school in Texas, and you know what my parents told me to do? Go read a book, or focus on all the other things that are more important than just academics. And then at Harvard, I was able to balance school and life way better than most. Maybe I didn't go on to get a super-prestigious job, but I'm quite happy! That's important, too, no?

(5) Your text about the "connected family Zoom" with Sawyer: there are no words. Are you supposed to get dressed up for a Zoom meeting with a prep school? Can you at least please show up pantsless, a little screw you to the man? They'll never know but WE WILL. It's a silent protest. Protect your dignity!

More updates from me soon, but I have exactly forty-five minutes to cook a big one-pot pasta thing to take to our block's block party before Elio wakes up from his nap and we go for a walk in Muir Woods. I'm such a caricature, I know.

Complimenti, you bitch (lol),

Xo

Camila

P.S. Two words: CHEWING GUM. Don't bite your own body off! Please!

• • •

"You're seriously going to insist on conducting this meeting in your underwear?" Dan scoffed, as Annie adjusted her crisp white blouse and angled the camera just slightly away from her, so she could continue to drink her wine off-screen.

But before she could reply, the Zoom opened, and the computer screen flooded with tiny little squares—Sawyer's head of school, who'd present first in this Zoom open only to parents who were alums themselves; then the head of the classics department, one of the most lauded in the city; followed by the diversity director; and, finally, the grand finale, the head of admissions.

Timmie Sullivan's legend preceded her. Of all the admissions directors at all the city's independent schools, she had held the position the longest, and the online chat boards Annie had checked out in preparation for this Zoom proliferated with queries on how not to screw up a coveted in-person interview. If you were to risk the first name address, better to go with Timmie or Timothea? (In the kaffeeklatsches that formed on the Upper East Side every fall, she was referred to as "Queen T," or simply "QT.") Use some sort of prefix when speaking to her—she did have that master's in museum curation—or just Mrs.? Or was it Miss? (She preferred the simple Miss, but pronounced with a Z at the end. She'd never married.) Was it appropriate to send a thank-you note, or gift? (Thank-you notes were fine, so long as they were handwritten, and gifts strictly prohibited, after an incident in which one art-scene-adjacent family offered exclusive access to the impressionist galleries in the Metropolitan Museum of Art, at whatever time was convenient for her, perhaps on Sunday mornings, first thing? They'd done their research and discovered that she headed straight for the Monets after her weekend coffee at Via Quadronno, a triple cappuccino, bone-dry. While it was the most difficult gift she'd ever had to turn down, she also had an impeccable sense of class and found it tasteless that her enjoyment of the paintings would deny other museumgoers access to the masterworks for her benefit. Not to mention creepy that this family knew her weekend whereabouts.)

In interviews with various media outlets, Sullivan always said the same thing: she understood the anxiety—on average, fifty children applied for every spot at Sawyer, a number that had risen after the most recent capital campaign—and felt it was her duty to disarm parents and children as much as possible, to get the best sense of whether the family was, truly, Sawyer material. This was partially why she insisted that interviews take place jointly with children and parents, a signature of Sullivan's that she'd instituted within a year of taking the head position. Other schools separated the children into "playdate" observations while the parents sat in the admission director's office, sweaty hands folded primly in their laps, desperately trying to seem normal and down-to-earth but also unique and spectacular, all the while panicking that their offspring might be throwing a career-ending tantrum next door—a tightrope that Sullivan didn't want anyone to have to walk. Merging the two, and having one of her admissions team in the room to quietly observe the child as he or she played on the rug while she spoke to the parents, she felt relaxed all parties and gave everyone his or her opportunity to shine. In her clip from the *60 Minutes* special put out a few years ago, Sullivan was shot from across her maroon leather-topped desk, a stack of manila folders to one side. As her segment faded to black and right before that stopwatch clicked its way to a commercial, the camera caught her rubbing her palms together before lifting one from the top of a pile. The next chosen child, or the next outcast? *Tick, tick, tick.*

Dan recognized about half of the other connected families on the Zoom. Leonard Mitchell's child was applying—Dan told Annie that he could remember, like it was yesterday, when Leonard walked onto the stage during Thursday assembly thirty years ago and conducted the high school orchestra in his original composition. He'd gone on to win an EGOT and become one of the most lauded songwriters in modern history. Yiwen Chao's daughter was also applying. She was now an international starchitect. Sitting in their old middle-school classroom was Yiwen's eighth-grade ancient history fair project: a three-quarter-size replica of King Tutankhamun's sarcophagus, complete with golden mask and crook, molded out of clay. It was one of her first known creations, and Sawyer was holding on to it with a vise grip.

"Man," Annie said, sipping her wine off camera, "seems like, um, this has way more to do with the parents than it does the kids, doesn't it?"

"In which case we'll crush the competition," Dan said through gritted teeth, face frozen in a smile for the camera. "You're a former *Times* reporter. And I'm *not* a hedge fund guy or an investment banker."

Annie snorted.

"Is there a difference between that and being a venture capitalist?"

"Jesus, Annie, are you actually serious?"

Mmmk.

For sure, Sawyer had in some file somewhere a whole section on the fall of Dan's father, which had happened Dan's last year there—a fall like Hemingway's famous quote, gradual, then all at once. A business tycoon who also liked to frequent the offtrack betting parlor by Penn Station to blow off some steam, Dan's father had gotten the family in deep enough of a hole that they'd had to sell off the apartment and downsize five avenue blocks closer to the East River—still comfortable, but no longer a player. His mother, in denial and trying to save face, had held a fundraiser at the Fifth Avenue maisonette a few days before the movers came. The divorce came shortly after. Annie, who had taken a few psychology classes, had a parlor Freud explanation for Dan's clearheaded goals, the methodical steps he took to achieve them, even his choice of Annie instead of a born-and-raised New Yorker: all of it was, in a sense, a reaction to his father's downfall and family's rupture. What calmed Dan more than anything was control and stability. One part of that puzzle: the apartment. Another: her. A third: a son at Sawyer.

"So anyway," she said, as the head of school put on a video about the school, the opening notes of Dave Brubeck's "Take 5" overlaid on top of a zooming drone shot that took them way up high over the turf, then swooped down to enter a music classroom, revealing the middle-school jazz orchestra playing the soundtrack, "I've started a draft of Sam's essay, his statement or whatever. I tried to capture his entire essence in five hundred words but feel a little bit out of my depth here. Like, do we want to present him as being insanely precocious, which he is, or should we have more humility? I was going to write about the lemonade stand, but then I thought—"

"No humility," Dan cut her off, a ventriloquist, his face still plastered into a smile. "And stop talking. They're watching. This is all part of the interview."

• • •

In five hundred words or less, please describe your child's strengths, weaknesses, and interests.

Recently, when putting away some of Sam's laundry, his mother came upon a drawer in his closet that had been repurposed, with a sign stuck on the front: this was no longer an underwear drawer, but in fact a "Spider Kingdom."

She opened it to find, inside, exactly that: webs made of string and tape, a small LEGO café that was hawking, according to the tiny chalkboard, "fryd antz" (sic), and a circular MagnaTile bath constructed from eight triangles, presumably so a spider might have adequate washing room for his eight appendages. When questioned about it, Sam explained that he'd lived his entire life in a world not built for him—the sink was too high, the clothes hangers unreachable. "Spiders have as much a right to live happily as we do," he said, exhibiting not just his newfound love of the insect kingdom, but also an inherent compassion that extends to all creatures.

Sam keenly observes his environment and delights in drawing conclusions, often with a knowing, wry smile. Spotting a picture-perfect spiderweb free of leaves or flies, he remarked that the insect must have mopped and vacuumed recently. And while his creativity, stamina, and precocity make us proud, it's his nascent value system—in which friendship and fairness are paramount— that bowls us over. Racing is fun, but better if you can hold hands at the end and "win in a tie." If you build a printer that prints out candy, you'd better take it to your friend's house to share. And if your little sister wants a lick of your ice pop, you offer it up—but only after demanding a thank-you, which you accept after sometimes aggressive attempts at manners coaching.

Of course, like any child raised in a capitalist society, his compassion and pure selflessness have limits. After learning more about his father's job, he asked to set up a lemonade stand this summer. Even as the sun continued to rise and the sidewalk baked, he remained in his chair, debating how much of his profits he should save to invest, and how much could go toward a toy. He sold out. After setting aside $1 for a new plastic bug, he scooted to the bank and opened an account, under the name of Samuel Bernard Lewin. The remaining $6.50 is now safely accruing 5% interest, which he plans to invest in Bitcoin during the next market downturn.

NOVEMBER

Dearest Mother Inferior,

We've been married for fifteen years and, two kids and a move to the 'burbs later, the romance has officially died. The idea of trying to look nice for him, or going through the hassle of finding childcare so we can go out every once in a while, is the last thing on my to-do list. Miraculously, my husband still seems to be attracted to me—the other night, when I told him my love language was cleaning, he responded, "My love language is f*cking you!"—and does his best to initiate, but when I give in, it always feels like a chore. Is there any hope?

Signed,

G-rated in Germantown

Dearest G-rated,

Fifteen years, you say? That is five thousand, four hundred, and seventy-eight days, give or take. Do you honestly think it's reasonable to expect that for five thousand days you'll wake up as bright-eyed and bushy-tailed as a twenty-year-old Victoria's Secret model? Absolutely not, *G-rated*. So I think for starters you should stop expecting those embers to be burning, and commit to working as a team to smack some rocks together.

As a mother, you know that children learn by mimicking. And so you, too, are going to have to start mimicking your much younger self, the self who'd willingly submit to having hot wax poured on her vajoon, simply to feel a thrill when those panties came off, because we all know no one enjoys those ten minutes of pretending to read the "Celebrities are just like us" part of *People* while a nice woman squints at your nethers. You are going to fake it until you make it. (For starters: just write *fuck*. We don't need an asterisk here, this is not basic cable.)

A few logistical pointers: in order to successfully mimic someone who wants to have sex, you have to method act—really inhabit the psyche of someone who is DTF, as the kids say these days, like someone who'd go on a dating app and start texting photos of side boob, right off the bat. Jared Leto, in preparation for his role as the twisted Joker in *Suicide Squad*, allegedly mailed one costar some used condoms, and another a dead pig. You don't need to go that far, but you do need to get a babysitter, at least once every two weeks. Put on some pants you haven't worn for a while (expandable not allowed), maybe do your nails, and commit to *not* talking about logistics.

It's like riding a bike. But just as it's critical for you to put the time in to raise good children, it is critical for you and your partner to put the time in to being sexy and appealing to each other, because happy parents make for happy kids.

Here's to an X-rated future!

J'Cheers* to you!

Mother Inferior

*This isn't a typo. Pipe up in the comments if you "get" this. I'm testing it out in lieu of *Complimenti,* bitches.

• • •

Before kids, the hours between five and seven p.m. used to involve putting the finishing touches on a piece, or getting a drink before a Broadway show she needed to see for work, or browsing for a bit in the bookstore before going to a movie. Now, the entire day hurtled toward that two-hour slot and filled Annie with a sort of amped-up anxiety bested only by the sight of two empty lunchboxes sitting on the counter at eight a.m. Each morning, she imagined those insulated narwhals as little Kevin Bacons in *Animal House*, assuming the position in their skivvies and muttering, through clenched jaws, "Please sir, may I have another," as they awaited their fate of being filled up with processed junk food and sun butter sandwiches, that gray, sorry, allergen-free substitute for peanut butter that tasted nothing like peanut butter. Belinda Brenner instagrammed overhead shots of the "bento boxes" she packed for Brando's lunch—a sandwich cut to look like a dinosaur over here, a skewer of fruit over in this compartment because "eating food on sticks is fun—plus great for fine motor development!," a make-your-own sushi with all the fixings, including a shiso leaf, a cookie that literally had eyes on it, as if cookies weren't appealing enough—which Annie regarded with a kind of sickening fascination. *Where, and how, did she find the time? Or, for that matter, the creativity?*

During dinner that evening, as with most of them, Claire was methodically embellishing the floor with Peppa Pig stickers while Max rubbed macaroni and cheese in his hair and Sam browsed a *Yoga for Kids* book. Dan had promised he'd be home for the kids' dinner but of course was running late, and Annie had let Maria go early because she felt guilty sitting upstairs not writing while her housekeeper-cum-nanny effortlessly fed and bathed the children, kept everything neat, and never once raised her voice.

"Claire, three more bites, because you're three," she heard herself chirping, idiotically. Claire ignored her.

"Claire, do you want to have three more bites, or four more bites?" Sam piped in, with a grown-up intonation it took Annie a moment to realize was a pitch-perfect imitation of her own. "Choose one or I'll choose for you."

"Three," Claire said, opening her mouth. In went a forkful of chicken. *They never told you that the vast majority of parenting energy would be expended at mealtime, as you cajoled young children to heed a basic evolutionary directive required for survival: to consume food.*

"There, that wasn't so hard."

Had she said that, or Sam?

Right before dinner, she'd had trouble locating Claire, getting increasingly panicked until Sam admitted that he'd convinced his sister to play a one-sided game of hide-and-seek to get her to leave him alone, which Annie was ashamed to admit she found brilliant. *Why hadn't she ever thought of that?* Claire had been perfectly happy, holed up in the bathtub, combing her doll's hair. Which was partially why the next moment, as she was cleaning up dinner, infuriated Annie so much. Claire piped up asking for a "treat," and then Sam asked for ice cream, and as she was scraping the plates into the garbage disposal and babbling on about how finishing dinner didn't necessarily result in a treat every time, and how if you had a treat every day, did that really constitute a treat?, she heard a high-pitched whine begin and turned around just in time to see Sam's face screw up into contorted agony.

"But I ate all my food, and you didn't even have to ask me, plus Claire only finished her plate because I HELPED! It's NOT. FAIR." Then, emitting a sound like a dying moose, he was suddenly lying face down on the floor, fists banging loud enough that the Olmsteds downstairs definitely heard. It shocked her, really, every time she caught Sam acting his actual age.

Within moments, Claire had joined him on the ground, writhing and mewling, a whole bevy of moose. Everyone got a bowl of yogurt with maple syrup and sprinkles on top, a compromise that was absolutely not a compromise—the yogurt's sugar content was likely higher than an equivalent amount of ice cream—and then, finally, sticky and sated, they tromped upstairs to the bath.

By the time Dan walked in an hour later, Max was asleep in his sleep sack, clad in some ridiculous startup onesie, "Infant-preneur" or "I.P.O.(oed) *poop emoji*" across his chest—*I'm sorry, bud*, she thought—and Claire was cuddled up in bed demanding a fifth last book.

"Hi, kiddo," he said, swooping down and kissing Claire on the neck until she collapsed in a fit of giggles. "Sorry, sweetie, we were on a call that ran late and they were in Brisbane so I couldn't—" He stopped midsentence, quickly scrolled through the tiny screen on his AppleWatch, then batted it away, killing another errant mosquito. Then, back to Claire: "We're doing *Little Fur Family* again? Okay, shove over, but I'll read it only if you let me expound on my theory that it's actually about Freud's concept of the id, ego, and superego."

Claire nodded gamely, having no idea what her father was saying, and scooched over to make room for him on the bed. Dan had never exactly figured out how to speak to young children, even his own, and often leaned on the kind of snarky, overly intellectual banter that would make other adults within earshot laugh. It was something many of the men in her orbit did, in fact, if they paid any attention to their children at all, and Annie surely preferred to its polar opposite—baby talk. Still, she couldn't escape the feeling that he was performing for an invisible audience while making ever so slight fun of his actual audience, genetically programmed to be rapt and smitten, but only for so long.

"I can take over from here," he said, snuggling in. "And you do Sam."

As she kissed Claire good night and headed to Sam's bunk bed, the bad taste in her mouth was compounded by this kind of military score keeping—*You take one, I'll take the other*—that felt both irksome and inevitable. Hadn't she "taken" all three of them starting at five, which should have earned her three units of caregiving that she could offload now, to take some time for herself? She'd half-heartedly read a book about how to delineate household to-dos across spouses, with "unloading the dishwasher" representing a certain number of chits, and "making the doctors' appointments" another, but, however well-intentioned the premise, she knew there was no way that would actually work. *How many chits were bestowed if you were the first person to spring out of bed at the cry from the monitor, without being nudged? If you were the one who made sure the baby was moving from the bottle to the sippy cup at the right interval? If you sent back the two other shoeboxes to Amazon because every brand measured on a different scale, so to save time you always had to order three sizes at once?*

The other problem with the chit stuff, with ejecting herself from bedtime upon Dan's arrival, was that Annie was always most happy at this moment, in Sam's room on the bottom bunk, as the warm smell of coconut lotion drifted off his damp skin, and they snuggled up together over a book. It was the one part of the day, right before she had to hurtle through a few pre-sleep hours of work, that didn't feel like part of a long-running to-do list, that had to be completed as efficiently as possible or optimized in some way. And now that Sam had graduated from shorter, simpler picture books to chapter books—books she'd started to gather were leaps and bounds more advanced than the ones his classmates were reading—she got the added benefit of actually enjoying the stories, too. She'd come across an article once that said reading aloud was linked to greater mind wandering than reading in one's head. *No wonder she was able to add to her mental grocery list while making it through* Little Fur Family *with Claire for the ninetieth time.* But now, with Sam, the two of them genuinely read together.

That night, they'd reached the chapter in J. M. Barrie's *Peter Pan* where Wendy, having been shot down by the Lost Boys at Tinkerbell's urging, awakes from her fainting and decides, unhesitatingly, to become their mother.

Then all went on their knees, and holding out their arms cried, "O Wendy lady, be our mother."

"Ought I?" Wendy said, all shining. "Of course it's frightfully fascinating, but you see I am only a little girl. I have no real experience."

"That doesn't matter," said Peter, as if he were the only person present who knew all about it, though he was really the one who knew least. "What we need is just a nice motherly person."

"Oh dear!" Wendy said. "You see, I feel that is exactly what I am."

"It is, it is," they all cried; "we saw it at once."

"Very well," she said. "I will do my best. Come inside at once, you naughty children; I am sure your feet are damp. And before I put you to bed I have just time to finish the story of Cinderella."

"Can Wendy *actually* be their mother?" Sam asked, gnawing on his teddy bear. "She's their age, right?"

Annie gently freed the damp paw.

"Well, what do you think?"

What he was really asking was, *What makes a mother a mother?* As Barrie laid out here, it was fairly straightforward: put the children to bed, tell them a story, darn their holes. In Neverland, you didn't need experience; you were just born, innately, with motherly characteristics. *If only that worked here on Earth*, Annie mused. She stroked Sam's hair and waited for him to think.

"Well, I guess if what she's doing is tucking them in at night, and making sure their feet are warm and dry, and telling them stories, then almost anyone can do that," he said, eventually, hugging the stuffed animal. "And if it's pretend, then it's kind of like me with Bear."

"I guess so, yeah," she said, pushing back his hair and giving him a kiss on his forehead.

Before Sam even asked, she turned back to the passage where Barrie sets forth the charming notion that as children sleep, their mothers go through their minds and organize them. As he did every night, he sleepily asked her if she did that with his own brain, and she said yes, of course, how else was he supposed to make sense of the world? And then thirty minutes later she woke up and inched her way backward out the door, vaguely entertaining the notion that she'd somehow internalized their nightly reading into her floating episodes. Could she, in fact, be channeling Wendy in her nightgown, floating to Neverland, or back? *A therapist would have a field day with that.*

Annie found Dan in the kitchen, pacing and staring into the middle distance.

"You know, I've been thinking, maybe we should at least look at that gifted and talented school, the free one with the IQ testing, Thatcher, is it?" she started to say, consciously not pointing out that Claire had been down for at least forty minutes, and he hadn't yet started dinner. She turned on the toaster oven and got some dry rotisserie chicken out of the fridge. "In case Sawyer falls through. He's just next-level bright—like, *Peter Pan* is certainly for kids older than four, but he just gets it, and this whole business of

recommendation letters, and statements . . . also, don't you think
he'd ace an IQ test? And maybe enjoy it?"

"Open kimono moment?" Dan responded.

"Um, sure?"

"We can consider that when we raise a half-billion-dollar fund."

Was he having a stroke? Annie looked up to find Dan's eyes sort
of looking at her but also looking, somehow, past her. When he
turned, she caught sight of a single AirPod locked and loaded in
his ear. *Oh. He was on a call. Of course.*

Later, in bed: "What's an open kimono?"

"You know, it means being super-transparent, showing all
your cards," Dan said, head bowed at the altar of Jobs, pecking
out a note on his phone.

"But doesn't it literally mean showing them your penis?"

That got his attention.

"Um, should I open my kimono now? You want an open kimono moment?"

She didn't.

• • •

From: Ash Wempole
To: Annie Lewin
Subject: Urns 'n' burns

Apologies for the ten-day lag but I just returned from a silent meditation re-
treat where I literally had to pantomime that I needed some Pepto one night
after I didn't react well to the carrot top pesto the chef had put on his chickpea
penne, and anyway, I have a newfound love of connection and just adore ours,
even though we've never met in person (ZOMG, amirite). I also am having renewed trouble understanding nuance, so if you were being mean with that "urn
full of wine" comment, I'm just going to ignore it. But srsly lol re: an urn full of

wine, getting SPICE-SAY! Love it. Love it, love it, love it (and loved seeing those order forms on my Etsy shop!). If you like your new urns, no pressure but I'm launching a new line of bread cloches for all that sourdough I'm sure you're kneading at home. I think next year is going to be the year of the cloche. (Do I sense a new viral hashtag? #Clocheencounters, boom!) *small explosion emoji*

So anyway I'm writing with absolutely fabulous news, and with no nuance whatsoever, which is to say that your numbers have NEVER *clap emoji* BEEN *clap emoji* HIGHER *three clap emojis*. (LOVED your use of vajoon. It's no j'bageled, but très millennial.) Did you see that your post got picked up by @Tequilamom?!! I mean, she only has 3,500 followers, but your numbers have been so low that even that moved the needle. And you know that saying "No news is good news"? Well, when it comes to social media, no retweets are bad retweets! (That's why the subject line—you're totally burning up on social!)

Just let 'er rip, gurl. Annie Lewin, 1; world, 0! Next step: a retweet by CHRISSY TEIGEN.

P.S. I still think we should try a TikTok. I saw a super-cute one recently with little kids playing "Single Ladies" on the marimbas, and something like that would be heartwarming. For sure, @Tequilamom would retweet!

Ash

She/They

Editress. Wordsmith. Potter.

@RiseFromTheAshes

Etsy store: TerraCottaAndAsh

From: Annie Lewin

To: Ash Wempole

Subject: re: Urns 'n' burns

Ash,

I just scrolled through @Tequilamom's Instagram feed. While I'll allow that I have no brand, whatsoever, I have no idea what *her* brand actually is.

Riddle me this: What am I supposed to take away from her latest post, a picture of three blond children tumbling on a large lawn, out of focus in the background, with a manicured hand holding a shot glass in focus, front and center, and an inspirational quote superimposed on top: "Always remember that I have taken more out of alcohol than alcohol has taken out of me—Winston Churchill"?

Is she celebrating drinking? Abstinence? Elder statesmanhood? It's all very hard to follow.

Best,

Annie

P.S. A bread cloche? I'll just leave that question there, hanging in the ether.

• • •

Annie unpacked her two urns, lugged them up the stairs, and placed them flanking her bed—interior design, check—then got dressed, kissed damp heads good night, flashed a prayer sign at Maria, and headed to SpaTinis.

Maya's "event space" turned out to be the apartment across the hall from her own—a tidy, spacious two-bedroom where her parents stayed when visiting from out of town, and where various twenty-four-hour staffers slept during their shifts.

"It popped up, and I didn't want anyone coming in and doing renovations on it for a year, so we just snagged it!" she said, taking Annie's coat and tossing it at a helper. "Christine is just now finishing up her massage, so you'll be up next. Now, let me get you one of these lycheetinis, and this is your 'tiny 'tini charm'—aren't you just dead, I totally died when I saw the name of them—and you can hang it on your glass so we know it's yours. They're all the major fashion labels! You can be LVMH."

Maya looped a charm with the Louis Vuitton symbol on it around the stem of a martini glass as Annie took in the cheese spread, which was in the shape of the Bartleby logo: a teddy bear wearing a mortar board.

"Wow, Maya, that is, like . . . it actually looks like a bear," Annie managed, dislodging a small triangle of truffled gouda from the animal's right toe claw.

"I know, right? I follow this account on Instagram, @Rhapsody InBleu, which went viral after they did this super-realistic skyline of New York City only in Cambozola. I reached out, *et, voilà!*"

About half the guests were already there, chatting stiltedly about their children, but it was clear that all the mothers were waiting to see if Shawn Axel's wife was actually going to show. Clementina, born in Milan to garment workers, plucked from obscurity as a nine-year-old, graced the cover of *Vogue Italia* at thirteen, had a thriving career until about twenty, when she famously proclaimed that she was leaving the profession to pursue a proper education. Became the poster child for reclaiming one's identity, enrolled at NYU, then mostly disappeared from the press. Some googling revealed that she'd actually attended NYU's extension school, online, for one semester before dropping out, but her reputation as the unlikely intellectual had already been cemented.

"Who's next?" Christine bellowed as she staggered into the room, adjusting her too-tight skirt, face sweaty and deeply creased from the massage table. "That was better than sex. Maya, we're doing this every night! Jesus Christ. Manjula, was that her name? Magic hands. Orgasmic."

Christine: loud, brassy, always the bridesmaid, never the bride.

"Annie, you're up!" Maya said, consulting her clipboard, as Christine popped the entire almond-crusted goat cheese round of the teddy bear's nose into her mouth and moaned in ecstasy.

Sweet.

So into the master bedroom Annie went, where the young masseuse introduced herself as the plinky-plonks of generic spa music played from a portable dock. When she excused herself to the bathroom, Annie slipped off her clothes and got under the crisp sheet, then lay there, skeptical she'd be able to relax while semi-naked in a house surrounded by other preschool mothers shrieking and laughing outside. But when Manjula signaled the start of the massage by waving a warm eucalyptus frond under the headrest, Annie almost instantaneously entered a half-awake limbo state, wondering if this was how those whales felt that Sam had talked about, floating around with their brain partially asleep, partially awake. As the masseuse started to knead through her knots, stopping occasionally to lube up her hands with massage oil, Annie started to float, pleasantly, languidly in a large dark pool, her mind a soup of images—Dan grinning at her from the airport lounge, Shawn pushing himself up from the school steps, Max's pillowy cheek resting on her chest after nursing, Camila walking through Muir Woods, Elio strapped in one of those chair things on her back, mouth open at the majesty of the towering trees. Gradually, as the plinky-plonks turned to a muted roar, the pool became filled with pinpricks of light, and she was irritated—and then, suddenly, quite scared—to find that she was bobbing, again in that damned nightgown, pedaling slowly at nothing. She couldn't place the source of her rising terror until she sensed that menacing, universe-sucking sinkhole just out of sight, its cosmic pull, its tentacles starting to grasp her body and squeeze her toes, her feet, and then it said, in a Sigourney-Weaver-as-Zuul voice, "Your time's up, ma'am." *What a polite sinkhole*, she thought, but then the light came rushing in, and she was blinking at a small face way down below.

"Are you okay, ma'am? It's been twenty minutes. You wouldn't wake up."

Manjula, Annie realized as she came to more fully, had slithered her way under the table, her back flat on Maya's silk rug, and was peering up at her through the hole in the headrest, a look of concern on her face.

Annie dressed, still part whale and willing her heartbeat to slow down, then made her way to the main room to find Laura getting a manicure at the kitchen table, a Givenchy charm looped around her glass's stem, while a little swarm of mothers flitted around the newest arrival.

So she'd decided to come after all.

"And this is Annie, mother of Claire, and our resident author!" Maya said, whisking over. "Annie, this is Clementina, Amelia's mother."

"Lovely to meet you," Annie said, wondering if perhaps she was feeling off-kilter now because of the unnatural angle at which she had to tilt her head upward to meet Clementina's towering gaze. Those enormous pouty lips, the cheekbones so chiseled they could cut MagnaTiles, those tresses. Even in a plain white T-shirt and baggy jeans, the woman couldn't make herself appear human. Her torso was so freakishly long, Annie wondered if Shawn's face was at boob level the entire time they had sex.

"So how are you liking Bartleby?" Annie finally managed, locating her LVMH and remembering that she'd seen Shawn at pickup the other day, immersed in his phone, crashes and bangs coming out of it—another TechCrunched viral video. *Washed-up celebrities, they're just like us!* Clementina sipped from a tallboy of Liquid Death artesian water as she folded her lanky frame into an Eames chair.

"Oh, it's just been so wahhhnderful, and Ellie *AH*lpert has been such a kind guide to this whole new world." An accent like a swan diving into a giant ball of warm burrata.

She sat there, beaming and blinking her eyes, as everyone else beamed and blinked back at her.

"Tell her about your new business!" Christine barked, breaking the silence and swilling back her martini.

"Oh, it's just a little"—rhymed with "beetle"—"thing I started when Amelia was born," Clementina said. "Because I found she really responded to candlelight. Even in the womb."

"Oh?" Annie said, nodding too enthusiastically. "In utero?"

"Yes, I am a firm believer in light *naturale*, not just for the environment but because it is how we are meant to see the world, gently," Clementina said. "When I'd light my candles before my morning and evening baths, Amelia would move in my stomach in such a calm, contented way, I just knew I was experiencing something primal."

Morning baths?

"So now she has a candle business just for children!" Christine said, unable to hold back.

"Yes, they are made from natural beeswax, and the children can roll different colors around a wick made of sustainably farmed cotton, or decorate them using wax they can cut out into shapes," Clementina continued. "All they need is the warmth of their hands to stick the decorations on."

The ladies appeared to be in a state of collective blind rapture, but Annie couldn't help herself.

"You're not, um, worried about fire and flames and stuff?"

"Oh, but this is a very *American* way of thinking," Clementina said, all the mothers now ringing the Eames chair, some curled up on the ground at her feet. "I grew up helping my parents on the floor of the garment factory, using big machinery when I was only, how you say in English, 'knee-high to a duck'? Is that the phrase?"

"Um, I think it's knee-high to a grasshopper," Annie said.

"And I'm taking this philosophy a bit further with my new line of toys," Clementina said, ignoring Annie and now speaking directly to her acolytes, her gaze moving to welcome everyone into this impromptu fireside chat. "I used to grind farina on my nonna's mill and got so much joy and purpose out of it. I was surprised that you cannot find a child-size mill here in America! So they are in production now. Along with my new favorite for the boys, a, how you say, quife-er?"

The acolytes were stumped.

"*Queeve*-er?" Clementina attempted again. "You know, for to hold the arrows if you are a hunter."

Annie drained her glass, then tried, "A *quiver*?"

"*Ah, brava*, yes, a quife-er," Clementina said, still not getting it, "made of the hide of a bull, to make the pretend play even more real. This is what we owe our children, no? The respect to help them make their worlds come alive."

The ladies swooned.

"And what's it called, the company?" Annie asked, popping a lychee into her mouth.

Clementina smiled demurely.

"You settle a debate for me and Shawn, okay? I spell it for you. It's L-U-C-E S-M-O-O-C-H-E," she said.

Long beat. Lots of squinting into the middle distance.

"Loose smooch?" Christine barked, finally.

"Loo-chay smoo-chay," Clementina corrected, placing an errant hair behind her ear. "*Luce* is light in Italian, and it's Amelia's middle name. I wanted to have a little fun with it, you know?"

Laura and Annie could barely make it to the elevator before doubling over in side-splitting laughter.

That night, Annie woke up to a crash.

"The hell is this thing?" Dan hissed. The light from his iPhone popped on, and a tiny beacon from a lighthouse swept stutteringly over the room.

"It's an urn. A funerary urn," Annie murmured. "I'm going to drink wine out of mine."

Then she rolled over and fell back to sleep.

• • •

BARTLEBY NEIGHBORHOOD SCHOOL

14a East 77th Street

New York, NY 10075

"Where Play Is Work"

PARENT AND CHILD INTERVIEWS: WHAT TO EXPECT

Dearest Fours Parents,

We hope to see you all at our annual pre-Thanksgiving Turkey Trot, held next Tuesday at 2:45 p.m., preceded by the threes' performance of their Turkey dance, which they've been working on all semester. It will begin promptly at 2:40 p.m. and lasts just a few short minutes (okay, likely just one minute, but what a charming minute!), so please do not be late!

Now that many of you are getting ready for in-person interviews, either with your children, or solo, we wanted to send along a few pointers:

1. *Child interview*: We urge you to include a distant friend, relative, or work colleague in the prep process, to get your children more comfortable speaking

to strangers. Make sure your child has never seen this person before. Think of this as a wonderful opportunity for you to reconnect with people from your past!

A few sample questions to help them get your child talking:

(1) What is the last book you read and who was your favorite character?

(2) What's lighter: a pound of feathers or a pound of rocks?

(3) Elsa or Anna?

When it comes time for the real child interview, make sure the parent who is bonded least with the child goes, to ease in separation. This should go without saying but do *not*, under any circumstances, send a nanny, housekeeper, chef, driver, or any other household help with your child. Your job is to present a united and loving family at every step of the process.

2. *Parent interview*: This begins weeks, sometimes months, before your scheduled in-person visit. If you attend any "get to know the community" Zooms, make sure you are engaged and paying attention throughout—they will be watching, particularly when they turn their own cameras off to show a film of the school. Some top admission's teams start files on prospective families even before application season, so don't be surprised if they seem to know quite a bit about you before you get there! Obviously, everything Google-able about you and your family will have been digested pre-interview, so use your time with them to impress them with your sophistication, intellectualism, and calm demeanor. Speaking of . . .

3. *Overall note:* Don't get emotional. Schools are hoping to bring people into their community for over a decade. These admissions officers have seen it all and have rejected many families more esteemed, in various metrics, than yours (see: Christiane Amanpour's son, Darius, and Hawthorne-Whitberry; Gwyneth Paltrow's daughter, Apple, and Sawyer; Jackie Onassis's son, John-John, and St. Edward's).

Happy almost Thanksgiving, and sending a warm Bartleby hug from all of us, to all of you—

The Exmissions Team

Bartleby Neighborhood School

• • •

A low fall light dappled the leaf-carpeted ground as Annie inconspicuously tossed Claire's enormous roll of artwork into the trash can—*Was she actually expected to take it all home, go through it, and pin it up on the bulletin board? Claire's artistic output was on par with Van Gogh during his manic periods*—then parked herself on a bench ringing the playground, where she could aggressively chew gum and scroll through her phone as Max took his catnap back at home under Maria's calm watch.

Someone had posted one of those daily poems on Instagram, ones she usually flicked right past, but the title caused her to stop: "What You Missed That Day You Were Absent from Fourth Grade." It was a list of all the imagined subjects the teacher covered, including "how to find meaning in pumping gas," or "ways to remember your grandfather's voice," or—Annie snorted with recognition—"falling asleep without feeling you had forgotten to do something else." But the last two couplets, about a math equation that focused on meaning, and psychology, and purpose, and not numbers or division or subtraction, cut to the heart of the questions she'd found herself wrestling with lately. In this imagined classroom, the math equation proved

> *that hundreds of questions,*
> *and feeling cold, and all those nights spent looking*
> *for whatever it was you lost, and one person*
> *add up to something.*

If only, she thought. *If only schools taught all the big stuff. Maybe they weren't just about academics and were also, as Dan kept underscoring, about social capital and mobility. But even so, then where, precisely, were kids supposed to learn how to live happy, meaningful lives, particularly if their parents were still figuring that out themselves?*

She looked up to see Sam swinging wildly from the climbing structure like a monkey hopped up on Ritalin. All year the kids had been playing some playground-wide game they called "War," which was, as far as she could tell, just different groups of kids pretending to be different animals and roaring, or tweeting. Sam, she noted, proudly, was a method actor and committed fully to his animal kingdom choice.

"I wanted to be a cheetah, but it's hard to walk on all fours," he'd told her the other week. Hence, a monkey.

Their local playground was located across the avenue from Mount Sinai Hospital at an intersection of neighborhoods: at the uppermost bound of a quiet, leafy one that had the highest percentage of city residents with a household income north of $200,000, and at the lower bound of a working-class one, known colloquially as El Barrio. Head there at three p.m. on a sunny afternoon, and it became a visual melting pot as the kids streamed in through the gates and then roved around, from the tire swings, to the sandpit, to the climbing structure, the private school kids' uniforms starting as tight color packs and soon all running together.

Surrounding the park were benches where parents and nannies sat, chatting with one another, taking hummus sandwich squares out of insulated unicorn lunchboxes, wiping snotty noses, applying various GOOP-approved organic sun creams to faces, and, apparently, wildly neglecting their charges, or so Facebook would have you believe. Vigilante justice was alive and well on the Upper East Side, as mothers skulked around, taking surreptitious shots of nannies and leveling varying degrees of horrific accusations at them, all under the guise of keeping an eye out for fellow "mommas."

How many posts had she read calling out a nanny for being

on her phone "the entire time"? For "not even getting into the sandpit once," for "having her AirPods in when she was pushing the swing, and not even facing her child"? How many times did she brace to see a photo of her very own self, doing any of these hateful things, and posted for all the world to see?

Speaking of, where was *Claire?*

"This one yours?"

As before, Annie recognized the voice before she looked up. And there was Shawn, Claire dangling over one shoulder and Amelia on the other.

Gut notwithstanding, he was still cute.

"Heh, yeah, kiddo, where'd you get off to?" Annie asked, taking Claire, then reflexively pulling a wipe out of the stroller and palming her daughter's face with it, like she was shining a squirmy bowling ball. She was about to mention to Shawn that she'd met his wife the other night, but then he said, with a smirk, "Found her starting to pour sand into her pants so, you know, I figured I'd save you some money in diaper cream," and she decided she'd just, well, not mention his wife. If only she could have told her fifteen-year-old self that Shawn Axel would one day utter those words to her. She raised a glass to herself in her head. *Complimenti,* bitch.

Amelia heaved one of Shawn's legs open into a wide straddle, and she and Claire started to crawl figure eights in between them.

"So, anyway," he said, after gesturing to the girls, cocking his head to one side, sticking a tongue out, shutting an eye, and twirling his fingers by his ears, in an effortlessly comic *welcome to the loony bin* expression, "I know all about you, Annie Lewin."

Huh?

"I used to read your *Times* pieces, back in the day. You were the only Arts writer I actually trusted. It's so comforting, you know, to be an actor in the industry and feel like someone in power has good taste."

The number of nice things he'd packed into that one sentence nearly caused Annie to choke on her gum wad.

• • •

That evening, she was already under the covers reading when she heard Dan making his way slowly up the stairs, breathing deeply. He finally came into view, lugging an enormous box.

"Hey, boo," he said, clunking it down and wiping a wrist over his sweaty forehead. "Sorry I'm late, I was just picking this thing up. You know that guy I was telling you about, who basically predicted that Peloton was going to take over the world?"

Nope. She'd been waiting to ask him about tomorrow's Sawyer interview, or bring up her burgeoning friendship—*Could she even call it that?*—with Shawn, whom Dan had been moderately interested to learn was a Bartleby parent, but could tell by his focus that this was not the time. She added it to the long mental list of to-dos to tackle later, right after getting more vanilla-flavored toothpaste for the kids.

"Anyway, he's invested like half his net worth in this new company. This is a beta-stage product they're letting me test out to see if we want to invest in the seed round."

She watched as he unpacked what looked to be a Kevlar vest, elbow-high black gloves, and a helmet—dominatrix meets combat marine. He then stripped down to his boxers and began to suit up, occasionally consulting the manual. Though she recognized that she still found his tall, strong frame attractive, and that this would be the perfect time to make a move, she simply couldn't summon the energy. As she stayed put, she could almost hear the moment flit by, with a mild *swoosh*.

"So you do your workout like you normally do, but the machine responds to the signals from your body and then sends shock waves to your muscles to activate deep twitch in the optimal way, at the optimal time."

He paused, glancing again at the manual.

"But yeah, in order for it to work, the sensors have to touch bare skin—the pitch is that you can get a two-hour workout in twenty minutes! Mind. Blowing."

Was the goal to get a two-hour workout? Hadn't Michelle Obama said all you needed was twenty minutes a day? Could a twenty-minute workout be completed in twenty seconds, then?

When he'd finished, Dan looked like he was going to report to dominatrix-combat duty, only through Zoom: completely leathered and military up top, boxers and chicken legs on the bottom. He checked himself out in the mirror, then pounded his chest like he was King Kong, grinning at her through his reflection.

"Okay, wish me luck, babe," Dan said, and off he went to do his workout in the next room, the high-energy exhortations of the virtual instructor punctuated by Dan's occasional yip.

Even as she allowed that this might be his way of psyching himself up for the interview tomorrow, Annie wondered just how many other couples were sharing their homes, their children, their lives, and yet had reverted to a developmental activity more appropriate to their toddlers: parallel playing.

• • •

From: Miss Porter
To: Annie Lewin
Subject: Lunch

Dear Mrs. Lewin,

Just a quick note that today when Sam opened up his lunch, we were all a bit perplexed to find a pair of socks, four MagnaTiles, and a teether in the shape of a small banana in there! (Sending a big hug to baby Max.) There was a cute penguin ice pack to keep everything cold, but, alas, nothing to eat. Parvati was kind enough to share some of her lunch with Sam, and we gave him extra Bunny Grahams left over from snack, but in the future, we're hoping we can work together to keep our young scholar powered up during the day with edible food.

Sincerely,

Miss Porter

• • •

From: Annie Lewin
To: Camila Garcia Williams
Subject: Losing it

Can you hear the crazy all the way in Berkeley? A sort of swirling, frenzied noise from the score to an M. Night Shyamalan movie, in which emaciated bony creatures zwoop from place to place?

Some supporting evidence that I am spinning out:

(1) A few days ago I was on a massage table at this SpaTinis get-together—please don't make me explain it, it was something organized by the class rep of Claire's homeroom—and I found myself floating up into space, in this darkness, trying to run away from some overpowering horrible sucking force and it happened a few weeks earlier when I was putting Max down in the middle of the night, and I don't know what it means but it terrifies me. Just for kicks,

I went to WebMD to see what symptoms accompany a nervous break, and check it out:

- Low self-esteem
- Fearfulness
- Irritability
- Worrying
- Feeling helpless
- Getting angry easily
- Withdrawing from family and friends
- Losing interest in your favorite activities

I mean, I exhibit all of these, but don't *all* mothers of young children? (No wonder the root word of *hysteria* is the Greek word ὑστέρα, aka *uterus*. Thank you, AP Greek.) Doesn't loving a human being so much that when they're gone it feels like you're missing a limb go hand in hand with fearfulness and worrying? Doesn't lack of sleep make us all irritable and shorten all our fuses? Aren't we forced to withdraw from friends and favorite activities simply because we no longer have the bandwidth to, say, go for a run or knit or play the piano or whatever anymore?? As for self-esteem, one look at my Mother Inferior inbox and it's ragingly apparent to me that no mother actually thinks she's doing right by her child. I guess my question is: Is this response to my life rational or a sign that I'm unraveling?

(2) I think Shawn Axel is flirting with me. I can't exactly tell, since it's been literally a decade since I've flirted with anyone (sob). And I keep being asleep, or almost asleep, by the time Dan gets home, and so our sex life is basically nonexistent. And then I fantasize about sex with Shawn. Though I'm pretty sure he's very, very dull. Like exceedingly dull. (Fun tidbit: his wife is a former model who makes children's candles for a living.) Anyway: This is normal, right? Not, like, hallucination-and-nervous-breakdown territory? I can't even tell anymore! I am losing my grip!!!

(3) My editor is twenty-three years old and their only real note is that they

want me to be more RAW and open, and honestly who wants to take advice from someone who is hallucinating that she's Wendy from *Peter Pan*? (I can't believe I put that in writing, but I think that's what is going on.) Everything is about clicks, and what headline is catchiest, so maybe it doesn't even fucking matter what I write. Shouldn't I just read the writing on the wall and accept that I'm going to be replaced by some sort of chatbot anyway? And yeah, my book. Ha. Won't chatbots be writing books, too?

(4) Do you remember that intro social theory class we took together, where we read about Veblen's theory of conspicuous consumption—that elite people preen by buying luxury items, fancy cars and whatnot, thus signaling to everyone how fancy they are? The Sawyer teachers do seem to be incredible, but in a way, aren't private schools luxury items, too, just status symbols? I brought this up to Dan the other day, and he said that maybe that's the case, but then, and I quote, "I just don't think guilt or shame about our ability to buy our way to an elite educational environment is productive." Wouldn't it be nice, to be able to reduce these big questions into streamlined ones about what is, and isn't, *productive*? And around and around we go.

(5) We had a parent-teacher conference yesterday. Apparently, Sam is "empathetic," "a natural leader," and (my favorite on the list of things he is being evaluated on) "plays well with others." Like a lil' puppy! We'll table the conversation about which, if any, traits he got from me . . .

(6) The interview is tomorrow. Wish me luck. And . . .

Never leave me.

A.

• • •

"Dan Lewin! And this must be the lovely Annie."

Her eminence herself, Timmie Sullivan, wearing a smart blouse and sensible shoes, walked out from behind her maroon leather-topped desk, a double orchid quivering in her wake, and reached out a warm hand. *Showtime.*

"And you must be Sam!"

She bent down just slightly, to shake his hand.

"Shake it like you mean it, kiddo," Timmie said, with a smile, and Sam, soft brown curls bobbing up and down, pumped away, immediately disarmed.

"Lovely to see you, Dan, and so glad we're getting another chance to reconnect," Timmie continued, somehow indicating with two tiny gestures that Annie and Dan should sit down in the chairs facing the desk, and Sam should make himself at home on the carpet, where stacks of books, toys, and dolls lay in wicker baskets. Effortless grace.

"Sam, we're going to have a little chat over here while you play with whatever you'd like, sound okay?"

Sam nodded quickly.

"Can I make a castle? For him?"

"Of course you can!" Timmie beamed, and Annie noted out of the corner of her eye that just as her son chose a baby to be his princeling, Timmie's associate, unobtrusively sitting on a chair in the corner, noted something down with her pencil, then flashed Annie that warm, Sawyer smile.

"So, I can imagine this process is all a little nutty to you," Timmie began, looking at Annie. "I understand you went to public school in New Jersey. The horror!" Then in a stage whisper, from behind her hand, "I also went to public school in New Jersey. Don't tell anyone." Hearty chuckles all around. "So, please, tell me a little about Sam here."

As Dan charmingly waxed poetic about his eldest, and the parts of Sawyer he'd loved the most—when the headmaster would dress up like Santa Claus and roller-skate around the gym before Christmas chapel, the thrill of getting onstage during assembly to debate a teacher on a topic of the student body's choosing—Annie looked around the room, taking in the old-school charm, the framed degrees on the wall, the various awards in thick plastic boxes. *What on earth were they for? "Most Graceful at Giving Rejections?"*

When they'd walked in the main entrance, she'd detected that generic and universal school fragrance that immediately whisked her back to those comparatively simple days of high school—clean and astringent, from some kind of industrial cleaner they likely used to mop the floors, mixed with the dank mist coming off the steam tables in the cafeteria, and a sprinkle of watercolor paint from the art studios. Hadn't she just been attending school herself, backpack slung over one shoulder? Wearing cargo jeans because everyone was wearing them to look like Joey Potter in *Dawson's Creek*, back when Katie Holmes was just Katie Holmes and not the collateral damage of Scientology and Tom Cruise? *Where did the time go? How was she old enough to have a child entering kindergarten, and two others at home?*

As her brain did loop-de-loops, Annie could sense, with nauseating familiarity, that damned tingling starting in her lower extremities, that dull roar beginning to drown out the cries of the children in the hallway outside, and she closed her eyes for a moment and, with great effort, willed it away, repeating a mantra silently in her head—*not now, not now, not now, keep it together, keep it together, keep it together.*

"And you, of course, have the pleasure of coming to Sawyer from the outside," Timmie said after who knows how many minutes, turning her attention to Annie, and wrenching her back, momentarily, from the abyss. "Can you tell me why you think Sam would be a good fit for our particular school?"

Annie inhaled for a long while. This was the softball question, the one she should have a quick and pat answer to, the *Why do you want to work here?*, the *Tell us why you'd be a good part of our co-op*, the easy one. She'd had some line she'd rehearsed, something about Dan's love of the school, and Sawyer's proven commitment to excellence, but after an awkwardly long beat, during which Timmie leaned forward with clasped hands, waiting patiently, she simply said, "Honestly? I don't really know."

The answer hung in the air, an errant message that Dan could not swat away. She saw his eyebrows squinch imperceptibly closer together, in what she recognized was her husband's attempt to disguise wild alarm as genuine concern. But the floor was hers, so, as the heat began in her chest, and started to spread its way up her neck and fan out over her face, she decided to embrace it.

"I'm sure every parent who sits in front of you believes that their child is God's gift," Annie continued. "I believe that about all three of my children. I also believe that Sam is a particularly focused and creative little guy." She turned to her son, who was now sitting next to the Timmie underling and sketching out an elaborate plan for a castle extension.

"And I can sit here and tell you how yesterday, we were walking around the conservatory pond and a quartet started to play Vivaldi's 'Spring,' and Sam looked up and said, 'That's Vivaldi!' and literally everyone within earshot stopped to beam at him, including the guys who were operating the little remote-control boats. Or how he cried at the end of *Charlotte's Web*, which I'm not sure every four-year-old has the emotional capacity to do. Or how he—" She stopped. *She would not cry in this meeting. That would be absolutely ridiculous.*

Dan chuckled nervously and put his hand on Annie's knee.

"We have a baby at home, and Annie is still nursing so, you know, sleepless nights and hormones!"

She was certain Dan was partially right, but still entertained taking the potted orchid from Timmie's desk and bashing it over his head.

Timmie smiled mildly at Dan and turned her attention back toward Annie.

"Mrs. Lewin, go on."

"Well, my goal is not to get Sam into the quote-unquote best school, which Sawyer clearly is, by many metrics, but to help him find his people. And people who know better than I do—the head of our preschool, my good friend who grew up here, Dan— say that Sawyer is that place. Intellectual but somehow playful, nurturing but also serious."

Timmie nodded at her, neither encouraging nor chastising, a Vegas dealer. Annie had to remind herself that she was at an interview, not a therapy appointment. Something about Timmie's demeanor conveyed, *I will not judge you*, despite that her job was, literally, to judge her.

The roar amped up in volume just slightly, and Annie refused to look down, afraid she'd see her bare feet floating there, beneath a swaying nightgown, and not the kitten heels she'd put on to convey down-to-earth professionalism. *She needed to wrap this up, and fast.*

"I mean, does a child need to know how to make shoes? I can't unequivocally say yes or no to that, and while I'm probably the only person to have ever admitted it in this room—I'm sure most of the parents who come in here have it all figured out—most of the time, I'm guessing when it comes to parenting." Dan cleared his throat quickly, eyebrows inching a millimeter closer and turning down at an angle, but Annie didn't acknowledge the signal, whatever it was trying to convey. "And I *know* I'm not alone. I just know it: my work inbox is full of other mothers who also have no idea what they are doing. So I figure, if Sam is going to be spending half of his waking hours in the care of others, *in loco parentis* and all that, the best shot on goal is the school where the professionals are the best in the business, where he'll be surrounded by people who know how to raise confident, uniquely bright individuals. If they think that involves making shoes, then, well, I guess I'm on board."

She wasn't sure, but she thought she saw Timmie's eyes twinkle.

"And I have a particularly personal glimpse into the school's successes, given that I married one of your graduates," Annie finished, with a long, protracted exhale, somehow remembering to wrap up with a point she'd rehearsed. Timmie gave her a curt nod and pushed back her chair, indicating the interview had concluded. In the midst of putting on coats, and listening to Sam tell Timmie about his building, Annie glanced at Dan, who widened his eyes ever so slightly, then raised his shoulders ever so slightly, a *What was that?* plus a *No idea.*

After the interview wrapped, Dan rushed to a meeting and Annie and Sam shared an ice cream cone. She sat there, licking and replaying the interview, certain she'd blown it all, and not exactly sure how she should feel about that, until that evening when Dan walked in the door, unslung his backpack from his shoulder, and kissed her on the mouth, hard.

"You're a knockout, Annie," he said. "I just got off the phone with Tom Paulson, who's on the board at Sawyer. Guy I know vaguely from work. Sullivan was blown away by our interview. Said it was, and I quote, 'One of the most memorable in her thirty years.' Something about this family treating the school as it should really be treated, as a partner, and not an employee, like the rest of the applicant parents. You knew what you were doing all along. Brilliant. Totally brilliant."

Annie didn't know what she was doing, knew that she certainly hadn't known what she'd been doing in that interview, but at bedtime, for the first time in a while, with the anxiety of the day dissipating around her, and a slightly fraudulent sense of accomplishment that she'd completed the task set before her, all five of them sat on the floor of Sam's room making an enormous whale puzzle. Dan didn't so much as glance at his watch. Sam let Claire put the final piece in, which she did with a triumphant crow—"Look," he pointed out to his little sister, as Annie and Dan raised their eyebrows in tandem, "look at the iridescence on his tail!"—and as Max let go of Annie's hand and stumbled his way two shaky, drunken steps to Dan, the first he'd ever taken on his own, all of them cheered. Dan found her eyes over the scrum of their children, now in a giggling pile together, and shot her a glance—*Look, just look at what we made.*

DECEMBER

Dear Mother Inferior,

My son's birthday is coming up, and our school policy is to invite no one, or everyone. He has five close friends—can't I just invite them? Separately, do we have to go to the twenty-four other parties? I don't want to buy gifts for kids I barely know! It's all so expensive. One parent sent out a registry accompanying the invitation. (A registry. For a four-year-old.) Anyway, I'm fine to celebrate my son's birth, but can't figure out how to do it.

Signed,

Party Pooper in Pawling

Party Pooper,

When I was ten years old, I attended a day camp I really hated, because my mother thought I should spend the summer outside, and not in the library with a book, which is what I'd have preferred. I'll never forget the day that all the other kids in my group came over to where I was sitting during a break and asked me to carry their invitations to Suzanne's birthday party, since "I had a bag" and they didn't. I was the only one not invited. I cried that night at home and felt miserable.

Suzanne, I recently discovered after minor internet sleuthing, is now a mid-market suburban real estate broker with a side hustle as a knitwear designer for pets, and, according to her website, KnittyKitty.com, lives in a charming colonial with her "three cats and multiple skeins of yarn."

Karma's a bitch, ain't it, *Party Pooper*?

The American birthday parties we all know and hate, the ones with the gifts and the annoying singers named Ramblin' Ray, and the pizza cut into tiny little kid-size slivers that flop on your shirt no matter how you hold them, are a relatively recent entrant into the annals of childhood—until about a hundred years ago, only royalty or super-rich people celebrated them. The consumeristic hellscape of gift giving and gift registries are fully American. Other countries seem to have figured it out better. In Canada, children are apparently pinned to the ground on their birthday while their noses get smeared with butter. In Switzerland, parents hire an evil clown to follow their kid around and torment them all day, which culminates in that evil clown smashing a pie into the kid's face. (Literally, google it.)

All of which is to say, you do you. You don't want to spend hundreds of dollars on balloons and a petting zoo that will give everyone ringworm? More power to you. You want to buck tradition and celebrate your child's birthday quietly, by smearing grease on his face and then terrorizing him with a clown that will send him straight from his fifth birthday to the therapist's chaise lounge? FINE!

But if I were you, I'd ask your son how he'd like to celebrate. On the off chance he says he wants to invite the entire class to a formulaic, boring party, sit him down and explain that he's going to have to start ranking his friends into tiers at some point—absolutely for his wedding, but likely before then, too—so he can start practicing now.

Peace out, *Pooper*, and assuming you end up excluding most of the other parents, *complimenti*, bitch!

Mother Inferior

• • •

Eleven a.m., Sunday morning, the Sea Glass carousel, the lower tip of Manhattan, towering mirrored buildings reflecting the sun off the Battery, a bitter wind whipping off the water. Someone's fifth birthday party, she couldn't even remember who, since there'd already been so many.

Now was the season of weekend birthday parties, each of which neutered part of Annie's soul in a different way. Yesterday, she'd taken Claire to one, held at a new play space with organic diapers in the bathroom and an aesthetic that might have reasonably been mistaken for a Berkeley community kitchen—bowls, crocheted avocados, and plush kabocha squashes. During the singalong portion, the chipper guitar player, facing a carpet of socked toddlers and siblings in various states of slack-jawed catatonia, switched up the lyrics to "The Wheels on the Bus." The wipers were still swishing, the babies were still crying, the mommies were still shushing, but instead of the daddies saying "I love you," something that always irked Annie—*Why were the moms the disciplinarians, the daddies the ones calming through love?*—he sang out, clear as a bell, "The nannies on the bus say 'I love you.'" The daddies, heads buried in their phones, keeping track of fantasy football scores and work emails, didn't so much as look up. But this wild recasting of the verse had snapped Annie out of her maracas-shaking lull to meet the gazes of other mothers, all of whom arched an eyebrow or rolled an eye, belying their obvious fear that their nannies were a more stable, capable force in their children's lives than they themselves were. When the singer wrapped up the song and moved onto a version of Darius Rucker's "Wagon Wheel," which everyone three to seventy-three dutifully belted out with him, including the raucously salacious chorus about someone rocking the singer "any way you feel," he hadn't even mentioned a mama on the bus at all.

"You want a juice box, sweetie?" she asked Claire, as Dan followed Sam to get in line for the carousel, which was playing Enya-style music and starting up its neon light show. Over Max's curls—he was strapped to her chest, asleep and serving as her own personal hot water bottle—she caught sight of the snot crusted to Claire's cheek and her eyebrow, due to the constant runny noses of the season, and a repeated upward movement of an open palm that Annie had learned, after falling down a Google rabbit hole the previous night, was called an "allergic salute."

Annie had eaten "breakfast," if that's what you could call hoovering up the soggy Honey Nut Chex from the kids' bowls, at six a.m. *Might as well do lunch now.* And so, she and Claire sat down at the picnic table and dug into a slightly congealed pizza slice together.

"You wanna see something cool?" a thin voice said behind her, as she flopped a pepperoni slice on a recycled bamboo plate.

Silent scream.

She knew before turning around that it was Belinda's husband, Greg, the shriveled eggplant emoji whom she'd never seen blink. Look up trustafarian in the dictionary, and there'd be his picture. He was the sixth—*Seventh?* Annie had poked around years before and never been able to figure it out—generation of a family-owned grain business, the largest supplier of livestock feed in the country. Whatever intrepidness had allowed his great-great-great-(great?)-grandfather to risk a trip through war-torn Prussia to buy grain with a sack of gold had, like a copy of a copy of a copy, dissipated in Greg's bloodstream, yielding a lost man with no discernible career, but a pedigree that had no doubt enticed Belinda when they met at an eating club at Princeton—or Annie could only assume, never exactly understanding why certain people ended up together, them perhaps more than others. According to LinkedIn, he'd ridden the tech wave a few years out of college and founded an incubator focused on start-ups that utilized augmented reality, a good decade before there was any demand. Then his résumé basically petered out. His lack of ambition didn't seem to matter much, though, as Belinda skyrocketed her way up the corporate ladder: she had enough professional drive for the two of them. Rumor had it Greg started off his days with a fistful of weed gummies and ran barefoot in Central Park, as part of some sort of caveman/paleo workout.

Did she want to see something Greg thought was cool? Annie plastered on a smile and pivoted on the picnic bench. *Hard pass.*

"Always!" she said, brightly, coming face-to-face with his crotch. She inched back.

"Okay, so look up there, to that tower. Do you know that migrating birds often fly into them at night, because all the offices turn their lights off, and they just see the sky reflected in the window, and so keep flying until they bash their little heads right into the side?"

She swallowed a chunk of hardened cheese and gave him, despite her best efforts, the same distantly encouraging look she gave Claire when she insisted on helping get Max dressed, jamming both feet into a single pant leg with a "ta-da!" as her little brother squirmed powerlessly on the changing pad, a human caterpillar. Dan and Sam, she saw out of the corner of her eye, were sitting together in what looked to be an enormous rainbow trout, twirling up and down as neon strobe lights flickered around them, too far away to rescue her.

"Yeah, yeah, I've heard of that happening," she said. "I didn't realize birds, like, migrated *through* New York City, though. You just think of that happening out in the country, not down Wall Street, right?"

Blank stare.

"So you really want to leave your lights on in the office, or at the very least put those reflective stickers on the windows, but of course none of these jerk bankers would ever think of marring their picture-perfect view," he continued, flatly. "So, anyway, you wanna see something kind of cool?"

Like in a horror film, it dawned on her that he'd been cupping his right hand around something that whole time, small and delicate. He sidled up closer to her, his hand right in front of his jean's zipper and level with her face, then unfurled his fingers. Inside, lying on the chub of his palm, was a brown-and-green bird with yellow fluff around its face, the real-life version of an avian Disney character who, in a pre-head-bash world, might have been helping sew her a new set of clothes for the ball as it merrily chirped along. But instead of sewing, this bird looked to be dead as a doorknob.

"So I found one on the ground; this is the real tail end of the fall migration season, she should have gone with her compatriots a few weeks ago. I can feel her heart fluttering a bit every now and then—I think she's still with us."

Oh. My. God.

Claire crawled up to get a better look, then capped off another wet and noisy allergic salute with a move to pet the bird who was, it appeared, indeed still maybe sort of alive.

"Oh no, no sweetie, that may have, um, diseases on it and stuff," she said, grabbing Claire's arm, heaving herself up off the bench, and pivoting them toward the carousel, Max squirming in response to the sudden movement.

"She's just dying to go," she explained apologetically, yanking Claire away, and leaving Greg there, next to her half-eaten slice of pizza, her custom-printed Pegasus-and-narwhal-stamped napkin starting to flutter away.

Near the end of the party, as she furiously chewed on a mouthful of gum, she ran into him again, hands now free.

"She's in here," he said, patting his back jeans pocket. "Rigor mortis has set in. She's definitely gone now. But I'll take a photo of her to put into my folder of birds. I blow them up, frame them, and put them in my office, urban nature at its finest. This one will be a beaut. Wanna see?"

Just then—*thank god*—her phone beeped with a notification.

"Sawyer Admissions decision" popped up onto her screen.

Annie's body flooded with adrenaline and she held up a finger. "Just one second, Greg, I'll be right back. Can't wait to see the dead birds folder."

• • •

From: Timothea Sullivan
To: Annie Lewin, Dan Lewin
Subject: Sawyer Admissions Decision

Dear Annie and Daniel,

We write with some disappointing and surprising news, which is that, after much deliberation, we won't be able to offer Sam a spot in next year's kindergarten class. We so enjoyed meeting him, and observing him at our interview, where he built such a lovely castle for his multiracial family.

Regrettably, the application competition was fierce this year, and there were not enough spaces for all the top-notch children who applied.

Sam is a bright child and will, we know, find a wonderful home elsewhere in the city. (And if not, there's always New Jersey! That one's for you, Annie. One must always have a sense of humor in these situations, which I know can be unduly stressful.) We look forward to a future date when we might continue our school's relationship with your family.

Sincerely,

Timmie Sullivan

Sawyer

Head of Admissions

• • •

Laura had texted early the next morning: *Check the Babes*.

Squinting into her phone from bed, Annie had reluctantly opened it up and learned why Sam—her charming, precocious little guy—hadn't gotten a spot at the school she'd naively considered a sure thing.

CHRISTINE: Guys, you'll NEVER believe what I heard this morning at Ralph's.

LEONORA: Ralph's?

CHRISTINE: The coffee spot across from Sawyer, part of Lauren B. Lauren's new eco-friendly lab-grown-cashmere store.

YAEL: *ear emoji*

LEONORA: 'scuse me, don't you mean Lauren LaurEN

YAEL: That lab-grown cashmere is srsly as luxe as Loro Piana

BELINDA: *flexed bicep emoji* *fist pound emoji* *small explosion emoji*

CHRISTINE: Okee, soooo I'm waiting in line and who comes in but the one and only Timmie Sullivan, and she's whisper-talking to her colleague, but of course I have ears like a bat.

MAYA: Bats have good hearing?

CHRISTINE: Parker is bat-obsessed now, so I happen to know they hear better than almost any other animal.

YAEL: *stop sign emoji* *bat emoji* *ear emoji*

LEONORA: OMG poor you, Harrison went through a bat phase, wait until he asks you for one as a pet.

YAEL: No one write until Christine is done. *angry face so angry it's blowing steam out the nostrils emoji*

(Flurry of thumbs-ups)

CHRISTINE: OK, so she tells this person that they now have enough money to fund their "Salve, Romans!" study abroad program and I looked it up on the website and it's this new initiative to have the rising sixth graders spend a month "living and learning in the Vatican to fuel a lifelong love of the Latin language." So they're gonna go chat with the pope, I guess? Anyway, Queen T is all, it used to be an anonymous donation, but the donor unanonymized it last minute because his kid was applying to kindergarten and he wanted a leg up.

(Flurry of exclamation points)

CHRISTINE: *stop sign emoji*

CHRISTINE: But the best part is she then says, with this little chuckle, "Let's just say it's not your money, it's AR-mani now."

YAEL: *omg emoji*

MAYA: OMG it's Giorgio Armani's grandson? *screaming cat emoji* *screaming cat emoji* *screaming cat emoji*

LEONORA: Isn't he bisexual with no children. . . . Hold up, googling.

CHRISTINE: Way ahead of you, it's gotta be his great-nephew, his sister's kid's kid.

MAYA: *screaming cat emoji* *screaming cat emoji* *screaming cat emoji*

Eh, Mamma Mia, there went Sam's spot. It was almost the exact same scenario as years before, with Annie's *Boston Globe* internship and the connected kid in her seminar—at least before Dan had encouraged her to play by a new rule book. *Was there another playbook for this situation, too?* As Annie lay in bed squinting at her phone, she shoved aside the dawning realization of how easily the Sawyer rejection had swung her along the pendulum from one side—thinking access to this world was unfair, unearned, and perhaps not even worth it—to the far end, where having it snatched away was inconceivable. *But, then again,* she heard Camila's voice in her head, *hadn't the pendulum started to swing its course long before, when she'd first met Dan, moved to New York, started to table her values and justify their life choices through pragmatism?*

The night before, after the kids were all tucked into bed and the Chinese takeout had been unpacked, Annie had watched, silent and fascinated, as Dan raced through Kübler-Ross's five stages of grief about the Sawyer rejection in an efficient thirty minutes.

Denial was dispatched of in two—"Are you certain Sullivan sent the right letter to the right people? She basically told Paulson we'd been accepted! What the hell happened?"

Anger lasted a solid five minutes.

"Show me one four-year-old, a single four-year-old, in the Tri-State Area who uses the word 'iridescence' correctly," he fumed, spearing a fried pork dumpling with his fork and aggressively dunking it in the too-small sauce container, splattering the kitchen island with black Chinese vinegar. "You think the Armani kid knows that word? *Stronzo!*"

Bargaining took up fifteen minutes, since he had to scan the Sawyer board of directors, cross-reference that with his LinkedIn network, and then do some background googling.

The verdict: "Our only real connection there is Paulson, but his hedge fund went belly-up last month, so I don't think we want our name linked to his in any way, even if he'd pull strings for us."

He allotted a brisk three minutes to Depression.

"Fuckers treated my family like crap after what happened when I was there," he said, morosely picking through piles of red chilies for a nubbin of dry-fried Sichuan chicken. Annie thought she saw a tear pool in his eye, though it could have been from the málà spice.

Acceptance got the remaining five minutes, but because it was Dan, he added on a personalized sixth stage: reframing, and spinning the narrative to his advantage. "It's way more interesting if we opt for the unexpected," he determined, crushing the take-out containers into the garbage bin. "The best all-boys' school is St. Edward's. Which would mean we'd have to apply from scratch for Claire, which, you know, ballsy. Two kids at the top two single-sex schools in the city trumps two kids at the top coed school, doesn't it? And if that doesn't work, screw it, we'll homeschool. It's all the rage in Silicon Valley now—it can be personalized, the kids can learn at an ideal pace, you can teach them *Huck Finn* if you want because the woke Mafia isn't on your homeschooling board, plus they learn actual skills. My buddy's kid can take apart a refrigerator."

First, cobbling shoes. Now, refrigerator repair?

Annie could tell, from the fevered pitch of his delivery, that now was not the time to tell him that, in the preceding twenty-four hours, with Sam's fate no longer decided for her, she'd actually started to form her own opinion about this process, and now had her heart set on Thatcher, its haloed IQ test impervious to bargaining by, well, people like her husband.

As for homeschooling, was Dan planning to step back from his career to develop units on Play-Doh and the Oregon Trail? *Fat chance.*

• • •

Beep. Beep. Beep.

She heard it later that night, after Dan went out for work drinks.

"They're in town from London, I have to," he'd said, as he'd whisked out into the freezing dark after dinner. She'd decided to use her pent-up energy to continue the now eight-months'-long process of unpacking, and had been up in the bedroom trying to figure out whether or not to keep the pumps she'd gotten with her first two pregnancies, along with the myriad parts that transformed her into a cross between Xena, Warrior Princess, and Gaia, Mother Earth, when she'd heard the chimes.

According to the alarm manual the previous owner had left them, three slow beeps indicated that a door had opened in the apartment. But . . . *which door?* There were three possible points of egress—the front door, the back door by the kitchen, and the door behind Sam's bathroom on the second floor. Three possible places an intruder could have come in, eluding, somehow, both the doorman and the elevator man. Unless, of course, the intruder came from inside the building. Annie snatched up the kitchen knife she'd been using to cut open boxes, which glinted in the moonlight streaming in through the double height windows.

As her heart began to race, she pressed herself up against the gigantic stone fireplace and leaned her hot cheek against the cool stone cheek of a cherub who'd been carved into the mantel. *A panic attack? Was this a panic attack?*

Wiping a sweaty hand against her jeans, she fished her phone out of her back pocket and dialed Dan, who picked up on the fourth ring.

"Hey, boo," he shouted over the din of a crowded restaurant. "You okay?"

"There was the beep, beep, beep," she whisper-hissed.

"Huh? I can't really hear you, sweetie, it's super-loud here."

Annie hung up and texted him, *There was a beep, beep, beep.*

To which she got an eggplant emoji in return.

There. Might. Be. An. Intruder, she typed out slowly. *The alarm system.*

Pulsing ellipses. Then nothing. The question of the hour: *Was she losing it, or was this a totally appropriate response to what was going on?* Recognizing that she was unable to calibrate, a flood of adrenaline swept over her body, releasing a fresh layer of sweat.

Beep. Beep. Beep.

Her phone buzzed, then a text bubble bloomed onto her screen: *The doormen are downstairs, and I just confirmed with them that no one entered the apartment. Home in an hr.* Pause. **eggplant emoji* *peach emoji**

Feeling a cosmic pull to be closer to her children, and ignoring what she grudgingly had to admit now constituted foreplay, she tiptoed up the newly recarpeted, plush stairs, feet making depressions in the thick pile, to find Max sleeping deeply in his crib, the smell of Dreft, that heavenly detergent, suffusing everything with a warm olfactory glow. Annie reached over, instinctively feeling the soft part on the top of his skull where everything was still coming together, then tiptoed down to the far end of the hall to Claire, who was splayed like a starfish, face up, on her polka-dot comforter. Then she backtracked to Sam's room, located right in between the two other bedrooms, strategically the best place to post herself in the unlikely event her panic attack was based in reality and not due to the most likely explanation: a glitchy alarm system. Up the bunk bed ladder she went, Sam curled around his teddy bear on the bottom, *Peter Pan* on his bedside table, a night sky full of projected stars twinkling comfortingly on the ceiling.

As she began to match his calm and level breathing, she loosened the grip on the knife's handle and pulled out her phone to open her text chain with Camila. *I'm lying on the top of Sam's bunk clutching a kitchen knife,* she wrote, *because the alarm went off and I kind of think someone might be in the house but I also know I'm super unhinged lately and D is downtown at a work thing and am I losing my mind?*

She waited for the read receipt to appear, but it didn't. Camila was three hours behind, safely ensconced in Berkeley life, and likely out in the backyard, picking lemons off her tree, or playing with Elio, or otherwise being normal and balanced. *Sigh.*

It was then that she heard the footsteps. Small. Mincing. Light. A floorboard creaked in the hall. *I knew it,* she thought, tensing. *Someone broke in. Well, you messed with the wrong unhinged mother.* She gripped the knife handle tightly and sat up hard in the bed, audibly smacking her head on the ceiling, right as Claire rounded the corner into the room. *Oh.*

"Mama?" her daughter said, at full volume. "What you doing up der?"

"Nothing, nothing sweetie," she whispered, blinking away the stars that whirled up with the projected ones, then gingerly making her way down the ladder and ushering Claire back to her room, the large kitchen knife behind her back, her other hand on that vaguely leonine, in-between-the-shoulder-blades part of her children that always reminded her of cartoon Simba.

She assumed the frozen sentry position that Claire favored, sitting back straight in the chair by the bed, both feet on the floor, and looked up at the stars projected on the ceiling. *She was just a little tired, that was all. It was fine. Everything was fine.* But just as she was starting to drift off herself, something caught her eye, jogging her back into highly alert mode. One of the stars—it looked to be jiggling. *Was something causing the projector to move? An earthquake?* She checked the bookshelf quickly to confirm that nothing seemed awry, but then again, if the projector was moving, then all the stars would be moving, right? *And when was the last time an earthquake struck Manhattan?*

Squinting up, she zeroed in on that one star again that now— she couldn't quite believe it—appeared to have dislodged itself from its coordinate in the sky and was making little loop-de-loops on the ceiling, a tiny Tinkerbell beckoning her to follow. *No way. Perhaps the settings on Claire's projector were just a little different than Sam's? Perhaps she was lucid dreaming. That was a thing, right?* She glanced at her phone, lit up with timely *New York Times* news updates that confirmed that she was not, in fact, dreaming, then shut her eyes, hard, willing the sky to return to normal stagnancy when she opened up her eyelids again—but when she did, she audibly gasped.

She was no longer sitting in the chair, but whooshing upward, the eight or so feet between the floor and the ceiling taking ages to cover despite the whooshing because she'd shrunk in size, that damned nightgown fluttering behind her (*she hadn't even put on her pajamas yet! she'd been wearing jeans and a T-shirt that night, of that she was sure*), her bare feet no bigger than snaps on a newborn onesie. As she zoomed up past the bed where her gigantic progeny was now breathing deeply, she caught sight of the teddy bear, a menacing mound of fluff, and the pink hippo night-light, now horrifyingly the size of a Buick. *Where was she whooshing to?* She didn't know, and could no longer look ahead because she'd had to close her eyes tight against the wind, which was whipping across her body, making her shiver—but she sensed it. That black hole, that place all the other nightgowned people had been furiously pedaling away from. What on earth would she see when—*if?*—she got the courage to open her eyes again? Trembling like a tuning fork, she braced for impact but suddenly, with the chiming of three tones, everything ceased, nearly as immediately as it had all begun.

Beep, beep, beep.

"Mama, what's going on?"

Light now streamed through the windows and Sam was peering down at her, his bear trailing on the ground next to him.

"Is . . . everything okay?"

Annie peeled her cheek off the carpet and rubbed her jaw, brain still a million foggy miles away. *She must have passed out, then fallen asleep?*

"Mama, is that a knife?"

That snapped her to attention. She snatched up the weapon and affected a studied nonchalance, heart racing.

"Everything's fine," she whispered, to herself as much as Sam, as she gestured at Claire, spread-eagled on the bed, mass of curls haloing her cherubic face, and tiptoed back into the hall. *Keep it together. Keep it together for the kids.* "I was just unpacking and then your sister woke up and I ended up in here and, you know,

I had to cut through packing tape and stuff. C'mon, let's get you some cereal."

"Mmmkay," Sam said, with a smirk, not buying a minute of it.

Downstairs, Dan greeted her with an eyebrow cock and told her that the alarm system had indeed been on the fritz last night—a window had been blowing open and shut, triggering the beeps—but he'd fixed it from his phone at the bar when he'd gotten an alert. Yes, he'd been a little surprised to return home to find their bed empty, and his wife sprawled on their daughter's carpet with a kitchen knife by her side, but she'd been sleeping so deeply, and so in need of sleep, that he'd decided against rousing her.

Practical, and likely right, but as he kissed everyone goodbye and the kitchen door swung behind him, Annie couldn't help but wish she'd woken up in his arms, being carried to their bed.

•••

BARTLEBY NEIGHBORHOOD SCHOOL

14a East 77th Street

New York, NY 10075

"Where Play Is Work"

HOLIDAY WASSAIL REMINDER AND BENEFIT UPDATES

Merry Christmas, Happy Hanukkah, Blessed Kwanzaa, and Feliz Our Lady of Guadalupe Day to all who celebrate (that last one actually falls today!).

Before we bid adieu to this year and head to locales near and far to cozy up with grandparents, friends, and family, don't forget to celebrate with your Bartleby family first! Two very important upcoming events to add to your calendar:

1. Our annual wassail will be taking place next Wednesday, at 3:30 p.m., and will conclude with a party in the gym. As per previous years, we will form a group of "wassailers," or carolers, on the school steps, and then knock on each of the classrooms and sing to the beloved staff and teachers behind each door. This is one of the most joyous days of our year, and we hope you can join us. Younger siblings and alumni welcome.

*Headmistress Halpert wants to reassure everyone that though wassailing is traditionally accompanied by a cup of "wassail," or mulled, spiced wine, this will be a strictly teetotaling affair.

**Note to parents bringing treats for the celebration: please remember that we are an allergen-free school, which means any baked goods you bring for the celebration must be nut-free, grain-free, legume-free, and vegan. (Note: many gluten-free mixes contain pea and chickpea protein, so we kindly request you check the ingredient list fully and *confirm the product was made in a legume-free environment*.) (Second note: *few apartments are legume-free*.)

2. Our annual benefit (Gatsby *by Baz Luhrmann*! Not the Robert Redford version! So put away those baker boy caps and get out your pocket squares!) is just one week away, and we're gunning for 100% participation. To get a preview of our silent auction items, click here *hyperlink*. There's something for everyone—theater geeks, sports enthusiasts, and wine lovers alike. Per PTA president Leonora Linsby, this will strictly *not* be a teetotaling affair. Get ready to party like it's 1920 (*after* the flu pandemic)!

Lots of love from the Bartleby family to yours—
The Bartleby Neighborhood School PTA

N.B.: To our families who will be remaining local this holiday season, please be reminded that our neighborhood playground will be closed until mid-January so the park's team can install a new rubberized surface that is much safer than concrete. Here's to a new year free of scraped elbows and knees!

• • •

At pickup, she heard it before she located the source.

"Annie Lewin! What a treat!"

Goddamnit. Belinda. It was 2:30 p.m. on a Monday. *Wasn't she supposed to be shrieking at some underling at her air-conditioned, glassed-in office, while cracking the leather whip that matched her leather tuxedo?* Annie riffled through her tote bag and popped a few pieces of chewing gum into her mouth.

"I'm *so* jealous that you get to do pickup whenever you want! So deluxe. Brando has a concert after school so I cleared my meetings, *just* for two hours, then back to the grind the minute that violin bow is dropped!"

"Right." *Again with the subtle career digs.* She looked past Belinda to the school doors, willing them to open. Then, trying her best to feign politeness: "What's he performing?"

"Paganini! Brando's teacher told me he was nicknamed 'The Devil's Violinist,' because they said he got his skills from the devil, but I think it's because it drives Greg crazy when he has to play along!" Maniacal cackle. Pause. Then barreling ahead, "You know, I'd absolutely *kill* to be a creative, to be able to just fashion the day however I wanted it. But I've always needed structure. Bam, bam, bam!" Belinda punctuated each bam with a clap then, with a final David Copperfield–style flourish, flipped her hands over to reveal nothing inside. "Otherwise, poof, I don't know where I am!"

Annie had gone through a phase of playing *Mortal Kombat* at a friend's house when she was in grade school and always chose to be the girl player with cascading skunk-like hair whose secret move involved snapping her neck forward, ensnarling her opponent in her mane, then violently bashing them onto the ground with it, exposed thigh muscles quivering afterward. Precisely at that moment, the long-ago vision of that character and her quivering thighs flitted into her mind. *Could she flip her hair over, entangle Belinda, and toss her up over Central Park?*

But just as Belinda took in a big gulp of air to continue speaking, she heard a voice from behind her.

"Yep, those long endless, structureless days when you question your very existence and purpose on a minute-by-minute basis and wait desperately for your weekly therapy appointment—the dream." *Thank god.*

And then Annie and Shawn were standing side by side, a few steps below Belinda, who was giggling like a schoolgirl.

"But I'd imagine when you're shooting a movie, you must work like a dog!" she replied, then in an exaggerated stage whisper, "I mean, we *can* admit that we all know you're an actor, right?"

"Guess the secret's out!" Shawn replied. "And yes, working like a dog. I think I remember those days. Do I?"

Belinda's schoolgirl giggle evolved into her patented half laugh, half shriek.

"You should have had me represent you in your last divorce," she said with a wink, then morphing into a high, singsong voice, "I could totally have gotten you the Miami pad." But before a shocked Shawn could reply, Brando bounded out next to Sam.

"Look, Mom," Brando said, "I made an ornament for the Christmas tree!" Inside a Popsicle stick frame, painstakingly painted to resemble a candy cane, Brando had drawn a remarkably realistic violin.

"Wow, kiddo, that's super-cool," Annie said to him, as she wrapped Sam in a bear hug. But behind, she caught Belinda shaking her head and pursing her lips.

"Haven't you read the article?" Belinda said. "The *New York Times* one everyone is talking about?"

Annie looked at her blankly, pushing Sam's curls off his forehead and kissing the bridge of his nose. He dangled his Jackson Pollock ornament in front of her, all random splatters.

"You're not supposed to praise them," Belinda said, stage-whispering again.

Now Shawn was also looking at her quizzically.

"Yeah, it's this whole philosophy that has taken over child psychology," Belinda continued, dropping Brando's masterpiece into her massive leather tote. "You don't praise them for any-thing that isn't truly astonishing, because you want them to be intrinsically motivated, and not overly invested in the outcome—it's more about the *process*."

Long pause.

"So, um, what *can* you say?"

Belinda fished the ornament back out of her bag, looked at it for a solid beat, then turned to Brando.

"I see that you painted an instrument," she said. Brando shrugged, noncommittally. Back to Annie: "You're allowed to ac-knowledge what the child did, just not put any sort of value judg-ment on it."

"Can you say 'good job'?" Shawn asked. Belinda inhaled sharply.

"Absolu*te*ly not. Those words are verboten in our household. We don't want Brando to grow up trying to please us, and we don't want him to think our love is conditional. If we say, 'We love that painting so much, it's so great,' all we are telling him is that if he makes another painting that isn't that great, we might not love him as much."

Shawn and Annie stood there, deer in the headlights. She imagined Belinda's head starting to spin around, then popping off and skittering down Seventy-Seventh Street.

"Like, the other day we went sledding, and parents were liter-ally saying 'Great job!' to their children at the bottom of the hill,"

Belinda continued. "They were praising them *for responding normally to gravity.*" Her eyes got big with a *can you believe that shit?* look, and Annie squinted, settling her gaze just behind Belinda as she remembered jumping up and down and shrieking in real elation the previous afternoon when Sam and Claire shot down Dog Hill and catapulted headfirst into an igloo another child had made.

"What are you going to say after Brando's concert?" Annie managed.

"I'm going to praise his *effort,*" Belinda said. "It's all based on this Stanford researcher's longitudinal study, I'll WhatsApp it to the Babes. Saying 'You played so well!' is such a controlling remark! It doesn't allow him to just be proud of the act of playing and makes it all about *my* enjoyment of hearing him play. So instead, I'm going to say something like, 'I can tell you worked really hard to play that piece!' Because he does work hard, don't you, sweetie?"

She and Shawn were knocked out of their dumbfounded silence by Claire and Amelia barging down the stairs. Each was clutching a thick roll of painting paper in a chubby fist.

"Look, Mama, my art!" Claire crowed.

Annie unrolled the outermost layer and looked at the wide, thick strip of brown paint with goldfish crumbs embedded in it. *Screw Belinda and all the women like her who study parenting obsessively,* she thought, *who theatrically perform the act of parenting, who think you can research your way to optimized moments, who never act from the gut, since their gut, and any instinct that goes along with it, has all but evaporated in Pilates class. Surely she must find it exhausting to filter every interaction through some nebulous arbiter of what is and isn't socially acceptable?* It occurred to Annie that Ash, and her entire generation, constantly seeking rawness, might actually be onto something.

What would happen if everyone just stopped bullshitting already? Just tell the kid you like his fucking Christmas ornament! Live a little!

"Claire," she said, zipping up Sam's coat and affixing helmets, willing her two feet to remain firmly on the ground, "that is the greatest painting I've ever seen. I love it. Let's go frame it. Enjoy the concert, Belinda."

• • •

From: Annie Lewin
To: Ash Wempole

Ash, I took your advice and really am letting 'er rip, as you say, in life, on the page, wherever the fuck. And in the spirit of that, can we just pause for a second on your sign-off?

"Editress."

Do you actually believe you are an editor, Ash? That what you do constitutes anything remotely resembling what editors have done for years? That you deserve to put yourself in the same professional bucket as Maxwell Perkins? Go ahead, look him up. He edited Fitzgerald, Thomas Wolfe, all the biggies.

Sorry to be so direct, but j'fold.

Annie

From: Ash Wempole
To: Annie Lewin

Annie, I am going to need to take a minute to process the hostility you conveyed in your latest email, which I'm not prepared to talk about until I've had my weekly session with my Zoom therapist (who conducts what I'm now calling my ZoomIllume sessions, lol), but I just wanted to let you know that at the virtual editorial meeting today, this week's column was called out not only for having gotten the most clickthrus of any article on the site all week, but also for its tone, which our EIC wants us to encourage writers to emulate. He specifically used the word "raw" a lot. I counted 45 "raws" in his rant.

Really rawly yours,

Ash

She/They

Editress. Wordsmith. Potter.

@RiseFromTheAshes

Etsy store: TerraCottaAndAsh

• • •

When Annie had gone to retrieve Max from his crib the next morning, they discovered, rolling up the shade, that they were under water. The humidifier, pumping full blast to counter the building's ancient heat system, which had kicked on a few weeks ago and turned every room into a crackling cauldron, had frosted the interior windows over with condensation.

"Oooooooh," he crooned, pointing at it in wonder, and then she propped him up on the sill in his sleep sack, a little perfect parcel of baby, and they swirled patterns into it with their fingers as the sun rose and the rest of the city woke up, Annie's second-guessing chatter about where she was supposed to be and what she was supposed to be doing blissfully quiet. Then Claire barreled in, and the day hurtled forward to its inevitable conclusion: Annie in uncomfortable heels at the preschool benefit. She had no interest in going, but now more than ever, adrift like the rest of the—*What had Belinda called them?*—unconnected families, she needed to show commitment to the school.

Laura had informed her that the Bartleby Babes had been in a tizzy about costumes for weeks, with most opting for flapper dresses. But by the time she got her act together and went on the "Great Gatsby Party" tab on Rent the Runway, everything had been scooped up save for a sequined maroon jumpsuit that she rightly suspected would make her look like a disco Neil Armstrong.

"Gorgeous, but only downside was going to the bathroom," read the first comment. "Slightly tight in the crotch, but doable," read the second.

Skip.

She was tucking Sam in that night, wearing the same simple black cocktail dress she'd had, literally since college, when she saw the oversize pair of glasses on his desk that went with his detective kit.

"Mind if I borrow these?"

Sam shrugged, sleepily.

"Is there a mystery at the benefit?"

"Kinda."

Up the dramatic curving set of stairs, the DJ was leaning hard into the Baz Luhrmann soundtrack, which mashed up old-timey crackling 1920s swing and ragtime records with rap and electronica, in a genre known as "electro swing."

We're all alone,
No chaperone can get our number,
The world's in slumber,
Let's misbehave!

Irving Aaronson's trembly voice soared over the gala, the pounding of an 808 drum discordantly pulsing underneath the 1928 recording and through the floor of the Cosmopolitan Club straight into her chest. Yet somehow the shriek pierced through, in another register.

"Annie Lewin, looking FABULOUS! And what are you, lemme guess, you're . . . that guy who plays the piano at his mansion, with the glasses!"

"Klipspringer. Almost!" she said, taking in Belinda's costume, her hair pinned up in a crisp bob, with a beaded cloche hat just skimming her eyebrows, a peacock feather grazing her ear. Greg, wearing a tuxedo with his bow tie undone, stood idly by, staring into the middle distance. "I'm Dr. T. J. Eckleburg," Annie went on. "And you are . . ."

Belinda coyly produced a golf club from behind her back, then flipped it over her wrist and leaned against it, like Fred Astaire with his cane.

"Jordan, of course. Good on you."

"I figure this'll come in handy during the auction," Belinda said, raising the club above her head. "The intimidation factor." Pause. "Look, I heard about Sawyer and Sam; what absolute idiots they are!"

Annie shrugged, grabbing an overflowing coupe from a circulating tray, feigning nonchalance but comforted in the knowledge that Belinda could keep the conversation going with or without a partner. Didn't Belinda remember their altercation on the school steps the other day, when she'd spat that praising philosophy bullshit back at her face? Or had it not registered as an altercation to the woman whose entire career was built upon the nastiest of nasty altercations?

"But at least now, Brando and Sam have a shot at going to the same school next year! Saint Edward's and all their literature about raising boys to be kings! I mean, I married one, so I know from kings!" This, she punctuated with a small butt squeeze, Greg's eyes widening like one of those Panic Pete dolls. *When was the last time she'd been moved to squeeze Dan's butt? Was this what was missing in her marriage?* "And Thatcher, what a dream, right? If they both got in, and it would *entirely* be on their own merits?"

The WhatsApp chain had lobbed up a choice morsel of information that afternoon: that as part of Brando's kindergarten application, Belinda had procured a letter of recommendation from the current district attorney of Manhattan.

"Letters of recommendation are neither required nor encouraged." Annie had just about memorized that sentence from the common application portal, and it had been making its way through her brain, as if on a looping chyron. Now she'd have to get one of those for Sam. *Damnit. Maybe she could just forge the thing.*

Sam's giant dress-up glasses started slipping down the bridge of her nose, and she shoved them up, rather violently.

"Those glasses!" Belinda purred. "So chic. You know, I don't remember the doctor character in Gatsby—"

Annie deposited her emptied coupe on the next circulating tray, scooped up two more, motioned to Belinda that she'd be right back, then, slipping into the protective sea of sequins and white tuxedos, quickly downed her next glass. Laura was at an academic conference, so not attending; Dan was, of course, late; and *Kiss from a Rose* was nowhere to be found.

There's something wild about you child,
That's so contagious,
Let's be outrageous,
Let's misbehave!

Thump. Thump. Thump.
The bass of the music beat through Annie as she made her way

around the silent auction table, full of the usual offerings of theater tickets, already expensive bottles of wine that would sell for two times their worth, and framed art from the classes. Dan had donated Presidents' Day Weekend in his uncle's timeshare in the Bahamas. They'd been once—a condo with linoleum flooring a seventeen-minute drive to the beach, down a stretch of desolate highway bordered by tin-roofed shacks that had reminded her of the valley of ashes. (How apropos, given the benefit theme.) Of course Clementina Axel had contributed a basket of her candles from Luce Smooche, with an option to preorder a miniature farina mill or leather quiver (starting bid: $200). Annie stopped at the placard for dinner with Bartleby's head of school, Elizabeth Halpert.

"Need we say more?" it read. "Okay, we will! Fours parents, use it as a strategy sesh for kindergarten applications! Threes parents, start that strategy sesh early! And twos parents, celebrate that you don't have to really think about this for another two years! Anyway you cut it, delightful conversation will abound with our dearest Mrs. Halpert, aka the woman with the golden phone."

Annie tipped back the rest of her third glass, then set to work downloading the complex app that would allow her to scan the placard's accompanying QR code. With Sawyer no longer happening, she'd need all the help she could get, and Halpert, who'd worked in the independent school system since the Carter administration, was regarded, citywide, as one of the most effective connectors in the business. She knew all the heads of admissions and traded in social capital—connecting prestigious families with prestigious institutions—with the discretion and skill of a high-end madam. After the Bartleby bear logo loaded fully on her screen, Annie entered in an opening bid of $100.

"Surely Mrs. Halpert is worth more than a C-note," she heard Dan say, as a hand cupped the small of her back and another appeared floating in front of her face, proffering a glass of champagne. He yelped when she turned to face him.

"What's with the glasses?"

"I'm the billboard they drive past on the way to the city," she said, receiving his offering and dispatching of it as he stood there, eyebrows a Kabuki mask of confusion. "You know, the one that maybe symbolizes God?"

His confusion turned to concern.

"You're God from *The Great Gatsby*?"

She waved him off and beckoned over a waiter carrying blinis with caviar.

"Are these particularly small coupes?" she asked, gesturing with her glass, the last dregs of bubbly sloshing out. "And wouldn't we raise more money if we did this in the school gym and nixed the caviar? Anyway, you look dashing, as ever. Meyer Wolfsheim, I presume."

"They asked me what they should start the bidding at for Tierra del Sol," Dan said, ignoring her. The waiter moved to keep circulating, but Annie motioned for him to stay there.

"We should pay *them*," she said, as she squished together a tower of blini sandwiches. Then, in a radio announcer's voice: "Slightly moldy towels, an abundance of mosquitoes, and the sound of cars thumping past on the road outside—almost as soothing as the sound of waves, but with *this* condo, you're a safe seventeen-minute drive from the beach, which makes it more financially practical, but then you're literally in a shitty apartment *near* the water, which is probably what you already have in Manhattan, but without the four-hour plane ride."

"Okee, I can see we are in a charming mood," Dan said, setting the waiter free and guiding Annie toward the stage. Then: "We didn't have *such* a terrible time there when we went, did we?"

Christ, Annie thought to herself, as the auctioneer started to tap on the mic to get everyone's attention. *That had rolled right off her tongue, no problem at all.* And no, they hadn't had a terrible time at all. Sure, they'd been in the phase of courtship where they were having sex anywhere—they could have been at an airport motel in Detroit. But she remembered thrilling at the prospect of a weekend at the beach, sweating it out in the sun when people back home were slogging through gray slush. *Am I the metaphoric frog?* she wondered. *Has the water reached the boiling point? Have I been cooked?* She'd email Camila later.

The flappers swished their sequins, the tuxedoed Gatsbies checked their phones, and Mrs. Halpert launched into a long soliloquy on the importance of small community schools like theirs.

"With an endowment that rivals the GDP of a small African nation," Annie whispered to Dan, who put an arm around her shoulder and raised his champagne coupe at someone across the floor. Annie saw a seven iron rise slowly out of the crowd in response. *Belinda.*

"Oh yeah, toast Belinda for nabbing the D.A. as her letter of recommendation writer for Brando," she whispered. "Didn't you hear? Why don't we one-up her, get someone absolutely *huge* to write Sam's letter. Like Elon Musk."

Dan gave her a sharp look, pursed his lips, and shook his head disapprovingly, Jay Gatsby as schoolmarm.

"I was giving her advice today about this crypto billionaire she's representing, and I think I helped her, that's all," he whispered back. "We have another call set up for later this week— she's vicious, that one, but razor-sharp. Um, anyway, and setting aside for the moment if we'd actually want to be associated with him, just how do you expect us to get a letter from Elon?"

Annie snorted and tossed back another coupe.

"We can just forge it, who'll check? And can we at least agree on one thing, which is that Brando is someone's *last* name?"

Dan ignored her.

Tierra del Sol popped up on the screen with a picture of the main pool.

"Calling all golf lovers!" the auctioneer barked out. "Calling all parents who need a little fun in the sun! Pack up the kids—or ditch 'em!—and treat yourself to a long weekend at one of the Bahamas' most treasured communities, a home away from home. Direct flights, one of the Caribbean's most lauded golf courses, a stone's throw from the beach, and endless sunshine. Opening bids starting at $3,000 for four nights."

"A stone's throw if you're Goliath, maybe," Annie hissed.

A paddle, featuring primary-colored handprints made by the twos class, went up in the back.

"I hear $3,000 from the fine gentleman in the back, that's $3,000, can I hear a $3,500, I'm looking for $3,500, let me see $3,500 and *bam!*, we've got $3,500 from the lovely lady, $3,500 from the lovely lady, and can I hear $4,000—" And just as it appeared the auctioneer's patter was going to slow down, a golf club went up from across the room. "And we've got $4,000, four thousand from the golf enthusiast, she's ready to go right from here, folks, right from the Cosmopolitan Club to the first hole, and can I hear a $4,500, I'm lookin' for $4,500"—and then, almost as if she were watching someone else raise her hand for her, Annie stuck her paddle up. *What the hell,* she thought, *let's misbehave.*

"And we've got $4,500 from the bespectacled brunette, this is for the school, folks, it's a good cause, we've got $4,500, and can I hear a $5,000, yes, our golferette is back for more, flying on a direct flight from the Upper East Side to the links, $5,000, and can I get a $5,500—"

"What are you *doing*," Dan spluttered, after doing a literal spit take, his last sip of champagne filling up the coupe with a plop. "You *hate* it down there!"

Annie ignored him, waved her little handprint paddle at Belinda coquettishly, who was now lasered in on her from across the room, then shot it up high over her head.

"Fifty-five hundred folks! We've got $5,500 for a fabulous four nights in the *Ba-Ha-Mas*, and does Tigress Woods want to get her hole in one, can we get a $6,000, are we going to get that hole in one—"

The crowd started to murmur, the Gatsbies looked up from their phones, and the school administrators, standing together near the bar, perked up as a unit, little meerkats.

Belinda squinted across the floor at Annie, turned her club into a sword, did a few jousting quicksteps, then with a triumphant flourish, flung the club into the air.

"And that's $6,000, we've got $6,000 folks, I haven't seen this kind of heated bidding since Leon Black bought *The Scream*, folks, and can I hear a $6,500, $6,500, don't leave me hanging, ladies—"

"This is *our* donation, you do realize that?" Dan hissed, flabbergasted. "You don't bid on your own donation! You know it retails for $600 per night on the open market?"

She should have just let Belinda win, schlep poor Brando and his violin down there where it would no doubt swell in the humidity as he practiced Suzuki over the backdrop of cars rumbling outside. But she already had that letter from the D.A., and now that Sam had been rejected, throwing into relief just how ludicrous the whole process was—unfair in ways big and small, no matter how telescoped in or out you were—a crystal clear urge rose from Annie's bowels: to protect her young, and to do that by crushing Belinda and her conscious parenting and bento boxes and flapper cloches, all of it.

She'd felt a variant of it earlier that week, when she'd mistakenly thought someone had broken into the apartment, but in the clear light of day, she was starting to recalibrate her internal compass. The city existed, for her, like it did in the Saul Steinberg cover in the *New Yorker*, with Canada, Japan, and Russia all somewhere vaguely across the Hudson River. You opted to live here because it was the center of the world, because of its benefits and access, but that came along with a skewed eat-or-be-eaten mentality and a scarcity of resources, be that of square footage, parking spaces, or spots at top-notch schools. Perhaps, in New York, protection had less to do with wielding a knife. Perhaps it was more about leaning into your primal instincts, fairness be damned.

It was something lower-level inhabitants of the animal kingdom had drilled into their bones: to protect one's young at the expense of nearly everything else. The moment Sam had been born, she'd been granted a backstage pass to their atavistic world. For those first few months, any higher-level interests—debating the artistic choices of various directors over dinner; spending hours cooking a perfect meal—had been replaced, instead, with the world's most base concerns: sleep and food. The older her children got, the further away she drifted from the stage, up through the orchestra and into the cheap seats. But at this precise moment, fueled by a cocktail of exhaustion, anxiety, and alcohol, Annie thrilled at a sudden clarity of thought and purpose—one she assumed graced Dan's every day, even if it lacked one iota of nuance. If anything, it sure was a simpler mindset.

Annie raised her hand one final time and watched the auctioneer's gavel come down on his pulpit, as if in slow motion.

"And SOLD! To the woman in the enormous glasses, to Bartleby's own Iris Apfel, for $8,800!"

Complimenti, bitch.

The crowd whooped, and Dan looked at her, incredulous.

"The fuck?" was all he could manage.

Dinner with the head of school, she later learned, just inched past them as that year's highest bid, closing out at $9,000.

Second Semester

JANUARY

Dear Mother Inferior,

My son is fifteen months old. I went over to my bestie's house for brunch with some other neighborhood moms and all the other kids were walking, and clapping, and he just sat in my lap, gumming an old Sophie the Giraffe. He isn't even pulling himself up yet, and I'm not sure his grasp is as firm as it should be. I told a friend I was getting concerned and she pointed me to a subscription service that sends you developmentally appropriate toys every few months so you can work on skill-building. Should I sign up?

From,

Behind in Brattleboro

Dear Behind,

I just looked up some of those subscription services. Good grief. One of them promises toys that will "build motor skills via hand-to-hand transfer, to promote cross-body coordination." Are you raising a baby, or a baby triathlete competitor?

I think this is about as good a time as any to let you know that "Mother Inferior" is going to be shifting gears, because New Year, New Me. The reason I was hired at this website was to be real, to tell it like it is. Instead of those other advice columnists who pen pieces about how fierce we "mommas" are, or how much various "mother warriors" in the community have your back, and basically don't wield any judgment or give you any hard-and-fast advice—because we're all millennials and got a part in the school play and heaven forfend someone criticize us for doing something clearly idiotic with our children, like alternating bites of dinner with fistfuls of M&Ms—my promise was to be as raw as cookie dough that might actually give you salmonella. And I failed. To peel back the shallot here, I think the problem was that I couldn't even take my own advice.

Let's play two truths and a lie:

1. My kids are sleeping through the night.
2. My husband and I regularly have screaming red-hot sex.
3. I didn't invite my kid's entire class to his birthday party.

Okay, fine, it's actually two lies and a truth.

Maybe it's three lies and no truths!

We can come back to this later!!

Anyway, as I approach my fifth decade on this planet, I'm beginning to realize that everybody is faking it—particularly when it comes to parenting—and so, after sensing renewed engagement as I've steered the ship away from rah-rah momma warrior crap and closer to No Fucks Given territory, I've decided that henceforth, I'm going to tell it to you straight. There will be opinions. There will be judgments. And for those of you who need the advice but don't want the color, there will be a Too Long, Didn't Read (TL;DR) sentence after my column's sign-off, summing everything up in a tidy manner. (Thanks to my Gen Z editor, Ash, who urged me to make my advice "snackable," to compete with withering attention spans that can focus on a video of a cat being groomed by a parakeet for a mere fifteen seconds before clicking away. And thanks, too, to her for allowing me to place it at the end of the piece and not the start, as is TL;DR convention, a concession to my hope that people might actually read my words.)

For the rest of you, who like their advice with a side of actual writing, let's turn back to *Behind*'s plight.

What is happening with these subscription services, *Behind*, is that, similarly to the bagel slicer PR teams that convince you a single-use item will ward off a visit to the hospital before brunch (just use a knife!!!), Silicon Valley and various marketing gurus have convinced you that something is wrong with your child, that he is the kind of snowflake that will never clap a day in his life. But maybe he just doesn't want to clap, randomly, in a sea of strangers at brunch. Maybe your child hates brunch! I have no idea. But don't spend your hard-earned cash buying him toys that will inch him along some developmental timeline that he will inch along, all on his own, with time. Give him some mixing bowls and a pitcher of water and set him up in the bathtub. He'll be fine. In short, I'd recommend that you go gum your own maraca for a while. And by "gum" I mean "drink," and by "maraca," I mean "goblet of pinot grigio."

Love,

Mother Inferior

TL;DR: Unless your pediatrician tells you otherwise, your kid is fine, and if you're intent on signing up for a subscription service, wine.com has a new one, just sayin'. *chef's kiss emoji*

• • •

ADMISSIONS CRITERIA FOR THE THATCHER SCHOOL FOR THE GIFTED AND TALENTED

Welcome to this year's admissions season, which will be open until March 1. Thatcher was founded in 1954 with the express purpose of providing a rigorous home for intellectually gifted and curious children in the greater New York City area, at no charge to families. We routinely teach one to two grade levels ahead of the standard state curriculum. As such, we evaluate each child solely based on his or her merit. No preference will be given to siblings, legacies, or staff member children. No recommendation letter will be required or accepted. No essay or formal statement about your child will be required or accepted. For the purposes of our admissions season, your child will be assigned a number that will follow him or her until the end of the process, to ensure no preferential treatment.

The first round of testing requires that your child visit a certified psychologist, trained to administer the Stanford-Binet V IQ test to young children. The test is normed for ages two to ninety, meaning that adults taking the test will receive the same set of questions as your child, but your child may hit his or her ceiling more quickly than older test takers. Upon submitting your contact information, we will email you a list of the approved psychologists, with whom you must schedule an assessment independently of the school. Parents must wait outside the room during the duration of the test, and if it becomes apparent that applicants have been coached in any way, the child will be automatically disqualified. We regret that we cannot retest or accommodate children who have an off day or exhibit what we understand is completely developmentally appropriate stranger-danger. As we are sure you can appreciate, building out the idealized kindergarten class is rife with challenges.

The top-scoring 200 applicants from Round 1 will advance to Round 2, and specifics about that process will be released only to those families. Fifty students will ultimately receive a spot in our rising kindergarten class, and twenty students placed on the waitlist. Since our school's founding, the waitlist has moved at most by one spot per year.

No tours allowed.

Scientia omnia vincit (Knowledge conquers all),
The Admissions Team

• • •

Now that Sawyer was no longer in the cards, Bartleby had set up a weekly strategy session for Annie, Dan, and Mrs. Halpert to discuss the best plan of action. Her office became, in her words, their "war room." At their first meeting, Halpert—a gray-coiffed Nancy Pelosi, all pantsuits and four-inch heels—made the convincing argument that no coed school would fairly consider Sam's application, since they'd correctly assume he'd been rejected from Sawyer, knocking his status down ever so slightly. The only one that might was Hudson-Green, a safety school she described as "charming" in the same way *New York Times* real estate listings describe two-hundred-square-foot one bedrooms as "cozy." Thatcher, she stated perfunctorily, was out of her jurisdiction, as the process was "entirely opaque" and involved numerical scores that no one, save for the admissions officers themselves, ever saw. So for now, she was going long on boys' schools, particularly St. Edward's. He was patron saint not just of royals, the reason for the school's pretentious tagline—"Raising boys to be kings"—but also, Annie had discovered while googling before the meeting, failed marriages. This fact was completely exempt from the school literature.

Halpert pulled up the school's admissions page and read aloud from the tab titled "Why St. Edward's?" in that elder Katharine Hepburn accent that was vaguely British, vaguely Swiss, and thoroughly patrician.

"For a century and a half, St. Edward's boys have followed a core curriculum," she began, "which includes

- committing to memory forty sonnets, half in Olde English;
- singing in four-part harmony to hospital patients over the winter holidays;

- spending three full school days per semester in Central Park, observing and sketching the city's native avian species in the style of great landscape artist John Constable;
- marching across the field of Antietam while reciting a poem by a favorite Civil War poet;
- drawing, accurately and from memory, pre- and postcolonial maps of Africa when supplied with a date;
- studying the etiquette of a proper handshake, table manners, and how to properly employ honorifics;
- learning to lead a partner in the cha-cha, jive, foxtrot, Viennese waltz, and both bolero versions (Spanish and Cuban);
- reading Homer, Virgil, or Chekov in the original language;
- subscribing to three publications (print only), and being conversant in both the business and arts issues of the moment; and
- developing a lifelong love of learning and a clear sense of purpose as he takes the St. Edward's legacy to schools secondary, tertiary, and beyond."

Dan nearly collapsed into tears afterward, he'd been so moved. What could be a better indication that he'd inched closer to that white-hot center than his son, clad in culottes and a tiny blazer, tromping over the mud of a Civil War ground, reciting Walt Whitman?

Whatever. Dan could handle that application, and the accompanying ninety-second video she'd heard other people had hired professional film editors to cut.

Annie would make an appointment for a tour at Hudson-Green, but it was in these war room meetings, when St. Edward's took center stage, that she found herself trusting her gut even more. The Wikipedia entry on Thatcher had a list of successful alumni who spanned heads of state, inventors, and stars of stage and screen, and though the school had its flaws—rumor had it there were no windows in any of the classrooms, and the pressure cranked up in the older years—she loved how the student body was wildly diverse, and the application she'd filled out almost monkishly ascetic. Thatcher didn't care where she went to college. Didn't care where she lived. Didn't care how many higher degrees she had. Didn't care what she thought Sam's strengths and weaknesses were. Didn't care if the D.A. knew your family. What they cared about was the raw intellect of the child, which could be reduced to a number. And while that number likely missed all sorts of important things about one's child, and was based partially on questions she'd come to understand were both biased and dated, at least it was concrete. The rest of this process had become so nebulous and fuzzy, she could barely stand it. As one reporter had written, accepted Thatcher children seemed to "acquire something like a reverse mark of Cain, a sanctification that will stay with them forever, whether they live up to that early promise or not."

Sam would live up to the promise, she just knew it. *And didn't he deserve to spend eight hours a day in a place that encouraged him to lean into his eccentricities, that didn't press him into a mold forged over a century and a half until every uniform-clad boy spat out was a carbon copy of the same generally excellent, and entirely indistinguishable, young gentleman, fated to pass one another on the dance floor at various benefits, twirling through passable versions of the Spanish bolero?*

The email from Thatcher about next steps came with the names of five certified IQ testers—four women and one man.

Noah B. Siegler's website was bare-bones. There was a small, fuzzy photo on the "About Me" page of the rumpled, professorial midsixties doctor, straight out of central casting. Under the "Testing" tab was a bulleted list of the assessments he was qualified to administer. There wasn't just the Stanford-Binet and Rorschach, both of which Annie recognized, but also the DAS, Kaufman, Beery, Bender, NEPSY, and over twenty more.

"Beery and Bender and DAS, oh my!" she whisper-sang to herself, to the tune of "Lions and tigers and bears." *People sure like having different ways to rank their children.*

It was possible to buy an IQ test on the black market—the Bartleby Babes considered it every admissions season. The test had not changed in two decades, so there were many floating around.

"Stanford-Binet V complete test, $3,000, no questions asked" was just one of a handful of posts Annie found after a cursory look on Facebook Marketplace.

And yet, there was that sentence from the Thatcher admissions page:

Parents must wait outside the room during the duration of the test, and if it becomes apparent that applicants have been coached in any way, the child will be automatically disqualified.

A safer bet: heading to Amazon to buy a bunch of IQ-tangential activities for Sam to do, like the tangram puzzles, made of various shapes you could combine to make images, or the "IQ FUNPACK" from Korea that promised to familiarize children with the parts of the test, both in English and Korean. Before buying it, Annie clicked through the product's images.

"Tell us what is silly about picture!" one photo blared in Comic Sans font, over a painting of a one-legged little girl with three pigtails, eating sushi with a spoon while standing on what looked like a 1980s-era Nordic Track. *Where to begin?*

• • •

From: Annie Lewin

To: Camila Garcia Williams

Subject: Intelligence quotients!

OK I found this question online somewhere, can you do it?

How would this paper look if cut like this, then unfolded?

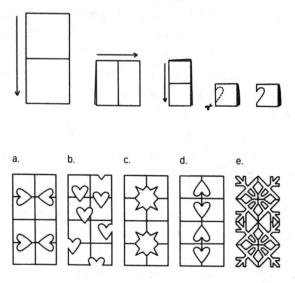

I def can't, but fingers crossed Dan passed down some visual and spatial reasoning skillz.

Latest in the kindergarten application saga: Sam is going to have to take the Stanford-Binet IQ test to apply to Thatcher, and while they have this crazy eugenicist background, they are kind of *fascinating*. I went down a rabbit hole on my phone last night after Max woke me up for a wee-hours-of-the-morning nurse and came upon this quote from Lewis Terman, who created the test way back in 1916:

"High-grade or borderline-deficiency . . . is very, very common among Spanish-Indian and Mexican families of the Southwest and also among negros. Their dullness seems to be racial, or at least inherent in the family stocks from which they come . . . Children of this group should be segregated into separate classes . . . They cannot master abstractions but they can often be made into efficient workers."

Maybe he should have met you and your Mexican-Phi-Beta-Kappa brain?

True story: a six-year-old got a whopping 298 on an IQ test, one of the highest scores ever recorded. One of the country's premier gifted and talented testers herself confirmed it! This boy wonder became the poster child for gifted children the world over, gave speeches in front of packed auditoriums, and enrolled in college at just seven years old. But when he started to exhibit severe psychological issues—like suddenly wetting the bed again—the authorities started to investigate, and eventually the boy's mother admitted that she'd stolen the test and had her son memorize it.

See: CRAZY PARENTS. No wonder Plato argued in *The Republic* that elite children should be taken from their parents and raised by teachers. Ho-hum.

Anyway, I've gotten Sam a bunch of tangrams, this ancient Chinese puzzle made up of seven different shapes that you're supposed to use to replicate a pattern. How being able to form a giraffe out of a triangle and diamonds indicates that you have high spatial reasoning capabilities, or what high spatial reasoning capabilities might allow you to do, other than interior design your apartment, I can't tell you. But I found a website where you can print out super-hard ones, like literally the Last Supper. Judas's head is a trapezoid.

Cute/sacrilegious? Who's to say!

Anyway, tomorrow: the safety school tour. Apparently they have alpacas?

A.

P.S. I've sort of let it rip in the column. Did you see the latest? My inbox is now flooded with mothers asking questions, or writing just to commiserate.

Like . . . I got 100 inbound emails yesterday. *Yesterday.* It's overwhelming but maybe . . . the point of all this?

P.P.S. I promise I'm not ignoring what you said about going to speak to some-one. But what, precisely, am I going to tell them? That I am having visions I am a character from *Peter Pan*???

From: Camila Garcia Williams
To: Annie Lewin
Subject: re: Intelligence quotients!

Um . . . I don't even know where to begin.

Memorizing IQ tests? Judas's head as a trapezoid? Alpacas?? (!) My immi-grant Mexican Catholic grandmother just rolled over in her grave, three times. (And no, I have no idea what the hell that diagram is.)

At the beginning of this year, you asked me to let you know if you were headed off the reservation . . . Well, the anxiety radiating off this email nearly short-circuited my computer. Sam is a good, exceedingly bright kid. I'm sure he'll do just fine on this test. And if he doesn't, so fine, he hangs out with al-pacas (??) all day, or (gasp) heads off to public school like you and me. It could be worse, right? Dare I point out that your New York City bubble is, maybe, totally warping your sense of what the rest of the world looks like? (A snapshot: spending the morning making mud pies in the backyard, then gathering ingredi-ents at various places for the new *Times* recipe everyone is talking about, falling asleep in your son's bed during his nap time, worrying that you're not equipped to run a nonprofit even though everyone is encouraging you to apply for the executive director position, etc. Suffice it to say, it doesn't involve alpacas.)

Another point: if Sam takes a spot at Thatcher, that means another child who can't afford private school no longer has an amazing option. Which is an issue all its own. I'm not saying you need to solve the problems of the educa-tional system with Sam's enrollment, I'm just afraid the pot is heating up and you're luxuriating your frog legs in it like it's a hot tub.

Maybe you should, seriously, consider writing something meatier, if only to ground you a bit? I also happen to have come up with THE PERFECT title for a book, assuming you want to expand your op-ed and explore how mothers feel they're going crazy but in fact are just coming to terms with their new roles. OK. Are you ready. Is this thing on? (clears throat) *Maternal Combustion*.

OK, you don't like that one? I've got another. Wait for it . . . *In Loco Parentis*. Mic drop.

(Come ON, that is golden.)

Anyway, responding to your P.P.S.:

1. Huge congrats re: the column. At a bare minimum, those hundred emails mean that you are connecting with people, making them feel less alone. *That's* what it's all about. Who cares about clicks?

2. I doubt any of your hallucinations would ruffle the feathers of a New York City therapist. Lena Dunham and Prince Harry both go to therapy. For sure, their shrinks have heard some things. (See: the ramifications of a very public social media presence that focuses largely on endometriosis; leaving the British monarchy.)

Sending love,
Camila

One P.S. of my own: if you are, indeed, Wendy floating off to Neverland, where no one grows up, and you're trying to escape the pull of being sucked down into its opposite pole, what is that exactly? Adulthood?

• • •

A banner with
   Students
   Making
   Intelligent
   Life Choices
   Extemporaneously

fluttered in the breeze over the main gate of the Hudson-Green SMILE Academy when Annie and Dan walked onto the campus, bustling with activity on the sunny, clear-skied winter day of their tour. Annie had briefly been on the website, paying only half attention to the description of Sam's safety school: an "astonishing haven on the city's Upper West Side, with multiple playgrounds, fields, outdoor art studios, and three resident alpacas, named Beowulf, Wolfgang, and Phil." Students were encouraged to wear long underwear throughout the cold months, since the school had adopted a kind of Scandinavian "there is no bad weather, only bad clothes" mentality, in order to allow a freedom of outdoor exploration that "made them children of the world." There appeared to be as much going on outside as in. A class rehearsed a play in the outdoor amphitheater here; another painted a still life of a bowl of vegetables gathered from the school's greenhouse over there; older students led an alpaca by on a soft, knitted leash.

Dan flinched as the alpaca tried to nibble his Sorel laces. Then, a little tyke excused himself from a nearby class, all clad in togas, and came up to them, proffering a small hand, which Dan, awkwardly, shook.

"Can I help you get to the office?" the pip-squeak squeaked and then led them across the grass to a large stone building. "Sorry for my outfit, we're pretending to be the Roman Senate today, and debating whether or not to overthrow Caesar."

"Oh, wow, lovely, and how old are you?" Annie asked. *This was a safety school?* She thought of her own suburban, John Hughes–esque high school, with one grubby outdoor field full of so many holes that the soccer players routinely sprained their ankles.

"Eight. Did you know that one of the Roman emperors elected his horse to the Senate?"

"I did!" Dan said. "Caligula."

"Yeah! Gee, you must be pretty smart, mister."

Dan beamed.

Ladies and germs, my husband, who can never let another person one-up him, no matter how unthreatening or short.

"Anyway, one of my classmates put in a motion to vote Phil into the Senate—Phil's one of our alpacas—because he calms her down, he's kind of a support animal, and even though it was pretty silly, we wanted to show our classmate that we valued her needs. Part of our philosophy is that we make intelligent choices. So now Phil is part of the Senate! He just ate his ballot."

"Not such an intelligent choice, huh?" asked Dan. The child furrowed his eyebrows, pointed at the building in front of him, then scampered off.

"Don't be an asshole," Annie muttered, as they walked up the big stone steps, though she couldn't help but feel that the child was, indeed, speaking oddly, stiltedly, like he'd just come back from a self-help conference.

Full of the sons and daughters of Columbia professors, non-profit lawyers, and social activists, the school had but one immutable tenet that the students, who held a 51 percent block to the faculty and staff's combined 49 percent, could never vote out: no grades.

"All grades serve to do is elevate the teacher above the student, and quantify the unquantifiable: a child's curiosity and innate creativity," the president's letter read.

"But *isn't* the teacher elevated above the student?" Dan had asked before their tour. "And if the point of school is to prepare a child for the real world, just how is a no-grades environment going to do that?"

After the tour guide introduced herself as the mother of two current students, one of whom occasionally popped up to give her a hug as they made their way through the campus, she began.

"We owe our school's name to a successful campaign by the students in the '90s," she said as they looped around the amphitheater. "It was originally simply 'Hudson-Green,' after the two progressive educators who founded the school in the 1910s. But the students decided it best that we be explicit about our values, so after campaigning and putting it to a vote, we added SMILE"—here she gestured to the banner—"to the end."

"Bit of a clunker, that name, no?" Dan whispered to Annie as they passed the new double-height-ceiling library, replete with wipeable walls that students could draw on and then clean off at the end of the day, and the lounges that were neither student- nor teacher-specific, to promote the cross-pollination of ideas across generations.

"If we're being literal about it, shouldn't it be Hudson-Green *SMILCE*?" he murmured to Annie as they reached the cafeteria, where every student held a shift each week, freeing workers to use the school's well-equipped gym, should they so desire. She silently shook him off.

In lieu of grades, each teacher sent home weekly tomes on the children. Parents would never be asked to participate in bake sales and fundraisers, as at other independent schools, due to a gargantuan endowment that was rumored to have received a critical influx in the 1980s, after the death of one of America's most famous and wealthy pop artists, a childless man whose niece attended Hudson-Green. But they would be required to sign an oath, upon accepting a spot for their child, that they'd actively participate in their educational journey, which meant reading those tomes, and responding. One parent estimated it was twenty single-space pages per week.

They'd barely made it outside the school's gates after the tour before Dan had pulled his phone out of his pocket to address the incessant pings coming through from his work email, while muttering about the alpaca who'd almost eaten his laces and the gall of expecting him to consume the equivalent of a *Power Broker*'s number of pages per year on his son's progress.

"It's not like just because the school is less prestigious, the tuition is any cheaper!" he scoffed, tapping repeatedly on the screen. "We're still going to be forking over $58,000 per year. Aren't I paying for them to educate my child? Or will that go toward alpaca upkeep? Damnit, I thought these were touch sensitive!"

Fed up, he ripped off a glove and pecked out a note with his index finger.

"Tonight we're filming Sam's St. Edward's video. And we're gonna crush it."

• • •

SAM LEWIN'S ST. EDWARD'S APPLICATION
90-SECOND VIDEO

Camera opens on a young boy, four or five, sitting in front of a page of blank paper.

"Okay, so, should I do it in green or brown?"

Tiny voice, off-screen: "Puh-ple!"

"Okay, Claire, we'll make it purple. I know that's your favorite color."

Hunts in marker bin.

"You know some beetles are actually purple, but it's mostly their iridescence." Charming little embarrassed smile. He knows that's a big word. "I learned that from my insect encyclopedia."

Boy's hair flops over his eyes as he hunches over the paper.

"So there are three parts to every insect: the head, which is, well, it's the head, the top part. Then the thorax. And then the last part is the abdomen."

Looks up.

"Wait, should I demonstrate?"

Man's voice, off camera: "Sure."

Camera moves to capture boy getting off his chair and heading over to younger sibling, playing with MagnaTiles nearby.

"Claire, can I just, do you mind?" Boy lowers her onto her back.

"So, here's the head, here's the thorax, and our abdomens are different than an insect's but an insect abdomen would kinda, well, it would be—get up, Claire—okay, it would be here." Tap on the butt.

Younger sibling in uncontrollable giggles.

Panning back to follow boy to his paper.

"Okay, so you start with the head, and I mean that isn't really a great one, but it's okay, and you want to make the eyes super-big, that's the trick, and then—" But then the boy becomes lost in his world, eyebrows furrowed, and stops narrating, occasionally and adorably biting his lower lip. The grip of his pencil is perfect, his focus palpable.

A solid beat of drawing. Camera comes from above to show a remarkably lifelike beetle.

"And Claire, what else do I have to put on here to make it an insect? What is missing?"

Curly hair appears at the bottom of the shot.

"TONGUE!"

"Insects don't really have tongues! They sort of smell and taste with their antennae!" Boy makes his two pointer fingers into antennae and wiggles them at younger sibling, who guffaws. An engaged, patient, and natural teacher, the kind we all wish we could be.

"No, we need wings." Flourish on the paper.

"And I present to you, the purple beetle."

With a yowl, younger sibling tries to rip the paper from the boy's hands, and the screen goes black.

• • •

The baby's checkup: an appointment Annie was sad to admit was the highlight of her month, and not just because it had absolutely nothing to do with kindergarten admissions.

Then again: *What mother didn't have a crush on her pediatrician?*

She, and most of the other neighborhood mothers, saw Dr. Rapaport, a man from the old guard who still wore suspenders and whose best joke was to pretend that various wild animals had taken up residence in his patients' ears. A mix between Mr. Rogers and George Banks from *Mary Poppins*, he held all the sex appeal of a Supreme Court justice, and yet a visit to his office always resulted in a Bartleby Babes flurry.

LEONORA: Bebz, don't get too hot and bothered but news flash: I'm omw to Rapaport for flu shots.

CHRISTINE: SWOON.

MAYA: OMG I could watch that man give shots all day.

YAEL: *puke emoji*

(Onslaught of question marks)

YAEL: OMG OMG mistake mistake, was typing too fast, meant to text *doctor emoji* *small explosion emoji* *sick person with a thermometer emoji* *tongue hanging out drool emoji*

LEONORA: So last week, I noticed that Brock's left eye was a little droopy and I googled it—

CHRISTINE: NO! You never google!

(Thumbs-up galore)

LEONORA:—and it said he maybe had a brain tumor or at least a low-grade neurological disorder and I brought this up with Chris and he insisted I was being crazy but I just had this *sense* and so I took him in for an emergency same-day appointment with Rapaport and you know what he said?

YAEL: *ear emoji*

MAYA: *ear emoji*

CHRISTINE: *ear emoji*

LEONORA: "A mother's instinct is a doctor's first line of defense."

CHRISTINE: I'm dead *skull and cross bones emoji*

YAEL: Be still, my heart. Preach, doctah!

CHRISTINE: [GIF of Patrick Dempsey as Dr. McDreamy, raising a glass and smizing]

LEONORA: Brock ended up being totes fine, but since I was there I had him check out a rash and confirm it wasn't scabies. So, *chef's kiss emoji*

BELINDA: *flexed bicep emoji* *fist pound emoji* *small explosion emoji*

As Annie pushed the stroller down Park Avenue, passing other children similarly bundled and strapped in at shocking angles that made them look like little ice luge competitors, she wondered just how often the pediatrician realized he'd become a stand-in for a romanticized, though not romantic, partner: someone who could calm you down while simultaneously focusing, fully, on your child.

Now that she had three children and no longer fell into the new mother camp, she had a whole new appreciation for Rapaport's calm demeanor, since she'd often be the first call or text from new parent friends about small medical issues.

"Found three dots on Theo's arm. Worth sending a photo to the doc or . . . ?"

"Switched her from the swaddle to the Merlin but now she wants to flip over. But isn't she supposed to sleep on her back? Do I, like, go in there and keep flipping her over?"

"Want to wean her down to just one session but afraid my milk production will go down! Checked both MilkyMamas and LecheBitch but they give opposite recommendations! What should I do?"

The concerns were minuscule and often ridiculous—*How many of these did Rapaport have to field every day,* Annie wondered, *while also attending to actual pediatric emergencies?*

She parked the stroller, extracted her hands from the enormous winter gloves that attached to the handle and made her look like a prizefighter, fished Max out of the snowproof winter bunting every mother on the Upper East Side of Manhattan had, then peeled off his puffer suit and tiny trapper hat to reveal, finally, her sweaty one-year-old. He immediately heaved his whole body toward the floor, a squirming, dense kettlebell. Annie couldn't remember the last time she'd exercised, but surely schlepping the baby around had to be as good of a workout as Dan's zapper suit.

Tinsel was still strung up over the nurses' station and holiday cards were plastered on the bulletin board. As she waited to be called, she watched the older toddlers push those rounded wooden pieces over the metal curves of a bead maze as Max, who after his two solo steps had reverted fully into cruising, made his way hesitatingly around the office, from plush chair to beanbag, toward his Valhalla: the fish tank, where a few flint-eyed neon tetras darted around in a school. Annie was about to pull her phone out to text Camila that the fish, on high alert and extremely busy, reminded her of Dan, but then something caught her eye: a holiday card with a picture of a family she recognized. The Brenners.

JOYFUL ran in huge letters underneath a black-and-white photo of Belinda, Greg, and Brando, standing on a beach and being joyful—or, at the very least, feigning it. Belinda's head was tossed back and her mouth open, in what was either a laugh or that signature hyena scream. Brando and Greg were standing on either side, wearing matching polo shirts and looking up at her in wonder, delight, or perhaps sheer terror. Ringing the card was a border of tiny birds, each holding the scales of justice in its beak.

Annie got up and squinted at the card. Monogrammed into each polo shirt was a small insignia: "Lyford Cay."

You've got to be kidding me.

She pulled out her phone and sent a photo of the card to Laura.

ANNIE: Look what I found at Rapaport's!

LAURA: OMG she's def hyena-screaming there.

ANNIE: OK but zoom in. Lyford Cay.

LAURA: ?

ANNIE: It's a members-only resort in the Bahamas. SHE'S A MEMBER.

LAURA: Umm . . . I'm ready to get enraged, but explain it to me like I'm a kindergartner.

ANNIE: She pays some ungodly sum of money to be able to go to Lyford Cay, and she was bidding on Dan's shitty Tierra del Sol thing at the benefit?

LAURA: *quizzical face emoji* Like I'm in nursery school.

ANNIE: SHE WAS ONLY BIDDING TO SCREW WITH ME. Lyford Cay is a ten-minute drive from his family's timeshare, and is *significantly* nicer.

LAURA: Oh! Oh. That's so . . . weird?

ANNIE: Also who puts a black-and-white photo of a *beach*? Isn't the point of a beach that there is color and warmth and not just grayscale expanses? The day could be totally overcast!

LAURA: Totally.

ANNIE: And who sends a holiday card to their DOCTOR?

LAURA: I mean . . . Many people? There's a whole wall of them at Rapaport's.

ANNIE: *angry red face emoji*

LAURA: No, you're right, it's entirely ridiculous and awful.

"Um, ma'am? Is he yours?" Annie turned to find a nurse in scrubs, and Max sitting on the ground, gumming an old surgical mask. "And if this is Max Lewin, please come on back to the purple room! We're ready for you."

Annie heaved her squirming kettlebell up off the floor, feeling her lower back scream in pain, and took Max back to the room, where he was measured and, thankfully, didn't pee when the nurse de-diapered him for the weigh-in. As she waited for Rapaport to come in, her brain started to rev up into its fast cycle. *Lyford Cay? Seriously? Why did Belinda have it out for her? Why this new interest in applying to Thatcher? That was* her *thing! And why did it seem like Dan was scheduling every-other-day calls with the Divorce Doyenne to discuss nebulous cryptocurrency issues?*

As she distracted Max with a tongue depressor, her mind drifted back to the previous weekend. She'd woken at dawn to face another bitterly cold gray-sky day full of MagnaTile castles and guilty pockets of screen time. The winter's first snow had long ago melted, and the blow-up sled she'd gotten the kids for Christmas was still sitting in the hall closet, so she'd reserved them all tickets to the American Museum of Natural History. In the steamy auditorium where she remembered sitting as a schoolkid decades before, the five of them had gazed up, slack-jawed, at the forty-foot screen as it took them on a journey across the Serengeti for thirty-eight minutes.

"Unlike baby cheetahs, which must be taught how to hunt, wildebeest are born with the tools to survive," the deep-timbred narrator had intoned, over footage of a slimy baby wildebeest, all limbs and joints, trembling on its hooves just minutes after birth.

Did that wildebeest's mother feel pride when her baby pushed himself up? Annie'd wondered, as the duo galloped off down the plain. *Did she feel satisfied, intuiting which direction to go, where to find the grass and water her young would need? What must it be like to have an innate impulse toward right and wrong and priorities, all clear as day, even without the help of an analyst?*

As the camera had held on a crocodile ingesting a snack of a baby wildebeest that had unsuccessfully tried to cross the Mara

River, the narrator had intoned about the cruelty of raising young in the Serengeti. Annie's own three offspring had been in various phases of attention—Sam riveted in the seat next to her, Claire's head lolling forward in a state of semiconsciousness on her lap, Max standing in the aisle, his back to the screen and gumming the armrest. She'd looked over at Dan, wanting to make a joke about raising young on the plains of Manhattan, or hoping he'd also be filled with some overwhelming, immense sense that their job was connected, through millennia, to the job of parents before them, wildebeestian and crocodilian alike. But as she'd moved her eyes from the screen, she'd found his illuminated in the glow of his phone, where he'd been furiously pecking away, there but not there. *What the hell had he been up to then? Texting Belinda?*

"Oh, my. Annie, have you been giving him his cute pills? You must have because would you *look* at this little guy? A carbon copy of you, and of his siblings! Miraculous, isn't it?"

Dr. Rapaport was suddenly walking through the door, scooping Max out of her arms and tickling him under his chin, making him giggle, and squarely depositing Annie back in the present. His hands were so smooth, and always warm.

"So, first off, congratulations on surviving year one! Huge achievement. And I see here you're still nursing him. Well done, Annie, well, well done."

She nodded perfunctorily to tamp down an unexpected surge of emotion, which kept building anyway.

"And you know, the first year can be particularly hard on the mother, so I always take a few minutes at the start of the appointment to make sure you're doing okay. How ya doin'?"

He continued bouncing Max in his lap and looked at her. Calmly, not rushing, just patient. *When was the last time Dan had looked at her like that, with no Jobsian gadget in the way, with no sense of looming time pressure?* She felt it about to happen, and then the dam broke, which Rapaport seemed to have anticipated. He had already grabbed the tissue box for her.

"I'm fine! I'm totally fine," Annie said, briskly wiping her nose on her sleeve, then sheepishly accepting a tissue.

"I just, I don't know, I know we're going to start talking about weaning, and maybe it's that I can't believe he's already one, or maybe it's hormonal, or that he'll likely be my last so I won't nurse ever again and I sort of really enjoyed it, or it could be this whole kindergarten application thing, or that Dan is working so much and three kids is a lot, or I honestly can't remember the last time I slept more than three hours uninterrupted, and I just have no idea."

She gulped in some air, blew her nose loudly, and recovered, partially. She declined to mention that there were, perhaps, more unique and alarming things that kept happening to her. The hallucinations, sure. Or yesterday at the playground, when Claire had asked her for a snack, and she'd rummaged around in the lunch box she'd packed that morning to unearth a package of ground cinnamon and a box of instant mac 'n' cheese. Claire was non-judgmental when it came to snacks and had happily eaten the packet of dried cheese powder. *But, still.*

"I'm so sorry. I'm so embarrassed."

He smiled at her and handed Max back so he could ready his stethoscope.

"There's absolutely nothing to be embarrassed about," Rapaport said, listening to Max's chest while mesmerizing him with the little tube of glitter that hung around his neck. Annie assumed he hung this dissonant accessory around his neck expressly for this moment, but liked to entertain that he was secretly an after-hours raver.

"Yes, you are hormonal, and yes, it's hard to wean, and yes, it's stressful to apply Sam to kindergarten, and yes, you are a mother of three and have a very busy life! Of course you're going to burst into tears! I imagine not that many people have asked you how you're doing in the last, oh, three months . . . since I last asked you."

Could that be right? Yes, yes it could. He smiled, put the stethoscope down, and eased Max onto his back on Annie's lap.

"I've been doing this for almost forty years," he said, stretching Max's legs out like a little frog, then pressing them in again. "And your generation has got to be the most anxious of them all. I always tell Elsie how glad I am that we raised our four before iPhones. Just the constant interruptions, and the social media, it's too much, you know? It's too much for us adults, so no question it's too much for our children."

He tapped Max's belly, like he was testing a melon for ripeness, then righted him and headed to get his syringe.

"I swear, the number of parents who come in here jangled and anxious, it's an epidemic, I'll tell you that for free. And I'm going to recommend that you find some time to speak to someone, and I already know you're going to tell me you're too busy, but I'm going to recommend it again. And we'll do that dance for a while, until you decide to take my advice, or you end up in the psych ward at Mount Sinai after a psychotic break, okay?"

Annie nodded, cocooned in the warmth of his voice, half expecting him to put on his cardigan, get out his guitar, and sing-ask her if she'd be his neighbor.

"Speaking of, before I forget, can I put you in touch with my son? He has his own pediatric practice across town and wants to write an op-ed about the anxiety he sees in his adolescent patients. It's all related. I figure you know people who might be able to help him place it somewhere."

She nodded—of course she'd help this man, and anyone he was related to, it was the least she could do—as Rapaport, true to his Bartleby reputation, quickly dispatched three syringes, one in Max's left shoulder, one in his right, and one on his left thigh. By the time he'd finished with the second, Max had just gathered the air in his lungs to let loose an infuriated, indignant yowl, then the Band-Aids were on.

"I'm here, Annie, if you need anything," Rapaport said with an avuncular shoulder squeeze, as Max turned beet red with un-fettered fury. "But, for the record, this kid is top-notch, just like the other two you've got at home. You're doing something right."

• • •

From: Miss Porter
To: Annie Lewin
Subject: Sam's wardrobe

Dear Mrs. Lewin,

Just a quick note that our pajama day is held once a year, in the spring. It confuses the other children when Sam wears his pajamas multiple times per week. So please, if we must go that route—I realize at this age, day clothes are virtually indistinguishable from pjs—let's just make sure the tops and bot-toms are different!

Sincerely,

Miss Porter

• • •

She heard the yelp piercing through the playground white noise of shouts and laughter and knew who it was before she'd looked up from her phone: Claire. It wasn't the irritated cry she gave when she was tired, or the exasperated one when she couldn't get up on a climbing structure without help, or the indignant one when Sam ran off with friends and didn't include her, all ignorable. This was the one that blared HELP, HELP, I AM REALLY HURT.

Annie was up like a shot, tripping over the knobbly mini-hills of the playground, homing in on the sound like a missile, straight toward the monkey bar area, to find Claire, arms akimbo, on the thick ribbons of rubber mulch that cushioned the ground, Sam kneeling at her side, eyebrows furrowed in concern.

"Baby, baby, what happened, what happened," Annie said breathlessly, stooping down and brushing Claire's hair out of her hot, red face. Some of her curls were stuck to her chin, adhered by the remnants of a peanut butter and jelly sandwich.

"He bit me." Her daughter winced, from a hair dislodging or simply general pain, Annie wasn't sure.

"Who bit you, darling?"

Annie followed her daughter's chubby pointer finger straight up above them, until her gaze intersected with Brando Brenner, crouched on the top of the bars, and peering down—with concern, curiosity, she couldn't tell. Once again, Annie found herself looking up in supplication at a member of the Brenner family.

"What do you mean he bit you?" Annie eased her daughter's head onto her lap, and sat there, cross-legged, not sure what to do. *Shit, shit. That little shit. He bit Claire?* Suddenly, someone was crouched down next to her, hand on her shoulder.

"Hey, brave girl, that didn't look like a fun fall, huh?" Shawn, who then whispered to her, "I wouldn't move her, in case she broke something. I've called an EMT." Her body flooded with adrenaline, and Sam, intuiting some emotional shift, promptly burst into tears and put his head onto the remaining part of Annie's lap that was not covered in Claire's curls. Amelia, awkwardly circling, patted Claire's kneecap with a gloved hand.

"We playin'," Claire managed, through sobs, "and he was a tiger, and he bit me, and, and, and, and"—hiccupping sobs punctuated each word, then, eventually—"I fell."

Where the fuck was Brando's grown-up?

"Shhh, shhh, it's okay, it's okay," Annie said, like a mantra, as she looked at the children in her lap, the mulch digging its way uncomfortably into her butt and scraping her ankles. After a solid beat, she squinted up at Brando, now silhouetted against the sky and immobile.

"Brando," she said, as evenly as she could manage. "Come down here, would'ja?"

Both Sam, snuffling hotly into her pants, and Claire, lying face up, limbs splayed, flinched. The boy hesitatingly made his way down the ladder until he was standing a few feet from the little pietà, Annie cradling her children protectively in her lap, Shawn kneeling protectively behind her.

"Can you tell me what happened?" she asked him.

The boy looked down at his feet, digging the toe of his sneaker into the mulch until it reached the concrete underneath. His hair was gelled up in some sort of Elvis-type pompadour that stood stiff against the cold gust of wind that whooshed up, scattering leaves.

"Did you bite her?" she asked.

"——," he muttered, unintelligibly, continuing to scuff his shoes.

"You're gonna have to speak up, bud," Shawn said. "We just want to figure out how Claire here fell down."

After a big inhale, Brando managed, "I'm a tiger. Is Claire . . . is she okay?"

There was a long beat. Then Annie felt a hot voice vibrating into her leg. She nudged Sam's head up so he could say it again.

"We were just playing," her son said, furiously wiping tears out of his eyes with balled-up fists. "Brando was being a tiger, and I was being a monkey, and Claire was being the little bird that hangs out with the monkey and grooms him, I don't actually know if monkeys need birds to groom them but I know that hippos do and I didn't want Claire to feel left out—" Annie's heart swelled; she could never exactly believe how good-hearted Sam was, with no prompting whatsoever, plus, when he started to talk like this, he was so much like his father, so focused, so levelheaded. "And I was swinging down below, and Claire was crawling on the top part, and Brando was going to eat me, but tigers don't have opposable thumbs so can't use the monkey bars, but they can climb on the top, and then, and then I guess he bit Claire." He loudly wiped his snot into his sleeve. "And tigers are *allowed* to bite."

Claire nodded, meekly, corroborating the account.

"Where'd he bite you?" Annie asked, and Claire moved her shoulder a bit. *Sam had a point. Kids played. They learned by mimicking. It was all part of the natural developmental progress.* Annie slid her daughter's jacket and sweatshirt and long underwear to the side to reveal a raised red welt, oblong, with distinct tooth marks in it, right on the roundest part of her shoulder. A wave of nausea overtook her, but she steadied herself by kissing the side of Claire's face, wondering, *Just how hard did a kid have to bite to get through three layers of winter clothing? Just how much anger had to be welling up inside that little body to erupt in that particularly primitive way?*

Which was basically what she heard herself saying a moment later, when Greg Brenner finally appeared, sheepishly admitting to having been absorbed in TechCrunched videos on his phone on the far side of the playground this whole time.

"They've been playing this game of 'animal war' or whatever all year, and no other kid has actually bit another one!" Annie hissed up at Greg, now standing with his hands on Brando's shoulders. Her reasoning from a moment before became warped and sharp, a dagger to use against him. "Kids mimic what they see around them, it's how they learn. What on earth is he learning at home? How come he thinks it's okay to actually bite another child?"

Greg looked at her, emotions passing over his face so quickly they blurred together, like when Claire added too many colors from her paint palette just to see what would happen to her picture and everything ended up a muddy brown—discomfort, sure, but also defensiveness, and confusion, and some sadness, along with an undercurrent of general haziness, like, *Why am I here, and is this my son, and what, precisely, am I supposed to say now?*

Finally, after an awkwardly long beat: "I'm sure Brando didn't mean to bite hard, he probably was just having fun, you know?" And then he shrugged.

No *Is there anything I can do?*, no *I'm so sorry this happened*, no acknowledgment, actually, of Claire at all, who was still lying in a tangle on the ground, wincing anytime she moved.

The reason your son is biting my child is because there is something deranged with you, or your wife, or, likely, both of you! Annie raged internally, her brain whirring into protective mode. *You are both unhinged! That holiday card in the doctor's office! The way you gel your child's hair! The bento boxes for lunch! The violin playing! The not praising him! What the fuck do you expect is going to happen? He's going to get hotter, and hotter, and hotter, and hotter, and then he's going to blow, like one of those balloon animals that hits wet grass! They are born perfect! They* become *damaged! And now my little one, my perfect little girl who'd never bite any-one, is collateral damage?!*

But instead, willing herself not to cry or get overly emotional, she went with, "You have to get your child under control," though even as she said it, she didn't believe it. Brando was a docile kid. An obedient kid. He looked ashamed, embarrassed, not trium-phant or gleeful. A good kid, swimming upstream in a house full of crazies. *Had* he just been playing? But even so, you don't chomp *that* hard. *Three layers. Three full layers.* So they stayed frozen like that, two little dioramas—standing father and son, crouching heap of limbs—until it was clear there was nothing else to be said, at which point Greg and Brando shuffled their way to the play-ground gate, passing the EMTs who were just arriving.

"Wow, what a weird dude," Shawn said, letting out a low, long whistle, then beckoning the EMTs over.

Two paramedics gingerly moved Claire's limbs, had her wig-gle various toes and fingers, and said that she'd likely fractured her elbow. "If we got rid of monkey bars in this city, I swear the Hospital for Special Surgery would have half the traffic," one said with a sigh, turning back to his van. "Take her to the ER, they'll do a quick X-ray."

The prediction was verified by the transparent sheet the doc-tor smacked up on the illuminator a few hours later: a hairline fracture that would heal in four weeks. Annie had tried Dan re-peatedly in the cab to the doctor, receiving a text back after the third down-buttoned call that read, *In a pitch meeting, important?* When she responded, passive-aggressively, or perhaps aggressive-aggressively, *At the hospital with Claire, you tell me,* he'd finally Face-Timed, wanting to know what had happened and asking to speak to his brave girl, but after Claire lost interest and demanded to start a game on the phone, he told them he loved them and that he'd meet them at home later. Then his face vanished with a bloop. And—as Anne sat petting her daughter's head, and feeding her Swedish Fish from the vending machine, and waiting for the cast guy to fit neon pink plaster on her soft baguette of an arm—that bloop ignited the adrenaline of the afternoon, of the last few weeks or months, who knew, where it crackled deep in her gut, gaining heat and power until, once Claire was safely tucked into bed, it finally exploded.

"You seriously didn't come to the ER?" Annie blurted out in the kitchen, startling Dan out of his computer focus.

"I mean, you seemed to have it totally under control," he said, eyebrows furrowed in confusion. "Plus, my afternoon was packed. What, precisely, would you have expected me to do? Just be another warm body in the room? Claire didn't even want to talk to me after a few seconds."

This poured a nice little glug of gasoline onto her crackling flames.

"*Do? Do,* Dan?" she sputtered, pacing back and forth, jaws clenched. "What would I have expected you to *do*?"

"Sweetie—" he began, but Annie held up a hand. She was thinking back to that system of chits the parenting book had recommended.

"Daily unpaid labor—the washing, the cooking—often falls to women and is time constrained and repeated," the writer had pointed out. "Other types of unpaid labor—the mowing of the lawn, the paying of the taxes—can be less frequent and completed on one's own time. Statistically, this work is often shouldered by the male in the household."

But what about the other stuff, the stuff that happened with no warning, and derailed days? How many chits had she earned by accompanying her daughter to the hospital? How many chits had she earned by wanting to be there, and nowhere else?

"Okay, fine, so your afternoon was 'packed,' whatever," she barreled on nastily. "What are you going to do about Brando, about the Brenners? About this situation? Now that your precious afternoon commitments have been taken care of?"

Dan squinted his eyes slightly, unsure what land mine he was about to walk into. Then he let out a long sigh. He was never one to take the bait—he was too reasonable, too measured to put himself in a situation where he might lose his cool.

"I don't know if there's anything to be done," he said. "Kids get hurt all the time, they fall, they bite, they're testing boundaries, right? Isn't that all part of childhood?"

"Oh, give me a break," Annie spat out. "Your child was *bitten*. She *broke her arm*. Is there any nuance there? This kid is just going to get off, scot-free? What if he bites another child? What if he bites Claire *again*?"

"Let's not blow this up, it was a hairline fracture, not a break," Dan countered, irritatingly precise, "and yeah, I guess I think it's okay if a preschooler gets off scot-free. He's . . . a preschooler. What do you want me to do, have him thrown in solitary confinement in the LEGO closet?"

The gall, Annie thought. *To joke now.* When Dan put Claire in Sam's shoes and took her to the playground after weekend naps looking like a clown, when she watched her daughter trip her way to the swings as her husband protested that all the shoes looked so similar, how could he reasonably be expected to tell them apart?, that she could laugh off. Those few and far between mornings when she asked him to pack the kids' lunch, only to discover that he'd sent them off with a slice of ham in a ziplock bag, a handful of grapes, and a cheese stick—she'd dig deep to make a quip about a baby charcuterie platter, and let it go. They weren't going to starve. *But this moment? If there was ever a time for Dan to rise up, to dial into parenthood, to lose his cool just a little bit, to access the kind of passion and emotion that poured out of her in parabolic increases at the birth of each child, wasn't it now? He'd worn that wedding band before they'd gotten married to command respect at the negotiating table. Surely he hadn't had his children for optics, too?* The thought was too devastating for her to contemplate.

"What, you don't want to make *Belinda* look bad or something?" she snarled. Dan's eyebrows shot up. *There. She'd done it. She'd provoked him into the fight. Finally.*

He slammed his laptop shut.

"*Belinda?* Oh, Jesus Christ, Annie. I'm sorry I can't be free to hang out at the playground at three p.m. on a Tuesday like your new bestie Shawn fucking Axel, okay? This has absolutely nothing to do with Belinda. Or me. This has to do with you."

"Oh, yeah, how's that?" The blood pulsed in her ears.

"It's like you have this crazed notion that I should, I don't know, go out and fight Greg Brenner to save the honor of our family! We live in Manhattan, not the Serengeti, okay?" *So he had, partially, been watching the museum film after all.* "When Sam first started at Bartleby, you made fun of women who acted like this!"

"Like what?" she spat out, bracing for the answer.

"Like, I don't know, the ones who chose to escalate every tiny thing about their child into being as important as the, the . . ."—he paused, searching for the perfect way to finish the sentence, methodical even in the midst of a raging argument—"the Oslo Accords! This is a playground dispute! Literally! Just relax!"

The truth of what he was saying nearly knocked the wind out of her. Dan took a sip from his Coke Zero, something Annie knew indicated a long night ahead for him and the need for an extra burst of caffeine, then continued, in a more measured tone.

"Annie, you've never once showed any interest in my work—I don't think you even know what I do all day. But this next decade is critical for me, for our family. It's when investors set the foundation for the rest of their careers. I have to push hard now, so that I can coast later—Why else do you think I'm waiting up until eleven p.m. to do a call with Korea?" He exhaled, slowly. "I am sorry that I wasn't there for you and Claire today, but I had back-to-backs, and honestly didn't know what the ROI would have been. And I don't know now."

Annie had stopped really listening after "decade," or else she would have erupted that he'd had the nerve to insert business jargon into this particular conversation. *Another decade of this?* In her mind's eye she saw that nature documentary once again, that image of the knobby-kneed wildebeest newborn taking his first few stuttering steps then, moments later, running up the hill and away with the pack. His mother gained so much, giving birth to a self-sufficient baby, but she lost so much, too. She'd never get to watch her child work and work and work to get the proper balance, to take that first step solo, to be proud and giggling and astonished as he did so. She'd never get to see her child evolve from utter helplessness to full independence, an iterative process that would crack her heart open, again and again, a state Annie was starting to internalize would be ongoing, constant until the day she died. *What did you lose*, Annie mused, *if you sprang into parenthood when your children were ten?*

Before she made her way to the door, to leave Dan haloed in the blue light of his many devices, she paused.

"You asked me what I'd have expected you to do in the waiting room. I guess I would have expected you to have *wanted* to be there. Parenting isn't always about, I don't know, taking action. Sometimes, yeah, it's just about being a warm body." She expectorated the last two words with a vitriol she didn't know she'd possessed, recognizing that while part of him was right, part of what she was saying was right, too. *Didn't a parent's role often boil down to just that? Being a warm body, on days when you'd rather be doing something else, when you had other commitments, when your afternoon was packed?* Warm bodying was constantly demanding, often monotonous, almost entirely disrespected by modern society, something that Dan seemed to think was merely an optional part of parenting—but it, too, composed a large part of a child's foundation of love, of that she was sure. *That was the ROI.*

The next morning, as Max cooed his morning song from the monitor, Dan had pulled Annie close to him in bed, whispered that he was sorry, that he'd challenge Greg Brenner to a duel in broad daylight if that's what she needed him to do, and, too exhausted to start a fight up again, too scared that if she did start it up again, she still wouldn't reach him, she'd murmured noncommittally, and then the fight was over. But, like the bruise from Claire's bite mark, which worked its way slowly up through her flesh, turning from a blue gray to a sickly yellow, it took some time before Annie could stop fixating on it, worrying it over in her head. And when the bruise cleared entirely, the fight still lingered deep beneath the surface of their interactions, one inextricable thread in the myriad ones that made up the fabric of their marriage.

•••

From: Ash Wempole
To: Annie Lewin
Subject: New Year, New US!

It's a new year, it's a new me, and it's definitely a new YOU.

But first, I wanted to tell you what happened to me over Christmas break, because my therapist told me during our ZoomIllume that the best way for me to start the new year off right was to be honest with myself, and being honest with myself means being honest with you. So step into the cone of truth. #truthcone

First, I was so offended by your implication that I am not a real editress that I read *Max Perkins: Editor of Genius*. (Well, first I read his Wikipedia entry, then watched the Colin Firth film where he plays Perkins. I'll read the book later.) And second, I devoted the last few ZoomIllume sessions to speaking, almost entirely, about you.

Together, both acts helped me realize that my job is to nurture your talent, and if that means being a punching bag every now and again, fine. Well, better than fine, because something has opened up in you, and I'm not saying it has anything to do with me, but I'm not not saying that.

Since you avoid all social media, I wanted to share a smattering of comments from your new fans.

"I feel like you're a friend. A real, actual, friend I can turn to. How sad is that? If you ever make it to Sidney Center—a tiny town filled with Trump supporters that you can't really call a town, there's just a post office, but anyway I was forced to move here because my grandmother died and gave us her house and it's considerably bigger than our place was in the city— please call me."

"I would give my right hand to be able to channel your no-bullshit confidence. So long as I could train my left hand to hold a wineglass."

"Mother Inferior, my ass. All hail Mother Superior!"

A movement is building, Annie. Your fans are beginning to call themselves "The Inferior Bitches." Given my interest in promoting female and nonbinary empowerment, I'm not sure how I feel about this, but I could get behind it if you think it's more about owning something bad and turning it into something empowering. Like those garden urns.

Xo

Ash

She/They

Wordsmith. Potter. MP2.0 (IYKYK).

@RiseFromTheAshes

Etsy store: TerraCottaAndAsh

FEBRUARY

Dear Mother Inferior,

This morning, my daughter wanted to watch more *Paw Patrol*, but I really couldn't bear to hear the soundtrack one more time, so I told her that unfortunately the iPad had died. Sometimes she asks me to have a bite of the candy I'm eating, and I tell her it's spicy. Things just randomly close when I don't want to go to them—parks, stores, playgrounds. Am I irreparably damaging her? When, if ever, is a lie okay?

Sincerely,

Deceitful in Darien

Dearest Deceitful,

When I was five years old, I had two gerbils, Saturday and Sunday. I noticed that Saturday was getting bigger, and bigger, and bigger, and then one day I came home from school to find five tiny gerbils in the cage, which I named—obviously—Monday through Friday.

The next morning before school, I ran to the cage, excited to see how the new little ones had gotten on, and arrived to find just three babies. Where were the other two? I asked my father. After a long pause, he said—and I remember it like it was yesterday—"Saturday ate two of her children, and honestly it's sick, but it's part of evolution, and it's time you learned that it's a gerbil-eat-gerbil world out there."

Naturally, my next question was whether he would ever eat me.

And again, he answered me truthfully: he wouldn't eat me both because cannibalism is illegal, and because he didn't need to save resources for the rest of the family, which was what Saturday was doing. We had enough Cheerios to go around. Then he sent me off to school.

Was this the right tactic to take with a young child? I don't know, but I can tell you for sure that I have no plans to welcome any pets to my family anytime soon.

Deceitful, you can find just about any study you want out there to back up any point you want to back up. I can cite research that says if you lie to your children, they'll be more likely to grow up to be liars. I can cite studies that say white lies, known as "instrumental lies" in the developmental psychology literature, have absolutely no effect on the child, and make life easier for the parents.

So, the question no doubt burning a hole through your internet browser: Do I lie to my children?

Of *course* I lie to my children! The world is full of lies, *Deceitful*, and our job as parents is to prepare them for the world. When my three-year-old came into the kitchen after bedtime the other night to find me standing over the sink eating a pint of ice cream, I just straight up denied that she was witnessing what she was witnessing and told her the ice cream was broccoli soup. She was tired enough, I think it worked.

In any case, if you don't want to take the kids to the park, or the toy store, or you want to keep that candy for yourself, that's your right! When and if they find out you've been lying to them, they'll push back, and you'll have a conversation about it, and you know what will happen? They'll grow up a little bit. Which is what they're going to do anyway! But this way, you get to maintain a shred of sanity as they do.

And with that, I'll sign off with a rousing *complimenti,* bitches!

Mother Inferior

TL;DR: How else do you think you're going to prepare your child for a world of lies without lying to her yourself?

• • •

"Welcome to the Bahamas, folks, where the current temperature is a sunny 82 degrees and it's always a good day to hit the beach," the captain said over the intercom as they touched down in Nassau, Max squirming in Annie's lap and Claire sucking on the Water Wow! Pen that had lost its luster within four minutes of takeoff. *So long as you're less than a seventeen-minute drive away and don't have three children under the age of five,* Annie thought to herself.

A sad steel drum band greeted them in customs, playing a languid, Carribeanified version of "Get UR Freak On," and forty minutes later, past the valley of ashes, with Max strapped to her front and Claire valiantly lugging along a tiny backpack filled with her essentials—a baby doll, a harmonica, and a yo-yo she could not yet use—they trudged up the outdoor staircase to the third floor. She'd forgotten those stairs, and stood there, heaving and batting away flies as Dan found the keys. The steady *thump, thump, thump* of passing cars filtered in from the road, and the smell of petroleum mixed with the dank tinge of warm garbage.

"YEEEAAAAAAAGH!"

Her shriek ricocheted through the apartment complex.

"WHAT?" Dan gasped, keys swinging from the lock.

"I thought that was a scorpion, sorry," she said, holding on to Max's two dangling legs for dear life and gesturing to the langoustine-size flat bug that was skittering up the wall. Sam leaned in close.

"Look, Mama, you can see its thorax!"

The pool was as she'd remembered it—shallow, just warm enough that you actively wondered how much pee was circulating in it, and crowded to the brim. This time, though, she had not one, not two, but three children who had to be sprayed top to bottom with sunscreen, and two of whom had a death wish.

From under her umbrella, she felt exhausted just watching her husband, as he threw Sam up in the air, then chucked up Claire, then stopped to check and swat away his watch mosquito, then swat away an actual mosquito, constantly in motion, constantly multitasking. A lubed-up Max sat in her lap, gumming a sunscreen bottle, the heat gradually turning his chub lobster-colored. When a gecko skittered by, he emitted a deep belly laugh that nearly tipped him over. Annie smirked and kissed him in his sweaty neck rolls, straining to remember how their last trip to Tierra del Sol had gone, just a few years, yet a previous lifetime ago. *Was the water already boiling then, around her unsuspecting froggy limbs?* she wondered. *Perhaps someone had struck the match?*

After a dinner of chicken fingers from the pool bar, they hosed the kids off, shoved Max in a Pack 'n' Play in the closet, put the two older ones to sleep in a queen-size Murphy bed that released a spray of sand as it swung down from the wall, and prayed for at least four hours before they rolled into each other and woke everyone up. Then they tiptoed across the linoleum floor to their room. Annie peeled back the covers and got in, wincing slightly. *Perpetually damp.* She knew she wouldn't get one iota of sleep in this room, but if she was being honest with herself, she wasn't getting many iotas in her own bedroom, either.

"Your uncle still hasn't replaced the air conditioner?" she whispered to Dan. "It still only chills the one-foot radius around it."

"Look, Annie, not to point out the obvious, but the reason we are here is because of *you*, okay? If you hadn't gone totally batshit at the benefit, Belinda would be here now, and we'd be home, in our icy cold apartment."

Annie heard something flit from one side of the room to the other and shivered.

Then an insistent buzz, coming from Dan's wrist.

"I have to take this."

Dan tiptoed into the bathroom and closed the door. She could hear his conversation, just slightly muffled, and was pretty sure she heard him ask, toward the end, "Do you want me to put my balls on the table?"

Moments later, after he got into bed next to her: "Did you ask someone if they wanted you to put your balls on the table?"

"Yes."

"What does that even mean?"

"It's something my Italian colleague told me is a saying over there. Like, *I'm just gonna put all my cards on the table, say it like it is.*"

"There's no way that is a saying. Even in Italy." Pause. "What happened to opening your kimono?"

"Our Gen Z intern called me out for cultural appropriation on a Zoom. So, *sayonara*, kimono. And *buongiorno, cajones!*"

"*Cajones* is Spanish."

He sought out her hand under the covers as the creature flitted back the other way.

"Sweetie, are you okay? You're just so tightly wound lately. It's like if I touch you, you'll spark. The urns, the framing of that painting of Claire's with the cracker crumbs in it, all this kindergarten stuff. . . ." Annie could feel little grains of sand on the sheets that she was pretty certain had been made into the bed however many months before. "You know Sam is going to be fine wherever he goes, right? He's a spectacular child. Plus, the whole point of these schools is to be feeders to college, and honestly I don't even know if college is going to be worth it in thirteen years when he goes. I was talking to Belinda yesterday afternoon—"

Annie cut him off with an exasperated exhale. He'd been talking to Belinda a lot of yesterday afternoons lately, sharing intel that would help her win back the majority of the fortune her client's husband had amassed seemingly overnight.

"It's just . . ." Annie started, wanting to nip a Belinda conversation in the bud. Every time she thought of her, she saw that raised bite mark on Claire's shoulder. "I guess for years, from when I was very little, I felt like if I put my head down and studied anything hard enough, I could learn it—and not just academic stuff. Like, one Friday the big kids on the bus were blowing bubbles with chewing gum, and I locked myself in my room and spent literally hours teaching myself over the weekend, so I could impress them on Monday. And it worked. But now—with my career, with the school stuff, with decisions I feel should be straightforward and obvious—it's like everyone is blowing bubbles, and I'm in the back of the bus, but instead of Bazooka, I have . . ." She paused, seeking the right analogy. "A mouthful of sawdust."

Dan squeezed her hand, to tell her to keep going.

"I even wrote the letter."

"What letter?"

"From Elon."

"From *who*?"

She fished around in the dark and found her phone on the bedside table, scrolled through a few notes, then handed it to Dan.

To Whom It May Concern, it began,

It is my immense honor to write a letter of recommendation for the kindergarten admission of Sam Lewin, who befriended my eighth child, X Æ A-12, this past summer.

Sam spent a short but impactful week at space camp outside of Los Angeles, where he and X Æ A-12 became fast friends. X can be a bit of a wallflower, and within a few tearful moments at drop-off on the first day, Sam had made him feel comfortable, indicating an emotional maturity beyond his years. He came to our house for playdates every day after camp that week, and I had the distinct pleasure of turning my "question philosophy" on him. When I founded Tesla, I didn't ask how I could make a better car company. That's a small question. The big question I wanted to answer was, how can we change our very understanding of what it means to be mobile? I believe understanding the heart of the universe and consciousness boils down to asking the right questions, and so Sam and I spent long afternoons just asking questions of each other, and never once answering them. He is the reason I decided to pursue the Twitter acquisition, which we both still maintain is a good investment.

In any case, I know Sam will be a critical part of any community he joins.

Sincerely,
Elon Musk

Dan guffawed, handing her phone back.

"This is ridiculous, Annie."

"I know, I know, it's not even Twitter anymore, it's 'X, formerly known as Twitter.' In the next month it's probably going to be 'a hologram of Elon Musk popping out of your phone and talking at you, formerly known as X, formerly known as Twitter'—"

"I mean, for starters," Dan jumped in, saving her from her sped-up babbling, "this letter fully misunderstands the 'question philosophy.' And Elon publicly renounced all physical possessions and no longer has a home, so I'm not sure how they could have had 'playdates at the house.' Not to mention that he prefers to keep all correspondence to under 280 characters." Pause. "But back to my original point: Do you really think Sam needs any help at all?"

It was then that the dam broke, and she found herself gasping through ugly, heaving sobs, tears streaming down her face and dampening the already damp pillow.

"Yes, that's the point, of course he shouldn't need any help, I've never met a brighter kid," she managed, before a shuddering sigh. The thing flitted back across the bed again, raising the hairs on the back of her neck. "But then shouldn't he have gotten in at Sawyer? Even though I was ambivalent about it from the get-go? It's like I'm riding a pendulum that is swinging a million miles a minute!"

Another hand squeeze, during which Annie could almost hear Dan's brain starting to whir into problem-solving mode.

"Honestly, Dan, what am I even *doing*? Not just with Sam's admissions. With everything! I write an advice column and don't even follow my own advice, plus everyone knows that advice columnists never have their shit together! The job I loved basically became untenable when the kids were born, and now it seems like it's going to be untenable because of chatbots that will render my skill set completely irrelevant, so what's even the point? I need to work to feel like myself, but if the world no longer needs my skill set, then do I need to confront, head-on, that I may never feel like myself again? And you're working so hard, I barely see you!"

She blew her nose loudly into the corner of the bedsheet.

Then, through slightly waning sniffles: "I'm probably, clinically, losing it. Like, how many more hallucinatory episodes do I have to have before they admit me to the psych ward? Dr. Rapaport said if I didn't get a handle on this, I'd end up at Mount Sinai! Just like Great-Aunt Esther!"

Dan exhaled, long, his thoughts arranging themselves in his brain, ammunition being slotted into place to be deployed to greatest effect.

"You're likely right about the future of arts reporting and coverage," he said, finally. "I saw a beta-stage product the other day that was able to generate a Pauline Kael review of an imagined film of *Fiddler on the Roof*, performed entirely in Aramaic, starring Hugh Jackman opposite Zsa Zsa Gabor, and directed by Wes Anderson."

Annie involuntarily emitted a noise that was part snort, part moan, like a bull penned into a cage before a rodeo. It was too scary, too ridiculous, to contemplate.

"She did not give it a starred review. On the plus side, I'm pretty certain advice has to come from an actual human for it to be considered authentic," he continued, "so you could go long on Mother Inferior. I mean, you're obviously crushing it! I still don't get why you didn't participate in the *Post* article that's coming out"—some reporter had been hounding her on email to respond to comments about an upcoming profile, which both titillated and terrified her—"but if that isn't a stamp of approval, I don't know what is!"

"Yep, recognition from a conservative tabloid, all I've ever wanted," she deflected.

"Oh, c'mon, Annie, all press is good press! But whatever, you could always wildly pivot to a field that is bulletproof from AI. Psychiatry will be pretty safe from automation, because of that authenticity marker."

"I thought everyone is betting on the future of therapy being *entirely* AI-run," Annie said, bitterly, recalling a recent news segment touting the benefits of rolling out chatbot psychiatrists to those most in need.

"Well, yeah, but I follow this futurist on Twitter, and he ran a simulation at his lab that predicted that in the not unlikely event that Elon Musk became tech czar to a president like Jeff Bezos, Musk would turn off the internet for a day—some sort of warning cry to the nation—which would upend the banking and security systems entirely, and then he'd blame his AI psychiatrist for the idea in front of the Supreme Court. At which point Bezos would mandate that AI and psychiatry no longer mix in America. Which is both far-fetched and, like, totally plausible."

"Seriously?!" Annie spluttered, even though she intuited that what he was saying was likely not as ludicrous as it sounded. Dan's career hinged on making bets on the future. *How many times had he done it successfully? Too many to count.* "Do you even hear yourself? You want me to be a psychiatrist? If I feel like I'm losing my own mind, how on earth can I help other people sort through theirs?"

Dan put his hand on her head and started to stroke it, absentmindedly, at the clinking-the-champagne-glass-to-get-everyone's-attention stage of the conversation. Annie heard the thing fly back, hitting the far wall with a smack.

"Annie, both of us know you're not *actually* losing your mind," he said, after clearing his throat. "That's ridiculous. You're just anxious about things—the kids, the apartment, work, whatever—but if you think pragmatically about each bucket, I bet we can knock them off one by one. Isn't this sort of what your op-ed was about? Matrescence? It's misunderstood, women think they're losing their minds but in fact are handling what is being thrown at them in a totally reasonable way?"

He had a point.

"Look, the kids are knockouts, the apartment is luck, if writing is replaced by chatbots, we'll make a plan for career number two, which, I'll point out once again, you no longer need to pursue for financial reasons," he continued, picking off her anxieties like they were unsuspecting waterfowl in a game of *Duck Hunt*, then, with a little flourish, blithely throwing into relief how little he understood about her internal drive—and psychological need—to write and create. "These hallucinations must be partially, like, you relaxing into them. I bet you can tamp them down if you try hard enough."

How wild, Annie thought, *to be confident enough to think you could reason your way to serenity. Wasn't there an entire medical field built upon the understanding that you couldn't, a medical field her husband apparently thought she should join in her second career?* But it was just like him, to think this was all controllable, that his father's gambling was a choice and not a disease, that emotions and impulses were obedient and not innate, that you could always, always, rationalize your way to an answer or solution.

"Like, you want to solve your most immediate fear, which is that we won't set Sam up in the best environment for him to thrive?" Dan continued. "We can solve it. My work actually has direct relevance to this kindergarten stuff."

"Oh?" Annie fumbled around on the bedside table for a weapon to smack the thing with when it made its next pilgrimage across the room.

"Crypto founders saw the current financial system and decided they could do better, they could free it from the authorities, the traditional banks and regulations. The entire model is a rejection of the status quo. But it requires a huge leap of faith."

Long pause. She grasped a magazine and rolled it up. Then: "I don't follow."

"All these private schools, they're like the banks: J.P. Morgan, Goldman Sachs, Bank of America—all the same. It doesn't really matter where you bank, it doesn't really matter where Sam ends up. I liked Sawyer, yeah, because I went there, but you want to take a bet on the future, you take Sam out of this entire crazed process and we homeschool him."

Again with the homeschooling?

"You want to exit the system, why not, say, send him to the public school down the block?" she countered.

He reached for an accent pillow—one that had actually made Annie snort when she saw its little crocheted message, "Why can't you go big AND go home?"—jammed it under his neck, and sighed.

"You enter the grand experiment of education only when you have to, Annie," he said in the measured tone she'd heard him employ on Zooms with non-native English speakers. "Sam is already reading. We need him in an environment that will challenge him. My grandfather was educated solely through the public education system and put himself through medical school afterward. It's hard to see that happening today, with it all in shambles, catering to the lowest possible denominator and not the unusually bright." He paused. "One day down the line, I'd really love to get into city politics, try to change things back to the way they used to be, or could be. Now, homeschooling? That's interesting."

But before she could weigh in on the hypocrisy of his pushing homeschooling when he'd previously gone long on the notion that schools allowed individuals to build networks, or that she was pretty sure his "down the line" was way later than hers, Dan was barreling ahead, now onstage at a TED talk, picking up speed, leaving her infuriated responses to float around in her head, unvoiced but echoing nonetheless.

"You want the best environment for Sam, you immerse him in what the city has to offer. He's interested in bugs, you take him to the natural history museum and have him meet with an ornithologist."

(Why would I take him to a bird expert to study insects?)

"He wants to learn jazz, you set him up with Juilliard's best jazz teacher. He wants to explore volcanoes, you take him to Mauna Loa. He's interested in cars, you take him to a garage and he learns how to build a car from *scratch*."

(You take him to a garage? Or me? And how, exactly, does your seventy-hour workweek and my desire to write something meatier than a short advice column fit into this?)

When the creature looped back across the bed again, it was so close to her face that its beating wings ruffled her eyelashes. Annie thwacked her magazine sharply in the air, making solid contact with something. *Finally.*

"OWWWW!"

Dan's head.

As Annie fell asleep that night, and for their remaining two days of schlepping lubed-up children back and forth from the pool, a thought flitted around her, another buzzing insect. Maybe, as Dan had said when Claire had been in the ER, the ROI on his presence would have been minimal. Maybe home-schooling would be a wonderful option for a kid like Sam. But his clarity—however false—that he knew what goals to achieve and how to achieve them, which actions mattered and which didn't, reduced a vast swirling mass of complex questions into a neutral algorithm, where different inputs resulted in different outcomes. *With big, messy stuff, could you even do that?*

Their last night, as she was packing damp bathing suits into ziplock bags, she caught sight of a water bug out of the corner of her eye, making its way, stutteringly, around the TV console. Instead of calling Dan in to fill the role of conquering hero, she grabbed his book, the latest Yuval Harari, from the bedside table and threw it so hard across the room that it knocked the TV remote to the ground. By the time Dan burst in from the kitchen to see what all the commotion was, she had dropped Max's infant car seat on top, to be extra-safe, and was standing on it with one foot, grinding down as hard as she could.

"Sorry," she wheezed out, unearthing the book, the bug's guts smeared red and brown across the pull quotes on the back.

"Whoa," said Dan. "Aggressive much? What did he ever do to you?"

She wasn't sure if he was referring to Harari or the bug, but she sensed neither of them were fully considering a third possibility: Dan himself.

...

Mom's Advice Column Goes Viral— Is She Spinning Out, or Dear Abby 2.0?

By Jennifer Westin, staff writer
New York Post

They're talking about it over calamari salads at E.A.T. on the Upper East Side; at the opening of the new De Kooning show at the Whitney; around the swings in Central Park; at drop-off and pickup.

"I've never been one to read advice columns, but I literally hit refresh until the latest Mother Inferior arrives in my inbox each Monday morning," said Pauline Harmon, 38, mother to four in Tribeca. "I sent a link to a friend in San Francisco, and apparently it's all anyone is talking about there, too!"

Just a few months ago, Annie Lewin was known mostly to the cultured elite of Manhattan, those who read the Arts section of the *New York Times* on the weekends, looking to scout the next best play or up-and-coming actress. But after she stepped back from the position when her youngest child, now one, was born, and the success of her *New York Times* op-ed, "Mother Nature's Myth," which investigated changing understandings about motherhood, the journalist was hired by the new media startup, RAWr.com, to pen an advice column for millennial mothers. Calling herself, cheekily, "Mother Inferior," she spent her first few months tackling the kind of bread-and-butter questions that advice columnists, or "Agony Aunts," have addressed for decades. And, according to her editor, Ash Wempole, the response was respectable, but not noteworthy.

"I knew there was this raw energy deep inside that we just had to unlock," they told the *Post*, "and given the mission of RAWr.com, which is to 'view the world through no-colored lenses,' we worked together to harness Annie's natural frankness. The numbers speak for themselves."

Mother Inferior now boasts over half a million views per post, with readers duking it out in the comments section, and waiting, with bated breath, for the next column to drop.

"It's the utter no-bullshit quality that I appreciate," said Trisha Walters, 34, mom of a six-month-old in Chelsea. "It's refreshing to have someone who is in the trenches with us, telling it like it is."

The evolution from staff journalist to viral sensation happened seamlessly and remarkably quickly given Lewin's minimal use of social media, with numbers starting to skyrocket toward the end of last year. One column, in particular, her followers point to as being the inflection point. In it, she counseled the advice-seeker to shirk the rules of a school that might require parents to invite the entire class to their child's birthday party, referencing not just the "consumeristic hellscape of gift giving" but a Swiss tradition in which parents hire a clown to terrorize their children on their birthday.

Perhaps the simplest example of how Lewin's tone has changed is her use of the phrase "*Complimenti,* bitches," which she often uses to sign off her columns. It's a small tweak, as any of her followers know, on a sentence that Ezra Pound wrote to T. S. Eliot after reading the first draft of *The Waste Land*. (Full quote: "*Complimenti,* you bitch. I am wracked by the seven jealousies.") Last year, she deployed "You got this!" as a sign-off, but her new one has a sassy fierceness that her readers are eating up.

What Lewin seems to have tapped into, more than any parenting advice columnist before her, is that mothers of the Digital Age are in desperate need of community. They are far from their own parents, they spend much of their time buried in their phones, and the concept of "It Takes a Village" just can't be translated online.

Christine Alvarez, a well-known New York City area psychiatrist and expert in women's mental health, said that Mother Inferior effortlessly vocalizes many of her patients' concerns, in a brassy style that disarms readers.

"Your own mother, your best friend—hell, even your own psychiatrist—can tell you till the cows come home that what you're going through is part and parcel of becoming a mother," Dr. Alvarez said. "But there's something about Lewin's tone—approachable, yet just a little messier than you—and her delivery—funny, sharp, real—that makes the message land. She has a knack for capturing the specific kind of free-floating anxiety experienced by many upper-middle-class mothers."

Her most avid followers have even given themselves a name: the Inferior Bitches.

Of course, as with anything that goes viral, there are haters.

"Yes, I read it to laugh, to get some practical advice, but part of me wonders if Mother Inferior should be on meds," said a mother who requested anonymity, since she knows Lewin through the school their children attend. "If we lived in the dog-eat-dog world that she envisions, society would crumble. What if it's your child that is excluded from a birthday party? Then the calculus changes, and these glib lines, which she writes for laughs, become damaging."

Lewin did not respond to repeated requests for comment. But, doubters notwithstanding, it appears that her star is continuing to shoot upward.

TBD whether she takes the suggestion of one of her commenters: "It's about time she changed her name to Mother Superior!"

• • •

It always *seemed* like a good idea, merging families for Sunday morning brunch—everyone needed to get fed and the kids could play with one another. And yet, no matter the configuration—which family, whether it was held at home or in the park, if the children were the same ages or not—it inevitably felt like a version of sensory assault torture, where you couldn't finish one thought before being interrupted, some electronic toy or book was repeatedly being whacked such that its musical phrase was truncated and restarted myriad times, and the baby was at constant risk of smashing glass on a tile floor.

"Welcome to the chaos," Annie said, opening the door to Laura as Jack barreled through, a homing pigeon to Sam's room. She'd texted Laura late on Friday night, faced with yet another weekend of juggling the kids while Dan was traveling for work, and she'd happily agreed to come—not just because it would allow her to skip out on a birthday party that her husband would now take their daughter to, solo. But, as Laura kicked off her shoes, Annie wondered if she should have just huddled up with the kids and flung food at them while they zoned out in front of cartoons.

She'd slept a fitful four hours until Claire roused her at six a.m. and demanded a blueberry bagel, so they'd been first in line at the bagel store, Max in his stroller perch, Claire on the rumble board, Sam scooting up ahead, Annie's lower back crying out futilely, everyone in pajamas and rain boots, like lunatics who'd escaped the asylum. As she turned back to the apartment, she was forced to admit that the house *did* in fact, look like an asylum. Scattered on the rug were the tangrams she'd ordered in bulk from Amazon, alongside cards with increasingly difficult images of everyday items—a house, a flower, a little girl with pigtails—you could replicate with the seven distinct polygons. Either because tangrams originally hailed from China, or because these ones had been made in China, the writing on the cards was both in English and Mandarin.

"I'm, um, not even going to ask," Laura said and made her way to the kitchen.

"You know, tangrams actually are super cool," Annie found herself saying, at 1.5x speed, as she sliced bagels and popped them into the toaster, except for Jack's mini plain, which he insisted be microwaved with butter. "They're dissection puzzles from ancient China, and the point is to replicate a pattern or shape with all seven pieces, but there is something called a 'tangram paradox,' where it appears like a similar shape made with all seven pieces is in fact missing a piece, but it isn't."

Laura looked at her curiously. Annie's movements had quickened to match the sped-up pace of her voice—milk in this cup over here, purple plate for Claire over there, orange juice back in the fridge, pivot, pivot, pivot. She took a sip from her coffee. *This couldn't be her third, could it? Already?*

"So, like, Sam has been creating all sorts of wild shapes out of them—he made a whole garden with all these flowers and even a chipmunk out of it. His IQ test is tomorrow."

"You okay?" Laura asked, putting a hand on Annie's shoulder, then doing a double take of the living room.

"What's with all the urns?"

Annie waved her off. "Look, not all of us have children who are taking high-school-level math before they're out of Pull-Ups, okay? And I'm competing against people who literally get the Manhattan D.A. to write kindergarten recommendation letters. The Manhattan. District. Attorney. *That* is ridiculous, Laura. Not to mention that some of these children are *biters*."

Laura nodded, a barely perceptible flash of irritation cross-ing her face, the one that appeared whenever she had to put up with someone who wasn't acting reasonably. Annie saw it most frequently when Laura was flicking through emails on her phone from tightly wound students requesting extra time on papers, or lobbing bullshit excuses about why they'd have to Zoom into class, like that they were pledging fraternities and hungover.

"I mean, yeah, of course, but he was her professor at Yale however many years ago, and then her boss at the firm," Laura said, placing butter pats on Jack's bagel and putting it in the mi-crowave. "It's weird, sure, a bit of an aggressive status symbol, but I think he actually knows Brando. And at the playground the other day, two other kids got kinda rough with each other, and we pulled them apart. Even Jack, with all his haywire emotions, recovered okay. Kids . . . play. And test limits."

Long beat. The microwave beeped.

"Jack, Sam, breakfast is ready!" Annie screeched. Laura flinched.

"And look, I get it," Laura continued, composing herself. "A lot of stuff happened this year. Max was born, the new apart-ment, the column blew up, which I realize is overwhelming but ultimately, like, every writer's dream, right? Plus Dan became a master of the universe . . ."

A wave of shame coursed through Annie. *Why couldn't she just be honest with Laura? Tell her about the post-bite blowup, that meander-ing conversation in the Bahamas, Dan's frequent calls with Belinda, which might add up to all sorts of things, or nothing at all? Why couldn't she admit to her fear that, though she had a hairline now speckled with actual gray and white hairs, just lurking there under the surface, she feared she was bungling the things in life that grown-ups were supposed to just know how to do?*

But, like an exhausted toddler who screams bloody murder

when presented with a warm, cozy bed in a darkened room, in that moment her psychological bandwidth allowed her only one course of action: to dig in her heels. So she snapped, "Not all of us have everything wrapped up with a bow, okay? Cut me some slack, Laura, c'mon."

Then, changing her tone as the boys walked in, "Sam, sweetie, do you want plain cream cheese or scallion?"

After the meal, a tense affair during which Annie over-animatedly led the children in a frenetic game of "Rose, Bud, and Thorn"—where you had to name the best part of your day, the worst, and what you were looking forward to tomorrow (Claire's answer for all: having a donut)—and Laura sat there as if run over by a Mack truck, Sam got down on the rug with the tangrams.

"You ever seen these before?" she heard him ask Jack as Laura excused herself to the bathroom.

"So, you try to make this picture but just using these few shapes."

Annie had barely put the top on the cream cheese container before she heard Sam yelp in delight.

"That was so cool! Mama, Jack just did that, in, like, two seconds."

Her heart started to clippity-clop. She came to take a look. *Yep. Perfect house.*

She bent down over the pile of cards and picked out an inter-mediate card: a bunny with floppy ears. Jack looked at it for a moment, fished out some pieces, and assembled it almost instan-taneously. Sam yelped again.

"AWESOME!"

"What about this?" she said, nonchalantly tossing out a card with a turtle on it, marked "高難度" which she now knew meant "advanced" in Mandarin.

"Um . . ." Jack said, sitting on his hands and starting to rock back and forth, a clear indication, so Laura had told her after a doctor's appointment, that he was "becoming emotionally dysregulated."

"Can we go back to Sam's room?"

"Just, like, *try*," Annie pushed, knowing, even as she did, that she shouldn't. "Then you guys can go. Just *one* more."

When Laura walked back in moments later, laid out on the carpet was a procession of Jack's creations—the house, the bunny, the turtle, the rose with multiple petals, the stork with one foot tucked up underneath, the Sydney Opera House, and Annie was holding out a piece of paper.

"Okay, Jack, what about *this* guy?"

In two strides, Laura was next to her, ripping the computer printout from her hands.

"*The Last Supper*? You're asking him to re-create *The Last Supper* out of tiny hexagons?!" Laura's voice had gone up a full octave and was loud enough that Max, sitting nearby and gumming a board book, burst into tears. Jack was now rocking back and forth like a metronome, tiny front teeth biting the chub of his lower lip.

"Come on, sweetie, we're going," she said, scooping her son up under the arms and carrying him like he was a much younger child. "You've lost it, Annie. You've got to get a grip. Like, soon. Or else you're going to succeed in alienating literally everyone around you. I'm done."

The door slam echoed in the cavernous room, ricocheting off the chandeliers and back, like Laura had just slammed the door to a deserted cathedral. Annie turned back to see Sam sitting there, dumbfounded. After a beat, he got up, walked up the stairs, and quietly shut the door to his room, where he stayed for the rest of the afternoon.

• • •

From: Ash Wempole
To: Annie Lewin
Subject: BIG NEWS!

Did you know that Perkins wore a fedora everywhere he went? And do you know that before I started throwing pottery, *I knit fedoras as a side hustle*?! I mean, you can't make this up, Annie. We have some sort of across-the-space-time-continuum connection. It's CREEPY!

Want another sign? OK, so that instinct I had, that we needed to include a TL;DR sentence at the end, so we could access all those mothers who are so time strapped they can't find the time to read through 400 words? (BTW, thanks for the shout-out in the last column! What a thrill to see my name in print!) Brace j'aself, because check out what Thomas Wolfe wrote to Perkins at the beginning of a manuscript for *Look Homeward, Angel*:

"Generally, I do not believe the writing to be wordy, prolix, or redundant."
stop sign emoji

It was obvs all those things (prolix means wordy, I looked it up, which really makes the word kind of redundant, even in that sentence!), which is why he had to pare 90,000 words from that crazy tome! And from a writer who famously treated every word like it was a bar of gold (I started reading the biography! The actual biography, not the Wikipedia entry), no less! Anyway, I, too, see the value in truncating good ideas into punchy takeaways.

OMG would you look at me, I've totally become Thomas Wolfe and am just rambling on! Prolix, amirite?!! LOLZ. And let us raise a glass to Annie Lewin, for bringing the joy of epistolary communication into my life!

Anywho: the point of this email is to inform you that our EIC is so psyched about your *Post* article and all the traffic it's driven to the site that he wants to open up a Twitter—'scuse me, 'X'—feed full of your snarky, snackable little pieces of advice. I told him you'd be cool with it, so long as it didn't involve you dancing on-screen.

Xoxoxo

P.S. You haven't even commented on my new signature!

Ash

She/They

Wordsmith. Potter. MP2.0 (IYKYK).

@RiseFromTheAshes

Etsy store: TerraCottaAndAsh

From: Annie Lewin

To: Ash Wempole

Subject: re: BIG NEWS!

Ash,

Wow. There's a lot to unpack here. I'm so glad that you're finding kinship with Perkins, but just one small note (in the spirit of being RAW and everything): Perkins famously did *not* want his name to be called out in print. He basically wanted to remain anonymous and behind the scenes as much as possible. And while I can appreciate that you want to truncate 400-word pieces into one-sentence takeaways, that is hardly the same thing as taking a manuscript of 300,000 words and shortening it by 90,000 words.

Anyway, re: Twitter/X/whatever it's going to be next, I'm of course happy that my column seems to be resonating now, but I am hanging on by a thread here. I feel like I exist in twenty-minute chunks: nurse the baby here, put Claire down for her nap there, cut up an apple here, sift through my Mother Inferior email account to find a letter to respond to—I'm getting hundreds every week, Ash, it's super overwhelming, including someone asking me what to do about the fact that she and her husband are thinking about swinging! How is that my realm of expertise?!—all while trying to apply Sam to kindergarten, sleep, maintain a marriage that isn't only about logistics, and invest in friendships that actually matter to me! It's too much! (I don't even know why I'm writing this all to you, but it does feel like a safe space.)

Anyway, Sam's IQ test is tomorrow, I am (clearly) overwhelmed, and I think I'm gonna have to pass on the Twitter offer. I seem to be filing pieces you like—it's sort of like writing a diary entry I don't think anyone is going to see, and then just blasting it out to hundreds of thousands of people, and trying not to care that I'm capitalizing on my own insecurities simply for clicks. Is this how it works? Is this how social media influencers treat their careers?

Best,

Annie

P.S. What is IYKYK? I see that and think, *ah-yik-yik*.

From: Ash Wempole
To: Annie Lewin
Subject: re: re: BIG NEWS!

So glad you view this as a safe space! And whoa, momma. Gonna glide right over all that deep stuff for the time being cause I wanna make a live streaming meditation class that's gonna drop in four mins, but just a quick note to say it totes doesn't matter if *you* actually write the Twitter account. There's this new AI chat-generator that can spit out basically anything you want, like yesterday I asked it to write a haiku about urns in the style of Chrissy Teigen and it was SPOT ON, check it out:

Urns on a shelf, so still
Silent, yet full of memories
Forever holding love.

Only issue is that the syllables are off, it's 6–8–6 instead of 5–7–5 but whatever, point is that you can so totes see her writing that, can't you? And sending that to John?

Anywayz, we can get some intern to read over whatever the chatbot writes to make sure it won't land us in any sort of legal hot water, and then tweet away.

And don't worry! We won't replace you with a bot. Your rawness is unparalleled. (At least for now. Until the algorithm gets better.)

Xo

P.S. LOL ah-yik-yik. You're too much!

P.P.S. (If you know, you know. That's what it means.)

P.P.P.S. (Now yk.)

Ash

She/They

Wordsmith. Potter. MP2.0 (IYKYK).

@RiseFromTheAshes

Etsy store: TerraCottaAndAsh

• • •

IQ FUN PREP FLASHCARDS

1. What is wrong with this picture?

2. Which image comes next?

3. Define jitters.

4. Define hornswoggled.

5. Define bedlamite.

6. Make this image out of tangrams.

• • •

From: Dr. Noah Siegler, M.D.

To: Thatcher Admissions Committee

Subject: Sam Lewin IQ Test

Esteemed Members of the Thatcher Admissions Committee,

I write to you regarding an exceedingly unusual situation involving Sam

Lewin, currently a student in the fours class at the Bartleby Neighborhood School, who came for an IQ test yesterday. I have never had a visit unfold quite like ours. As such, though I know you are expecting a succinct report, I entreat you to take the time to watch the accompanying video and transcript—which I've given to a third-party psychologist to annotate—as evidence of why, though Sam technically scored remedially, I believe him to be one of the most gifted children who's ever passed through my waiting room.

By way of brief background: though many seasoned IQ testers will be able to tell, within a handful of seconds and simply by looking a child in the eye, if he or she is gifted, our work is to prove this numerically, which is an entirely separate issue. To do so, we must master all sorts of tactics to make young children feel comfortable.* Often, particularly bright testees will just stop trying once they realize that the questions are getting progressively harder. Only once, though, have I met a child who knowingly threw it away from the start.

In the video, you will see me employing tactics that are questionable—scaffolding, skipping ahead without proceeding properly through each round, et cetera. But I am putting my job on the line in the hopes that you see what I saw in this child: unfettered brilliance.

Best,

Dr. Noah Siegler, M.D.

*As an example, I've had one child get up suddenly and make for the door. When I asked why she was leaving, she said, "I lost my focus, I have to go find it in the waiting room." I acclimatized her, and she scored in the top decile. She was what I call a "hand on the armer": a top performer, often with advanced mathematical abilities, who becomes so enthralled with the test that she'll absentmindedly rest a hand on the tester's forearm when answering a question. (Please keep an eye out in the video.)

• • •

FILM: SAM LEWIN IQ TEST

DATE: FEBRUARY 15

LOCATION: DR. NOAH SIEGLER'S HOME OFFICE

Shot on two cameras: one overhead, to take in a table with two chairs, and one mounted on a tripod, trained on the chairs.

An adult (Dr. Noah Siegler, M.D., henceforth referred to as DOCTOR) and child (Samuel Lewin, henceforth referred to as BOY) walk into frame. The setting is stark, no friendly pictures on the walls or beanbag chairs. On the edge of the frame, you can just catch the barred windows overlooking street level.

Doctor: You can take a seat over here.

Boy (assessing room): Not a lot of bright, friendly colors, huh?

Doctor: I'm going for a more Soviet aesthetic.

BOY squints, then hoists himself up in the chair and sits, hands folded in lap, feet swinging languidly below.

Doctor: So, I don't know what your mother told you about what we're going to do here today.

Boy: She said you'd ask me a bunch of questions and that it wasn't a big deal.

Doctor: Exactly right.

DOCTOR starts to unpack testing materials and lay them out on the table.

Boy: But I got the sense it was a big deal.

Doctor: It's not a big deal. We're just going to do a few games and puzzles. It'll be fun.

BOY shrugs, noncommittally.

Doctor: Okay, so for starters, can you tell me what this is?

DOCTOR holds up a card with an apple on it.

Boy: Something you eat.

Doctor: Right, can you tell me more about it?

Boy: Um, no.

Doctor: You were eating one of these in the waiting room a moment ago. You gave the core to your mother.

**Note: Technically, this is known as scaffolding, but we can understand why DOCTOR is engaging in this method. For a child to earn the full score for each verbal answer, he needs to say very particular words. There is no wiggle room. BOY obviously knows that this is a picture of an apple, and that the apple is a fruit, but will not say it.

Boy: A kumquat. That's a kumquat. Okay? Can I go now?

DOCTOR sighs. Roots around in his bag and pulls out a different section. Clearly deciding to skip to the next subtest, though technically, he is not supposed to do this until the child has scored a zero on four consecutive questions in a given subtest.

Doctor: Okay, how about this. Can you look at this picture and tell me if there's something silly about it?

DOCTOR holds up a card showing a boy eating cereal with a comb.

BOY does not respond.

Doctor: Is there anything odd about this picture?

Boy: Did you know that in Australia, in the 1940s, they invented something called the sporf that is part spoon part knife and it was supposed to change the way people ate like, forever, but it never caught on?

Doctor (dryly): Fascinating.

DOCTOR taps the picture on the tabletop again.

Boy (finally): Maybe that person likes his cereal just a little bit damp, and so he's devised the perfect way to eat it. My sister likes to dip each Cheerio into slightly warmed milk each morning. It drives my mom nuts, but she lets her do it because it makes her happy. So who's to say if that is silly behavior or not. Maybe it's just silly to you, because you only know of three utensils, whereas in fact there are many more.

DOCTOR guffaws. Then clears his throat. Shifts his posture.

Doctor: Okay, you wanna play? Let's play.

BOY sits up straighter in his seat, watches DOCTOR expectantly, as he flips forward to SECTION FIVE of the FLUID REASONING SUBTEST. It looks like a chalkboard in an advanced mathematics grad school class—intimidating, gnarly, ridden with x's and marks, some at angles, some straight on.

**Note: Fluid reasoning measures a person's ability to detect the underlying conceptual relationship among various images and identify and apply rules to them. It begins with visual analogies: this big circle is to this small circle as that big square is to X, with the possible answers being (A) a small triangle, (B) a big triangle, (C) a small circle, or (D) a small square. The answer, in this case, would be (D). And so on.

Level five is appropriate not for a four-year-old brain, but a fully developed one. Once a testee has progressed to this point in the test, pattern recognition becomes less important than identifying the salient feature in each image; i.e., this shape is colored in and that one isn't, but more important still is that the borders of two in each row are curved instead of straight. What is critical is being able to zero in on what is important. High fluid reasoning is linked not only to an individual's ability to process novel information quickly, but the ability to predict what might happen in the future.

The little legs stop swinging below the chair.

Doctor: Got any thoughts on this one, Sam?

BOY squints, then scoots up ever so slightly in his chair, until his chin is resting on his hands on the table, eyes moving up, down, left, right, back and forth from the answer list to the blank square. There's a sharp little intake of breath. BOY's eyes move, repeatedly, from the far left corner to the blank square, then across each row one last time, to confirm he hasn't missed anything. Then back to the far left corner, where (A) shows the correct answer. BOY smiles. He's landed on it, and done so in less than a minute.

**Note: This is absolutely astonishing.

The slow swinging starts up again, along with a shrug.

Boy: I dunno, Doc. D? Maybe it's D.

Doctor: You sure about that, Sam?

Boy: Maybe I can see the next one, just in case.

DOCTOR turns the page over to reveal another mess of lines and symbols—circles and squares juxtaposed around an axis, some filled in, some hollow, yet others mirror images of the previous square, but with no obvious relationship. BOY stares at it for a solid sixty seconds, biting on the wristband on his sweatshirt.

**Note 1a: The answer to this particular question hinges on the test taker's ability to shift the reading progression from left to right, and look, instead, from top to bottom. Both ways work, but it is significantly easier to see the pattern if you start up top and work your way down. One's instincts, though, work against you here, with the eye naturally following left to right (at least if you are a reader, which few children of this age are). Like an optical illusion, once it has been pointed out to you—assuming you have a natural proclivity to score quite high on this type of reasoning problem—it is impossible to unsee.

**Note 1b: Grit, or "stick-to-it-iveness," is one of the defining characteris-tics of highly successful individuals, and at a young age like this, stamina is the leading indicator of grit. How many four-year-olds can sit still for one minute, looking at a completely abstract set of pictures? This sustained attention, testers know, arguably indicates more about the child than whether or not he eventually lands on the right answer. Even the fiercest adherents to the test admit that it is imperfect, and this is one of the reasons.

The clock is inching up on seventy-five seconds. With the time almost up, DOCTOR appears to throw in the towel.

Doctor (softly): What if you read it top to bottom, instead of left to right?

BOY flinches, startled out of his concentration.

Boy: Are you allowed to help me? Isn't that against the rules?

Doctor: Just look at the card, would'ja?

It takes BOY only about ten seconds after the prompt, his eyes darting from top to bottom, three times in the grid, back again once more, then straight to the correct answer, smack-dab in the middle of the answer line. He absentmindedly places a hand on DOCTOR's forearm.

Boy: It's . . . it's C, isn't it?

DOCTOR exhales, long.

Doctor: Yes, buddy. Good job. Correct.

DOCTOR starts to pack away the cards. The test seems to be over. Then he pauses.

Doctor: Sam, one last question.

DOCTOR rises slightly to dislodge his wallet from his pocket and places a handful of dollar bills on the table.

Doctor: If I ask you to tell me precisely how tall you are only using these dollar bills, each of which is six inches long, how would you do it?

**Note: This is completely off-script for the IQ test. It appears DOCTOR is trying to ascertain the child's real-world problem-solving capabilities.

BOY stares at the money for a beat.

Boy: I'd go downstairs to the doorman and say, "I'll give you this if you can find me a measuring tape."

DOCTOR barks out a laugh.

Doctor: You can go back out to your mom now. Test's over.

BOY seems startled, then quickly recovers and jumps off the chair. But as he reaches for the doorknob, he turns.

Boy: Dr. Siegler?

DOCTOR looks up from his pad, where he's furiously scribbling down notes.

Boy: Trying to quantify a person's current intelligence and future potential is . . . silly, right?

BOY scuffs one sneaker against the carpet but continues to look at DOCTOR directly.

Boy: Like, if I'd had a bad day. Or wanted to prove something to someone. Then I'd blow it, and you wouldn't know what my IQ was. It would just be some nonsense number.

Long pause.

Doctor: Sam, would you mind sitting in here for a few moments? I'm going to chat with your mother for a second.

Boy: Can I look at the rest of the problems?

DOCTOR smiles.

Doctor: Of course.

DOCTOR picks up the box of questions and places it back on the table. As DOCTOR makes his way out of the room, BOY, head bowed in concentration, starts flipping through the book. When his mother calls him out, five minutes later, BOY has to be wrenched away, like a magnet off a fridge.

. . .

They were one block from Dr. Siegler's office, standing at a cross-walk, when Annie asked Sam if he'd like to stop for a hot choc-olate on the way home. When he didn't answer, she bent down to ask him again, only to come upon the sight of tears streaming silently down his little face, now a rictus of grief.

"Oh sweetie, sweetie, what's wrong?" she said, stomach dropping as she crouched down to his level, balancing precariously on her snow boots.

Sam shook his head quickly, hiccuping as he swiped his gloves across his nose.

"Was it the doctor? Did something happen in there?" she prodded, suddenly primed to march back into that little cramped office and give the doctor a piece of her mind, but Sam managed a muffled "No," and she squinted at her son, the gentle taper of his furrowed eyebrows flooding her with a love that moved her to put her hand on his flushed cheek, just to feel his skin. *Her deep little guy, her deep little genius—that's what the doctor had told her moments before, right? That he'd never met a kid as bright as her son?*

They'd been together for all of eight minutes. Barely. When the door opened and the doctor had emerged back into the wait-ing room, she'd been convinced Sam had flubbed the test, be-cause all the chat boards said that if your child was in with the tester for fewer than thirty minutes, he was toast. But then Siegler had started to say all sorts of things about risking his career to make sure Sam got a fair shot at a school that would be lucky to have him. And she'd just stood there, holding the gross brown apple core Sam had been eating because she couldn't find a gar-bage can, combatively chewing her gum as her mind spun.

What kind of child can give that sort of impression after just a few min-

utes? she'd wondered then, and once again as she fished a napkin from her bag and wiped her son's nose, feeling a pang when she realized that, when she got home, she could no longer call Laura to hash it all out. There was so much she wanted to make sense of. *What was the difference between raising a child like Sam, and one like Brando, who could bite through three layers of winter clothes? Just a smidge more exposure to derangement from the generation above? What did it even mean that Sam had scored in the top decile of all children his age, and did that change the calculus of where he should end up? And perhaps most importantly, was he like this because of her, or in spite of her?*

They held hands the whole way home, then she decided to blow her column deadline, and the two of them spent the afternoon building bug castles together on the rug.

• • •

From: Ellie Halpert

To: Annie Lewin, Dan Lewin

Subject: Thatcher

Dear Annie and Dan,

Thank you for forwarding me the email about Thatcher—what wonderful news that Sam passed through the first round! We are, of course, not in the least bit surprised, as he has demonstrated brilliance since he first set foot in the building as a two-year-old.

But, as nothing in the city comes without a catch, I also write with complicated news. Sam is not the only one of our students who got through the first round at Thatcher, and Sam and this other student are *also* in the front running for St. Edward's. What a year for little old Bartleby, I must say!

In an effort not to pit parents against each other during a process that is already unduly stressful, in these types of situations we find it best to have a frank and open conversation with all relevant parties, to collaboratively make a coherent plan of attack moving forward.

Please let me know if you are amenable to schedule a tea with the other family and discuss next steps.

Best,

Ellie Halpert

Head of School

Bartleby Neighborhood School

"Where Play Is Work"

MARCH

Dear Mother Inferior,

The other day at the playground, my son was bullied. I saw the whole thing: an older, stronger, bigger kid from his school shoved him to the ground and then riled up a few of my son's classmates to make fun of him. It broke my heart, but when I found the bully's mother at the playground, she said she hadn't seen it happen and it wasn't a big deal and went back to scrolling through her phone. By nature, I am a very gentle person, so I let it go, but I was livid. What should I have done?

Tyrannized in Tacoma

Dear Tyrannized,

I went online to the Child Mind Institute, one of the most esteemed places for information related to childhood development, to get some pointers on how to advise you on this heartbreaking problem, and found a five step to-do. First, you're supposed to "forewarn" your child and talk to them about bullying. Then you're supposed to "fortify" them and ask them to resist joining in on bullying; then "practice an appropriate response"; then urge them to "find allies"; and, finally, talk to the school.

You know what I'd say to that five-step plan, *Tyrannized*? What if we meander away from the Institute and straight on over to the animal kingdom.

Google "mother animals protecting young" and you'll find clip after clip of sloth bears tearing shit up when a tiger wanders near their cubs, or ducks flapping away dogs that threaten their ducklings, or teensy-weensy ghost spiders, who'll spin vast webs of silk to buttress their eggs from the outside world.

Look very, very close to our own species. Baboons are known bullies. They bully other baboons in their cohort by snarling at them, slapping them, or biting them, all in a bid to assert dominance. Years ago at the Detroit Zoo, the staff had to remove all the males because the veterinarians on-site were so overwhelmed with sewing up scratches and bites. And one of the remaining females, absent any male bullies, put on weight and started to bully the others in the enclosure. I read about this recently in an essay written by an anthropologist, whose takeaway was that bullying is hardwired into us—even with no "need" to bully for food, or to assert sexual dominance, we'll do it anyway.

Now, forgive me while I zero in on one key aspect of the story that may get elided over in other publications for reasons of propriety: this oversize female baboon did not just gain weight and start fights, she apparently (and I'm going to quote here directly from the essay) "developed a false scrotum" *hyperlink*.

And so, *Tyrannized*, I urge you to follow in the steps of that monstrous lady baboon, and grow a scrotum. Next time you see that mother at the playground, you threaten her with the wrath of a thousand suns. Watch that sloth bear video to pump you up before. Put the fear of god in her.

Happy scrotum-growing, *Tyrannized*. Go to the ends of the earth to protect your young. It's just what mommas do.

Complimenti, etc.

Mother Inferior

TL;DR: Grow that scrotum.

• • •

Of course it was Belinda and Greg in the War Room that afternoon.

"I realize this could be considered slightly uncouth," Ellie Halpert said, as Annie sat down at the table facing the Brenners, a tiny Dan propped up on her phone, FaceTiming in from a crypto conference in San Francisco. "But let us first raise a glass to all of you, for the hard work you've done so far as parents, and to your sons, for being so wonderful. They are the shining stars of the school, and it is a privilege to serve as their stewards during their early childhood."

Annie realized this was the first time she'd seen Greg since the biting incident. Belinda had given her a quick, dismissive acknowledgment at drop-off a few days after, then nothing.

"Sam and Brando have apparently gotten over it," she'd said condescendingly as Brando yanked her up the stairs, "so can't we just cut each other some slack? We're all doing our best here, Annie." Annie had been able to muster not a single reasonable response, so had done everything to avoid Belinda in the intervening weeks. But she could hide no longer.

They all raised their small teacups of tepid tea, and the meeting began.

The facts, as Halpert laid them out: both boys were front-runners at St. Edward's, and both had also gotten through to the second round at Thatcher. The schools offered about the same odds: the math was transparent at Thatcher—the second round would consist of two hundred high-scoring applicants competing for fifty spots—but St. Edward's was as competitive. The odds became significantly higher in St. E's favor, though, when you factored in that Halpert had known its head "since before Giuliani took office and packed all the homeless people into buses and shipped them to the outer boroughs." Which meant that she'd recently been the recipient of a phone call from Headmaster Loren Fitzhughes, formerly don at Magdalene College in Cambridge, with insider information.

"I've seen this happen just once before in my tenure in this position," Halpert continued. "But he's guaranteed your boys spots, so long as they *both* commit."

Dan, tinnily from the phone: "Why? I don't get it."

"Daniel, there is something called a 'first choice letter,' which we urge parents to write if they think a given school is a particularly perfect fit for their child," Halpert explained, squeezing a thin wedge of lemon between her pinched fingers. "Basically what Headmaster Fitzhughes is asking for is two first choice letters, which he will accept as a pair."

"And only as a pair?" Belinda asked, eyebrows furrowed.

Halpert sighed.

"Unfortunately, yes," she said, pausing to take a sip of her tea and collect herself. "It has to do with the makeup of the class, which involves a complex calculation that factors in diversity, fundraising, and the overall 'yield' of acceptances. Fitzhughes has a particular knack for constructing the ideal class each year, and he rarely accepts more than one child from Bartleby. But he seems to believe that your two sons' traits complement each other."

Here she picked up a piece of paper and began to read from it.

"'Sam helps encourage Brando to participate and thereby boosts his confidence, Brando gives Sam a quiet space in the classroom to regulate his emotions'"—paper down, no explanation if those were Fitzhughes's words or her own, then back to the group—"so it appears that just this year, he'll make an exception. Which is exciting, but leaves us in a bit of a predicament."

"And if neither of us writes the letter?" Annie asked, pulling a pen and notebook out of her bag and starting to jot down notes, certain she'd misremember key parts of this conversation.

"St. E's will reject you both," Halpert responded. "Their class is entirely made up of first choice families, so if you don't want them, they won't want you."

"And how does Thatcher play into all this?" Belinda asked, pulling out a tablet and stylus and starting to take notes in some sort of bizarre digital cuneiform. Then, aside to Annie with a little patronizing wink, after Annie's jaw dropped open: "Oh, this is an amazing tool, it converts shorthand to Word documents that I can email to myself. You just need to know courtroom shorthand."

Just that.

"Well, of course if you commit to Fitzhughes, you'll be out of the running for Thatcher," Halpert said, "and historically, Thatcher has never accepted more than one of our students. They have a strong commitment to diversity, and accepting two children from our preschool, when the incoming class is so small already? It just wouldn't be in line with their value system. Which is not to say that their tuition isn't just a tad more palatable, heh, heh." Halpert chortled quietly to herself as she poured another tiny cup of tea, each chortle making the gooseneck spout clank against the cup. "Now, you both also applied to Hudson-Green which, as a safety, will likely accept you both. Except, of course, should you write the first choice letter to St. E's."

Annie's piece of paper was a tornado of scribbles and arrows. She flipped to the next page, as Belinda silently pressed her stylus, revealing a clean digital page.

"It's a *safety* school," Dan piped up from the phone. "Why would they care if we wrote a first choice letter to another school? And how would they even know?"

"Well, even the humblest among us still have some pride, you know," Halpert said, dabbing a lemoned finger on her tea towel. "And everyone talks, all the heads of admissions and their deputies, there's a whole shadow economy of information passing from school to school during the application season. Since you don't technically *have* to write a first choice letter anywhere, they'll take it as a snub."

Dan: "And from Thatcher's perspective, we'd be increasing our odds if the other party commits to St. E's, right?"

"Oh, certainly," Halpert said. "Chances are if one boy were out of the running at Thatcher, the other boy would be accepted. Your children are just each such strong candidates that they're bound to take one, just not both." She finished her dabbing, and took a deep breath. "Over my decades helping shepherd families through this process, I have come to realize that, like with tipping doormen at holiday time, opacity never serves the greater good. As such, it's better we openly work together for a mutually desired outcome that will benefit the school and all outgoing families equally."

She opened her palms upward, ceding the floor.

"And there you have it. Now, let's make a deal!"

There was a long pause, as Belinda scribbled furiously on her tablet. Then Annie heard Dan clear his throat.

"B.B., you thinkin' what I'm thinkin'?"

B.B.?

Belinda barked out a laugh in response.

"Oh, I think so, I think definitely maybe totally YES!"

The two of them hyena-ed together, as Halpert, Annie, and Greg—whom Annie had not seen blink the entire meeting . . . *Was he high? Catatonic? Part-reptile?*—sat there, completely confused. Annie missed Laura, deeply. If only she could see her after this, maybe Laura could reel her in, could help her find the humor in it all.

"Hey, my brotha, lookin' good, loved your TED talk—sorry, I'm literally walking through the Moscone Center, guys," Dan chirped up, "but I believe what you're saying is that we've found ourselves in a real, live prisoner's dilemma."

"A what?" Halpert asked, eyebrows forming a right angle.

"Mm-hmm," Belinda nodded, writing out a quick grid on her tablet. "I do believe this is a *perfect*, but perfect prisoner's dilemma, Danny. Classic."

Danny? Annie couldn't be sure, but she thought she caught Halpert shake her head in a demure tsk-tsk motion. *This wasn't in her head, was it? How jokey the two of them were with each other? Just how many crypto-based conversations had they been having lately?!*

"BOOM!" Dan shouted from the phone, the vibrations causing it to slide off its propped-up perch. Pause. "I'm looking at the ceiling here, help a guy out?"

Annie righted the phone, as she felt her stomach heave. She heard a distant roaring. *Was that from her phone, or her conscience?*

"I'm not exactly sure I follow."

"Look—sorry for the background noise, it's a zoo here"—*it was from her phone!*—"but I'm gonna open my kimono, okay?" Dan's voice piped up, the FaceTime image a blur of carpet, suits, and people. "Or, um, sorry if that's culturally insensitive, I'll put my balls . . . Whatever. What we're talking about is trying to predict how rational actors behave when presented with a Faustian bargain."

He went on to explain, as Belinda nodded along, an eyebrow arched coyly the whole time, that this setup could have been lifted out of a game theory textbook. As with the prisoner's dilemma, which involved the fate of two connected felons, and whether or not they confessed or remained silent, Halpert had given them two actions to take: writing the first choice letter, or not. And, as with the prisoner's dilemma, there were four possible outcomes: There was an option for a tie, in which both people wrote the letter to St. Edward's, thus sealing their child's fate. There was an option for a worse tie, in which neither of them wrote the letter, thus preserving the slight possibility that one of them would get into Thatcher, and their spots at Hudson-Green.

"And the situation in which one writes the letter and the other doesn't?" Annie asked, struggling to keep up, the skin around an offending hangnail beckoning.

"Oh, then there's the clear winner and the clear loser," Dan responded. "It's zero-sum. The person who writes the letter, and does the 'right thing' by mutual standards, gets super-duper punished, by taking themselves out of the running for Thatcher, Hudson-Green, and St. E's, all at once."

"Leaving them with what outcome?" Annie asked, still lost.

Halpert gasped, having put it together. She leaned forward conspiratorially and dropped to sotto voce as she morphed into Dowager Countess Maggie Smith.

"Exactly the situation we are hoping to avoid."

"Public school," Belinda barked out, eyebrows shooting up in emphasis.

The words reverberated in the air above the tepid tea.

"But how on earth are two acceptances to St. Edward's a *tie*?" Halpert asked, shaking her head, incredulous. "Wouldn't that be a win for us all?"

"And how is it rational for me to give up a chance at Thatcher?" Annie asked, flummoxed, as Belinda nodded along. Thatcher had been her port in the pounding storm of kindergarten admissions that tossed values, guilt, and fairness together until they became an indistinguishable wintry mix of swirling mayhem.

"Ladies and Greg, I have to go present," Dan said. "Annie, we can talk tactics tomorrow, I'm red-eyeing it back tonight unless I can get a seat on Josh's PJ. Sayonara, ladies!"

The screen went black as Greg sat there, quiet, immobile, lizard-esque.

Tactics?

Belinda locked eyes with Annie, a spotlight haloing the two of them as the rest of the scene faded to black. Annie could sense the pinpricks of light starting, that weightless feeling, could hear the swirling swish of white noise again, which was now definitely not coming from her phone, and shut her eyes for a solid beat.

"You okay?" Belinda asked, not a shred of genuine concern in her voice.

Annie snapped her eyes open, her gravity correcting, the roaring shutting off.

"Yep, fine. So, where were we?"

Belinda threaded her fingers together and, with one brisk motion, cracked her knuckles.

"Can I speak bluntly here?" Then, without waiting for a response: "I know you. We're the same—both type A. We both want to win."

The same? Annie thought, alarmed, her body now hovering just a few inches above the table, her son floating off somewhere in the ether, behind her, lost and pawing his way toward her. *They may both be type A, but they were not the same.*

"Game theory dictates that even though we should both commit to St. E's, and guarantee ourselves the second-best outcome, we won't—and it's second best simply because we both happen to agree that a spot at Thatcher far outweighs one at a school where the child is judged not just on their own merit, but on their parents'." *Since when did Belinda care about merit? Wasn't her whole job to twist facts to make them fit whatever truth was most convenient to her desired outcome?* "BUT, and here's where it gets fun"—she punctuated the word with another loud knuckle crack, making Annie wonder if she'd somehow managed to uncrack her knuckles in the intervening fourteen seconds, just for effect—"since we are not separated into different interrogation rooms, we actually have a shot at acting in our mutual best interests, and not just going for the self-interested maneuver."

"Oh?" Annie asked, struggling to keep up with the confusing permutations of the prisoner's dilemma, accept that she was basically married to a disembodied voice, and respond appropriately to the straightforward acknowledgment that they were actually playing with her beloved son's future as if it were one big game.

"Oh, this is where lawyers get their rocks off," Belinda barreled ahead. "What we're trying to do here is predict what the other party is going to do. If I say I'm going to commit to St. E's, will you commit? Because if I say I'm going to commit, and then I *don't* commit, you're screwed, and I win."

"Ladies, ladies!" Halpert could sit idly by no longer. "I think we can all agree that I've offered you a completely palatable outcome that would benefit us all! If this is about 'rational actors,' as Mr. Lewin kept saying, then can't we all agree that the most rational thing for us to do is send two bright boys to take two spots at a fabulous school, and be done with this rigamarole? Wouldn't that be the, um, the 'tie' that we're all hoping for?"

Annie thought back to Sam's charming phrase, the one that had ended up in his application essay: *winning in a tie*. It had sounded so sweet and innocent when he'd said it.

"Ellie, apologies, but be careful who you call rational! Right, Annie?"

As Annie looked up at her rival, she was grimly unsurprised to find that she actually had to crane her head down toward the table, now miles below her, nightgown swaying behind her in the breeze, as she tried to home in on her son—*Hadn't he just been behind her?*—the cackle of Belinda's deep throated hyena-laugh piercing through the roar.

"I'm not quite sure what is going on here," Halpert said, pushing her chair back with a squeak that squarely landed Annie's feet on the linoleum tiles. Halpert, seeming to recognize that she was exceedingly out of her depth and no longer able to orchestrate her players as usual, moved to stand up, indicating the meeting had come to a close. "But if you want to submit a first choice letter to St. Edward's, you must do it by next Friday, to give Loren adequate time to organize the new class. Please have a hard copy in my mailbox, signed, and in an envelope addressed to Loren Fitzhughes, care of me. No questions asked if the letters don't arrive, but I believe I've made clear what I think is best for not just Bartleby, but most importantly, your beautiful and brilliant young sons. Let's not forget about Brando and Samuel!"

But Belinda and Annie were already out in the hallway, striding to the exit, each trying to overtake the other and failing. They ended up walking side by side the whole way, faster and faster, the dot-paint collages that decorated the hallway fluttering in their wake.

• • •

To: Bartleby Parent Community
From: Bartleby Parent Teacher Association
Subject: Luncheon Honoring the Efforts of Belinda Brenner

Dear Parents,

Since our founding in 1973, one parent each year has received the Bartleby Brooch, awarded to those who embody the values of our cherished community—integrity, joy, and generosity—and have exhibited an unparalleled commitment to the school. It is my great pleasure to invite you to a luncheon honoring this year's recipient, the lovely, indomitable Belinda Brenner.

As many of you know, she not only spearheaded this year's gala but was out in the rain with her umbrella, greeting prospective parents this fall; has been school treasurer for all three years of Brando's enrollment here; and put in motion the conversion of half our rooftop turf into a garden, which she'll see through next year's completion, even though Brando will be graduating this spring. We envision it both as a respite from the classroom, and a place for our little learners to explore, plant, dig, and build their way to a better future, one tulip bulb and kale plant at a time.

Save the date: April 10. (Yes, fours parents, I realize this is shortly before acceptance letters are sent out, but this should be a lovely and welcome distraction for us all!) The wonderful Leonora Linsby has graciously offered up her new apartment, even though she warned us the paint might still be drying!

With love and good cheer—
Ellie Halpert

• • •

"Mama, I have to pee."

Annie looked up to see Claire standing there in front of her at the playground, sand caked to her leggings.

"With Maria we always have da widdle potty," Claire said, face screwed into an almost-cry, then she started to whimper. Annie always just let the kids pee off to the side in the dirt. Natural fertilizer. *If it was good enough for the squirrels, why couldn't it be good enough for them?*

But apparently Maria was in the camp of super-organized women who always brought along a little portable potty and then were stuck lugging around knotted plastic shopping bags sloshing with pee and poop.

In that moment Annie had one goal: to avert the kind of sudden tantrum Claire had unleashed on the way to the playground, wherein she'd refused to scoot and lay down on the sidewalk instead, forcing Annie—who had Max strapped to her chest—to drag her by the armpit the remaining two blocks, flashing sheepish *It's just one of those days* looks to passersby. (It was that, or literally sit down on the pavement next to Claire to embrace the teachable moment and talk it out, something she was sure was recommended in gentle parenting books about how to raise resilient toddlers, but which also mistakenly assumed an ability to maintain a Zen-like calm in the face of an irrational tyrant. That, and a center of gravity that would allow you to heave yourself upright after lowering, respectfully, to toddler level.)

"Okay, sweetie, but we left the potty at home and we're going to go right over there, sort of near the woods, okay?"

She scurried Claire over to the edge, whipped Claire's pants down, straddled wide with a straight back, and held her daughter under the armpits, like in a trust fall, all the while accounting for her sleeping son, a dense watermelon in between them.

A pause.

"You done, sweetie?" Her back was about to give out.

"Gotta poop, too," Claire grunted out.

Sweet. Her abs started to cramp.

"Annie Lewin!"

Oh good lord.

"Belinda, we're sort of in the midst here," Annie said, gesturing with her chin.

Belinda shrugged, unimpressed.

"You know, for years Brando withheld poop, it's an actual term, where kids refuse to poop in the potty during potty training," Belinda said. "My doctor told me it's a way to exert control. The only way he'd poop was outdoors. So that's what we'd do, take him out on the street before bedtime. You do what you gotta do, right?"

Belinda, trotting her son outside to relieve himself before bed, like a cocker spaniel? Annie thought. And a human shone through. *Perfect mothers, they're just like us.*

"Look," Belinda began, ignoring Claire completely, "I wanted to apologize for two things. For the biting incident, which I realize we haven't really discussed face-to-face, at least not without the rush of drop-off in the mornings. I am totally mortified about what happened, and Greg and I have spoken at length about it to Brando—I mean, praise be to husbands that actually engage in the granularity of the day-to-day together with you, right?— and I really do believe he was just playing, but also we've been putting all this pressure on him with the violin, and kindergarten admissions, and he just picks up on everything, you know, they are little sponges, they suck up all the emotions in the room."

She shook her hair and fluttered her lips, as if resetting.

"I have already petitioned the parks department to remove the monkey bars at this playground, since I believe they are one of the most dangerous pieces of playing equipment and should totally be verboten."

Annie nodded, feeling an unexpected rush of catharsis. *So Belinda did, actually, take the biting incident seriously.*

"Second, I wanted to apologize for the tone I took at the meeting with Ellie the other day," she said. "I spend so much time at work just grinding that sometimes I go on autopilot, you know?"

Annie didn't.

"Done, Mama."

"And look, I know you and I haven't always seen eye to eye over the years," Belinda continued, her perfectly coiffed hair swooped behind her ears into a perky ponytail, as Annie wiped Claire's butt. "I realize I'm a little . . . intense, you know. Tiger mom, rawr!"

Annie yanked her daughter's leggings back on and finally stood up straight, with an audible groan.

"RAWWWWR!" Claire responded, running away to join the animal war game.

Annie stood there awkwardly, holding the wipe, not sure if she was supposed to wait for the rest of the speech or go over to the trash can, but then Belinda whipped out a little baggie from her jacket pocket.

"Carry these with me all the time, you never know when you'll need one!" she said, proffering it to Annie. "They're technically for dog poop but they come in handy for all sorts of things, you know, like when Brando drops his Goldfish on the ground and I have to clean them up quick."

"Oh, you, um, clean up dropped Goldfish?"

Annie just left dropped snacks on the ground or kicked dirt over them. *Didn't everyone?*

"Well, of course I *used* to just leave them, but ever since I read this article in the *East Hampton Star* about how all the ducks at the nature preserve were getting sick—not to mention obese!—because they were eating so many crackers and snacks from the kids, all full of processed wheat flour that really doesn't have any nutritional value in it, or at least no *avian* nutritional value, anyway, I just can't live with myself if we litter like that. Like, we share this city with animals, we have to respect them, you know?"

This, this was the person Dan made the time to chat with after hours? Unable to come up with a single duck-related response, Annie put the dirty wipe into the bag, kissed the top of Max's sweaty head, and decided it best to pivot the conversation.

"So, I see you're getting the Bartleby Brooch next month, how exciting!"

Demure little smile.

"Well, you know how much I love that school," Belinda said, ponytail swinging back and forth. "I arrived from Connecticut a country bumpkin, and all the Bartleby Babes just became my backbone you know? My support system. I *do* wish Ellie could work her magic and just get both our boys into Thatcher, but I guess there are a few things that even Her Majesty Halpert can't do!"

Oh. This is what this conversation was about. Obviously.

"Anyway, speaking of, I did want to touch base about all that." Belinda waved her hand at nothing in particular. "And I was wondering if you'd thought any more about sending a letter to St. Edward's. Because I spent the last few days on their website learning more about the school, and it really is just phenomenal. Did you know it has graduated more Supreme Court justices than any prep school in all of America?"

Annie knotted the baggie, sure there was some tactical maneuver happening but not exactly clear on what it was.

"You know," Belinda continued on, "I grew up in a small town in Connecticut, a country bumpkin." *Hadn't she just said that?* "So this is all new to me—the first choice letters, the negotiating with a preschool!" She exhaled a long, protracted sigh. "I always thought my kid would go to public school, just like I did. But then I got to New York, and our local school wasn't nearly as good as the one I'd gone to, and I got introduced to Bartleby, and my whole worldview shifted a little bit, and now I'm, like, treading water as I figure out how to give Brando everything he needs, even if I'm second-guessing myself every step of the way!"

She laughed lightly as Annie considered, then rejected the idea that Belinda and she weren't, actually, that different after all.

"I realize my parenting style might seem a little, well, *unorthodox*," Belinda continued, shrugging her shoulders in an *I can't help it!* motion. "The violin lessons and all that. But I've been in therapy for years—years!—and my doctor has helped me understand that it's rooted in my work. I spend my days with people who start out being in love, only to wake up a few years later realizing that love only works if there's thought and planning and practicality undergirding it all. So I try to be super-pragmatic about everything with him."

Belinda went to therapy? To think that she'd just started to come to terms with the earlier reveal: Brando's pooping en plein air.

"Like, you can love your kids to the moon and back, but day-to-day, you are dealing with logistics and plans, and those logistics and plans better be super well thought through, or else you'll be sending them out to sea in a little raft made of newspaper, and hoping for the best. Violin gives him grit, a love of music, an appreciation for hard work. You don't just, like, get that stuff via osmosis."

Didn't sound totally insane, actually.

"Anywhooo," Belinda said, with a little whistle, "I spent all weekend thinking about it, and came to the conclusion that I kinda wanna go in on St. E's together, and have the boys go to chapel on Fridays, and all that." Then she reached for Annie's poop bag and tossed it into the trash, a good four feet away.

"College basketball," Belinda said, with a self-deprecating shrug. "Anyway, it could be fun. Parts of it are kind of stodgy, but, I don't know, we could liven it up, couldn't we?"

Annie felt entirely off-balance, but she could no longer only blame Max, just now starting to squirm awake out of a nap and blink out at the world with a single fish eye. She responded to the simplest point.

"Look," she said, "we are Jewish, not particularly religious but still culturally so, and I'm not sure our family is the right fit for a school where chapel is held every week. Pedigree and prestige entirely aside."

Belinda laughed warmly, not a hint of hyena in it.

"Totally, but did you know that the student body is now over 60 percent Jewish? And honestly, as far as I can tell, chapel talks are just one way of many that the school tries to teach the boys how to be leaders in their community," she said. "They're each expected to organize one chapel in their final year, writing and delivering a speech about a value of St. Edward that they want to emulate, and honestly, that doesn't strike me as being such a bad thing."

Well, maybe, yeah?

"And the school is serious, really academically serious," Belinda continued. "Wouldn't both Brando and Sam do well at a place like that? They're both such smart little guys."

Belinda sighed as Annie, buying herself some time to figure out how to respond, squinted out at the playground as if trying to locate her children. She just saw a sea of bodies hurtling around, seemingly the physical manifestation of her own psyche.

"But bottom line? This shouldn't be a game, it shouldn't be about winning. Just look at them."

She directed Annie's gaze to the sandpit, where Brando was riding on Sam's back, Claire flapping her arms around them in circles, committing hard to being her bird. The kids had bounced back, quick. Didn't seem like the bite had had any real lasting trauma. *Maybe Belinda was right. About it all.*

"We need to be harnessing their natural curiosity," Belinda continued. "We need to just place them in a good environment, and let them do what they're innately programmed to do, which is learn and create. Let's not miss the forest for the trees."

Annie had been getting so many things wrong lately—everything from small stuff, like how to keep Claire in her room through the night, to the biggest of the big stuff, like navigating her marriage, her career, her friendships. Laura still wasn't talking to her, and Annie feared, despite a history of loyalty on both sides, that she might be on borrowed time with Camila. *Had she bungled this, too? Was Belinda, in fact, just another human being struggling to keep her life together? Letting her son poop out in the open, because it made him comfortable, and then snuggling with him at night, because she loved him so much?* The mother-on-mother crime she'd written about in the op-ed, it didn't just happen on social media. It happened right here, in this moment. *Couldn't she do her part to stop perpetuating it?*

"Anyway, if you sign it, I'll sign it, too," Belinda said, "and we can both drop our letters in Ellie's mailbox next week. No pressure, but you have my word that if you decide that's best for Sam, I'll jump in with you, feetfirst. And then we can take St. Edward's by storm. And if not, let's just communicate so that one of us isn't entirely left out in the cold, okay? In this insane cauldron of competition, it's hard to remember that we're just people. I'm just a mom, standing in front of another mom, asking her to do right by her kid."

Wasn't that from Notting Hill?

But Annie found herself nodding along, tears starting to sprout in her eyes, and then the boys barreled over, saying they were hungry, and then they were heading out of the park in opposite directions, the kids waving at each other until they were so far apart, they each disappeared into the backdrop of the darkening city.

• • •

From: Ash Wempole
To: Annie Lewin
Subject: Scrotum love!

OH. MY. GOD. CHRISSY TEIGEN JUST LINKED TO YOUR POST.
I was totally hesitant to publish the word "scrotum" but . . . Annie, could Kim K be next?!!
Ash
She/They
Wordsmith. Potter. MP2.0 (IYKYK).
@RiseFromTheAshes
Etsy store: TerraCottaAndAsh

From: Annie Lewin
To: Ash Wempole
Subject: re: Scrotum love!

Ash,

I realize we are from different generations (and maybe also planets?), but, maybe because I've never met you in person and envision you as a floating internet body, I feel comfortable laying all my shit out for you. I don't even know where in the world you live! Or where you're from!

Speaking of floating, I googled what it meant that I keep having these recurring dreams where I'm floating off in space, escaping that sinkhole, and the general consensus seems to be that floating dreams indicate a "loss of control," and I have to be honest, I definitely feel out of control, and very much regret writing that rant advice column that involved the word "scrotum," and I got an email from a mother whose kid has been bullied for ages and she said I was off my rocker, that I fundamentally misunderstood what it is like to be in her shoes, that it breaks her heart every day, that she works hard to keep her son safe and be a good example, that she can't just grow a scrotum because she's an adult woman with responsibilities in the community and . . . what if I've made a massive mistake?

SOS.

A.

From: Ash Wempole
To: Annie Lewin
Subject: re: re: Scrotum love!

Annie Lewin, I thought you'd never ask! Pull up a chair and gather 'round! I am from a little town on the Upper Peninsula of Michigan, which means I am, yes, a Yooper! (Yoop!) I was weaned on pasties (say it with me, *pass-tees*), which are meat hand pies. My mom used to make the world's best pasties stuffed with meat from the animals my dad would shoot in the woods or run over with his car by mistake. Ya'ever eaten a squirrel pasty? Don't knock it till ya try it, is all I'm saying! I live in Bushwick now, though, so spend much of my time trying to pretend that I didn't grow up eating sustainably gathered roadkill and am vegan and gluten-free. Tried to make a cashew cheese pasty with a rice-potato-sorghum-flour dough, and, man, that did NOT taste like it came from my mama's kitchen!

In any case, re: your floating dream, I am honored that you feel I am close enough to you to share your deepest fears, but I gotta say, I love a good floating dream! I'd look at it in a totally different light. What if you're not losing control, you're just ethereal and becoming closer to the stars? INTO THAT. HARD. Speaking of being from different planets, did you know that Pluto is in retrograde now? Everyone always talks about Mercury being in retrograde, but Pluto is the planet of rebirth, and when Pluto is in retrograde, it's an opportunity to take stock of all the things in your life you don't like, and flush them away. Maybe your subconscious is telling you that what you need to be getting rid of is earthly concerns that weigh you down! I subscribe to an astrology substack that delivers mantras to my inbox daily (today's is the navagraha chandra shanti mantra, which translates to "the resplendent moon god emanated while churning the ocean of milk by the gods and demons in pursuit of the immortal nectar," which, I mean, I don't even get half of it but SHIVERS amirite?) and seems totes plausible to me.

(Also, this more-than-280-character epistolary thing we have going has really underscored for me how much I love the written word! Look how much I can convey!)

As for haters, haters gon' hate! We need to feed the click beast, gurl. Welcome to the 20th century!

Ash

She/They

Wordsmith. Potter. MP2.0 (IYKYK).

@RiseFromTheAshes

Etsy store: TerraCottaAndAsh

From: Annie Lewin

To: Ash Wempole

Subject: re: re: re: Scrotum love!

21st. 21st century.

• • •

The night they finished *Peter Pan*, both Annie and Sam cried.

Wendy, of course, grows up, and though Peter promises he'll come fetch her once a year for spring cleaning, he forgets, and one sad evening while they're waiting for him and he doesn't come, Michael says, with a shiver, "Perhaps there's no such person, Wendy!" and their childhood begins to slip away from them, just like that.

The last sequence has Wendy and her daughter, Jane, cuddled under the sheets and telling stories about Wendy's magnificent run with the magnificent Peter from long ago. And then Peter flies in, right at the end, and is so startled to find a grown Wendy—who admits to Peter that she is "ever so much more than twenty"—that he sits on the floor and sobs, which awakens Jane, who knows precisely who he is and within moments is flying about the room, having taken the mantle from Wendy to become Peter's own mother.

"Of course in the end Wendy let them fly away together," Barrie writes. "Our last glimpse of her shows her at the window, watching them receding into the sky until they were as small as stars."

"So Wendy can still *see* Peter, even though she can't *get* to Neverland?" Sam asked, lower lip trembling.

"Yes, because—and at least I think this is one way to read it—when we grow up we still remember our childhood, we still have access to that imagination, we just don't use it as well or as frequently as we did as children. So she can't, like, get all the way there. But she wants her child to go."

"So if I use my imagination every day, and work at it, maybe I can make it to Neverland forever?" Sam asked, eyes big and round under the sheet, which he'd pulled up just as Wendy did for Jane. A single tear slid down his perfect, downy cheek. "And maybe if I know the way, I can bring you there with me?"

"It's worth a shot, right?"

Yes, he'd agreed. Annie read the passage about Miss Darling

arranging the contents of her children's brain once again, reflecting that if Barrie had known anything, he'd have had the pure, clearheaded, unmarred children arranging their parents' brains for them and not the other way around, then headed down to the kitchen, where Dan was pacing, AirPods locked and loaded. He silently beckoned her over and gestured to a piece of paper sitting on the island.

"Prisoner's dilemma, mapped out," he whispered, sotto voce, then turned back to the call. She picked it up.

	BRENNER FAMILY WRITES LETTER TO ST. E'S	BRENNER FAMILY DOESN'T WRITE LETTER
LEWIN FAMILY WRITES LETTER TO ST. E'S	Both get into St. E's (second best option, tie)	Letter writer: Public school (worst option, loser) Abstainer: Highly increased odds at Thatcher (+ no tuition!), accepted into safety school (best option, winner)
LEWIN FAMILY DOESN'T WRITE LETTER	Abstainer: Highly increased odds at Thatcher (+ no tuition!), accepted into safety school (best option, winner) Letter writer: Public school (worst option, loser)	Both accepted into safety school, possibility of increased odds at Thatcher for one family (third best option, tie)

Starred underneath was an underlined note: **<u>Rational Actors Act In Self-Interest</u>**

Over lukewarm leftover chicken fingers, Dan laid out the various scenarios.

"Game theory is just a probabilistic framework, a way to strategize if you're trying to figure out how rational actors would make decisions," he said. "What you're trying to do here is not put yourself in someone else's shoes, but predict what they'd do if you actually *were* them. Get it?"

Sort of?

"Look, do you remember that day last year when I came home and you were cleaning up all the kids' toys and complaining that they never cleaned up after themselves?"

She nodded.

"And how we instituted that policy? That if they helped each other clean up, and did it fast, they'd get some sort of prize, and if they didn't clean up at all they wouldn't get anything, and if one cleaned and the other sat out, the cleaner would get an even bigger prize?"

She nodded again.

"So that was the prisoner's dilemma. I set it up like that. Because I knew that it would incentivize them to cooperate with each other and clean up together. Sam wouldn't want Claire to get a bigger prize, and Claire wouldn't want Sam to get a bigger prize, so they'd end up working together for a mutually beneficial outcome."

"I thought you said rational actors act in self-interest, though, and don't cooperate with each other?"

Annie moved on from chicken fingers to eating chocolate chip cookie dough ice cream straight from the carton, vegetable intake a distant pipe dream.

"Totally, BUT," Dan said, mid-chew, finger in the air, "the clean-up scenario only works because it's what's known as an *iterated* prisoner's dilemma. If you know the same situation is going to happen again, and again, and again, you'll come to realize that the best thing for you to do is cooperate, and both remain silent. Then you both get the second-best outcome."

The spring semester they'd met, Dan was taking the class that ended up dictating the rest of his career—an upper-level seminar on game theory, taught by a legend in the field who'd worked in various presidential administrations and even had an obscure theory named after himself. He'd made her laugh with his talk about stochastic outcomes and combinatorial games, such a geek behind his confident, a cappella singing exterior, an onion of layers, waiting to be unpeeled and understood. Watching him here, now, at the kitchen table as their three babies slept upstairs, Annie felt a rush of love—for his charm, his smarts, the way he could become completely immersed in a subject or task, with a confidence that lit up a room. As she'd learned more about his family, she'd grown to understand that he'd been taken with game theory not only because it was intellectually engaging, but because it imposed rationality on an inherently irrational world, on a world in which a father could squander everything away even while convincing everyone that he was a business titan, on a world in which a mother could continue to host fundraisers at her apartment while she was quietly selling off antiques and artwork to keep the children in private school, until the whole house of cards fell down.

But as he became a father himself, she'd watched his desire for control pivot ever so slightly, into a reflex to amass as many wins as possible, to create a world in which even if irrationality reared its head, he'd be so impervious to it, it wouldn't matter. They'd reached the core of the onion, his myriad interests reduced to one, his desires and motivations singular and, more pressingly, so foreign to her now. Annie knew Dan loved his children, that he loved her, and perhaps they were, actually, the reason he was working so hard, even though it often felt like he was advancing his career at the expense of all else. But she also could no longer ignore the thought that had reared during the fight they'd had the night after Claire fractured her arm—that he'd just as soon put parenting on hold until he'd handled his career, at which point he could tap into a life with three almost teenage offspring. Whether or not he'd actually take that option if it were offered, she was certain that the twin goals of maintaining control and parenting three young children were inherently at odds—*Which meant what, exactly, about the next ten years? That she'd tread water until he dove in?*

"But this isn't iterated," Dan continued, gesturing for the ice cream pint. "You are only doing this once. Well, at least until Claire goes through it. But you'll only be playing against Belinda this one time."

This, this was how she could reengage with her husband. Strategy.

"Okay then, so why was Belinda all gung-ho about St. E's today in the playground? She kept telling me how good it would be for the boys to be together, how solid the school's reputation is, how they've graduated more Supreme Court justices than any other prep school in America; it actually sounded kind of nice," Annie said, tossing her spoon in the sink with a clatter.

Dan barked out a laugh.

"She's playing you, Annie!" he said, digging into the pint. "She's a snake. Weren't you the one who told me her name literally means serpent? Anyway, she's one of the most tenacious negotiators in the entire country. You know what she told me the other day? In mock trial in law school, she apparently got Dax Shepherd full custody of his children by accusing Kristen Bell of neglect. Kristen Bell is *Elsa*." *Anna*, Annie thought, but this wasn't the right time to correct him. "She's about as threatening as a puppy! Her side hustle is running an organic children's lotion company! Anyway, you actually think Belinda'd settle for second best, if she has a shot at winning it all?"

Oh. Clearly that made more sense.

"She's a chameleon, Annie, that's her job," he continued. "She takes adorable clients and makes them hateful. She takes hateful clients and makes them adorable. She shape-shifts until she can strike. She's playing you! I've been on the phone with her almost constantly the last few months, advising her on this crypto divorce. I should know. What she's going to do is *not* write that first choice letter, but try to convince you to do it. That way, she'll get Brando into Thatcher with a nice backup of the alpaca safety school."

"And if I don't write the letter, either?"

"We'll likely both end up at the alpaca school," he said. "Which is fine. So long as you're the one to read the hundreds of pages on Sam's progress each week. And: there's always homeschool."

Annie grabbed the closest vessel from the drying rack—the neon blue bottom of one of Max's sippy cups—and poured herself a few fingers of bourbon as Dan turned back to his watch, slapped away an errant mosquito, then flipped up his laptop, getting ready to lock in for the night. But just as he started to respond to a Slack message, something occurred to her.

"The prisoner's dilemma only works because you're separate,

because you can't force the other person to do anything, right?" she asked, after her first sip. He nodded, sucking backward on his ice cream spoon, not following. "But, like, if you *could*, you'd force your partner to remain silent, and then you'd rat them out, and be guaranteed a win, right?" He nodded again, still not following. That quote from the *Financial Times* popped into her head: Belinda "bends the law, but would never break it." She'd never risk disbarment. Her entire life hinged on her professional success.

"Okay. Got it." She drained her bourbon, tamping down first the urge to pursue a detente with Laura and just text her already, and the wave of loneliness that followed once she realized that she was far too ashamed to break the truce. Then she tossed the sippy cup in the sink and headed upstairs.

• • •

From: Miss Porter
To: Annie Lewin
Subject: Snack week

Dear Mrs. Lewin,

Quick clarification for snack week, when each student gets to "host" snack time with treats from their culture: I hope you understand why we were not able to serve the family-size Flamin' Hot Cheetos you packed in Sam's bag for today, and not simply because we were all a bit flummoxed about how they fit into your ancestry. Not only do all snacks need to be individually portioned, we request that they be nutritious and, due to various allergens in the school, free not only of legume proteins, gluten, lactose, and soy, but also artificial colors like Red 40 Lake and Yellow 6 Lake, something we never write out explicitly in the Bartleby literature. Just to spark your imagination, Parvati packed samosas, Marcus served soup dumplings (his mom brought a portable steamer, which the students loved!), and Josephine brought in homemade milk bread with passionfruit curd.

Please let me know if you'd like a chance to rehost snack next week and I'll slot you in!

Best,

Miss Porter

• • •

"Welcome to Spring Curriculum Night!"

The banner hung above the entrance to Bartleby, parents sipping room temperature white wine and holding tiny tea plates of sushi underneath. Undoubtedly the least practical stand-around-and-mingle food—to chopstick or not?—but a tried-and-true indicator of conspicuous consumption, and thus a Bartleby staple.

Curriculum, for a preschool that billed itself as being "strictly play-based," seemed like a stretch—*What could that even mean? Two periods of blocks, one of slime, and three of stickering?*—but as they inched their way toward admissions D-day, Annie knew she should make an appearance. Dan was, naturally, about to get on an overnight flight to Dubai, so she had to represent them both. Even though there were indications she absolutely shouldn't be in public. That evening, while washing the kids, she'd eyeballed the bubble bath wrong by an order of magnitude, placed Max in the tub with the water running, pivoted to yank Claire's shirt off, and turned back to find Max's head just barely peeking out from a mountain of white, a baby Martin Sheen crocodile-eyeing it out of the muck in *Apocalypse Now!* She'd accidentally popped an instant hot cocoa packet in the microwave instead of popcorn the other night, too, returning to the singed smell of burned chocolate that she still couldn't get out of the kitchen, lingering olfactory proof of her unraveling. But, as far as she could tell, she didn't really have a choice, and so she'd asked Maria to stay over, put on some non-expandable pants and a swipe of lipstick, and here she was.

Her phone buzzed with a FaceTime right as she made it to the drinks table. Dan.

"Hey, boo," he said, an airport lounge behind him. "Getting ready to board in a bit, just wanted to say hi and see how everything is going."

Pause.

"Where are you?"

She panned the phone to the Bartleby entryway.

"Curriculum night," she said. "It's been on our joint calendar for months. One of the school events you told me in August you'd make."

"You knew the first quarter was going to be a doozy for me!" he protested, a small, childlike whine in his voice that always made her blame her mother-in-law. "Also, isn't it the end of the year? Why do we need to have curriculum night now?"

"It's to preview *next* year's curriculum," she said. Even as she said it, it seemed ridiculous. *Did they really need six months to prep their three-year-olds for the fours class?*

"Don't we already know what the curriculum is? We did go through this with Sam, right?"

"Yes," Annie allowed, "but isn't now the time to perform support and commitment to Bartleby?"

Dan shrugged, then perked up, suddenly remembering something.

"Wait, but I wanted to tell you something sort of ridiculous but maybe amazing. You remember that workout suit thing with the electrodes?"

How could she forget.

"Okay, so, the guy who wants me to invest in it says that if you change the settings down to low, you can essentially work out in a low-grade way as you *sleep*. So I'm going to try it on the flight."

He paused, eyebrows raised, mic dropped.

She squinted at him.

"Sorry, you're going to get naked, put that suit on, and zap yourself throughout the night while you're thirty-five thousand feet in the air? Sure you're not going to, like, short-circuit your brain or scramble the pilot's communication?"

"Annie! This guy predicted Peloton, remember? Anyway, I thought you'd be excited. I honestly don't have any other time to test the thing, and I figure if it works, that means I can exercise in my sleep, then free up way more time with you and the kids during the day. I'm gonna try to figure out a hashtag for it, something about sleeping but pumping iron."

Thankfully, someone started to clink a glass and ask them to head to their assigned classrooms. She waved goodbye, and the screen went dark. But instead of pouring herself a single glass of tepid wine, she thought better of it and snatched up the nearest bottle by the neck, along with a tiny plastic cup. So much classier than a Solo cup, but so much smaller.

"So first thing at circle time, we ask them to describe what the weather was on their way to school—Was it sunny, rainy, cloudy?—and then enter that in the weather chart," Miss Thornton, Claire's threes teacher, was saying moments later, her overgrown audience shifting uncomfortably in their munchkin seats as they looked at the presentation projected on the smart board. "Part of the reason we do the weather every morning is that it helps children feel in control to name things about their environment."

"Wine," Annie whispered to herself as she gulped back a full cup in one swig and poured herself another (*What were these, thimbles?*). She waited expectantly for a sign that she now felt in control. *No dice.*

"And next year, the children will be able to really take ownership of that exercise, by drawing their own weather cards and taking turns being class meteorologist, one of the most sought-after jobs in the fours classroom!"

Miss Thornton clicked through to a few more slides.

"Here, you'll see the children using the dramatic play area," she continued, making her way through the slide show as "Here Comes the Sun" played from a tinny portable speaker. There was Claire, sitting in front of two untethered computer keyboards, two babies in her lap, a large slice of plastic pizza clenched in her teeth. "Dramatic play helps them prep for how they'll feel in various situations and makes those situations less scary. Next year, dramatic play will shift into a whole new caliber, as they start interacting with each other more, and parallel playing less."

As far as Annie could tell, Claire was reasonably acting out life as a working mother. *If only she'd had more dramatic play as a three-year-old*, she thought, as she took down another thimble. The next slide showed Claire with a girl who looked familiar. *Who was that? Amoeba? Was that her name? Oh, right.* She hadn't seen him since the biting incident. She twisted into a stretch, feigning discomfort in her tiny seat, to see if *he* was there, and almost immediately they locked eyes. He gestured toward her wine bottle and raised an eyebrow, lip curling into a half snarl, half smile. She shrugged, as her heart fluttered.

After the forty-five-minute presentation that, yes, involved full sections on block building and the importance of gross motor skill development—meaning, as far as Annie could tell, walking and running around—the lights came back on, and the parents were encouraged to mingle, take in their children's artwork, and eat more sushi.

"So, down the hatch, huh?" Shawn said, coming up behind her as she stood squinting at Claire's dot painting. She looked down at the now empty bottle, then threw it, underhand, into a nearby tiny trash can, where it made an unexpectedly large crash. Other parents, milling nearby and straining to keep the conversation going about their children's dot paintings, looked up, startled. Ignoring them, she chucked her plastic cup after it. "You know, my wife really likes your columns," he went on, smirking.

Annie turned around quickly to face him.

"Your wife, huh," she said, eyes swimming ever so slightly—because of their proximity, or the alcohol, or the distorted way she felt whenever she stepped into this shrunken world, she had no idea. "That's nice. Where is she?"

"Milan. To check out scents for her next candle line."

Right.

"Anyway, I started reading them last night, and they are a riot; really, you're quite talented," he continued. She was close enough to see which bits of his salt-and-pepper stubble were salt and which were pepper. "Granted, I'm not really the target demo for Mother Inferior, but you already know I'm an Annie Lewin completist, from way back."

"Yeah, my *Times* stuff, you mentioned at the playground," she said, leading them to the sushi table, where one lonely bottle of wine remained. She picked it up and, finding no more cups, took a swig. "Wasted potential. Something you're probably familiar with." Then she gasped.

"Oh my god, I'm so sorry. I can't believe I said that out loud."

But he just laughed.

"It's refreshing to have someone call a spade a spade," he said. "Mind?" He reached over, slipped his fingers around the wine bottle, and took a swig himself. As his hand brushed hers, she felt a titillating little rush.

"Gotta love that cheap pinot," he grinned. "I'm a sucker for it."

"I thought you, uh, were totally sober after all the, the stuff."

"The arrest? Yeah, I went cold turkey after that. I mean, I was just a kid, how else could anyone have reasonably expected me to respond to that level of attention and fame? So yeah, I did some drugs and other things I regret, but that was decades ago."

How amazing, to be able to brush an arrest, multiple misdemeanors, and being publicly lousy to his first wife under the rug.

"Now I'm a devoted father and husband," he went on. "I literally google how to make bacon, because Amelia really likes bacon. I've found that if you do it in the oven it gets the crispiest, so I lay out the bacon the night before so I can just pop it in the oven when Amelia wakes up, first thing. I'm at curriculum night for a preschool that doesn't really have a curriculum, for chrissakes. If that isn't turning over a new leaf, I don't know what is."

Annie stood there nodding along. Even tipsy, she registered that a monologue about breakfast meats would be deeply boring if it weren't for Shawn saying it.

After a beat: "So I told you where my wife is. Where's your husband?"

She hadn't been lying to Camila—the last time she'd flirted with a guy had been a full decade before. But even so, there was zero ambiguity here. *That was definitely a come-on. Like with a sledge-hammer.*

"Dan?" she said, buying time. "Um, Dan is lying in a first-class suite on an Emirates flight to Dubai, with some sort of electrode suit strapped to his body, working out as he sleeps. So that's what we're dealing with." *She was a creative person. Creative people needed other creative people to thrive, right?*

"*Annie.*"

Laura was suddenly next to her, pulling her gently aside and flashing a weak smile at Shawn.

"I think it's time I took you home," she said.

"Laura! Laura, always here to rescue me at the right time," Annie said, then conspiratorially to Shawn, "even when we're not really talking. That's how good of a friend she is. Shawn, meet Laura, the one non-crazy parent at this school. And Laura, meet, well, let's be honest, we all know his name and have been texting about him nearly constantly since the first day of school, so whatever, that's over."

Shawn snorted, loving it.

"She's a live wire, this one, isn't she?" he said to Laura, then jiggled the bottle. "Wine?"

Laura shook him off, turned to Annie.

"I just, I mean . . ." Annie trailed off. "How does a person become who they are, you know? Like, how are you, one minute, a young writer with all this potential," she said to no one in particular, "or an actor with all this potential"—she gestured at Shawn, eyes locked on her and flashing that devilish, Jack Nicholson grin that had graced his early film posters—"and then suddenly you're spending a Wednesday evening in a preschool classroom, and you're gonna stay here simply because the idea of going back to your apartment fills you with dread, and you're part of this massive game without rules that is called Parenthood that you're certain everyone else is playing better than you?"

Pause, then she heard: "You wanna get out of here?"

Her eyes focused on Shawn. *He'd actually said that. To her.* Oh, to show this clip to her teenage self, sitting alone in the high school library during lunch period.

"Um, no, I'm going to take her home," Laura said firmly. Then, into her ear: "Don't do something foolish."

"*Foolish?*" Annie squawked, yanking her arm out of Laura's grip. "What are we, out on the heath in *Jane Eyre* or something? And anyway, I thought we were 'done,' after the tangrams thing." Her stomach churned with a feeling of part regret, part excitement she imagined bullies knew intimately. "Sure, Shawn. Let's get out of here."

Ignoring Laura's jaw-drop and grabbing her bag, Annie followed Shawn down the hall to the school's front steps, where a car slid around the corner from wherever it had been lurking and whisked them across town then down the West Side Highway, the tires thumping rhythmically as they passed the lights of the Intrepid, Chelsea Piers, a lit-up soccer field where a late-night league was practicing in the cold, the Hudson black and menacing beyond. Annie hadn't been outside after dark south of Fifty-Ninth Street since before Sam was born. *What a thrill.* And then Shawn was knocking on a metal door, and they were ascending a flight of stairs, and she found herself in a sort of speakeasy, a DJ spinning jazz records in one corner, red plush couches and chairs surrounding tiled café tables in little clusters. A group of beautiful people beckoned Shawn over, and then she was surrounded by what could only be termed an entourage, hearty back slaps between the guys, double air kisses for the willowy women. She thought she recognized a few from somewhere—and was that the new director everyone was comparing to Tarantino?

"And this is Annie, my new friend," Shawn said, sinking with her into the nearest couch. As the entourage flopped down around them, he turned to her, close enough she could smell the wine on his breath. "I sometimes just, like, need a break, you know? From all the bullshit. Sometimes I just see something I want, and I just take it."

She had no idea if he was talking about her, or the drink that was put in his hand, or breakfast meats, but she responded, nodding, "Totally." *Totally?*

No one paid much attention to her, Shawn included, which allowed her to sit back, sip her bourbon, and observe the beautiful people from the center of it all. She was surprised at how comfortable she felt, until she realized that she'd spent years doing this, just with a reporter's notebook in her hand.

Well, not exactly this.

A few hours in—she'd completely lost track of time, could have been one hour or four—Shawn put his head in her lap and said, to one of the laughing entourage, "Why won't she just flirt with me?!" and she'd put her hands on his head and felt his thick hair and realized she hadn't touched another man's hair in fifteen years. She thought of Dan, working out in his sleep at thirty-five thousand feet.

"Just flirt with me!" Shawn said again, now a hot whisper in her ear. "You can, you know, just take what you want—sometimes." *Could she? Had she ever, before, taken what she wanted? Had she ever, before, known what she'd wanted?* And then she was floating up above the two of them, looking down at herself, the wisps of her nightgown fabric fluttering in the air around her feet, gravity warping, time simultaneously contracting and expanding, living in Claire's long five minutes. Everything around her went fuzzy and out of focus, and as she leaned down, she wasn't sure if it was her leaning down or her ethereal self, wasn't sure if she was there or not there, wasn't sure if she was imagining his hands hungrily under her shirt, his stubble scraping her chin, his teeth tugging at her lower lip, her body pulsing, and then the whole universe starting to pulse, and then buzz, and then it was buzzing insistently.

Her phone.

A text from Laura.

"You know his wife is pregnant. And whatever Dan's flaws are, he's doing his best."

That was all it said.

Annie disentangled herself from Shawn and went to the bathroom, sitting down, hard, on the toilet as the world swirled drunkenly around her. She just needed a minute, one moment, to pull herself together and figure out what, exactly, was going on here. The night could unfurl in any number of directions, and even through her haze, she sensed that she had total control in the outcome. She just didn't know what she wanted that outcome to be.

As she gathered her thoughts—*His wife was pregnant? Really?*—she pulled out her phone to see a few more alerts behind Laura's.

MARIA: All babies asleep, see you in the morning.

DAN: About to take off. Abs on fire. Will call later.

She scrolled through some emails. Popped through Instagram, to Shawn's feed, which mostly featured pictures of his two rescue dogs. "Adopt, don't shop!" read one caption. *That made him a good person, right? He showed up to curriculum night, and adopted puppies?* Then back to her main feed, where Belinda's latest, an overhead shot of Brando's bento box lunch from yesterday, was the top image.

"PRAISE BE to this special Japanese warmer I found on-line that you can put into the lunchbox right before sending your littles off, to keep empanadas and mini hand pizzas warm for hours!"

Precisely what was a "mini hand pizza"?

Pause.

After a quick visit to Amazon and a search for "Japanese mini lunchbox warmer," which had received a whopping 17,000 five-star reviews, she ordered two. The pair was only $9.99, and would arrive before ten p.m. the next day.

She scrolled down to Leonora's latest post, a photo of the family on a boat taken the previous weekend, crystal blue waters all around, geotagged "Antigua." "So grateful!" the post read. Leonora was always so grateful to be on vacation with her family on non-holiday weekends.

Then, a bloop.

LAURA: Don't do anything stupid.

It was when Annie was about to flush, when the room had stopped spinning sufficiently to give her the gumption to go back out to Shawn and see just what might happen if she took what she wanted—which, she now knew, was to act on her impulses for the first time maybe ever, without any consideration for the downstream consequences, just like everyone else seemed to do—that she saw a new post from the TechCrunched channel. A few weeks ago, she'd joined the millions of other tightly wound basic people who got a legitimate reprieve from their tightly wound days by watching others destroy expensive objects. Though she'd stuck her nose in the air about it months before, she'd come around to its benefits: unfettered catharsis. In an introductory college psych class, she'd learned that the idea of releasing one's anger to calm down, as if from a spigot, was a crock of horseshit. The more anger you released, the angrier you got. But the professor had never discussed the benefits of watching someone *else* release anger. With an *n* of one, she could unequivocally report that it did the body good, and not just because it made the watcher immediately feel smug. You might be angry and nuts, but not so angry and nuts you'd actually do something like *that*.

The latest post featured what appeared to be a scuba diver detonating some sort of explosion underwater. The camera panned up to reveal a yacht, being blown to high heaven. Liked by over half a million people.

Staying cocooned in the bathroom for a few more blissful moments, her life safely hovering at a fork, Annie found herself clicking through to the main TechCrunched page, and scrolling down a few weeks of postings. A Ferrari meeting its demise over here, a Peloton bike crashing into the bottom of a ravine there. And a few flicks of her finger down, she saw a post that stuck out, for its stark cover photo: a black-and-white violin, shot overhead. Though it had hardly any views—a mere 5,000—she clicked on it.

It took her a moment to understand exactly what she was looking at. The camera was in a dark, hollow space, a few primal bongs reverberating the image, and then the perspective suddenly whooshed upward, past what appeared to be large metal wires, until she was looking at a violin from above. Decent production value, for something clearly done in someone's house. She popped an AirPod in and turned the sound up ever so slightly.

The image stayed stagnant as the first famous bars of Paganini's Caprice no. 24 in A minor began to play. The piece was widely considered to be one of the most difficult ever composed for the instrument. There was the speed, but more to the point, the relentless onslaught of changing techniques, a veritable candy store of sadistic ones—parallel octaves and fast arpeggios, double stops and pizzicato—that led violin students to proudly post bloody Paganini fingers online, as proof of having survived a classical music hazing period. But even if you knew nothing about violin, the diabolic melancholy of the music was unmistakable.

Clear, piercing, the spiraling notes continued to play as a man's hand came into the frame wielding a pair of garden shears. Snip, went the strings over the instrument's bridge, just as the first wild arpeggio sequence began.

Oh my.

Then out came a hammer, smashing off the chin rest, which went spiraling out of the frame.

As Paganini's creepy, distorted sliding began, as if to herald the arrival of a slippery monster, a coping saw arrived, and very methodically began to slice the violin into pieces. The destroyer's face was obscured, but you could see that he was wearing protective eyewear. At one point, the saw stuck, and he simply took the remaining shell of the violin and bashed it, repeatedly, methodically, on the floor until it had completely crumpled.

Sick and twisted, like an Almadóvar film. Heartbreaking, because it was a musical instrument and not some generic status symbol. Like burning a book. Something that should be impervious to destruction because of what it represented: freedom, creativity, joy, beauty. Yet impossible to look away.

As the parallel octaves began, the wood went into a garbage can, marching toward the video's finale.

With the pizzicato, a match sparked to flame, the camera zooming in to see the strike up close.

And then, the camera panned to get the flames beginning to lick the rosined wood, and the sound of crackling finally joined the demonic music, as the piece and video raced to its inevitable conclusion.

Wait a second.

She paused the video. Dragged the time backward so she could look more closely.

Yes. There it was. Just as the camera panned to the match, in passing, and only for a split second, it had captured the wall behind. And on it, barely visible unless you knew what to look for, was hung a full gallery of framed photos—large, small, some triptychs.

All of birds.

No. Fucking. Way. She felt her world upheave, but instead of continuing to float up, as she had been doing for months, she came to with her feet firmly planted on the tiled bathroom floor. She knew exactly where she was. No whooshing void, no weightlessness.

She should have known. There had been signs everywhere. The hyena laugh. The wearing of leather in 75 degree weather. The withholding poop story. The dead birds (shudder). The damned obsession with violin. The biting. *Of course. Of course Greg was filled with rage.*

If only she could send this to Dan, to Laura, to someone, to help her sort through her chaotic mess of feelings. One of those, for sure, was triumph. *Just look! Your perfect marriage, Belinda? The one with the perfect husband who's interested in all the granularities of raising children, whose perfect butt you can't restrain yourself from squeezing in public? It's actually a trash fire!* But, perhaps in equal measure, she felt a rush of pity. *Poor thing. In an unhappy marriage and living with a constant, sizable chip on her shoulder that she's perpetually trying to shrug off, Atlas on Park Avenue.* Then, the pendulum swung way back again. Pitiable or not, there was no way she could remain in the same orbit as Belinda, that Sam and Brando could end up in the same school together next year. That, she just couldn't bear.

Like a backward time-lapse shot with her at the center, she saw herself standing up and leaving the bathroom, catching Shawn's checked shirt blending into the sofa—but he didn't even see her, another woman was already on his lap—and then she was rushing down the stairs out of the speakeasy, and she was outside, the cold air slapping her awake, the sun just starting to come up, a bakery wheeling carts out to a waiting truck.

Just as Annie was letting herself into the apartment, after an eyebrow raise from the elevator man, another alert popped onto her home screen.

Calendar alert: First choice letter due tomorrow.

Head still spinning from alcohol, Annie tiptoed up the stairs and opened her laptop. It came so easily, she'd finished with it before Claire staggered out, Pull-Up weighing five pounds, asking for cereal.

• • •

Belinda Brenner
Brenner and Associates
11 West 57th Street, 40th Floor
New York, NY 10021
BB@Brennerandassociates.com
@BBgun

Headmaster Loren Fitzhughes
St. Edward's School for Boys
10 East 94th Street
New York, NY, 10128

Dearest Headmaster Fitzhughes,

It is with sincere excitement and great joy that I write to you on behalf of our son, Brando, and the extended Brenner family, to let you know how blown away we have been by your school, and what an honor it would be to become part of its community.

As we await your final decision, I will be in court, continuing my quest to give my client her due after years of playing second fiddle, but my husband will be at home actually playing the fiddle with our pride and joy and taking photos of various birds—dead and alive—that he finds around the city, so he can totally step back from those responsibilities should you need anything from us to move this forward.

Cheers,
Belinda Brenner, Esq.

• • •

From: Camila Garcia Williams
To: Annie Lewin

Annie, can you pick up your phone? I can't do this over email. I can't understand half of the things you wrote in your last email, or your texts from 4 a.m. (4 a.m.!?) but please, please call me? Just take a deep breath. You told me to tell you if you were headed off the reservation and I think the answer is a resounding YES. Come back? I tried to reach Dan but it went straight to voicemail, and his Instagram from eight hours ago indicates he was in some sort of hotel suite on an Emirates flight, getting ready to fall asleep with sensors and a combat vest strapped to his body. Is he okay? What does #DrillWhileYouChill even mean???

Xoxo

APRIL

Dear Mother Inferior,

Lately on my Mommas Facebook group, I've seen entries in which members post pictures of nannies in playgrounds, accusing them of neglecting or mistreating their charges in some way, and asking the group for help locating the parents. They follow the same general format, anchored by a photo of the person in question, with big rounded yellow stars plastered over the faces of all the children, like a dystopian Keith Haring painting. This is vigilante justice, right? Which is something that I find questionable, but I'm not exactly sure why. Do you think these posts are appropriate, and if not, how should the community be handling them?

Sincerely,

Vigilante in Ypsilanti

Vigilante,

Before I launch into a tirade about how totally and utterly insane this practice is, with the same raw honesty that has, somehow and against any master plan, made this parenting advice column one of the most read in recent history, let us first turn to the words of the mighty Arthur Miller. Though writing about the Salem witch trials in *The Crucible*, he might as well have been referencing the Wild West world of Mommas groups.

Is the accuser always holy now? Were they born this morning as clean as God's fingers? I'll tell you what's walking Salem—vengeance is walking Salem. We are what we always were in Salem, but now the little crazy children are jangling the keys of the kingdom, and common vengeance writes the law!

Little crazy children, jangling the keys of the kingdom! That is what we have become, Mommas!

For those of you who are not part of a virtual community of mothers who have too much time on their hands and enjoy pretending that they are sunnier versions of Batman, clad in cable-knit pastels instead of black rubber, and driving electric SUVs instead of flying Batmobiles, let me share with you an actual post I plucked, at random, from one of my groups just this very morning! Strap in, ladies.

If this is your nanny, or you know this nanny, please reach out to me in a DM. She was with an adorable little boy who was wearing blue jeans, a red hoodie (with ears—love!), and holding a Thomas train. Brace yourselves, because I saw him be ABANDONED for literally forty-five minutes. The nanny was finally found leaning against a tree by the sandpit, AirPods shoved in and yapping to someone. If I were the parent, I'd want to know, so I'm posting about it here. As Hillary Clinton once said, it takes a village!

For starters, before Hill it was an African proverb. But more to the point, can we actually unpack what it is that this person is accusing the nanny of doing? Talking. On her AirPods. While at a playground. Was the child actually at risk? Was he within eyeshot or earshot of this nanny, who was right there next to the sandpit? We don't know, Mommas, because our poster has crawled up on her supremely small soapbox, now not so small, thanks to the Internet, which has frayed all our relationships and turned us into info-addicted automatons, to accuse someone of behaving the way we all do at the playground. Sure, you might be one of those mothers who follows her child around, narrating in slightly sped-up chipmunk speak every damn thing he's doing because you read somewhere that exposure to language would help him get into Harvard. But if so, you can't sit with us.

Honestly, *Vigilante,* you're "not exactly sure why" you find this Motherhood Police State questionable? You have no opinion whatsoever about your fellow mothers prowling playgrounds on the hunt for weaklings to crush? Perhaps the path of least resistance is to join them, to bring Shirley Jackson's lottery to the monkey bars as you team up to gather bits of anxiety to feed your collective neurosis. Or maybe, just maybe, you want to grow the hell up, and start thinking for yourself, instead of asking me for advice. Because if anything actually deserves a *complimenti*, bitch, it's that: becoming an adult who can make her own decisions, without writing to a mother who is clearly as unhinged as the rest of you!

Mother Inferior

TL;DR: Grow up! *peace fingers emoji*

From: Ash Wempole
To: Annie Lewin
Subject: WARNING: TOO RAW

Gurl, I can't believe I'm saying this, but we gotta crank this baby down a few notches. Poor Vigilante in Ypsilanti. And not just because she lives in Ypsi, amirite? Bottom line: I can't run this. We gotta have a little compassion. Sending you a link *hyperlink* to my daily meditation live stream, *highly recommend* you join.

Xo
Ash
She/They
Wordsmith. Potter. MP2.0 (IYKYK).
@RiseFromTheAshes
Etsy store: TerraCottaAndAsh

From: Annie Lewin
To: Ash Wempole
Subject: re: WARNING: TOO RAW

Dear Ash,

My numbers keep going ever higher the more outlandish my columns, I just figured I'd let my freak flag fly? But I see what you're saying. Will rethink and revise and send back to you shortly.

Just checking, though: I read that Elon Musk was in talks to buy RAWr.com. According to some *Post* article, he has grand plans to reduce the head count to one or two humans, who'll oversee a "newsroom" of fifth-generation chatbots. Is that . . . real? What does that mean for you? What does that mean for . . . me?!

Gotta go to a preschool luncheon, but will be ohm-ing with you in spirit.

J'hugs from afar. (Did I do it right?)

Best,

Annie

• • •

The Bartleby Brooch luncheon was held at the new apartment of one of the PTA chairs, Leonora Linsby, who had been a member of the PTA for nine years running and held the president's chair for four—a Bartleby record on both counts.

"Welcome one, welcome all," she called, as Annie and an elevator-full of others stepped out of the sliding doors and directly into the floor-through apartment. She'd rather have been anywhere else, but did not want to raise any suspicions from Belinda, so had dragged herself to attend in the spirit of community support. Their hostess breezed toward them, arms outstretched and with a conspiratorial *it's finally happening!* look on her face, floral gown fluttering behind her, silver mules clicking on the tile floor, Bartleby Brooch from the previous year pinned prominently to her collar and festooned in emeralds and diamonds, the school's colors. *She must have embellished that herself,* Annie thought. *The things people had time to add to their to-do list.* "You can give your spring coats to Marcia here, she'll have them back to you at the end!"

Air kisses all around. Annie didn't have a coat, spring or otherwise, so nodded at Marcia, who was wearing a doilied apron and small cap.

"Apologies, apologies, the painters literally left *yesterday,* and we're nowhere near ready to host, but I'll do anything for my Belinda!" Leonora said to no one in particular.

Annie let out an involuntary guffaw, but luckily Leonora had breezed away, a tiny dog clickety-clacking behind her, to take care of the passed hors d'oeuvres. Not yet moved in? *She* was the one still unpacking boxes a full year after move-in day, and from what she could see, Leonora's house was a Nancy Meyers film, everything cream colored and plush, with so many cashmere throws casually draped over various upholstery, she wouldn't have been surprised to find one of Leonora's children enveloped in one and wriggling to get out. *Sucked down deep in the cashmere again? Come out, you silly thing.*

Annie made her way to the deck, where the lady of honor was holding court, Central Park stretching out in three directions like a green carpet, with pops of white and pink where the cherry blossoms had started to bloom.

After awkwardly standing there for a few beats and weighing the pros and cons of entering the nearest conversation, which appeared to be about hiring a new "high-end picnic service" to bring bales of hay to Central Park for a seated rustic lunch, she felt an arm on her shoulder. There was Laura, wearing, like her, a simple skirt and blouse, her expression one of forgiveness, and calm, and everything Annie craved right then.

"Oh, thank god," Annie said. She hadn't seen Laura since curriculum night, hadn't *really* seen her since that awful brunch, mostly because Annie felt terrible and embarrassed and didn't know how to come back from her horrendous showing. Grabbing two glasses of sparkling rosé, she ushered Laura to a corner of the deck away from the others and said as much.

"I'm a terrible person, and I'm embarrassed, and I cannot believe I behaved that way at brunch, and god, I hope you forgive me, and Jack forgives me, because I need you in my life, you're a grounding force, and—" And then Laura just pulled her in for a hug. And they stood like that for a markedly long time, but to Annie, it felt like stepping into a decompression chamber. Her shoulders relaxed for what seemed like the first time in weeks.

"So we left your apartment after brunch and I was enraged, yes I was, totally and utterly," Laura said, pulling back and taking a sip of her drink. "But then I was at Jack's weekly therapy appointment with his counselor the other day—so we now take him to see an occupational therapist and she's a gem, she really works wonders, like, how is it that this person who is basically a stranger can parent my child better than I can?—and we were discussing tactics for how Jack can feel safe even when he's in an environment that threatens him—and I mean, you've seen him, when he feels anxious he starts rocking back and forth, or kicking the floor, or whatever—and it all sort of aligned for me."

Annie wiped away her tears—she hadn't even realized she'd been crying—and shrugged, confused, and humiliated when she remembered little Jack's body, on the floor of her kitchen, tangrams strewn around, morphing into a metronome.

"This is just not an environment where you feel safe," Laura said. "So you're sort of . . . spiraling. Like what happened at curriculum night. That's not you. We just need to get you on solid ground. I know you're in there, somewhere."

It all sounded so simple, so straightforward.

"But more to the point, I can't navigate the Bartleby Babes without you," Laura said. "I tried, trust me. But Team Belinda can't win. You and I both know that."

"I've been having the most insane episodes, Laura, I almost texted you the other night but then felt . . . too ashamed," Annie said. "I don't think this is the right place to get into it, but can we, later? Just you and me and some wine and Goldfish and Fruit Roll-Ups and no tangram puzzles and no kindergarten talk, like old times?"

"Hard yes," Laura said, then drained her bubbly.

A gentle wind blew across the balcony, giving Annie brief shivers, and Laura, seeing, said, "What, you didn't bring your spring coat?" and the two of them burst into uncontrollable laughter, after which Laura went inside to find a snack, and Annie leaned against the stone railing, taking in the majesty of the city on the cusp of warm weather, feeling like everything just might work out, like maybe, at long last, she'd figured out how to play the game. Her phone buzzed, and she was so happy, oh so happy, to see Laura's name on her WhatsApp again.

LAURA: OK, so does Leonora's maid opt into wearing that doily outfit, or does Leonora ask her to?

ANNIE: OMG I was wondering the same thing.

LAURA: Like, how does that conversation go, even?

ANNIE: "Welcome to my manse, where we expect you to channel the cook from Mary Poppins."

LAURA: *laughing so hard you cry emoji*

LAURA: Apparently Brock is the only kid at St. E's who doesn't dress down on dress-down Fridays? Like, he shows up wearing a blazer.

ANNIE: *stop sign emoji*

ANNIE: OK, I can one-up though. I heard for her daughter's fourth birthday, which was Beauty and the Beast themed, that all the staff had to dress up like staff. From. The. Movie. Like the cook had to wear a candlestick costume. And someone had to dress up like a teapot. While serving the kids tiny bonbons. *upside down crazy smiling face*

LAURA: NO.

Pulsing ellipse, then:

LAURA: OMG, check out the Babes, they're having a collective aneurysm.

Annie toggled over to the chain that she hadn't checked since the Armani information had been revealed and scrolled down. *Bloop, bloop, bloop.* The messages were coming in hot, even as the people writing them circulated on the balcony feet from her, surreptitiously texting as they clinked glasses, delicately crunched on crudités, and made actual in-person small talk. PTA Cocktail Hour Kabuki at its finest.

YAEL: Could NOT be more proud of you, B!

CHRISTINE: Also, no doubt, gonna be the best brooch speech EVER.

MAYA: You guys know there's gonna be a special guest, right?

BELINDA: *shh emoji* *wink emoji*

YAEL: *stop sign emoji* *warlock emoji*

YAEL: Sorry, sorry, mistake.

(A riot of ha-ha's)

CHRISTINE: We love you, Queen B!

(A flood of hearts)

CHRISTINE: TEAM BELINDA!

YAEL: Rah rah!

Annie toggled back.

ANNIE: OMG, I can't.

LAURA: I invite you to consider how I've felt the last few weeks, navigating this alone.

Laura had just made her way back onto the terrace, handing Annie a plate of cucumber-wrapped tuna sashimi bites, when Leonora clinked her glass with a rounded butter spoon to ask everyone to please sit down, but as Annie turned to follow the crowd inside, she felt a thin, icy hand on her shoulder.

"Mind if I borrow her for a moment?" Belinda said to Laura with an eye squint, then guided Annie over to the corner, right next to the balcony's railing. *What on earth is she going to do, chuck me off the edge?* But Annie calmed herself with the knowledge that, in a scenario with asymmetric information, she held more of it. *Might as well lean into the game.*

"Belinda, hi," she said, inching her way slightly back. "What an honor, you must be so proud."

Belinda's face split into a cold smile.

"Well, this community has really been a lifesaver for me," she said. "Without the Bartleby moms and teachers and administrators, who am I? Just a girl from Connecticut who doesn't know the first thing about how to raise a kid in the big city."

At what point did saying something repeatedly make it true? Never?

"Nice to know that we have a shot at re-creating that at St. E's, right, together?" Annie said, trying to tamp down the rising hysteria in her voice, eyes darting back to Laura, who was flashing her a *What's going on?* look as she reluctantly allowed Leonora to shoo her inside. "You did drop your letter off with Ellie?"

"Oh, of course I did, Annie," Belinda said, one eyebrow raised up devilishly. Her eyes settled on the horizon, way across on the Hudson River, as she took a deep breath, then turned back to Annie.

"I heard that gibe you and Laura made about spring coats," she finally said. "And honestly, Annie, I'm just. Fucking. Done."

Spring coats? That's what this was about? A laugh erupted from deep in Annie's belly. *How exhausted this sad, bitter woman must be, putting on facades to the outside world while her son and husband quietly spiraled out at home!* But Belinda's eyebrows inched closer together and she continued, "Since day one your superiority has been impossible to escape. It's so tasteless, Annie, how you so obviously think you are better than all of us, than all of *this*. But *you* chose to send Sam to Bartleby, *you* chose to live in this world, *you* chose to come to this luncheon. No one forced you. You're here: so behave." She paused as if contemplating whether or not to go on, and then it came. "Just once, okay, don't be such a selfish whore."

The record scratched, immediately wiping Annie's incredulous smirk off her face as her body flooded with adrenaline, her primal instincts kicking in.

"I'm sorry, Belinda, what the hell did you just call me?"

Belinda turned toward the horizon, shaking her head, and fished her phone out of some hidden pocket in her ruffles, then started to scroll, and scroll and scroll.

"I never meant to actually show this to you, but you know what, fuck it. I'm just so tired of your . . . your *everything*. Here."

She shoved the phone at Annie, where a photo took up the screen. At first, she wasn't sure what she was looking at—a bunch of people on a couch, in a dark place, lots of limbs intertwined and draped over others, like a human octopus with multiple extremities.

"Belinda, what—"

"Oh, I can go ahead and zoom in for you," Belinda said with a little simpering smile, as she leaned down, squinted her eyes, and pinched the image apart. And there, now fully in focus, was the big reveal: Annie, herself, sitting on Shawn Axel's lap, head tilted up to his, him gazing down at her, eyebrow cocked and lip snarled, like she was a baby wildebeest, and he was an alligator, lurking in the water beneath her scrambling legs. *Lust. That was what appeared to be pouring out of the image like lava.*

Belinda deftly slid the focal point down half an inch, then zoomed in again.

"And I believe that's your hand grazing Shawn Axel's crotch," she said. "Imagine my surprise when I found it this weekend, innocently checking out Shawn's page," Belinda purred, her second eyebrow rising to meet its pair, in mock horror. "Just there on Instagram, for anyone to see."

"But this, this isn't on Shawn's page," Annie protested, her heart continuing to clippity-clop, certain she'd checked it that very morning, as she (sadly) did every day.

"Oh no, it isn't dear, he wouldn't be so stupid as to post something like this *himself*, what with Clementina pregnant and all," Belinda continued, eyes flashing, "but he was tagged in it. Time stamp is in the wee hours of the morning after spring curriculum night, presumably a few hours after you chugged a bottle of wine and then disappeared with him and his entourage. It's all anyone was talking about."

His entourage: that large group of willowy women and five o'clock shadowed men.

"Belinda, I don't get where this is going." Annie's brain was looping around in circles, so tired of strategizing that she didn't even know what game they were playing anymore.

Belinda snorted, snatching back her phone.

"You don't? How sweet, Annie. I've taken people to court and wiped the floor with them with less." Belinda was emanating so much power, so much anger, it crossed Annie's mind that she just might be able to pick her up with her perfectly coiffed hair and flip her high up over Central Park and straight into the East River, *Mortal Kombat* in Manhattan. Like a flourish to underscore her point, she reached over to the cocktail plate Annie was holding, grabbed the last tuna sashimi bite and popped it, whole, into her mouth. Then Annie saw something flash briefly over Belinda—*sadness? despair?*—before she set her face back to its resting grim mask and took an ugly swallow.

"In divorce court, you can't build a case on spurious allegations," she resumed. "'He said, she said' will only take you so far. Evidence. That's what cases hinge on. And this here, it's evidence of what I knew all along—you're selfish, thoughtless, and honestly, just as lost as the rest of us, despite this ruse you've drummed up online that you're open and honest and *real*. So maybe you wanna step down from your high horse, just once, huh? I can see right through you. And it's just a matter of time before your husband, your readers, your children do, too—if they all don't already. You're smarter than to delude yourself otherwise, aren't you?"

But before Annie could sputter back a response, Belinda was flouncing into the apartment, where she was quickly enveloped in a sea of shimmering silk, leaving Annie alone, trembling and flushed with sweat. She pulled her phone out, and with shaking hands, typed out a message.

ANNIE: She fucking threatened me. My marriage. My career? I think. I can't even process it all.

LAURA: What?!

ANNIE: She found a photo. Something on Instagram. From the other night.

LAURA: Oh shit.

ANNIE: I'm on his lap, that's all. It's not . . . a great look. But I didn't do anything, I promise. I really didn't. I almost did. But I couldn't!

LAURA: I believe you.

ANNIE: NOW WHAT? Do I call Dan? Has she already called Dan!!?

LAURA: Deep breaths. Ellie has to talk, then Belinda, then everyone needs to applaud, so . . . Calm down. Come inside.

ANNIE: Right. OK.

After the amuse-bouche—a shot glass of white gazpacho topped with peeled and quartered grapes—Leonora stood up to give a few remarks. Annie felt it inconceivable that no one else could hear her heart pounding. Belinda, she noted from across the room, was quietly laughing and making small talk, not a hair out of place.

"Distinguished members of the Bartleby community," Leonora began, "you'd better believe that when Ellie asked me to host this luncheon way back in September, before the votes had come in, I told her I'd have to see who got the brooch first!" Tittering laughter rippled out among the tables. "I'm bad, I'm bad, I know, but *seriously*! Now, I wanted to start with a special shout-out to Christine's housekeeper, Ayu, for overnighting fresh basil leaves from her family's farm in Indonesia, which are part of the microgreens salad you're about to enjoy." She pressed her hands together like a yoga teacher in deep gratitude, eliciting a polite smattering of applause for Christine, who raised herself off her seat slightly and gave an ironic queen's wave.

ANNIE: I need a breather. *peace out emoji*

LAURA: *flexed bicep emoji*

The powder room smelled of Molton Brown Sandalwood and Bergamot hand soap, and the toilet paper edge had been folded into a perfect little triangle. *Did Marcia pop in here after each pee?* Annie wondered. *Or was she the first person to use the facility, since none of these Stepford wives ever seemed to need to relieve themselves?* As she started to pee, up blooped the Babes. *Jesus. They were inescapable.*

MAYA: OMG I'm sorry but WUT is in this salad dressing? *drool face emoji*

LEONORA: So glad you asked, I snagged it from a GOOP Insta post a while back. Two secret ingredients.

CHRISTINE: *ear emoji*

LEONORA: liquid aminos and chlorella

MAYA: Chlorella? Is she the latest Real Housewife?

(Onslaught of ha-ha's)

LEONORA: It's a powdered algae that is super-earthy and funky, a little sprinkle and this basically becomes a detox salad!

BELINDA: *flexed bicep emoji* *fist pound emoji* *small explosion emoji*

(Flood of hearts)

What non-mayonnaise-based salad wasn't a detox salad? Annie raged, silently. With a quick, satisfying flick, she flung the Babes into the ether. Was now the time to unleash it, her own little personal Fury, pent up in her phone for weeks, just raring to pour some gasoline on the trash fire that was her life, fraying at the seams? But even as she contemplated it, she knew she didn't have it in her. And yet: she couldn't die being the only one on Earth to have proof of Belinda's phony existence.

When she came out of the bathroom a few moments later and made her way back to her seat, she found Brando sawing away, joylessly but skillfully, at the violin. *Of course, the special guest.* His hair was gelled into an immaculate swoop, his culottes red, and the brass buttons on his blazer gleaming.

ANNIE: I found something.

LAURA: Is it weed gummies in the downstairs powder room *fingers crossed*

ANNIE: No, no, it's from a while back. When we weren't talking.

Long pause.

LAURA: . . .

Annie saw Maya, beaming at the little child prodigy, demurely type a quick note into her phone. Momentarily, it appeared on Annie's home screen.

MAYA: What an absolute angel!

CHRISTINE: *angel emoji* *music notes emoji*

This poor kid, Annie thought. This poor little human, whose joyless face was so dissonant on his little body, an innocent, perfect, immaculate little child with a wellspring of potential, whose father was losing his damn mind and had posted it for all the world to see, whose mother was a monster. An actual monster who thrilled at the prospect of blowing up another woman's marriage, another woman's career. A tactician whose entire brand was a mirage, who treated people as pawns in the big game of life, with no care for the consequences. *The hypocrisy!*

Under the heavy tablecloth, Annie flipped her phone up again, scrolled until she found what she needed, then typed to Laura in a crazed rush, ignoring Maya's infuriated sigh, a performative gift at the altar of the etiquette gods.

ANNIE: You will NOT believe this. A TechCrunched video. [Hyperlink]
But: It's GREG BRENNER. Seriously. Remember the dead bird thing from
the birthday party? Anyway, it's him, burning a fucking violin. On the
internet. Like, holy shit? Belinda's life is a trash fire!!! LITERALLY. There
was a trash fire In. Her. House! Team Belinda my ass. And she threatens
ME? And MY MARRIAGE? With an innocuous photograph? Where I'm not
even DOING anything? Fuck that.

She toggled quickly to her GIPHY app to insert a "rubbing
hands together" GIF. The first one she found was, weirdly, of
Jerry Orbach in *Law & Order*. Toggled back. Inserted. Sent.

ANNIE: How'd you like dem *red apple emoji*?

She glanced across the room at Laura, awaiting a flash of recognition or glee or widening eyes, but instead saw a look of stark
concern cross over her friend's face.
Then a buzz from her phone.

LAURA: WRONG CHAIN.

As Leonora welcomed Belinda up to the dais, the ripples
began, from Maya at her table, to Christine at another, to Yael
nearby, the gasps audible, the hands going up to cover mouths,
Belinda still oblivious for a few moments more, her phone sitting
next to her untouched salmon, but Annie had already fled, heart
racing, nightgown floating up over her head as the elevator
whooshed down, and she spiraled, doing backward loop-de-loops
in the air.

• • •

From: Annie Lewin

To: Ash Wempole

Subject: re: WARNING: TOO RAW

I won't be able to file the vigilante rewrite in time. We need to have a bigger conversation—about my tone, my brand, all of it. I don't even know if you speak by telephone, but could we try? I think I need to actually, like, hear your voice. (What if you're just a bot?!)

Best,

Annie

From: Ash Wempole

To: Annie Lewin

Subject: AUTOMATIC REPLY re: WARNING: TOO RAW

I will no longer be responding to emails sent to this address, due both to a restructuring in the newsroom and a professional rebirth, of sorts. I am applying to an MFA program, where I plan to immerse myself in great literature and live off the grid and will spend the summer back home with my parents, cleansing my mind and body in preparation. Ta-ta, for now, virtual world. Real world, here I come.

If you are a writer with queries about an outstanding piece, please email the main newsroom address. I'm sure someone (or something!) will get back to you shortly.

If you are writing with regards to my ceramics, particularly the best-selling "j'caffeinated" or "*Complimenti*, bitches" mugs, please send a query through my Etsy shop portal, which I will be checking periodically.

Ash

She/They

Wordsmith. Potter. MP2.0 (IYKYK).

@RiseFromTheAshes

Etsy store: TerraCottaAndAsh

• • •

From: Camila Garcia Williams

To: Annie Lewin

Have called you repeatedly and can't reach you. Why aren't you picking up your phone??? I booked the first flight out in the morning.

• • •

As if swimming up from underwater, Annie heard someone calling her name.

"Mama? Mama?"

After a few echoes, her eyes focused, finally. Claire, her face haloed in curls, was looking at her in jubilant disbelief.

"*Dat's* for bweafist?"

Annie glanced down to the cereal bowl she'd just filled with Cheerios to see, instead, a heap of rainbow sprinkles. Outside the kitchen window, Decisions Day had broken clear and warm, a harbinger of summer. *And in here, we're apparently flying over the cuckoo's nest, right next to Nicholson,* Annie thought.

"You want some broccoli instead?" she asked. She felt hungover, her stomach lurching as if strapped to the hull of a motorboat.

Claire, sensing an opening, shook her head fiercely and scurried off with the bowl.

About an hour after her performance at the luncheon the day before, Annie had clicked into her WhatsApp to find that she was a Bartleby Babe no longer—it had been scrubbed from her chats. She'd gone back to sobbing in Laura's lap, blubbering that it had been an honest mistake, she'd just been so furious at Belinda for threatening her, she hadn't been thinking straight. She hadn't *meant* to send it to everyone, just to maybe use it as collateral, or something, if Belinda actually went ahead and did something with that photograph.

"But are mistakes like this ever truly mistakes, or just your unconscious poking through?" Laura had asked, gently, stroking her hair. *Fair point.*

But Annie couldn't very well keep her children locked up in the apartment, Dan was hurtling southwest in an air-conditioned car across the desert from Dubai to Abu Dhabi to meet with potential investors for dinner, and what was done was done. She was a pariah from Bartleby, fine. She'd never felt part of their crowd anyway. She'd have some hard conversations with Dan later that night, once he landed. So, after hearty breakfasts of sprinkles, off they went.

"Claire, c'mon, fly after me!" Sam shouted, scampering off as Annie unbuckled her daughter at the playground. Once her feet touched the ground, she skipped after her brother, wildly flapping her arms toward the sandpit.

Annie settled herself into the most secluded bench, her greasy hair shoved into a ponytail, her feet jammed into old, salt-stained winter UGG boots, and took a look around. Most of the working moms had taken the morning off, unable to focus on anything but what fate the day would hand their child—the single-sex school with the dress-down Fridays? The coed relaxed school with the headmaster's dog that roamed the halls and was considered prestigious because Tobias Wolff had spent a year teaching there, decades ago?—and so the swings were already packed at nine a.m., phones fully charged, cappuccinos extra-large, the kids shot up on sugar from pre-celebratory donuts. The anxiety was as palpable as the weight of the oversize sunglasses on 90 percent of the noses, of the knobbly feel of the pebbled driving loafers on 80 percent of the feet.

Gmail refresh. An email loaded. Her heart skipped a beat.

"40% off GAP Swimsuits!!!!"
Was anything at Gap ever full price? Delete.

The tulips had bloomed over the weekend, and the perimeter of the playground was an explosion of pink, orange, and yellow, a loud proclamation of the dawning of a new day. At the far edge, she could see Belinda, sipping her travel mug of scalding Red Bull as her minions fluttered around her, occasionally shooting daggers at Annie. So be it. She deserved it. Now, all she had to do was wait for the acceptances to come through from Thatcher and Hudson-Green, then feign confusion if Belinda ever confronted her. Unlike WhatsApps and emails, her hard copy forged letter had no duplicates. It was in some folder in Headmaster Fitzhughes's office, or long gone, in the St. Edward's shredder. She'd win either way, having finally figured out how to play the game after all, and no one would ever be able to prove why.

And so she passed the morning slumped in the corner of the playground, refreshing her email inbox, offering snacks up when Claire ran by, and scrolling through her Facebook feed.

Hey, Mommas, getting ready for the summer and on the hunt for matching Daddy-Son swimming trunks, but bored of Vilbrequin, any other brilliant suggestions? J'love y'all!

Desperate for some gluten-free focaccia for my son's bday party which is TOMORROW? HALP! Need recs stat.

The day has come. Kids need braces. Can they do tiny Invisalign? Are they fated to look like Nelly in the *Grillz* video? Am I about to go broke? Need an orthodontist that people LOVE.

"Mama, I have to pee." Annie looked up to see Claire, knees knocked together. "Now. Right now."

It was a moment later, with Claire's pants down around her ankles and Annie's core starting to give way, that she felt a presence behind her.

"Hello, Annie."

What was it with this woman and the al fresco potty chats? Some sort of tactic she'd learned in her negotiation classes at law school, to always approach your enemy when they were in a weakened position? She wiped Claire quickly, yanked up her leggings, then turned around, prepared for . . . she had no clue. Annie had toggled between anger and ecstatic joy, perfect certainty and wild anxiety, hallucinations and reality for almost eight full months at this point, and felt utterly and completely spent.

"Look, Belinda," she began with a sigh, "I already tried to explain that it was a mistake, okay? I'm angry but I'm not that angry."

"I know," Belinda said, hair in a perky ponytail, all smiles as Claire scampered off. "I come in peace. Believe it or not, I just wanted to apologize."

Yeah, right.

"Look, if you'd threatened me like I threatened you on the terrace, I would have done the same," she continued. "My marriage to Greg, I mean, I know better than anyone that marriages are built to fail. I just didn't necessarily want that broadcast to the school. And honestly, I wasn't planning to actually use that photo of you in any public way, I just wanted to make a point."

Annie waited, certain that Belinda would continue talking, which she did, after hocking something up and spitting it on the ground, where it landed with a splat.

"It's all rather Shakespearean, isn't it? The divorce lawyer whose marriage has been a mess for god knows how long?" Bitter laugh. Annie noted that Belinda's ponytail appeared to be vibrating behind her.

"So, what happened to the, um, carefully planned structure you talked about earlier, the one that needs to be in place for love to 'work'?" Annie said, slightly titillated that she no longer had anything to lose and could now poke the beast directly. "Like with Brando and his violin? Did you have that with Greg?"

Belinda chuckled, coldly.

"Our plan was always to leave. Greg wanted to leave the city basically from the day we got here, always told me it was no place to raise a child, that they need wide open spaces and unstructured time. I was down, I wanted that for Brando. But then my career took off, and you can't run a thriving divorce practice from Podunk, America—just like you can't be a *New York Times* staffer in bumblefuck." She sighed. "This city, it does a number on you, doesn't it?"

Annie stood there, idiotically, still holding the wipe. She wasn't sure what was going on, but remembered her conversation with Dan. Belinda was a chameleon, a shape-shifter ready to strike with poisonous venom whenever the opportunity presented itself. A killer. Any vulnerability she was showing right now *had* to be in service of something else. *But . . . what?* She could sense the other mothers in the playground, at a distance and yet ready to pounce if she so much as looked in the wrong way at their queen bee, iPhones in pockets like guns in holsters, ready to pull the trigger on the slightest infraction.

As she was contemplating her next move—to walk to the garbage and toss the wipe? To commiserate?—Annie felt the energy shift, a wind sweeping through the playground, rippling the adults like they were pieces of grass. Suddenly, people's heads were buried in their phones, and then they were looking at her, and then they were once again looking at their phones, and then devices were beeping and buzzing. She barely registered Maria swinging open the gate and waving, coming to relieve her with Max strapped to her chest.

"Go on, you should get your phone," Belinda said, eyes now twinkling in a deranged sort of way.

At first, she couldn't put it together. Nothing new in her inbox. But then something did pop up: a Facebook notification that she'd been tagged in a post, which happened not infrequently now that the column was so widely read. She clicked through to the homepage of the Facebook group she'd been scrolling before, assuming she'd find the little Mother Inferior logo that RAWr had designed for her—a nun in a habit pushing a stroller with one hand and guzzling a bottle of wine from the other. Instead, linked to her group, was a *New York Post* article.

"Upper East Side Mommas Implode Over Kindergarten Admissions."

As she skimmed the article, her vision blurred, and she suddenly found herself at the center of one of those Hitchcock shots where the background recedes scary quick.

"Unhinged mother" . . . *"Preschool feeder to independent kindergartens"* . . . *"Crackling wood of the destroyed violin"* . . . *"Annie Lewin's wildly popular Mother Inferior advice column"* . . . *"Bartleby Babes WhatsApp chain"* . . . *"Shawn Axel's friend's Instagram feed"* . . . *"Jerry Orbach"* . . .

Annie's brain whirred frantically. *Someone had leaked it. Someone had taken the Babes chat, had found that photo, and sent it to the fucking* Post.

"Oh my god, Belinda," Annie whispered, actually clutching her heart like an old lady as she continued to scroll and that gaping sinkhole started swirling closer and closer, the subway rumbling crescendoing into a constant dull roar. "Someone got hold of the WhatsApp chain. Who would do this? *And why??*"

But as Annie's world started to list, she heard another sound pierce through: a full-throated hyena laugh, loud and staccato, and when she looked up to find its source, there was Belinda, a figure in the whirling darkness, head flopped back, face turned toward the spring sun, ponytail swishing, mouth open, letting loose that sick cry.

"Belinda, what are you, why are you—"

"Oh, Annie darling," she said, choking back her laugh and wiping some spittle off her lips. "*I* leaked it. I sent it right to that *Post* reporter who wrote that article about you."

"You? But why on earth would you want this in the *Post*?"

"Oh, babe, my shit is already out there. Once the Bartleby Babes read your note and clicked on that horrifying link, all New York City knew, and once New York City knew, the world knew." She jerked her neck to the side in a quick movement, cracking it as if loosening up before a tennis match, then smiled at Annie devilishly.

"Anyway, I figured I'd just burn this to the ground, and take you with me. Blow up the holding cells entirely, so it doesn't matter what the prisoners choose to do with their dilemma, you know? I wasn't gonna do anything with that photograph, honest, but you went too far. You don't get away with that kind of behavior without a rap on the knuckles, do you?"

Annie leaned over, resting her hands on her knees for support, not sure if she was going to throw up, or faint, or what. She'd sent that text by mistake, unconsciously, subconsciously, whatever. She'd flirted with a washed-up actor *once*, one tiny dalliance that wasn't even a dalliance in most people's books. She'd never done anything purposefully evil, like drive her husband to burn a musical instrument. Or force her child to play violin for hours every day when his friends got to be kids. Okay, maybe she'd pressured her best friend's child to do a tangram puzzle, and rubbed her hands in glee at the failure of another woman's marriage, and, um, forged that letter, but those had been little glitches! These women, they were the monsters, the slinky coven in *The Devil's Advocate* that had satanic hands rippling under their otherworldly skin. Annie wasn't that! *For chrissakes, she wrote a quippy advice column about how to get your kid to eat broccoli!*

The tang of bile rose up in her throat. All she'd ever wanted was for Sam to find a spot at a place where he'd thrive, where he'd be surrounded by his people, to feel like the decision to raise her children amid the rat race was, in fact, correct. *And she was rewarded how? By landing on the front page of the* Post, *her unintentional missteps laid out for all the world to see?*

Just as the roaring became loud enough to drown out the subway rumbling beneath them, just as she grimly acquiesced to the imminent hallucination, with the sinkhole getting bigger and bigger, a menacing, gaping maw that would finally swallow her whole and plunge her god knows where, two loud bells pulled Annie back to earth. Two notifications, one from her phone, one from Belinda's, chiming at precisely the same moment. She swallowed her bile and pushed up from her knees to see other mothers hugging, or jumping up and down in elation, or raising their phones to their ears, grim and straight-mouthed.

The acceptance letters. They'd dropped.

Sure enough, when Annie checked her Gmail, there it was. St. Edward's Admissions Decision, sent from the Office of Headmaster Loren Fitzhughes.

Except when she opened it, resolved that she'd done what she had to do to win, and bracing for Belinda's very public meltdown and the hellacious aftermath she'd no doubt have to wade through, it took her a moment to understand just what she was reading.

Dearest Lewin Family,

On behalf of the St. Edward's School for Boys, I am delighted to offer Sam a place in next year's kindergarten class.

The Admissions Committee was impressed with Sam's precocity, charm, and humility. Whether he's learning more about his beloved bugs, urging his younger siblings to be their best selves, or immersing himself in the cryptocurrency world with his father, we can tell that Sam is a remarkable four-year-old and will no doubt grow into a remarkable adult. It would be our absolute honor to help guide him on his path toward scholarly and ethical pursuits, with his dear friend Brando Brenner by his side.

Since you agree that Sam and St. Edward's are a match made in heaven—don't worry, we're not *that* religious!—please respond to the separate email regarding the enrollment deposit.

Sincerely,

Headmaster Fitzhughes and the St. Edward's Admissions Committee

What the . . . ? She looked up to see Belinda's face, also drained of blood.

"Brando got into St. Edward's," she muttered.

"So did Sam," Annie managed.

They stood like that, frozen, phones in their hands and eyebrows identical Kabuki masks of confusion, until Belinda finally broke the moment with a bitter laugh and a grunt, like a bull.

"You did it," she spat out, half laughing, half expectorating. "I can't fucking believe it! I, obviously, knew you weren't going to write your own letter, figured you'd lie to me and assume that if I were lying to you—*which well, yeah, duh*—then we'd both end up at Hudson-Green." She let out a long, low whistle. "But look at you. You finally grew some testicles. What's that phrase your followers all say? Oh, right. *Complimenti, bitch.*"

Which was when the maw finally opened up, big and dark and swirling, and as Annie fell feetfirst down its shoot—nightgown up over her head, stars turning from dots to lines, lines to searing light, so bright she could barely see, as the children faced off against one another at the sandpit, wild animals roaring and screeching, falling and bouncing up from the rubber ground, this next generation's world one big antigravity chamber—her brain put together what Belinda's had, moments before: they'd both forged each other's first choice letter. *She'd become a killer, no different than the rest of them.*

And then the lights swooshed off.

• • •

Annie's blurred vision focused first on the industrial-grade beige socks she was now wearing, complete with squiggly grips that stuck on the linoleum, like she was an overgrown toddler learning how to walk. Completing the scene, a small box of apple juice and packet of Oreos sat on the table next to her. Disoriented and blinking up at the fluorescent lighting shining down harshly from above, she momentarily considered that she was in Claire's preschool classroom at Bartleby. But no, across from her was a young man in a white doctor's coat, clipboard in his lap, even expression on his face, and she was clad in the papery yellow fabric of a hospital gown.

"Mrs. Lewin, as you came to, you were mumbling about hallucinations," the doctor prompted.

Oh, Jesus. In a rush, she remembered the soft feel of the knobby playground rubber on her cheek; righting herself from the thundering ground and seeing, as if in slow motion, EMT workers rushing toward her; the sickening feeling of understanding that something was terribly, terribly wrong.

After a protracted beat, the doctor consulted the clipboard and went on.

"You said these, um, these *Peter Pan* visions, where you're wearing a nightgown and floating around like Wendy, you said they've been happening for a while. Do you remember when they started?"

Despite her general disorientation—she didn't know where her children were; if she still had a husband, or a best friend, or a career; and she wasn't sure how much time had passed since she'd blacked out on the playground floor—Annie could serve up any number of distinct moments that signaled her unraveling. There'd been that morning at drop-off, when her heels had started to lift, just barely perceptibly, from her insoles. The evening in the nursery with Max, when she'd first sensed other figures in the ether with her. SpaTinis. The night when she'd been certain a perpetrator had broken into the apartment, before she shrunk into miniature and whizzed about Claire's room.

Where, though, had it all begun?

She took a breath, then picked the one she felt was easiest to explain.

"When a faulty alarm went off in my house, and I wandered around in the dark in my apartment with a knife, having what I think was a panic attack," she lied. "About six months ago, now."

The doctor betrayed no hint of concern or shock, as if deranged, knife-clutching mothers routinely hurtled their way from the playground into his office, and with a nod of his head, silently urged her to go on. But as she caught sight of the North Meadow in Central Park out the window behind him, her stomach instantly lurched along some otherworldly wave, a feeling not unlike when her babies used to flip inside her, rippling her shirtfront. She recognized the view. *Yes, she'd seen the park from just about exactly this spot.*

"I've been here before," she managed, swallowing down a fresh surge of bile. "Three times, in fact."

"Have you?" The doctor riffled through some pages, puzzled. "Don't have any record of that in your file."

"Well, to Mount Sinai. The labor and delivery floor. For my children."

But even as Annie said it, even as she felt the tears start to slide silently down her cheeks, even as she shivered, a film of sweat blooming on her skin, she was no longer in this room, she was no longer talking to this well-meaning doctor who would send her home after an hour of evaluation with a prescription for antianxiety medication, a list of therapists who took her insurance, and the reassurance that the right kind of self-care would lead her back to dry land and far away from the sanitorium— something Camila, just now landing at JFK, would underscore back at her apartment that afternoon, over a cup of herbal tea. The view had whisked her up and out of the window, then down a few floors and back a few years, and into the memory of a busy room where miracles routinely upheave the earth's axis. There, the wisp of an idea, of a new and profound understanding of what had happened to her, and when it had all begun—long before her feet lifted from her insoles—started to flutter about, busily gathering up moments from her past, and feelings in her psyche, to shape it all into a coherent narrative of just when she stopped recognizing herself and her choices, of just when her emotions became heightened, of just when her internal compass went haywire and her world started to heave, then came to rest at a new tilt.

For the second time that day, she found herself peering down curiously at herself from above. But instead of seeing her body face down like a chalk outline on a playground floor, this time she was lying face up on a hospital bed, time telescoping in and slowing just as a baby, red and squalling and having left behind the cocooned wet warmth of the womb just one breath before—a baby not yet Sam yet wholly in possession of the traits that would become him—was placed on her heaving chest.

And as she cradles him—as she takes in his tiny tricep covered in thin, soft hair, his mouth opening and closing like a little fish, the weight of his cheek against her clavicle; as the hormones flooding her body dull the physical pain and all but disassociate her from the swirl of activity she senses is happening down below—things being tugged and sewn up, catheters removed, pads changed, measurements recorded; as the sound of blood rhythmically thrumming in her eardrums drowns out the beeping of the monitor and she thrills to feel the world's newest heartbeat fluttering wildly against her own—she grasps something essential.

In that fleeting moment, as she and her child are still reflexively straining together to shut out the assault of the everyday, to re-create, for a moment, the dreamy simplicity of the before life, still within reach, just now slipping away, she understands something she will forget momentarily and struggle for years seeking to internalize again: that in that hospital room, not one person, but two people have been born. Her new role, she will know then with utter clarity, will be to absorb all the pain of the world to protect this new person, even if she'll lose herself in the process, even if she'll forget to be gentle and kind to herself as she endures the stumbling blocks of recalibrating to a wholly new existence.

But it will all be worth it, because barely a minute old, and her child has already given her the gift of a lifetime—the gift of being conscious as her world cracks open anew and she blinks, for the first time, into a bright and glorious light.

EPILOGUE

In Loco Parentis: Understanding Matrescence

by Annie Lewin-Rapaport

AUTHOR'S NOTE

I experienced an inflection point fifteen years ago that helped recalibrate my priorities in work, love, and life. It also gave me the seed of an idea that grew into this book, which explores the life stage called motherhood through reporting and memoir. My network was not only critical in helping me regain my footing, but also in ensuring that I'd see this to completion. And so, instead of beginning with a prologue or introduction, I want to start by calling out the people who inspired and encouraged me along the way. It's an act that seems particularly fitting given that, in the pages that follow, I underscore how critical a supportive community is to each of us, as we strive to be good, happy mothers.

First up: my editor, Ash Wempole, who has never once stopped being my cheerleader and has worked tirelessly to help me find my voice, even as they were building out the team at their new publishing house, which has fought the onslaught of AI-led content from day one. It is a privilege to join you in this new, golden age of publishing.

My dear friends Camila Garcia Williams and Laura Carter have been first readers and last readers, have grounded me, have always been on the other end of my phone, have saved me too many times to count. Should everyone be so lucky as to have friends like you in their corner. (And thank you, Camila, for the title!)

The father of my children, Daniel Lewin, who gave me the three greatest joys of my life, and due to the encouragement of his wife, Belinda, has channeled his charisma and expertise into the public sector, where he enjoyed a successful run in the Office of the Comptroller and recently accepted the role of special adviser to the chancellor of the New York City Department of Education. The city's children have a worthy advocate in you.

My husband, Marty Rapaport, has been a constant source of love, support, and calm—and not just because he's a pediatrician, which is nice to have in the house. (And a hat tip to my late father-in-law, my children's pediatrician, not only for introducing us, but also for being a port in the storm for so many New York City mothers. Dr. Rapaport Sr., you are deeply missed.)

And I would never have been moved to embark on this professional journey were it not for the three individuals who made me a mother.

As I write these words, Sam, Claire, and Max are hunched over a notebook in the next room, home from various schools on summer break, working together to develop a new and improved algorithm to predict what educational environment a child needs to thrive—one that will take into account not just a child's intelligence at a fixed moment in time, like the failed IQ tests of yore, but in five, ten, fifteen, twenty years, while adjusting for every possible

external factor that might affect it, from natural disasters to pandemics to wars to worldwide shifts in the understanding of various social mores. My generation was not able to fix the educational system. Maybe yours will. It is a privilege to have a front row seat as you three set the world on fire.

And there is a final group to highlight, a sisterhood I entered into that sacred moment when I gave birth to my first child. I remember some unseen, uncontrollable force urging me to whisper into Sam's tiny ear, during his first few moments on earth, *Tell me, tell me everything before you forget.* Because I felt it, in that moment—that this tiny child's conscience was as yet unmuddied by the onslaught of the world, all its pedestrian concerns and anxieties, that he knew the answers to all the big questions. As Buckminster Fuller once said, "Everyone's child is born a genius, but is swiftly de-geniused by unwitting humans."

Over the course of almost two decades learning, firsthand, how to be a mother—an ongoing process—I've come to realize that parents have but a single responsibility, one that is both maddeningly complex and profoundly simple. We may find it easier to focus on those quotidian anxieties and concerns than to confront the magnitude of our new roles head on, particularly when we live in a society that routinely undervalues the work we do. But with time, we'll grasp that parenthood has but one North Star: to fight tooth and nail to preserve the genius and infinite wisdom our children arrive on earth possessing.

And so, finally: to all the mothers out there who are riding alongside me on this deeply rewarding, wholly consuming journey, who are part of my extended community whether they know it or not, I hope you find encouragement and comfort in these pages. And I raise a glass to each of you. *Complimenti.*

ACKNOWLEDGMENTS

Like Annie, my support network runs deep and strong, and without it, this book would absolutely not have seen the light of day. And so, I give meaningful thanks to:

Amelia Atlas and Kari Stuart, my agents, and the rest of the team at CAA, for encouraging what felt like a wild pivot, and being a constant source of clear-eyed support.

My enthusiastic and thoughtful editor, Liz Stein, and the team at William Morrow, not just for believing in this project but also for being the ideal partner—smart, selfless, and collaborative—at every turn.

My children's preschool, which has all the wonderful and none of the terrible parts of Bartleby. I cannot keep having more children just to stay part of the community, but I'll always be grateful for our years with you.

Dr. Janet Jackson, for giving me a crash course in IQ testing.

Alex Testere, for his charming spot illustrations.

The staff at the New York Society Library, where I holed up in Stack 6 on a cold, hard, folding metal chair day in and day out writing, during some of the happiest hours of my professional life.

There's nothing like being physically surrounded by great fiction to light the fire.

The friends who helped me with everything from emotional support to game theory to line editing: Yaran Noti, for being a whip smart and unsparing reader; Seth Robinson, for consulting on myriad versions of my prisoner's dilemma grid; David Orr, for brainstorming walks; Greta Caruso, Sarah Gronningsater, Leticia Landa, Anna Moody, and Isobel Morton for lending your eyes to this thing in various stages, sharpening the manuscript beyond measure.

Peppoli, you know our WhatsApp chain is my digital lifeline. *Complimenti*, bitches.

My family: my father, Marshall, for countless park walks and conversations and mini master classes in storytelling—what luck, to have you in my corner; my mother, Nina, for raising me in a household I try to re-create, daily, for my own children; my sister, Jessica, and her husband, Michael, for title help and for bringing creativity into my kids' lives; my husband, Dave, for keeping me sane and happy, and for being self-confident enough to have parts of him fictionalized, parodied, amped up to an 11, and then laugh at it all. I love you.

And finally, to my babies: Ella, Charlotte, and Jules—it's all for you.

ABOUT THE AUTHOR

SOPHIE BRICKMAN is a writer, reporter, and editor based in New York City. Her work has appeared in *The New Yorker, New York Times, The Guardian, Wall Street Journal, Saveur, The San Francisco Chronicle,* the *Best Food Writing* compilation, and the *Best American Science Writing* compilation, among other places. Her first book, *Baby, Unplugged,* about the intersection of parenting and technology, was published in 2021. *Plays Well with Others* is her debut novel.